Imperfect Paradise

Fiction from Modern China

This series is intended to showcase new and exciting works by China's finest contemporary novelists in fresh, authoritative translations. It represents innovative recent fiction by some of the boldest new voices in China today as well as classic works of this century by internationally acclaimed novelists. Bringing together writers from several geographical areas and from a range of cultural and political milieus, the series opens new doors to twentieth-century China.

HOWARD GOLDBLATT

General Editor

Shen Congwen

Edited by Jeffrey Kinkley

Translated from the Chinese by

Jeffrey Kinkley

Peter Li

William MacDonald

Caroline Mason

David Pollard

General Editor, Howard Goldblatt

University of Hawai'i Press   *Honolulu*

Imperfect

Paradise

Selection and English translation © 1995

University of Hawai'i Press

All rights reserved

Printed in the United States of America

00   99   98   97   96   95   5   4   3   2   1

Library of Congress Cataloging-in-Publication Data

Shen, Ts'ung-wen, 1902–

    [Short stories.   English.   Selections]

    Imperfect paradise : stories by Shen Congwen / edited by

  Jeffrey Kinkley : translated from the Chinese by Jeffrey

  Kinkley . . . [et al.].

      p.   cm. — (Fiction from modern China)

  Includes bibliographical references.

  ISBN 0–8248–1635–8. — ISBN 0–8248–1715–X (pbk.)

  1. Shen, Ts'ung-wen, 1902– —Translations into English.

I. Kinkley, Jeffrey C., 1948– .   II. Title.   III. Series.

PL2801.N18A24   1995

895.1'351 – dc20   94–23488

CIP

University of Hawai'i Press books are printed on acid-free
paper and meet the guidelines for permanence and durability
of the Council on Library Resources

Designed by Richard Hendel

Dedicated to the Memory of

SHEN CONGWEN

Contents

Introduction

Shen Congwen (pronounced Shŭn Tsoong Wŭn; 1902–1988) is one of modern China's foremost writers and, many would say, one of the finest Chinese prose stylists of all time. His earliest and most enthusiastic readers were urban young people of the 1920s and 1930s – the first generation of Chinese to see themselves as moderns and the generation soon engulfed in Communist revolution, Nationalist counterrevolution, and war with Japan. Shen Congwen chose other battlegrounds. One was the Chinese language, whose modern spoken forms he labored to enrich and reconfigure into a literary language subtle enough to bear all the pathos and allusiveness of China's ancient poetry. Another was the idea of China itself. In the early twentieth century, China was a battered and decrepit nation. Shen Congwen wanted to reconceive it as a brash, young land still endowed with the idealism of knights-errant and tribal princes. He wrote novels, poems, personal essays, travelogues, literary criticism, and topical commentary, but his best works, and those that made him famous, are short stories and novellas. His most acclaimed tales conjure up a savage frontier land of warlords and aborigines or, contrarily, refined pastoral scenes where intimate human emotions flower and wither according to fate. This book enters both those worlds. It features selections from the polished Shen Congwen canon that in the 1980s finally made him one of the few Chinese ever seriously in the running for a Nobel Prize for literature. And, in illustration of the author's range, it contains some of his more outré and yet more autobiographical pieces, which earned him the reputation of "the Dumas of China," the adventurous ex-soldier of creole (part aboriginal) blood who had run with the warlords and sat in as court recorder while they tortured their enemies.

Shen Congwen thrived as a writer only in the first half of the twentieth century, when there were fewer political and ideological controls on writers. After the Communist revolution in 1949, he never wrote another major work of fiction. That could be said of most of China's veteran writers under communism, but Shen Congwen suffered an ignominy more profound than most. His works were banned, his name was removed from textbooks, and he was forgotten even in the colleges – and not only in the People's Republic, but in Taiwan as well, where, because of his refusal to follow the defeated Kuomintang (Nationalist) regime, he was branded as disloyal. Only in the 1980s, after the death of Mao Zedong, did Shen Congwen enjoy a second heyday. Some of China's most talented young writers, including Ah Cheng, Jia Pingwa, and a host of Shen's fellow Hunanese, credited him with influencing their development. So did the acclaimed Taiwan-affiliated writer Pai Hsien-yung (Bai Xianyong). When in 1987 Taiwan finally lifted its ban on mainland writers, it, too, experienced a "Shen Congwen craze."

What had Shen Congwen done to deserve the thirty-year eclipse of his reputation? To Chiang Kai-shek's Kuomintang government, Shen Congwen was ever the leftist malcontent, "like all the others," always criticizing the status quo. To the Communists, he was a bourgeois reactionary, "like most intellectuals," but even more forthright about refusing leftist leadership. Shen Congwen never supported any party. From his writings, his friends, and his life, one must suspect that he advocated liberal democracy like his colleague Hu Shi. But Shen was more libertarian, in some ways anarchist in outlook. Probably he was anti-Communist, although he was reluctant to say so as long as his idealistic Communist friends were threatened by Chiang Kai-shek's white terror, and he was even more reluctant when the Communists turned the tables and unleashed their red terror. His immediate response to the Communist revolution in 1949 was to attempt suicide.

Fortunately for Western readers, Chinese culture does not pose an insuperable barrier to understanding the outer structures of Shen Congwen's fiction. Like other Chinese writers of his age, he was heavily influenced by Western writers, particularly French and Russian fiction masters of the nineteenth and early twentieth centuries: Chekhov, Daudet, France, Gorky, Maupassant, Turgenev. Also influential were Shakespeare, Gide, and Joyce (while undergoing Communist political reeducation, Shen literally *confessed* to having been influenced by Joyce; see his story "Gazing at Rainbows"). Like his peers, Shen Congwen was a realist by persuasion and a romantic at heart. He diverged from them mostly in his linguistic and thematic experimentation and in his turn toward modernism in the late 1930s and 1940s, his last creative years. His themes, characters, and narrative style were also influenced by China's own "classic" Ming-Qing vernacular novelists, by Pu Songling, by the ancient sage Zhuangzi, by the ancient historian Sima Qian, and even by Buddhist Jataka tales of Indian origin. Yet in his later years Shen was engrossed in speculative philosophy, Freudian psychology, Western classical music, and a pantheistic, abstract idea of God. The vernacular Protestant Bible influenced his narrative style, and thoughts of God and Love remained with him to the end of his life, although he joined no church. It only seems strange that Shen Congwen never learned a foreign language (he tried, but he had a mental block) and never went abroad until 1980, when he was an old man and could bask in the international acclaim long denied him.

Yet it is Shen Congwen's pronounced Chineseness that really endears him to his readers, both Chinese and Western.

In his works, West Hunan, his native region, itself becomes a character, as Shen's romantic eye sensuously evokes the lush southern flora and natural rhythms of the countryside. And he delineates the customs, taboos, and folk sayings of the majority Han Chinese and minority aboriginal peoples, the Tujia and Miao (Méo, Hmong), with ethnographic concentration equal to his natural descriptions. As an adviser to the filming of his novels, Shen Congwen was known for criticizing the actors' ways of sitting, squatting, and carrying themselves because people did these things "differently" in West Hunan.

Shen Congwen's language most fully marks his legacy as "Chinese." This is a paradox, for Shen's generation and the one before it originated China's modern vernacular literature, remolding both its grammar and its vocabulary through native inventions, reworkings of classical Chinese figures, and massive importations from Japanese as well as literal translations from foreign languages. Shen Congwen's style is rightly called Westernized. Contrary to tradition, many of his sentences are very long; direct translation ends in what are run-on sentences even in our language. The translators of this book split them up to achieve idiomatic English, reasoning that the shock value of Shen's "Westernisms" can in any case be conveyed only to those with a sensibility molded by classical Chinese. Shen also uses the common twentieth-century lexicon of psychological, social, and technical terms from Japan and the West and eschews patterned idioms from classical Chinese, particularly four-character set phrases (*chengyu*). Above all, he takes plain speech, including sometimes his native West Hunanese dialect (a branch of Southwestern Mandarin), as the basis for his literary style. To some Chinese, that is itself a "Western" departure from conventionalized Chinese literary writing.

On the other hand, Shen Congwen's use of a modified speech-based style does of course make it indelibly Chinese, despite the opaqueness of the many regionalisms and "ungrammatical" sentences voiced by his characters and narrators. (We translators consulted West Hunanese informants for advice, but often they disagreed or threw up their hands in puzzlement.) Although Shen's sentences are long and periodic, they seldom use embedded structures and conjunctions in the tightly "logical" Western style. Like Chinese poetry, Shen Congwen's prose is rich in lexical meaning (using characters with many allusive, often abstract and ethereal meanings) but poor in syntactic specification – leaving sentence objects, subjects, or context to be filled in by the reader. Shen Congwen's lexicon is full of words not in any Chinese dictionary. But they are not always neologisms. Often they are two-character words he invented himself by juxtaposing erudite near synonyms having slightly different nuances. Hence, many readers accused Shen of writing classical Chinese, and for economy he did omit many syntactic words necessary in spoken Chinese. Constructing sentences using the word order of speech, while omitting syntactic words for the sake of "classical," native-style elegance; spinning out a poetically associative, classical feeling lexicon, while avoiding patterned clichés from the old language that even modern writers abused as well as their more blatant neologisms – this was the *Chinese* genius of Shen Congwen as stylist. But this, too, is a simplification, for Shen Congwen invented many styles for his variously lyric, satiric, and castigatory prose. The translators only hope that a hint of his lexical and tonal, if not his syntactic, range will be apparent in our renditions.

Pastoral, idyllic, and *lyric* are the words most often used to sum up Shen Congwen's literary achievement, both in praise and in disparagement. Those who love Shen's works are overwhelmed by the beauty of his style and the purity of his representations of human nature. His foes, mostly on the Left, have accused him of depicting the Chinese countryside as a paradise in order to disguise social oppression in the old society. Such views are now so hardened that this anthology takes the slightly contrarian approach suggested in its title. Acknowledging the element of paradise in Shen's style and in his alternately folkish and intellectual idealism, it also highlights the savagery and disquiet that make his imaginary world far from perfect, even "fallen."

The book addresses this question directly in its opening section, with four of Shen's beautifully crafted works from the 1930s, when he was at the height of his powers. Although these stories unfold in idyllic settings, they are riddled with conflict and hidden pathos. From there, the book's thematic approach is reinforced by chronology. The second and third sections are devoted to stories inspired by Shen Congwen's "roots": first his "barbarian" and folk cultural milieu and then his adolescence in a warlord military regime, a fallen institution if ever there was one, particularly to Shen Congwen, who grew up in a quiet frontier military colony, the son of a soldier. Tracing the author's original inspirations back to still rawer progenitors is an appendix at the end of the volume, which contains two of Shen's early nonfiction works: a personal and folkloric essay on his region's "mountain songs" and a humorous one-act folk play that he wrote, or perhaps simply rewrote from childhood memories.

Feeling himself on the outs with China's highly politicized literary milieu based in Shanghai, by 1930 Shen Congwen had begun to identify with China's country folk and to praise their virtues. Yet, as one sees in the fourth section, the country folk who really interested him are far from perfect. It was, however, in the cities that Shen Congwen found the most dramatic social decay and signs of impending upheaval – although he seemed still drawn to enacting his moral dramas in gardens, on campuses, and at seaside resorts, as is apparent in the fifth section.

The sixth and seventh sections represent Shen Congwen's last stage of writing, during the war and civil war decades of the 1930s and 1940s. The former group of stories is darker than ever in its view of China's future, despite expressions of forced optimism that may reflect the author's turn to religion. But he was still experimenting with new techniques. Hence, the seventh section presents Shen Congwen the modernist, still thinking about paradise, and still finding it nowhere but in his imagination. Escape through a gateway to a spiritual world – or through suicide – was on his mind.

Selecting the best Chinese texts of Shen Congwen's works to translate was a matter of judgment; the translations below draw on all known editions. The author, with help from his wife, carefully revised the bulk of his writings one last time for his collected works, the *Shen Congwen wen ji*. Ordinarily, those versions would be considered definitive. But in the 1980s Shen Congwen had been away from fiction writing for thirty years. The passage of time and the intervention of horrific events gave him, at the very least, a different mind-set from that in which he originally composed. Then, in 1983, as the *Shen Congwen wen ji* was being published, Shen was attacked again, this time by no less than Chen Yun, Deng Xiaoping's chief rival for power. Sensitive pieces were altered and abridged, reminding readers that Shen must have felt pressure to be discreet even in his own 1980 revisions. (And "Songs of the Zhen'gan Folk," "The Celestial God," and "Gazing at Rainbows," translated below, do not appear in the *Shen Congwen wen ji*.) We have consulted pre-1949 versions to restore "politically incorrect" phraseology and what the author and his wife might in 1980 have considered "too revealing" autobiographical passages (notably in "Eight Steeds") missing from the *Shen Congwen wen ji*.

Most of Shen's revisions were, however, small differences of word choice; curiously, he most often *added* words to his final versions, typically heightening local color or making ambiguous passages more specific. Whether that improved the Chinese originals is moot, but the increased clarity was a boon to translation. However, when interpolations appeared inauthentic or incompatible with Shen Congwen's original creative vision, we favored pre-Communist texts. The biggest and perhaps the only major intervention was my excision of a one-line paragraph added in 1980 after the tenth paragraph of "The New and the Old": "This was one of the many forms of ethnic oppression in a remote border area." (The story has no other reference to ethnic oppression. That the author added the line is an act of reinterpretation startling to me as Shen's biographer, so I note it for readers now.)

In general, our renditions err on the side of inclusiveness. We have favored free translation, if only as a corrective for the excessive literalness that has plagued renditions of modern Chinese literature in the past, but we have never presumed to "improve on" Shen Congwen by abridging his original creative visions, not even his topical satiric barbs in "The Inn" and "Meijin, Baozi, and the White Kid," which readers today may consider out of character. Our reasoning is that ours are translations of record for scholars and students as well as the general public; with imagination, a reader can blot out lines of text but cannot restore passages deleted.

The works in this volume were chosen for their literary merit, with occasional consideration also of thematic and historical interest and emphasis on pieces that have never before appeared in English. Nine of the twenty-six items here have already been differently rendered by others, however, so the translators of this book would like to acknowledge our predecessors: Gladys Yang, Di Jin (Ching Ti), Robert Payne, Wai-lim Yip, C. T. Hsia, and Yüan Chia-hua. Eugene Eoyang, Kai-yu Hsu, and Emily Hahn have also contributed impressive renditions of Shen's work; partly for that reason we do not retread ground that they have covered. Thanks are due Shen Congwen's widow, Zhang Zhao-he, who gave this book her blessing; Howard Goldblatt; our editor Sharon Yamamoto, who among many other things contributed the book's title, inspired by a phrase in "The Poems of Our Climate" by Wallace Stevens; our copyeditor, Joseph H. Brown; Zhang Zude, who, by involving us in translating works by Shen Congwen for publication in Nanjing, encouraged our own, more modest project; Fred Yong Gang Huang, Long Haiqing, and Wu Ningkun, who provided valuable assistance with texts, as did Di Jin, who originally intended to join this project and helped conceive it; and Wong Kam-ming, who consented to the inclusion of the piece that he and I translated together. I am particularly grateful to Mi Hualing, a West Hunanese educator now retired in Anhui. He procured the text of "Gazing at Rainbows," which I once believed might not be extant, fielded questions about Shen's dialect, and sent me his own mimeographed glossary of Shen Congwen's colloquialisms, even expanded it to cover the works in this book. To these special friends and colleagues, to my unflagging fellow translators, and to St. John's University as well as Chuchu and Matthew Kinkley, who each in their own way provided release time for this research, I give heartfelt thanks.

Having reviewed and sometimes investigated every line below, I am only too aware that mistakes and infelicities inevitably remain and that I am responsible for them. Whether or not "to translate is to traduce" *(tradurre tradire),* to translate Shen Congwen is surely to interpret; may these renditions inspire still other interpretations, not close the door on variant readings.

J. K.
Bernardsville, N.J.

New and Old;
Paradise and Perdition

The New and the Old

In the developed world today, unlike China in the 1930s, nostalgia so often makes us favor tradition above modernity that one is tempted to read "The New and the Old" ("Xin yu jiu") as a tale of paradise lost. But why did Shen Congwen embody tradition in a headsman (i.e., a decapitator), a figure from old China that his Westernizing generation of intellectuals, notably Lu Xun, found shameful? Lu Xun's recoil at "backward" and "uncivilized" behavior is now so widely shared that today it is Chinese cultural conservatives who decry Shen's story, for "putting China's old culture in a bad light."

The difference is that Shen Congwen could see executioners as his ancestors saw them. An older relative of his was a headsman; Shen Congwen as a child was proud of him, and in 1980 Shen still liked to demonstrate the technique. So "The New and the Old" probably is nostalgic. The era designated in the story ended at about the time Shen's childhood memory began, when Zhen'gan, the small town of his birth (today called Fenghuang), was still inhabited mostly by soldiers and their families. Owing to Miao rebellions a century earlier, it was the center of a Military Preparedness Circuit, a special unit of government below the province with troops under its own command, some of whom farmed public colony fields out in the country and manned nearby forts in case of war. But, by the time of the story, West Hunan's soldiers were as anachronistic as masterless samurai in a Kurosawa film. Beheadings by then partook of the decorum of civil society; the strange custom at the temple of the city god is a real one, witnessed in Yuanzhou as late as the 1920s.

Yet, when Shen Congwen wrote, he was not only a modernizer himself but a transcendental and relativist thinker, post-Kantian and post-Nietzschean — or post-Zhuangzian, he would have preferred to say, since his story "Knowledge" argues that Zhuangzi transcends Nietzsche. Shen Congwen said that Beauty was his God, a God that is not dead, and that Beauty exists in things apparently ugly, primitive, even abhorrent. Beheading, done well and in the proper spirit, *may embody such Beauty. Shen Congwen actually beckons us to look beyond custom, to embrace a truly transcendental morality that finds more Beauty in a spiritually examined Life than in the rationally examined life prized by the West.*

This story, written in the summer of 1935, has a topical meaning, too. By implication, it condemns the New Life movement, a 1934–1935 mass campaign of Chiang Kai-shek's that revived ancient moral maxims – in form, without the spirit – to modernize China and make it resistant to Communist revolutionaries such as the victims in this story. Hence, narrowing the field to politics, another subject of the story is hypocritical neotraditionalism: the false project of restoring a paradise that never was.

During a year in the reign of the Guangxu Emperor, 1875–1908. . . .

Horses were being raced in this little county town, across parade grounds drenched by the sun in shimmering yellow. Meanwhile men in military garb, outfitted in all the colors of the rainbow, gathered before the Martial Demonstration Hall to rehearse the eighteen different disciplines of the martial arts. It fell to the circuit intendant in this season of Frost's Descent[1] to inspect the drills as tradition required, set the ranks in order, announce promotions and demotions, and confer rewards and punishments. And so this army, of the Military Preparedness Circuit commanding the frontier prefectures of Chenzhou, Yuanzhou, Yongzhou, and Jingzhou, was stepping up its drills in preparation for examinations. Seated on folding chairs in front of the Martial Demonstration Hall, the patrol commander and drill instructor drank tea from covered bowls and called the roll from a register in red covers. Each soldier could select the gear that best suited him and have a crack at wielding his weapon, solo or against an opponent. When it came to the competitions on horseback, the mounts were given free rein to gallop like the wind, while the men demonstrated their skill at knocking off balls with long lances or revolved in the saddle to show off their archery – "puncturing the willow leaf" from a hundred paces. Each won hurrahs or jeers according to his prowess.

Warrior Yang Jinbiao[2] was under the command of the Miao Defense Colony-Field Affairs Office, Second Company. He had just hit some targets from horseback with his lance; now he was returning to the Martial Demonstration Hall to

[1] The beginning of the eleventh month.
[2] "Yang of the Golden Banner."

Translated by Jeffrey Kinkley

find a partner to take him on in "twin swords break the shields." Although the sword-wielding opponent demonstrated great skill and ferocity, Warrior Yang rolled and tumbled hither and yon with his leather shields. It seemed no blow of the sword could touch him, nor even a drop of water.

Just as the heat of battle was rising, a military courier clad in a red tunic rushed up and stood before the upturned eaves to report: "Yang Jinbiao, Yang Jinbiao, you have official business at the yamen. Come to the city wall, West Gate, at a quarter till noon to await further instructions!"

Hearing his orders, the soldier intentionally waited for a climactic moment to fall to the ground, as if felled by the sword of his opponent. Quickly he threw down his shields and came over to report. When the courier had left and Yang went to the stables to catch his breath, the others swarmed around him like bees. All knew that there would be a trial today at noon and that, at the appointed time, Yang would have to march out through the West Gate and cut off a man's head. Warrior Yang was known to them not only as a comrade on the drilling field and in the barracks but also as a servant of the big civil yamen in town. For he was not just skilled on foot and horseback; he was the most distinguished headsman in the district.

After the noon meal, the soldier donned his dress black tunic with the twin cloud design and wrapped his head in a crepe silk turban. Then he took his foot-long devil-headed sword through the West Gate to receive his assignment. Precisely at noon, three shots from "little piglet" cannon sounded from within the city. Soon after, a troop of men and horses dragged forth a man struck dumb with terror. He knelt facing west in the center of the grounds to await his sentence. Holding the devil-headed sword like a dagger, thrust backward to conceal it in the crook of his arm, Yang went to the tribunal's mat-shaded shelter, bowed deeply before the inspector of executions, hands at his sides, and inquired as to the imperial will. Then, with permission to proceed, he strode behind the criminal and paused a moment to take stock. A brush of his arm against the nape of the convict's neck, with the sword below coming straight down on it like a guillotine, sent the head falling to earth with a dull thud. The crowd of soldiers and civilians roared as one (they were applauding how he dispatched the man with a single blow), but this soldier had duties yet to perform; he ran head down, oblivious to everything, straight to the temple of the city god.

There he thrice kowtowed before the god, as was the custom, and quickly hid under the incense altar before the god, silent as could be, to await the next act.

Soon His Honor the county magistrate likewise honored custom by entering to offer incense to the god, his retinue of lictors proceeding in advance with gongs to clear the way. The incense presented, a fleet-footed scout rushed in, breathlessly, and knelt to report: "I beg leave to inform Your Honor, a commoner has been killed by the stream outside the West Gate – beheaded, in an affair most bloody. The whereabouts of the culprit are unknown."

Although the magistrate had signed the writ of execution in red with his own brush, clear as could be, just a short while before, he again followed tradition by pretending amazement, as if he had no knowledge of the event. "Can such a thing happen in broad daylight?" he shouted, rapping his gavel.

Thereupon he sent runners throughout the city to find the culprit, enjoining them to bring the man immediately to justice. Others he ordered to make ready the case so that the criminal could be interrogated before the god. When the soldier-executioner reckoned that the magistrate had taken his seat, he quickly crawled out from under the god's throne and knelt before him to confess and request punishment. He reported his identity and his origins, allowed as how the man outside the West Gate was his victim, and presented the bloodied sword in evidence.

Rapping his gavel, the magistrate began the interrogation with a great show of pomp and severity. The executioner came forth with all sorts of explanations for the killing, all the while kowtowing to His Honor and begging for mercy. At the end, continuously sounding his gavel, the magistrate shouted out to his runners to "severely punish this ignorant country fellow with forty blows of the red bamboo rod!" Clutching the executioner and forcing him down on the stone-cold brick floor, they counted out the blows by fives, "five, ten, fifteen, twenty," in reality delivering only eight blows, whereupon they respectfully informed His Honor that the whipping had been carried out. A runner handed the magistrate an envelope, which he in turn flung before the executioner. The soldier kowtowed in gratitude as he picked up his remuneration, repeatedly wishing this "eminent dispenser of justice" a "prominent and rewarding career." When all the necessary procedures had been performed before His Eminence the city god, His Honor the county magistrate returned to his yamen.

Since the tragedy had to unfold in just this way, the adage that "being an official is acting a part in a play" was not far off the mark. Legal and religious rites combined to make a drama, and the result was just as entertaining. For remote border areas are ruled jointly by men and gods; they can be controlled only when the two cooperate. Even such affairs as this were regarded very cautiously by the townspeople and the executioner. To the headsman, the admonitory forty blows of the bamboo rod seemed particularly significant. The rulers were determined to demonstrate to the citizens that even an executioner who served the officials sinned when he killed – bore some responsibility to the deceased. But this sin was brought openly before the gods and could be exorcised by the bamboo. This already being a tradition, it would of course be carefully preserved, until all social institutions collapsed or were reformed.

An executioner earned a third of a tael of silver for each

head he severed. The soldier who received the emoluments necessarily invited his brothers in the ranks to a feast of meat and wine after his return to camp. He told them about the knack of beheading and all about the victim and how he took it. He also amused the crowd by mimicking the bureaucratic airs of the magistrate as he had just seen him in the temple of the city god.

"Warrior Yang Jinbiao, hath thou not heard that, when a prince violates the law, he is punished in the same degree as any commoner? Yet you, a soldier, dared to murder a man with your own sword in broad daylight!"

"Your Honor, Paragon of Justice, have mercy – "

"By the gods above, confess before me!"

"Your Honor, Paragon of Justice, have mercy – "

Yelling out to have at him, the soldiers gathered round and pounced, poking and chopping at Yang Jinbiao with their chopsticks.

Yang Jinbiao was twenty-four and a bachelor. He cut a fine, healthy figure of a soldier, being free and without a care. He was known for his generosity and skill in all things. He had dreams of future glory: "A tower a mile high must start from the ground." His companions in the ranks, too, felt he was not a fellow to be underestimated.

In the eighteenth year of the Republic, 1929. . . .

The era changed; the last emperor's power was overthrown by the revolutionary party, and the miracle of the famous Qing dynasty headsman who beheaded six people in a trice without leaving any skin dangling would never happen again. But, when the era changed and "the court" became "the government," the local methods of killing became crueler. Small though the town was, it would usually dispatch eight or ten people at a time. The bravest and most dashing man around couldn't get through so many if they were as easy to slice as cucumbers. So the authorities just lined up the people and shot them. Yang Jinbiao became the old soldier guarding the North Gate, the one who bolted and locked it at night. His days of glory were past; as the seasons went by, he and his profession were slowly but completely forgotten.

Already sixty, Yang Jinbiao lived alone in a little gatehouse. On his wall still hung two leather shields, a matched pair of "tiger-head swords" with curved tips sharp as hooks, an old Guangdong Arsenal-style musket, and a pair of daggers – all the treasures that had made him fall in love with his profession in his earlier days. There were also a pair of poles, a forked spear, and a scoop net, all for fishing. His calabash was often half filled with strong corn liquor. And the precious sword that had beheaded so many people hung at the head of his bed. Thirty years before, it was said that the sword delivered a portent one day before the yamen was to order an execution. Now that the Republic had come and the sword lay unused, the portents came no more. But, when the sword was pulled from its scabbard, even today it gave off a terrifying, cold gleam, as if unwilling yet to despair of itself. On the edge of its blade could still be seen many a semicircular bloodstain that would not come off with grinding. Having nothing to do during the day, the old soldier took it with him to the top of the city wall, where he sat on a rusted cannon in the battery, stroking and admiring the sword as he basked in the warm sunlight. And, when he was in the mood, he put it through a few exercises.

Also stationed in the gate tower was a platoon of regular soldiers charged with defending the city. All troops in the city had long since been reorganized under the modern military system. But the old soldier still went to the Miao Defense Colony-Field Affairs Office monthly to receive his two and eight-tenths taels of silver compensation as a "warrior," plus old-style grain ration tickets. The silver was paid at the market price in currency, while the ration coupons could be exchanged for 8.4 pecks[3] of grain in the hull. His duty was to open the city gate in the morning and close and bolt it at night, which he did on his own initiative.

Being a drinker, he often went over to Butcher Yang's table to chat and wash his wine down with a bowl of soup flavored with pork bone marrow. Or he'd go to the table of Butcher Sha, the Muslim, and carry back a sheep's head or sheep's stomach to enjoy at home. He knew something of herbal medicine, so, whenever someone came down with a blister or a boil, he was happy to go off into the countryside to pick the healing plants. And, being a good fisherman, he often went by himself up to the mill embankment to fish in the reservoir. When his catch was stewed, he would carry it in its earthenware casserole up to the other soldiers in the gate tower, and they would all feast raucously together, playing the guess-fingers game as they drank.

In the dog days of summer, when it was hot as a bamboo steaming basket, he still lay down in a ventilated spot of the gate tower and snored away. While the soldiers practiced Chinese boxing, making him itch to join them, he, too, would take up his antique shields and practice "seizing the spear," "bringing down the flying-wedge yoked troika by cutting down the end horse at the knees," and other quaint exercises.

At the foot of the wall flowed a long stream. Innumerable women with bamboo baskets on their backs came from the city to wash their clothes there, pounding them with wooden rollers. Others stood midstream to rinse cotton yarn, the rolled-up legs of their trousers revealing the pale white calves of their legs. Upstream a short distance was a row of stepping stones spanning the river like a centipede. People coming to market from the Miao villages, others headed for the countryside to collect rent, still others coming to town to have their fortunes told – hay cutters, fish fry

[3]Eighty-four liters.

peddlers, bearers of messages or of manure – all passed over the stepping stones in a ceaseless parade lasting the whole day long. The vegetable gardens across the stream were Miao property; the glistening green plots, all laid out in neat squares, presented a beautiful prospect. Hillocks luxuriant with trees lay beyond the truck gardens. There were two main roads, one wending its way over the hills, the other following the river upstream. Both led into Miao country.

At the foot of the city wall was a clearing where firewood and fodder were exchanged; hence, there were also stalls selling beef entrails and others selling *baba* corn cakes and a soup of fermented glutinous rice. And there were several sheds with the furnaces of blacksmiths, who beat out every kind of sickle, firewood hatchet, and yellow-eel-tailed dagger, exclusively for sale to the country folk who came to the city to sell their firewood and hay.

When he was not fishing in the reservoir or drinking at Butcher Yang's, the old soldier sat atop the rusted cannon in the city wall, watching all the people come and go. Or he turned to look at the city in back, at the playground and classrooms of the primary school. The school was run by a young couple. From on top of the wall he could see very clearly when the children were having their lessons and when they were enjoying recess. They seemed to like their teachers, and the teachers loved their students. Sometimes the woman teacher brought her children up on top of the wall to play. When she saw the old soldier with his shields, she would ask him to go through his motions to amuse the children. (The tiger eyes painted on the leather shields so filled them with wonder and delight that, once the children had seen them, they would often sneak off to the old soldier's home for a look on their way home from school.) Sometimes as he watched them play soccer on the playground, the old soldier on top of the wall would bellow out encouragement to the losing side.

The old soldier rose early one morning, at the onset of the season of Frost's Descent. Seeing the fine weather and that so many people were busy with the traditional autumn housecleaning, he decided to give his own place a thorough scrub. He rolled up his sleeves and wrapped a colorful turban around his head. Then he moved all his things out of his room, made several trips to the river to bring up water, and set about scrubbing every wall and floor in turn. He was just going at it when the platoon commander suddenly appeared. The old soldier was to hurry to the yamen with his short sword. Urgent business awaited him.

At the yamen he found the adjutant of the day in his red sash. After quizzing the old soldier a bit and having him pull out his sword for a look, the adjutant ordered him to hurry outside the West Gate.

It all happened in such a rush, in such chaos, that the old soldier thought he was dreaming. Everything was hazy in this dream; he couldn't verify any of it, so he did run outside the West Gate. He saw no tribunal, no shed for the officers, not a single spectator. Apart from some dogs out in the open field, he saw only a dyer who'd been toting a load of white cloth, resting by the side of a pile of manure. Nothing gave any clue that an execution was about to take place. The sky was bright and clear. A magpie, shaking its long tail, flew overhead.

"Are they still killing people here in this day and age?" wondered the old soldier. "Am I dreaming?" Across the meadow was a tiny brook where children played. They were collecting stones and catching shrimp, with their book bags laid out on top of the pile of dried cow manure. The old soldier recognized them all from the primary school inside the North Gate, so he went over to address them.

"Young gentlemen, young gentlemen, better hurry and leave. Someone's about to be executed here!"

The children raised their heads all at once and laughed, "What, who're they gonna kill? Who told you?"

"Was I dreaming after all?" thought the old soldier. Seeing that the dyer was about to spread out his cloth on the meadow to dry, the old soldier went over to speak to him next.

"Master dyer, you must gather up your cloth. This is no place to dry it. There is going to be an execution here!"

Like the children, the dyer paid him no attention. He, too, laughed: "A killing? How's that? How do you know?"

"Could it really have been a dream?" thought the old soldier. "How should I know who's to be executed? If this really is a dream, I'll kill the next one I see."

As he prepared to return to town to inquire, he heard trumpets blaring the signal to charge. So they really were going to execute someone. The troops had already passed through the wall. One turn and they would be here. In a daze, the old soldier ran back to the center of the field. The troops had come. They quickly and silently formed a circle, each man raising his rifle and pointing outward as if ready to fire. Sure enough, there were two young people, bound and kneeling in the meadow, their faces deathly white. One was a man and the other a woman. Their faces seemed very familiar at first glance, but in the commotion he couldn't quite think why. An officer on horseback, holding the arrow with a pennant that in the past had symbolized the emperor's authority, observed the proceedings from an earthen mound outside the circle. Still thinking he was in a dream, the confused old soldier went before the inspector of executions to ask for instructions. But another soldier dragged him away, saying, "Get them on the first chop, old fellow, one each. Come on, hurry up!"

He went over to the criminals. Two swishes, and two heads fell on the ground. Seeing the blood spurt out made him think that this dream would soon be over, but force of habit reminded him of the tradition from thirty years before. Without so much as a look backward, he picked up his heels and ran. When he reached the temple of the city god, a group of women was praying there, and the priest was noisily shaking bamboo divination sticks out of a tube. Heedless of all this, the old soldier prostrated himself on the floor the moment he entered, kowtowing and crawling under the altar. When the temple crowd saw this man with his bloody sword, they thought he must be a murderer or a lunatic who had just killed his wife. Scared out of their wits, they ran outdoors to warn the neighborhood.

Soon the party from the execution ground arrived and was beset by people anxious to give them all their different versions of the event at the temple. Everyone agreed that it was the old codger who guarded the North Gate, that he had killed someone, and also that he was certifiably crazy. Like most of the elders of the town, the old priest from Yang Jinbiao's youth was already deceased. Nobody paid any attention to the old custom; nobody even knew it had ever existed.

Having established that the man was crazy and holding a murder weapon and that anyone who entered the temple risked being cut down himself, the crowd immediately latched the door from the outside to think up a plan for capturing the madman.

Hiding under the altar, the old soldier heard all the hubbub outside but could not imagine the reason for it. When after a long wait the magistrate still had not come, he became very anxious, not knowing whether to go out or to stay in place.

More time passed. He could hear people outside the temple pulling the bolts on their rifles and loading the magazines with bullets. Then he heard a very familiar woman's voice: "Don't go in, don't go in. He has a sword!" Next came the voice of the adjutant: "Don't be afraid, we have guns! As soon as you see the lunatic, open fire and shoot to kill!"

The old soldier was frenzied and bewildered, without a clue about what to do. He kept thinking, in his befuddlement, "This is truly a terrible dream!"

Then someone opened the door to the temple and

shouted, still without entering. He pulled the bolt on his rifle, as if about to fire. Yang could also hear, very clearly, voices of people he knew. Among them was that of a leather worker.

He heard the adjutant speak again: "Enter! Shoot the madman!"

Frantic, the old soldier shouted out, "Hear me, hear me, Your Eminence the City God, what's going on?" The people outside were making such a commotion that they seemed not to hear this.

Although the soldiers outside the door were in an uproar, each had only one life to give, so nobody dared to be the first to rush into the temple.

Suddenly an unidentified voice from the crowd bellowed out, angrily, "Madman, throw out your sword, or we'll commence firing!"

"If this dream goes on, it will be just too horrible," thought the old soldier. He did not want to be killed by a burst of gunfire in a dream. He simply couldn't stand it any longer. The sword clattered out on the edge of the steps. At the risk of his life, a soldier rushed forward and picked it up. Witnessing the murder weapon in custody, and fearing no longer that they were in jeopardy, the throng surged forth into the temple.

The old soldier was seized. In the confusion, he was given a sound thrashing, then thoroughly trussed up, hog-tied, and secured to a pillar of the stoa. He saw himself surrounded by hundreds of people, yet still he could not understand what he'd done wrong, why they took him for a lunatic, or what would be the upshot. All this proved that it was not a dream. So the execution a little while before must have been real after all. Could it be that no one had been killed here for so many years that he really was crazy? Doubts swirled about in his mind, and in the end he could not get a handle on it. Someone came up behind him unawares and overturned a bucket of filthy water over his head. He was drenched from head to foot; everyone broke out into uproarious laughter. Shocked and angry, the old soldier turned to look. So his tormentor was Cripple Wang, the town's stinky-bean-curd peddler. He was grinning at his foul deed, as if proud of himself. Furious, the old soldier cursed him roundly: "Fifth Wang, you dog-fucked bastard, so even you've decided to take advantage of me – me, your old forebear!"

That sent everybody into rollicking laughter again. Hearing him speak, the adjutant opined that the madman had been shocked into sobriety by the slop and was no longer befuddled. He felt safe to draw near and ask why, after the execution, he had run so insanely into the city god's temple. Had he seen a ghost, perhaps? Or run into some evil miasma?

"Why did I do it? Don't you know the custom? You made me handle the case, and afterward I followed tradition by turning myself in. But the lot of you surrounded me, wanted to shoot me. I came close to dying in a hail of bullets! You've done fine, really fine. You took me for a madman! *You're* a pack of ghosts. What other ghosts are there besides you? I ask you!"

So the local military who thought up this new gambit had put to death two Communists, not by firing squad, but by an extraordinary measure: they had asked the old executioner who guarded the city gate to cut off their heads, that they might be exposed in public as a warning to others. But the old soldier could not understand why the yamen wanted him to kill those two young people. The beheaded were none other than the two teachers from the primary school inside the North Gate.

Before their replacements had arrived, the office of keeper of the keys to the North Gate fell vacant, for the old soldier had died. From that time forward everyone in town – soldiers, citizens, everyone – knew the joke about "the last executioner." Moreover, it was said that the fellow in his befuddlement had been scared to death in broad daylight by a ghost.

The Husband

"The Husband" ("Zhangfu"), a finely crafted story from the start of Shen's mature period (written in Wusong, 13 April 1930) and one of his favorites, is a study in ambivalence – at first reading, a pastoral in reverse. If the placid mood and lovingly rendered local color reflect Shen Congwen's nostalgia for the docksides he frequented as an adolescent soldier, the human scene is clearly unwholesome, a case of city values corrupting the human spirit. Yet the flesh trade is described with surprising moral neutrality. And, although the river warden has the power to oppress and may be part of the underworld, he seems, not evil, but rather a protector, like Shunshun, the dockside hero in Shen's novella The Frontier City. The familiar is made strange, and the strange becomes familiar; prostitution itself becomes a natural way of life and the husband's rejection of it not a moral, modern, or progressive choice but the result of repressed passions and resentments that can be dammed no longer. Routine "nature" is rectified not by morality but by a transcendent Nature.

Certain images echo throughout the story, as small details describe an intimate psychological panorama of human relations. There are the hidden tensions over the gift of the fiddle, the prostitute's treating her husband like a child, the husband's newfound regret at having once scolded her over the loss of a little sickle, and his recurring visions of the red, orange-peel face he secretly resents. Although in his fiction inner emotions are typically revealed obliquely, through dialogue, Shen Congwen presents here one of the most probing portraits in Chinese literature of the private world of a peasant man.

Seven days of spring rains have left the river swollen.

Rising waters submerge the sandbanks where floating opium dens and brothel boats are used to mooring. They are close in to shore now, lashed to the support piers of houses hanging over the water on stilts, the "balconies with hanging feet."

A man sipping his tea at leisure in the Springtime All Over the World teahouse can lean out the riverside window and catch a wonderful vista on the farther shore, of a pagoda wrapped in "peach blossoms and misty rains." Looking down, he can also learn how the women of the boats keep their customers company as they smoke opium. The world above is so close to the world below that either one can hail the other just by calling out. When the one catches the attention of the other, they begin to talk and flirt with wild and raunchy words. Whereupon the one upstairs pays his bill and makes his way down a dank and fetid path, splashing through the filth and excrement until he's aboard the boat.

Once on board, having paid anywhere from a half dollar to five, he can smoke and sleep any old way that suits his fancy – can enjoy himself with the women as recklessly and wantonly as he knows how. The buxom, broad-hipped young women who live on the boats use all their womanly assets to keep their man pleased the night long.

The women of the boats call this activity by the same name as it is known elsewhere: *business.* Business is what they've all come for. It holds the same status as any other work, being neither offensive to morality nor harmful to health. These women are from the countryside, from families that farm the fields and dig in the gardens. Leaving their villages, their stone mills, their newborn calves, and also the embraces of their young, strong husbands, they go to town through the offices of an acquaintance and come to

Translated by Jeffrey Kinkley

do their business on these boats. Through their business, they gradually turn into city people. Slowly they grow estranged from their country villages, and slowly they learn the vices that are useful only to city folk. And then they are spoiled. But this happens very gradually. It takes so long that it goes unnoticed. Besides, there's no lack of women who can keep their country purity under any circumstances. And that is why there is never any lack of new young women for the brothel boats in this town.

It is all so simple. A young woman in no hurry to bear children goes to the city while her husband still earns his living by honestly and arduously tilling the fields back in the village. Her earnings from two nights in the city, remitted to him once a month, provide him a better life. He keeps the rights to his wife and the profits, too. Therefore many a young husband sends his wife away after marriage, while he stays at home farming and minding *his* business. It happens all the time.

When a husband in this situation misses the young wife out on her boat doing her business, or if it is New Year's or another holiday when he ought to arrange to see her, he'll put on his freshly washed and newly starched clothes, hang from his waistband the short-stemmed pipe that never leaves his mouth when he's working, shoulder a whole basket full of sweet potatoes, baked corn-and-rice biscuits, or the like, and set off for the city as if going to meet some long-lost relative. He'll ask for her at the very first boat docked at the pier, then keep on going until he recognizes the one that holds his wife. When he's sure he's in the right place, he'll go aboard, placing his cloth shoes ever so carefully on the awning over the cabin, and then, handing his gifts to the woman, start searching her whole body with his startled eyes. For by now the woman has of course entirely changed in the eyes of her husband.

The big knot of hair on top of her head, all shiny with oil, the long eyebrows plucked so thin by tweezers, the white face powder and crimson rouge, the city affectations and city clothes – these are enough to fluster a country husband to the point that he doesn't know how to treat her. The woman understands his perplexity, for she has seen it all before. Finally it is she who speaks. She might ask, "Did you receive the five dollars?" Or, "Has the sow given us any piglets yet?" Her manner of speaking is completely different from before. It is confident and easygoing now, like that of a lady from the city. She has hardly any air of the country wife about her.

From his woman's talk of remittances and raising the pigs back home, the husband sees that he keeps his status as head of the family even on this boat and that this city woman has not completely forgotten her home in the country. Emboldened, he slowly goes for his pipe and flint. His next shock comes when she suddenly snatches his pipe away and thrusts a delicate Hatamen-brand cigarette into his thick, coarse palm. But the surprise is only momentary. Soon he has it lit and begins to talk.

In the evening, after supper, he is still enjoying the novelty of those machine-made cigarettes. A customer arrives – a boat owner or a merchant sporting tall cowhide jackboots and a thick, gleaming silver chain that hangs out from his waist pouch. He staggers onto the boat, all liquored up. On board, he yells out that he wants a woman to kiss and to sleep with; in the mind of the husband, the loudness of the man's slurred speech and the pompousness of his manner evoke the self-importance of the village head and country gentry back home. The husband knows without having to be told to slink away to the back and crawl into the afterhold. Hiding out there with the rudder, out of breath and panting softly, he takes the cigarette from his mouth and gazes listlessly at the life on the river after dusk. The river has changed with the night. The shores, the river boats, all shine with lantern light. At this point the husband tends to think of the chickens and piglets back home, as if they were the only friends really true to him, his only family. Close now to his wife, he feels all the farther from home. A faint sensation of loneliness comes over him, and he wants to go home.

But does he? No. It's a ten-mile hike, with jackals and wildcats along the way, and militiamen on night sentry duty, all best avoided. Of course he can't go back. Besides, the old lady who oversees the boat naturally wants him to go with her to the night performance at the Palace of the Three Top Scholars opera house and then take tea and snacks at Springtime All Over the World. What's more, now that he's come all the way to the city, it would be a shame to miss all the bright city lights and crowds. So he stays seated in the afterhold, watching the activity out on the river until the old madam gets free. Finally he goes ashore, leaning against the awning frame as he sidles along a plank that serves as a running board to the bow. And, when his night of seeing the sights is over, he crawls back the same way, careful as can be not to disturb the cabin, where a customer may be lying on his side, enjoying a pipe of opium.

When it is time to retire, the watchman's clapper sounds in the city, and the great watch drum in the western hills can be heard rumbling in the distance. Peering through a crack in the boards, the husband sees that the customer is still there. The husband has no say in this matter; he can only crawl into the freshly padded quilt in the stern and go to sleep alone. Come midnight, by which time he may be asleep – or perhaps he is still brooding – his wife gets a chance to crawl back into the afterhold. She asks him if he'd like a piece of candy. She remembers how fond he is of candy. So, when he protests that he's sleepy or has already eaten some, she pops a piece into his mouth anyway. Feeling rather ashamed of herself, the wife then leaves him. As if this candy in his mouth could pardon his wife's behavior, the husband goes peacefully back to sleep, leaving her to go on seeing to her customer's wants.

There are many such husbands in Huang village. It breeds sturdy women and generous, honest men, but the place is just too poor. The lion's share of the meager harvests it does provide goes to the people on top. The country folk who find themselves bound hand and foot to the soil must stave off hunger by eating sweet potato leaves mixed with chaff three months out of twelve, however thrifty and hard-working they may be, and even then it is not easy to get by. Though it is up in the hills, the village lies but ten miles from the river port, so it is the custom that the women go away to make their living, and every male knows how much is to be gained from such a business. He reasons that his woman still belongs to him in name; the children she bears will be his, and, if she prospers, he will get his share of the proceeds.

The boats were all drawn up in ranks along the river, too many for any stranger ever to count. He who knew their number and the order in which they docked – who remembered every boat and every sailor on them – was the old river warden, *baojia* head[1] of the Fifth District, out on the wharves.

The river warden had but one eye. They said he'd got into a fight on the river during his youth and had it scratched out by the thug he killed in the struggle. But he seemed to see better with one eye than with two. The whole river was in his hands. His power over those little boats was more concentrated and absolute than that which any Chinese emperor or president ever had on land.

The floodwaters had made the river warden busier than ever. It was his duty to inspect everywhere – for shipboard babies, crying for milk while their parents went ashore; for

---

[1]Local governments organized citizens into mutual responsibility groups, called *bao* and *jia,* for self-policing. Influential private citizens were named as heads of these units.

on-board quarrels, which he must mediate; for unattended craft in danger of being swept away with the flood. Today, this patriarch had to go poking around everywhere to investigate an incident on land that now involved the world of the river. There had been three minor robberies on shore in the last few days. The police claimed to have combed every nook and cranny without turning up a clue. When all those nooks and crannies on land had been searched by those most reputable functionaries, it became the river warden's responsibility. He was notified, by those self-same lying policemen, that he was to meet with the armed river police tonight at midnight, to board and search every boat until the "scoundrels" were caught.

Having got word just that morning, the river warden had been kept busy all day. He wanted to do his duty by all those folk who were in the habit of treating him to fine wine and good food, so he boarded the boats one by one, starting at the first pier, and spoke with those on board. He had to begin by ascertaining whether the boat was harboring any unsavory characters from out of town.

A river warden was lord of the river, up on everything that went on there. Originally this one had made his living on the water like all the others, and on the wrong side of the law. The officials, then, as was their practice, used him to control the others. But he was getting on now, and he found himself wealthy, what with all the turmoil that had come to the world. Married, with a family, and fond of a drink or two, he enjoyed the good life. He had gradually become a peaceable and respected man. But, if his job was to help the authorities, his heart remained with the boat people. In these circumstances he had become a moral exemplar, every bit as respected as the officials, yet without all the fear and dread. He was godfather to many women in the trade. By dint of these social habits, his behavior and his way of handling things tended to favor the boat people.

Just now he was jumping from a wooden gangplank onto

the prow of a freshly painted "flower boat" tied up to the water stilts of an unobtrusive shop selling lotus seeds. He knew whose boat this was. "Maid Number Se-ven!" he called.

There was no reply. The young woman wasn't there, and neither was the old lady who managed her. The old fellow was wise enough to know that some young man might be on board sowing his oats even during the daylight hours, so he just stood there in the prow a while, looking about him.

Time passed, and he called out again, this time for the madam, and then for Wuduo, the boat's skinny little servant girl, an eleven-year-old with a shrill voice who usually looked after the boat while the grown-ups were on shore. Mostly she did the shopping and cooking; she was given to crying, for they often beat her, but then after a while she would be singing to herself again. Wuduo didn't answer, either. Yet he thought he heard the sound of breathing coming from the cabin, and the boat didn't look like they'd battened it down so they could all go ashore or to bed. The river warden bent over and peered into the cabin, asking who was there in the dark.

Still no answer came from within.

A little put out, the river warden shouted out, "Who are you there?"

"It's me," came a weak and timid male voice that was unfamiliar to him. "They've all gone ashore."

"All gone ashore, eh?"

"Yup. The women – "

As if scared to death that his curt answers might have given offense, for which on second thought he must make amends, the man crawled out of the darkness to the cabin entrance. Carefully, carefully rolling back the awning, he stared up awkwardly at the visitor.

His gaze traveled upward from the towering pigskin boots, glistening as if they'd just been rubbed with persimmon oil, to the soft, russet deerskin waist pouch, on up to his hirsute, folded arms, which had blue veins that stood out under all the brown hair, and a simply enormous gold ring on one finger of his hand. Still higher, he finally came to a square-jawed face that looked for all the world like it was pieced together from little scraps of orange peel. Imagining this guest to be a customer of some importance, the husband tried to mimic the expressions of the city folk, saying, "Pray take a seat inside, master. They'll be back soon."

The river warden could tell at once, from his speech and the way he wore his starched clothes, that this was a farmer just in from the countryside. Ordinarily the warden would have left after finding the women to be out, but something in this young man intrigued him, so he stayed.

"Where are you from?" the river warden asked in a soft, fatherly tone of voice, to put the young man at ease. "I don't think I know you."

It occurred to the young fellow that he didn't know this guest, either. "I just got here yesterday," he answered.

"Up there in the country – is the wheat in ear yet?"

"The wheat crop? Our wheat out front o' the mill – ha – that pig of ours – ha ha – and our – "

Suddenly realizing that he hadn't answered the question the eminent city man had asked, he remembered his place: he ought not to have talked about "our mill" and the "pig," and he oughtn't to have used such vulgar words. He found himself tongue-tied.

Words having failed him, he gave the river warden a timid smile, hoping that he would forgive him and understand that he was a good boy, not one for deviousness.

The river warden understood this. And he could already tell that he was one of the boat people's relations. "Where's Seventh Maid gone to?" he asked the young man. "When do you suppose she'll be back?"

This time the young man replied more carefully. But the answer was the same: "I just got here yesterday." "Yesterday evening," he decided to add. Finally he got it out that

Seventh Maid had gone with Wuduo and the procuress to worship at a temple on shore, while he guarded the boat. Feeling a need to explain why he could be so trusted, he then told the river warden that he was Seventh Maid's "man."

Since Seventh Maid called the warden "Godfather" and this godfather was getting to meet his son-in-law for the first time, he needed no invitation; a few words more, and both men had crawled into the cabin.

It was furnished with a little bed. Sheets of embroidered silk and red calico were folded and neatly stacked on top. The visitor sat on the edge of the bed, as was the custom. Light streamed in through the opening; what looked dark from the outside was plenty bright inside.

Fumbling for cigarettes and matches for his guest, the young man managed to upset a small jug of chestnuts. Big round nuts shining like black gold began to roll all over the dim cabin floor. Scrambling to stop them, the young man put them back into the jug, quite unaware that he ought to be offering them to his visitor. But the visitor just made himself at home, picking up a few from the floor to crack and eat. These chestnuts dried in the open air were wonderful, he added.

"These are delicious – don't you like them?" said the warden, noticing that his host wasn't cracking any open for himself.

"I like 'em fine. They're from the chestnut tree out back of my house. We got a lot of them last year. You should have seen how nicely they burst out of their prickly shells. Sure I like 'em!" He laughed, almost as proud as if he were talking about his own children.

"You don't often see chestnuts this big."

"I picked out the biggest myself."

"Did you?"

"Yeah, I kept 'em 'specially for Seventh Maid, 'cause they're her favorite."

"Do you have any monkey chestnuts out there?"

"What are they?"

The warden then told the country man the story: Up in the mountains there lived some monkeys who pelted chestnuts big as your fist at anyone who came to call them names. So, whenever anyone wanted chestnuts to eat, they just went to the foot of the mountains and let the foul words fly.

The chestnuts had helped the inarticulate young man find a friend. He opened up to the warden about all sorts of things having to do with chestnuts. He knew so much about country things. He told him all about a place called Chestnut Hollow and about how strong and handy were plow handles made of chestnut wood. He was desperate to get all these things out, for customers had come to drink and smoke all night long after his arrival the day before; pent up in the little afterhold with no one to talk to but Wuduo, he'd seen her drop off to sleep like a dead sow. This morning he ought to have had the chance to talk country talk with his wife, but then the women had announced they were going ashore to Seven-Mile Bridge to pray, assigning him to guard the boat. It felt like he'd been waiting in the boat forever, and still they weren't back. He had gone to the afterhold to watch the sights out on the river, and, new and different though everything was, it just got him even more in the dumps. Earlier on, sleeping in the hold, he'd dreamed of what would happen if the floodwaters rose all the way to engulf his village. How many carp would be trapped behind the fishing weir then! He'd catch them and hang them in the sun to dry, stringing them through the gills with a willow branch. He had tried to count them all, but couldn't get it right, when suddenly the visitor had arrived, at which point all the fish seemed to get away into the water.

Now he had company, and the guest seemed in the mood for such conversation, so the young man seized the opportunity and told the river warden all the things he'd been saving up for pillow talk with his wife.

He told the river warden about everything in the country, like his naughty little piglet, whom he'd named Lil' Darling, and the millstone that had just been whetted and fitted again by the stone mason, which reminded him of a joke about that trade. Finally there was the story of the missing sickle, a little sickle the likes of which the river warden couldn't imagine:

"Tell me, was that strange or not? I swear I hunted for it high and low – under the bed, on the lintel over the door, all over the barn – everywhere. It was hidden. Just like in hide-and-seek, it just vanished. I blamed Seventh Maid, and she cried. Still we couldn't find it. Devils' surprise, covered up my eyes – it was hidden in a rice basket up on a roof beam the whole time. Six months in a rice basket! Must have been hungry! Came out rusty as a man covered with boils. Tricky little bastard. Do ya see what I'm saying? How could it have been in a rice basket for six months? It was mostly an ornament, something we hung over the smoke hole up top. Then I remembered. I'd been whittling pegs with it when I cut myself. With my finger all bloody, I got mad and chucked it aside. Later I went down by the stream and ground away at it. It's pretty good now – sharp enough to chew into flesh again. If you're not careful, it'll draw your blood. I haven't told Seventh Maid about it yet. She's sure to remember how hard she cried over it. So I've found it. Ha ha, found it at last."

"It's good you did."

"Yes, I'm glad to have it back. Because I always suspected that Seventh Maid had dropped it in the stream and was too embarrassed to admit it. Now I know she wasn't lying. I know, I wronged her. 'If you don't find it,' I swore, 'I'm going to beat you.' Of course I never made a move like I was going to, but my anger frightened her. She cried half the night."

"Can't you use it to cut grass?"

"Huh? Why that? It has so many other uses. It's a little

one, so delicate – what do you mean, cut grass with it? You can use it to peel potatoes, carve flutes – that's what it's for. It's so tiny, and worth three hundred cash – made of wonderful steel. Everybody ought to carry a little knife like this on him, d'ya see?"

"I see, I see," said the river warden. "Everybody ought to have one, I follow you."

Thinking that he really did understand him, the young man shared all his thinking with the warden, even his hope for a baby in the coming year, and other thoughts that were best left to be shared with his wife in bed. He went on and on, no longer even afraid to use obscene and unseemly language, until the river warden got up to go and the young man realized he hadn't even asked his name.

"Sir, your honorable name? If you'd kindly leave your card, I can tell them you called."

"No need, no need. Just tell her that a tall man came to the boat, wearing these boots. And tell her not to receive any customers tonight. I'm coming here."

"No customers, because you're coming?"

"That's right. I'll be here all right. And I'll take you out for a drink, now that we're friends."

"Friends, yes we are, friends."

The warden clapped his big, fleshy hand on the young man's shoulder and stepped ashore from the prow. Then he boarded another boat.

When the river warden had left, the young man tried to guess who this giant fellow might be. It was the first time he had ever talked with such a noble person. He'd never forget this wonderful experience. The man hadn't just talked with him; he'd called him his friend and invited him for a drink! He figured he must be one of Seventh Maid's "regulars" and a big-spending one. Suddenly he was so happy he felt like singing. In a low voice he began to sing a folk song in the style of the people from Four Streams:

The river is up,
Trapping many carp in our weir;
Some are the size of big straw sandals,
Others the size of little straw sandals.

But he waited a while longer, and still his wife didn't
return, nor anyone else. He thought again of the big man's
sophisticated manners and speech. He recalled those shiny
boots. Only the very best mountain persimmon oil could
have made them so handsome, he decided. He remembered
the heavy gold ring, worth more than he could guess. He
wasn't sure why he was so attracted to it. And he recalled
this gentleman's every gesture and opinion – he had the aura
of a provincial governor, the dignity of a general – so this
was Seventh Maid's money tree! And he began to sing
another song, in the saucy style of Yang Village:

The militia chief burns charcoal in the hollow,
The town head crawls o'er his ashes down below!
It's them ashes makes a yam begin to swell, oh!
While charcoal burning only leaves you yellow.[2]

It was after noon and people were cooking lunch on their
boats all around. The husband's wet firewood refused to kindle; the smoke went every which way, causing him to cry
and sneeze, until finally it flattened out over the river water
like a piece of thin silk. He could hear the cooks' ladles
clanging against their woks in the eateries on the bank and
the sound of cabbages plopping into the pan on the boat
next door. Still no sign of Seventh Maid. Since the trick of

[2]"Crawling over ashes" is associated with "getting one's knees dirty" (wu
xi), which is a pun on "defiling the daughter-in-law" (getting her dirty,
wu xi). Hence, line 2 alludes to the town head (di bao, as in the baojia system) having an affair with the militia captain's daughter-in-law. If the
figure of a yam inflating while roasting in hot ashes needs further explanation, see the "Songs of the Zhen'gan Folk" below.

starting a shipboard fire with wet firewood was new to the young man, his little iron stove remained cold and mute. He kept trying without success. Finally he had to give up.

Helpless to take his meal, he sat hungry on a little stool, drumming on the deck, with something still on his mind. A hint of discontent had begun to grow in his heart. That waist pouch that had seemed so stuffed with money, so arrogant, reappeared before his eyes, and it robbed him of his peace of mind. The look of that square, red, orange-peel face, which now seemed made up of wine lees and dark blood, had become hateful to him, a look that was now burned into his memory. And what use was memory? He could still remember that command, delivered to his face – his, the husband's! "No customers tonight. I'm coming here." Damnable words, straight from that big, impudent, yam-eating mouth of his! Why did he have to say it? What right did he have to say it?

Wild thoughts raged in his heart, aggravated by hunger. The emotions of primitive man welled up inside the simple youth.

No more songs came to him. His throat was choked with jealousy, and he couldn't have got them out in any case. Happiness was beyond his grasp. Angry farmer that he was, he decided to go home the next day.

Naturally in this rage he was even more useless at lighting a fire. He ended up throwing all the firewood overboard into the river.

"Fuck you, firewood! Get lost in the ocean."

Yet the firewood hadn't floated ten yards away before people on another boat fished it out of the water. It was as if they were all ready for it, just waiting for some wet firewood to float down the river to them. Just as soon as they'd got it, he could see them kindling it with a length of frayed rope. Immediately the boat was blanketed in smoke, and the fire was lit, to the accompaniment of crackling and popping. The sight of all this heaped humiliation on top of the young man's anger. He made up his mind to head for home, even if the women hadn't returned yet.

At the end of the street he ran into his wife and the young maid Wuduo, laughing and talking as they walked hand in hand. Wuduo was carrying a two-stringed *huqin* fiddle. It looked to be brand new, a finer instrument than he'd ever dreamed of seeing.

"Where are you going?"

"I – I'm on my way home."

"Can't even get you to mind the boat – here you are, going home already. Are you angry at someone? Why so peevish?"

"I'm going home. Let me go on my way."

"Come back with me to the boat!"

He looked at his wife, and she appeared even more adamant than she sounded. And he knew for sure that that fiddle was a present for him. He had to give in. Rubbing his burning forehead, he muttered, "All right, all right, I'll go," and followed behind his wife to the boat.

Presently the old procuress caught up with them, carrying a pair of pork lungs. She'd run so fast her cheeks were flushed, and she was gasping for breath, as if she'd filched the meat from somebody's stand and feared they'd catch up and haul her off to the yamen. As soon as she was on board, the wife called out to her from the cabin, "Imagine that, Auntie, my man wants to leave!"

"What an idea. Leaving before he's even seen the opera."

"We ran into him at the entrance to the street, all out of sorts. He must be angry at us for coming home so late."

"It's my fault. And the fault of the gods we were praying to. And the butcher's fault, too. I shouldn't have haggled on endlessly with the butcher over so little money, and the butcher shouldn't have filled these lungs with so much water."

"No, it's my fault," said the wife, who was keeping her

husband company in the cabin. She sat down across from her man and began to undo her tunic, letting him see her coquettish bra of thin damask silk. Embroidered on it were a pair of "mandarin ducks dallying between the lily pads." She had made it herself, just the month before.

He eyed her in silence, while feelings beyond description raced and surged through his blood.

They heard the madam and Wuduo in the afterhold, talking about the provisions.

"Who stole all our firewood?"

"And who washed this rice?"

"I'll bet he couldn't light the fire. Elder sister's husband is a farmer; all he knows how to kindle is rosin."

"Didn't we just untie a new bundle yesterday?"

"It's all gone now."

"Go up to the bow and fetch another bundle. Don't say anything."

"Sister's husband only knows how to wash rice!" Wuduo giggled.

The young man listened in on all this without saying a word. He sat quietly in the cabin, looking at that new fiddle.

"It's all in tune," said the woman. "Give it a try."

At first he kept still. Then he put the fiddle on his knee to inspect the rosin on it. As he tuned, an unfamiliar tone flowed out from between his fingers. He smiled rapturously.

Soon the cabin filled with smoke. When the women called the man out to eat, he brought the fiddle with him. He continued his tuning in the bow of the boat.

As they ate their lunch, Wuduo said, "Sister's Husband, after a while why don't you play 'Lady Mengjiang Weeps at the Great Wall'? I'll sing."

"I don't know that one."

"I hear you can play it real well. You're fooling."

"No, I'm not. All I know is the melody to 'The Mother Sees Off Her Daughter.'"

"Seventh Maid tells me you play very well," the madam put in. "So, when we got to the temple and saw this fiddle, I thought of you and said we must buy it for you. We were lucky to get it so cheap. You couldn't get one for a whole dollar in the countryside, could you?"

"No. How much was it?"

"A hundred-string of cash and six. Everybody said it was worth it."

"Who said?" Wuduo put in.

"Who said it wasn't, you little brat?" said the madam angrily. "What do you know? Zip your lips!"

Wuduo stuck her tongue out at herself, ashamed of her slip of the tongue.

They'd got the fiddle absolutely free, from a friend in the trade. Seventh Maid was amused to hear the madam scold Wuduo for disputing her little fib. The man laughed uneasily along with them, thinking his wife was laughing at the old woman's ignorance.

He bolted down his food, the quicker to take up his new fiddle. Its tone was clear and bright. Beside herself with happiness, Wuduo put down her rice bowl and began to sing along, until the madam rapped her over the head with chopsticks. She had to gulp down her meal so she could clear the dishes and clean the wok.

That evening, when the awning was pulled over the front cabin, the man played his fiddle while Wuduo sang. Seventh Maid sang, too. The lamp shade over her Standard Oil kerosene lamp, made of red paper folk cutouts, bathed the entire cabin in the rosy light seen at weddings. The young man was as elated by the excitement as if it were New Year's. But it wasn't long before two roaring drunk soldiers heard the music as they made their way down the river street. The drunks staggered down to the boat, rocking it with their muddy hands, and yelled out, slurring their speech as if they had walnuts in their mouths, "Who's that singing? Tell us your name! Sing for us sweetly, and we'll give you five hundred cash. Hear me? Daddy's gonna give you five hundred cash for your trouble."

The music abruptly stopped, and the boat fell silent.

The drunkards kicked the boat repeatedly. Bung, bung, bung, dull and heavy it resounded. Then they tried to roll back the awning but couldn't find the seam. "So our money isn't good enough for you, eh, you whoring bitch litter!" one of them bellowed. "Playing deaf and dumb, huh? Who's fooling around with you down there? You think I'm worried about *him?* I'm not afraid of the emperor himself. Sir, you in there! Devil take me if I fear the emperor. Hell, not even our army commander or our division commander – sons of bitches both of them – bastards, turtle eggs. Yeah, chicken eggs, bad eggs, putrid rotten eggs one and all. They don't scare me!"

"Foxy whores," the other yelled in a hoarse voice, "come out of your cabin, and pull Daddy down on board."

Then suddenly they heard stones pelting down on the awning, accompanied by a flood of abuse against their ancestors. All on board were panic stricken. The madam hurriedly dimmed the lamp and went out to turn back the awning; the husband had crawled into the afterhold with his fiddle at the first truculent shouts. Moments later he heard the two drunk men enter the forward cabin, cursing and falling over each other to kiss Seventh Maid and even the madam and Wuduo. Then he heard them ask, "So who was it, making that music? Drag the fiddler on out here, so he can sing Daddy another song."

The madam was too scared to speak. Seventh Maid, too, was out of ideas.

Drunk out of their minds, the two men began to curse at the top of their voices: "Stinking bitches, get that cuckold bastard out here to play for us, and there's a thousand in it for you. Cao Cao himself, number one sport in the world, wouldn't be so generous! A thousand for you – a thousand yams! Hurry up and get him out here, or we'll set fire to your boat. Did you hear me, you old biddy? Right now, before Daddy really gets mad. What's wrong with your peepers, can't you see who we are?"

"Please, gentlemen, we were just having a little family fun. There's no one else here – "

"Oh no? Oh no? You're no good any more, you old whore! You old woman, you're shriveled up like a wrinkled orange. Get that fiddle player out here on the double, the bastard. I'll play the fiddle myself, and I'll do the singing!" Meanwhile he was standing up, getting ready to search the rear cabin. The madam's jaw dropped open with fright. Rising to meet the crisis, Seventh Maid caught hold of the drunkard's hand and laid it on her ample breast. He got the idea and sat down again. "Ah, that's good, that's really fine, and Daddy can afford it. This is where Daddy's gonna sleep tonight. 'In the Peach Blossom Palace I neglect my duty, / Smitten with Sumei's boundless beauty,' " he trailed off, singing Song Emperor Taizu's lines about his consort, taken from a Peking opera.

He lay down by Seventh Maid's left side, and the other followed suit without a word, flopping down on her right.

When things seemed to have quieted down a bit in the forward cabin, the young man whispered for the madam through the partition. She stealthily crawled back to him, still feeling the sting of the men's insults. Confused as ever about what had passed, the young man asked her, "What happened?"

"They're soldiers from the camp, drunk as skunks, but they'll be gone soon."

"They'd better. I forgot to tell you, a big, square-faced fellow came today – looked like a big official – and left instructions not to take any customers since he's coming tonight."

"Did he wear tall leather boots and have a booming voice like a loud gong?"

"Yes, that's him. He had a big gold ring on his finger, too."

"That was Seventh Maid's godfather. So he came this morning?"

"Came in person. He talked on and on before leaving and ate some of my dried chestnuts."

"What did he say?"

"He said he was coming for sure and not to take any customers. . . . And he said he'd take me out for a drink."

What was he coming for, the madam wondered? Surely the river warden didn't want to spend the night here himself? Might he possibly want the company of someone more his own age? She couldn't figure. Although an old procuress was accustomed to dirty things of every description, and nothing could make her blush any longer, being told that she was "no good any more" had really shamed her. She crept back to the forward cabin and made a face at the unseemly tangle there, calling the soldiers swine and dogs under her breath before returning to the afterhold.

"Well, what are they doing?"

"Nothing."

"What's going on, have they gone?"

"Nothing much, they're asleep."

"Asleep?"

The madam couldn't see his face very clearly, but she caught the tone in his voice, so she said, "Sister's Husband, it's not often you're in town, so let's go ashore. They're performing *Qiu Hu Plays Three Tricks on His Wife* tonight at the Palace of the Three Top Scholars. I'll get us box seats."

The man shook his head in silence.

The soldiers fooled around some more and left at last. The three women joked about it by lamplight in the forward cabin, making fun of their drunkenness. But the husband refused to come out of the afterhold. The madam twice went to the door and tried to get him to join them, but he ignored her. They couldn't understand what had got him so mad. She turned to inspect the four banknotes. She could tell a counterfeit; these were genuine. She pointed out the serial numbers and designs to Seventh Maid by lamplight and then sniffed at them, remarking that they must have come from the Muslims' eating house since they had the smell of beef fat on them.

Wuduo went over and tried again. "Sister's Husband, Sister's Husband, they've gone now. Let's finish our song. And then we can – "

She was stopped by Seventh Maid, who pulled her away, seemingly with something on her mind.

It was dead quiet now. The man in the rear cabin had been softly plucking the fiddle with his fingers, but now he stopped even that.

The three women heard the sounds of drums, gongs, and *suonas*[3] wafting down. A shopkeeper on the river street was getting married; guests had arrived to present congratulations, and they were making preparations for a big opera that would keep things hopping all night long.

Seventh Maid stole back into the hold after a bit, only to return moments later, her attempts at reconciliation evidently having failed.

"What's wrong with him?" asked the old lady.

Seventh Maid shook her head and sighed. "He's just bullheaded. Let him be."

Thinking that the river warden was not coming after all, they went to bed. The three women slept in the forward cabin, with only the man in the stern.

A search party led by the river warden came in the middle of the night, when the whole river was dead silent. Four fully armed policemen stood guard at the prow of the boat as the warden and the patrol leader shined their flashlights

[3]Brass-belled Chinese oboes.

into the forward cabin before entering. The madam turned up the lamp. She'd been through this before and knew it was routine. Throwing a jacket over her shoulders as she sat up in bed, Seventh Maid said hello to "Godfather" and "Your Honor the Patrol Leader," then asked Wuduo to pour them tea. Wuduo was half asleep, still preoccupied with thoughts of the spring country berries she'd been picking in her dream.[4]

Madam shook the husband out of his sleep and dragged him out. The sight of the river warden and the high official in his black uniform scared him speechless. He wondered what awful trouble they were in.

"Who is this?" demanded the patrol leader in a haughty voice.

The river warden answered for the husband. "Seventh Maid's man. Just up from the country, on a family visit."

"He arrived only yesterday, Your Honor," added Seventh Maid.

The official stared at the man a while and then at the woman. Then, as if satisfied with the warden's explanation, he said no more and began a perfunctory search of the cabin. The little jug of dried chestnuts caught his attention; when the warden grabbed a fistful and stuffed them into a big pocket of his smart uniform, the patrol leader beamed, still saying nothing.

Soon they were off to the next boat. The madam was about to put back the awning when a policeman returned to give her a message: "Madam, tell Seventh Maid that the patrol leader will be returning to give her a closer inspection. Understand?"

"Soon?" asked the madam.

"When the night patrol is over."

"You're sure?"

"When have I ever lied to you, old whore?"

_____

[4]"Third-month berries," yellow and sour, and smaller than strawberries.

The husband was puzzled by the old lady's delight, for he had no idea why the patrol leader would want to inspect his wife again. But the sight of his sleeping wife had dissipated his anger from earlier in the evening, and he was willing to make up with her. He wanted to go to bed with her and talk about family matters, for they had something to discuss. So he sat himself down on the edge of the bed.

The madam seemed to know what he was thinking, to understand his desires – and his ignorance – so she gave a hint that only Seventh Maid would understand: "The patrol leader will soon be back."

Seventh Maid bit her lip in silence and for a long while remained lost in thought.

The husband rose early the next morning to leave. Without a word, he made ready his straw sandals and searched for his pipe and tobacco pouch. When all was ready, he sat on the edge of the low bed, looking as if he had something to say but couldn't get it out.

"Didn't you promise Godfather last night you'd be going to his house today for the noon meal?" Seventh Maid asked him.

He just shook his head.

"He's preparing a banquet just for you! Four entrees, four side dishes, and a hot pot. This is a big deal – a lot of honor is involved. Don't you feel embarrassed to stand him up?"

He didn't reply.

"And you haven't even been to the opera yet."

He remained silent.

"What about those pork dumplings you love, at the Rosy Heavens restaurant? They don't begin serving them until noon."

He was bent on going. Seventh Maid didn't know what to do. She stood in the prow, then went back and retrieved from her purse the bills given her by the soldiers the night before. She counted them – four in all – then stuffed one of them into her husband's left palm. He said nothing. Thinking she knew what he was thinking, she said, "Madam, give me the other three bills, too." The madam handed them over, and Seventh Maid stuffed them into her husband's right palm.

He threw them on the floor, shaking his head. Cupping his face in his big, rough hands, unaccountably he started sobbing like a baby.

Wuduo and the madam knew enough to flee into the afterhold. Wuduo thought it strange, laughable, that a grown man should cry. But she didn't laugh. Standing in the stern by the rudder, she spotted the fiddle hanging from a beam in the afterhold. She wanted to sing, but somehow or other she'd lost her voice.

When the river warden arrived at the boat to escort his guest from afar to his feast, only the madam and Wuduo were on board. From them he learned that husband and wife had returned to the countryside together early that morning.

The Lovers

Limpid in style and bucolic in setting but without reference to specific regional local color, "The Lovers" ("Fufu") is a model pastoral, its apparent simplicity bearing rich allegorical overtones. (In a postscript dated 14 July 1929, Shen attributed its rural lyricism to influence from Fei Ming and regretted being unable to duplicate it in other works.) In her biography of Shen Congwen, Hua-ling Nieh notes his sensuous and ironic use of color symbolism and the importance of recurring details such as the crown of wildflowers forced on the girl in this story, which Nieh takes to be an emblem of the life force, as in D. H. Lawrence. We may add that, in local folk idiom, wildflowers denote a woman of fallen virtue. They are, then, beautiful things of nature that have been distorted by civilization into something that hurts.

When all is said and done, however, "The Lovers" runs quite contrary to Shen Congwen's love of "the bucolic." This is the rare piece in which he makes villains of country characters and a hero of a quintessentially troubled (indeed, depressed) city man. A member of the Kuomintang, like Shen's sparring partners on the Right, the man actually concludes that the city is more restful than the country. As usual, however, Shen Congwen shows evil to proceed from weakness and incompleteness (drunkenness and sexual frustration, in this post-Freudian story), not from any primal demonic urge. To analyze the story using Shen Congwen's usual iconography, it is the sensitive city man Huang who is really the "country fellow" of the piece: the one who knows and restores the workings of nature. The peasants are too benighted, too beset by their traditional ways, to understand behavior that "comes naturally under such fine weather."

Once again, Shen Congwen deftly shows his understanding of social manners, of how rural and urban classes of people interact, and of how primitive motivations masquerade as morality and refinement. In this story, better-off peasants (the lovers) appear more sympathetic than the peasant "masses," an inversion of contemporary ideology that could not have found favor with Chinese revolutionaries.

Huang had moved to the village in the hope that peace and quiet could heal his nervous depression. One evening at supper in the courtyard under a pomelo tree, already feeling helpless before a game hen set down in front of him by a hosteler who was a bit *too* concerned with his nutrition – a bird so underdone that he could see its blood – he found himself suddenly interrupted by shouts from outside. "Come on, go take a look. Two of 'em, caught in the act!" It sounded urgent, as if there'd been a catastrophe, something the whole village needed to see. Huang had never cottoned to such excitement, but for some reason he put down his bowl too and strode out the door to the little pond, chopsticks in hand, to see what the commotion was all about.

He saw people running toward the south, filling in bystanders in haste as they went: "Down by Eight Path Hill, Eight Path Hill – what a pretty sight! Go now if you want to see it. Don't wait around. They'll be turning them in to the militia any minute!"

He couldn't imagine what in the world it was about. He could only suppose that, since everyone wanted to see it, it must be pretty interesting. But, on second thought, what was interesting in the countryside was always obvious to a city man.

Maybe they'd caught a pair of wild boars, he thought; that was worth a look.

He followed after a man who was talking to the crowd as he went. They hurried up some hill paths that Huang seldom took, made a sharp turn, and there in a little hollow he saw a crowd. They were all strangely huddled together in a circle, for what purpose he couldn't fathom. The man who'd led him here plunged into the crowd audaciously, forcefully pushing people aside. Having noticed that he had Huang in tow, the clever fellow was removing them in the name of letting this city guest see what went on in the country. The

Translated by Jeffrey Kinkley

other country folk, too, seemed to think that this thing should be shown to the visitor, so they scurried to make way.

It was all laid bare before his eyes.

Much to the disappointment of Huang, who'd hoped to see wild boars in the flesh, the prey was just a couple of human beings.

Yet Huang's very presence heightened many of the onlookers' interest in the spectacle. They all exchanged knowing smiles, as if to say, "We have this city person as a witness." A country wife among them who took special interest in his "foreign" machine-made shirt seemed also to be asking, "Do you city people wearing these clothes of yours ever see such things?" Aware that the country people found his haircut, his leather shoes, and his light woolen trousers with their ribbed texture even more engrossing than the two captives, Huang made his way toward them. They were trussed up together with rope.

To his amazement, it was a young couple, a girl and a boy. They were country people, both so very young. The girl was silent under the merciless stare of the crowd, crying softly to herself. Some wag had thought to stick a funny little wreath of wildflowers in her hair, a tiara that bobbed in the air whenever she shifted her head, in a way that might have seemed quite beautiful in other circumstances.

The situation was clear enough without any explanation. Their crime was of the sort peculiar to young people.

But the clever man offered Huang an explanation anyway, for he was a "visitor from the city." Someone had been passing by a hollow in the hills and come on the couple in a haystack. There they were, doing something openly in broad daylight that was an outrage to the beholder. So the one who found them raised a crowd of men in the neighborhood and nabbed them.

Now that they were arrested, how were they to be punished? That sort of thing wasn't for them to decide.

Probably they'd have to call in the township head pretty

soon. He'd line them up before his table with red cloth over it and sit on his throne, wearing sunglasses to hear their case, or at least that was how all the country folk pictured it. Why the young people had to be captured in the first place wasn't too clear now, to either the captured or the capturers. Still, the young bucks who had brought the offenders in for public humiliation, themselves not having got in on the panting and sweating, looked on at the woman now with a kind of satisfaction that went beyond panting and sweating. The women in the crowd went up to the couple, scratching their own faces, "Tsk, tsk!" to shame them. Needless to say, it would never have occurred to them that this good weather in any way sanctioned certain kinds of behavior with a man. The old folk just shook their heads, evidently having forgot the follies and impetuousness of their own youth, and believing, now that they had children of their own, in the necessity of upholding local mores.

A gentle evening breeze brushed Huang's face. Hearing the sound of a flute playing up in the mountains, he raised his head to the skies and took in the peach-pink glow of the sunset. It occurred to him that such a poetic setting was incomplete without a woman.

Trussed up though he was, the young man seemed lost in thought. Huang thought there could be no harm in asking where he came from.

His head bowed, the boy had already noticed Huang's black leather shoes. They were something new to him; even in this predicament, he risked a longing glace at those ebony, square-toed shoes and marveled at the tapered pant legs above them. The question asked of him didn't sound like it came from a judge, so he raised his head and looked at Huang. This wasn't someone he knew, but already he sensed that Huang was a friend. The boy shook his head to indicate that he had been abused.

"Are you from around here?"

Someone answered for him: No, he wasn't. There wasn't a

chance that the one who spoke was mistaken, either, for that fellow had acquaintances that went even beyond these environs. The girl, in particular, was dressed differently than girls in the village nearby. He knew the names of all the women in the village anyway. Still, the busybody couldn't say exactly where they did come from, for a lot of people had asked them that before Huang ever came on the scene, and nobody had got an answer.

Huang examined the girl again. She was young, not yet out of her teens. Her outfit was impeccably clean, made of moon-blue burlap. Tall and rosy cheeked, she seemed handsome and well bred. From the look of her, she wasn't just an ordinary country girl from the neighborhood. And she seemed to be crying more out of fright than shame.

Suspecting that the young people had eloped to escape their families, Huang began to feel pity for them. He had to get them away from this hysterical crowd. But the friend who'd given him lodging was off to the city, and Huang had no idea who was in charge of the militia bureau. A crowd like this was capable of acts far stupider than what they'd done already. They saw nothing at all wrong with meddling in other people's business. His thoughts were interrupted by the voice of someone who had a suggestion.

A man who looked like he'd been drinking, with a face full of pimples and a red drunkard's nose, set down his bottle of liquor and came forward to get in on the commotion. Muttering to himself while he stroked the girl's face with his big, hairy paw, he proposed that the girl and boy be stripped naked and given a good lashing with thorny brambles before being packed off to see the township head. To him, this punishment was sensible and clever. He had no scruples about bellowing out this strange proposal to the others, and he might have gone and done it himself, without waiting for the crowd to agree, if someone hadn't tugged at his trousers and reminded him that there was a "city man" present.

The women nursed a grievance of their own, that this woman could so handily sleep with a man amid that idyllic mountain scenery. They were against the stripping, but in favor of the flogging.

The children, meanwhile, out of their heads with glee, scrambled to be the first to get the brambles. Having felt the lash of their fathers' cattle prods on their backs all too often before, they were always especially excited to see somebody whip a thief, a wild dog, or a feral cat.

Huang could see that the situation was getting out of control, but there was nothing he could do. Suddenly a man with the look of an army veteran came on the scene. His appearance raised a tumult from the crowd; everybody clamored to fill him in and give their own opinion. Seeing that they addressed him as "Captain," Huang figured he must be a man of influence in the village. He kept quiet, waiting to see how he handled the situation.

Imitating the manner of army officers he'd seen reviewing troops in town, the soldier frowned in silence as he solemnly gazed at the crowd. Then he looked around and caught sight of Huang. The presence of the "city man" made it all the more imperative that he assert his authority. So, when the women and children crowded in around him, he surprised them all with a shout of, "Stand aside!"

That sent them reeling backward, and it was with difficulty that they kept from laughing.

Flicking the aggrieved young man's face with a "dog-tail" bristle fern he'd picked by the wayside, the man began cross-examining him with the tone of a customs officer: "Where are you from?"

The boy hesitated. He looked at the captain's face and saw a scarlet mole near his ear.

"I'm from Yaoshang," he said.

As if satisfied to have this confession, the captain turned to the woman and asked her name in the same tone of voice.

"Your name?"

Instead of answering, the girl raised her head to look at her interrogator in the face, and at Huang. Then she shyly turned her gaze downward toward her feet. She wore shoes embroidered with double phoenixes, the sort that only rich families could afford in the countryside. A roguish man started praising her feet. Adopting the same insulting tone of voice, the captain asked, "Where are you from? Answer me, or I'll have you sent to the county magistrate!"

Country folk typically are scared of seeing officials, for to them officials are quite fearsome beings. But sometimes they have to see them, to settle a lawsuit, for instance, at which point they can rely on that very awesomeness of the officials to scare their opponents into submission. A lot of people were terrified just to think of going into town, afraid they might lose their way.

Helpless as she was, lashed together with the boy under the tree, the girl didn't seem afraid of the officials. She still said nothing.

"Flog them!" someone butted in from the crowd. It was the tried and true method for country people who liked to tell tales and could never get the truth out before an official without a little help from the wooden plank, the leather whip, or the bamboo rod. So some of them remembered that torture was the easiest method.

Someone else suggested finding a millstone so they could send them to the bottom of the pond. That was a threat.

Yet another person said they should make the boy drink urine and feed cow dung to the girl. That was a joke.

The discussion remained on this infantile level.

The girl and boy said nothing in reply, which made them appear unafraid. The captain was furious. His voice sterner than ever, he repeated the threats from the others, as if they were the majority's will after all and it were only right for those who had offended the many to be judged by the many — whatever they decided would be correct, which even the officials in town couldn't oppose.

"I was coming from Yaoshang, on my way to visit relatives at Huang Slope village," said the girl almost inaudibly, shaking her head.

Hearing her voice, the boy added, timidly, "We were going to Huang Slope together."

"Fleeing together?" asked their interrogator.

Finding the word *fleeing* quite inappropriate, the girl whispered, "No, just traveling together."

This differentiation of *traveling together* from *fleeing together* got the crowd to imagining that the two had met for the first time on the road and got it on right there. That sent everyone into titters.

The man who had caught the fornicators returned just now from the militia bureau. He had been looking for the captain for some time; he was as proud to have found him now as a subject reporting his triumphs to the king. Smirking and giving a roguish wink, he related everything that he had seen these shameless young people do under the afternoon sun. It was the part about "in broad daylight" that was so outrageous, for that was when everybody in this village was either working or napping – anything else was wrong, above all what they'd done, which was never done outdoors.

The captain naturally felt the couple should be turned over to the crowd to be stoned to death; he knew how to handle this situation. But, before sentencing, he wanted to know a little more about the boy's family background because custom and law might allow, in passing, that the boy be fined a hundred strings of cash or that an ox be requisitioned from his family – with the captain making a little something for himself. It was with this object in mind that he resumed the interrogation, rather tirelessly, and much more magnanimously than before.

The boy could no longer hold back.

Having managed to get everything out of the boy – his family's wealth, position, even how many there were of them – the man beamed with satisfaction. But then the bound boy caught him off guard. He said he was the girl's legal husband. They were newlyweds, on their first visit back to the girl's parents in Huang Slope. When they arrived here, the fine weather persuaded them to rest on a haystack of freshly mown rice straw, to view the wonderful scenery and all the mountain wildflowers. The sweet fragrances in the breeze, the hypnotic chatter of the birds, reminded them of what young people were here for. And then they were caught.

After that, the crowd could see for themselves that this was no spur-of-the-moment tryst. Yet, with the hint of wild passion gone, they felt all the more need to punish the couple. Those who knew they'd get no share of the fine insisted on a good beating at the minimum. And the captain, knowing now that the boy was a married man, became all the more conscientious.

The very fact that they were married and had done their thing in broad daylight without covering themselves was especially provocative and aggravating to the bachelors. Frustrated in their own desires for a woman, they naturally could never forgive this performance that had come before them.

Huang, who had got the whole picture though he'd at first been as surprised as anyone, now took the captain aside to beg for the couple's release. The captain looked him in the face, wondering if Huang was one of those interpreters for the foreigners. Finally, having just noticed the special Kuomintang badge on Huang's belt, and not wanting to look like a complete country hick, the man laughed and held out his hand to shake. When Huang didn't reciprocate, he rubbed it against his leg and said, slightly annoyed now, "We can't release them, sir."

"Why not?"

"We have to punish them. They've offended our village."

"Let them apologize for what they've done. Then let them go."

"That's no good," said the man with the whiskey nose, "this is our business." The men and women who had been listening in silence while Huang defended the sinners roared with approval at this. But, when Huang turned around to identify the dissenter, the red-nosed man had ducked down out of sight behind someone else and begun to smoke his pipe.

With the rout of the whiskey nose, others came forth to support Huang and beg the captain to show mercy on the couple. Women were among them, even the middle-aged ladies who were scared to death of the "city man" and nosy enough to deserve the epithet *shameless gossips*. Others, aware of who Huang was, tugged at the captain's lacquered black silk uniform and quietly clued him in. Thus informed, the captain realized that he could perform no extortion now. But, to keep up appearances before the crowd, even with the VIP standing in front of him, the captain continued the pretense of his official airs: "You are correct, Mr. Huang, sir. However, what happens here is not entirely up to me. There is also the head of the militia."

"Suppose I pay him a visit?"

"Of course. Let us go at once. I've no objection. Let's just not give the locals any cause for complaint."

Huang was well ahead of him; he knew what this crafty fellow was up to. He wanted to shift responsibility to the militia head. So Huang followed his lead. The onlookers made way for them.

They took the girl and boy with them. Some of the crowd followed after them out of curiosity, all the way to the militia bureau, many of them not content to go home even when they'd entered the compound.

It grew dark.

Negotiations at the militia bureau ended happily; the wily captain's tricks were of no avail with Huang intervening, so the young married couple were released from bondage there in the militia bureau courtyard. The captain sidled up to the young woman and said, hoping to ingratiate himself with Huang, "You owe this gentleman your thanks. It was he who saved you."

Just then removing the wreath of flowers that the country people had put in her hair to mock her, the young woman gravely saluted Huang with hands together. She kept hold of the flowers while making the gesture, instead of casting them aside. Her husband followed with a salute of his own. The captain begged off and went on his way. That rang down the curtain on this farce.

Huang accompanied the young rural couple outside. They went silently, past nosy fools still hanging around at the entrance who would have made more trouble without his presence. Escorting them up the mountain path, he paused and asked if they were hungry. The young man said they could make Huang Slope in time for supper. His father-in-law's house wasn't far, only two miles away; it was dusk, but they could find their way by starlight. At that, all three of them looked up into the heavens. Stars twinkled above the purple mass of mountains in the distance. It was a beautiful night.

"You should be all right now," Huang said. "They won't trouble you any more."

"Do you live here?" the young man asked. "I'll be back to visit you in a few days."

"Heaven protect you, good sir," the young woman said.

And then the young married couple went away.

Standing alone by the little bridge at the foot of the hill, Huang caught the fragrance of wildflowers in the breeze. Suddenly he thought of asking for a memento of the occasion – the wreath of flowers, which the woman still held.

"Hold up, there, hold up!" he called to them in the distance. "I'd like to have the flowers. Just drop them there for me."

She laughed as she laid them down by the road and

waited for Huang to catch up. Seeing that Huang was not coming up, the boy brought them down to Huang himself.

They disappeared into a thicket of bamboo. Mr. Huang sat down by the bridge with the handful of half-withered flowers whose name he didn't even know. As he smelled these blossoms that had been through such a strange experience in the woman's hair, vague pangs of desire unaccountably stirred in his heart.

Going over everything that had happened that day, he came to feel the narrowness of his world. If he had such a wife, invisible perils would be hovering over him, too. He decided he was tired of living in such a place. The surroundings were beautiful, but country people were as tedious as city people. He decided to move back to the city in a day or two.

Quiet

"Quiet" ("Jing"), written 30 March 1932 in Shanghai and revised 10 May 1942 in Kunming, is an elegant mood piece, but one with structure, even a "surprise" ending. Once again the setting is idyllic, yet the characters are refugees of the Sino-Japanese War, enmeshed in not one but several tragedies of death and silent frustration. In his History of Modern Chinese Fiction, *C. T. Hsia explains that the quietude that Shen Congwen here creates captures the helplessness of his characters. Their routines and small talk within the house of refuge appear constrained next to the scenery and signs of movement outside – kites, horses, the nun, and the bride – each of which becomes "a symbol of liberty and joy beyond the reach of the family." So, too, the kite whose string has snapped. According to folk belief, says critic Woei Lien Chong, such a kite bears away with it all the worries of its owner.*

This is also one of several stories in which Shen Congwen relies on "negative capability" to enter the mind of an adolescent girl, using dreams, daydreams, and subconscious exchanges of thought. From the story's postscript, "in memory of my elder sister's deceased son, Bei-sheng," one surmises that the characters here represented real people to Shen Congwen. But one need not have guessed that to feel his pain.

Hsia and William MacDonald, the translator, have suggested that a Daoist muse lies behind much of Shen Congwen's work, and here one sees the evidence, not so much in the story's philosophy as in its style. Apart from the overt dualism of war and nature, death and life – life appearing in images of youth, peach blossoms, and the spurting growth of the young female heroine Yuemin – nature itself appears in a dualist guise. It is quiet and reassuring, like the fortunetellers sought by the young women of the family, the soft, comforting conversation between mother and daughter that leaves fears unspoken, the magpie, bearer of good tidings, and the unheard flapping of a flag atop a grave. But to say this is to notice that quiet can be deceptive. Nature's other face is dynamic, even noisy: kites, flapping laundry, a girl grow-

ing like bamboo, echoes of the human voice. Where does true comfort lie? And what is one to make even of the innocence that is about to be lost – the innocence of the children, of the family unaware of the tragic fate of its father, of the nun who loves to hear the echo of her own voice? Besides the mundane questions of life and death, this story has intimations of a freedom in another realm, that of the unattainable. Perhaps after all innocence – indeed, "ignorance," Daoist ignorance – is bliss.

The spring day was very long. During the long daylight hours in this little town, old people sat in the sun enjoying the warmth or dozing. Young people with nothing to do were out on the porches or in the empty fields, flying kites. In the sky, the white sun moved along slowly; the clouds moved along slowly. Someone's kite string broke. Everywhere people looked up, searching the sky. Children made a great racket, jumping up and down and waving their arms to see the ownerless kite fall into someone's yard and catch on the end of a drying pole at the corner of the wall.

Yuemin, a girl of about fourteen with a pale little undernourished face, and wearing a new blue dress that went down to her knees, was just then on the drying porch behind the house. She watched a broken-stringed kite drift in from town. It floated at a slant over her head, the end of its string dragging over the roof tiles. Just as a fat woman on the porch of the neighboring house was awkwardly flailing to catch the kite string on a clothes pole, Yuemin heard a noise on the steps behind her. A little boy was climbing up the steps on his hands and knees. Momentarily a small forehead appeared at the head of the stairs. The child's lively eyes looked around, nervously and stealthily. He called out softly, before ascending the top step, "Little Auntie, Little Auntie, Grandmother is asleep. Can I come up for a while?"

The girl heard his voice and quickly turned her head. She looked at the child and scolded him softly, "Beisheng, you should be spanked! Why did you come up here again? Your mother will be back soon. Aren't you afraid of a scolding?"

"Just let me play a while, Auntie. Please don't make any noise. Grandmother is asleep," the child repeated in a pleading tone. His voice was very weak and gentle.

The girl frowned, scaring him a little, then went over and helped him up onto the porch.

This drying porch, like most of the drying porches in

Translated by William MacDonald

town, was made of wooden planks – most of them quite old – roughly arranged on a wooden frame. The two of them stood there leaning against the rotting, moss-covered railing, so rickety that it seemed about to collapse, counting kites in the sky. Beneath the porch was the slanting roof. Some tiles were missing, and green moss had grown in the places exposed to the spring rains. Roof touched roof, and on both sides of the porch were the rooftop porches of other houses. Clothing and sheets, drying on bamboo poles stuck up into the air, flapped like flags in the light breeze. Across from the porch was the stone city wall. You could see grapevines putting out new shoots in the cracks between the stones. Behind the porch was a small river, with gently flowing water that was clear and soft. On the other riverbank was a large field looking like a big green carpet embroidered with flowers of all colors. At the far end of the field were vegetable gardens and a small, red-walled convent. The peach trees beside the garden fence and inside the convent walls were just in bloom.

The sun was so warm and the scene so peaceful that the two children did not speak but simply looked on, now at the sky, now at the river. The river water was not the same shade of green as in the morning and the evening: some places seemed blue, others had turned silver in the reflecting sun. There were several patches of rape in the big field on the opposite bank, the flowers a clear golden yellow. Elsewhere in the grassy field, large pieces of white cloth being dried by people from the dye works in town lay stretched out, held down at the ends by large stones. Three people flying kites sat on a big rock in the field. One of them, a child, played wedding tunes on a reed whistle. Meanwhile, untended horses, three white and two brown, casually ate grass and moved along with their heads down.

Beisheng saw two of the horses begin to run. He shouted gleefully, "Look, Auntie. Look!" Auntie looked at him and pointed downward. The child understood that she was afraid they would be heard downstairs. He quickly pressed his hand over his mouth and looked at his aunt, shaking his head as if to say, "Hush, hush! We don't want them to find out."

They watched the horses and looked at the grass, looked at everything. The boy was wildly happy, but the girl seemed to be thinking of something far away.

They were refugees. This was not their home, nor was it their destination. In the whole group – Yuemin, her mother, her sister-in-law, her elder sister, her elder sister's son Bei-sheng, and the little maid Cuiyun – little four-year-old Bei-sheng was the only male. They had traveled in a daze for fourteen days under the awning of a little boat, intending to transfer to a river steamer when they reached here, but then, after repeated inquiries, they learned that Wuchang was still surrounded and none of the boats or vehicles going to Shanghai or Nanjing could get through. They learned that the news they'd heard upriver was inaccurate. They could not go on, and it would not be easy to go back, either. It was expensive, troublesome, and, what was more, unsafe. On the mother's suggestion, they had hunted up this little house to live in for the time being. They sent the soldier who had come with them back to Yichang, and now, having mailed letters to Peking and Shanghai, they awaited replies from all three places.

Mother and Sister-in-Law hoped someone would come from Yichang, Elder Sister hoped for a letter from Peking, and Yuemin thought only of Shanghai. She hoped a letter would come from Shanghai first so that she could go to school there. Going to Yichang to live with her father, a military attaché in the war ministry (her elder brother was an army officer, too), would not be as nice as going to Shanghai to live with her second elder brother, a teacher. But Wuchang had been under siege for a month, and who could say for sure when they would be able to get through on the Yangtze River? They had already been here forty days.

Every day she had gone in tow with the maid to the local newspaper office at the city gate, read the papers posted there, then hurried back to tell Mother and Elder Sister all the news. They either tried to find some comfort in the news or chatted about the good dreams they'd had the night before and from them tried to divine all sorts of impossibly good omens. No letter had arrived from any parts in the past month. Only a small portion of their traveling expenses remained.

Mother had always been in ill health. The added hardships of travel had quite naturally made her poor condition worse. Yuemin often thought, "If nothing happens in a couple of weeks, perhaps I'd better just go to the Party school." There were a lot of fourteen-year-old girls attending the Party school just then. Why couldn't a colonel's daughter attend, too? Once she was accepted they need spend no more money on her, and after graduation, in six months, she'd do her service wherever they assigned her and even get fifty dollars a month. She had read all about this in the newspaper but had kept it to herself, not daring to bring it up with her mother.

As she stood there thinking of the Party school and her future, the little boy kept listening intently. He was afraid that when his grandmother woke up she would find out he had climbed up onto the porch by himself, and then she would say that he could have fallen into a ditch and broken his arm. Just now he heard his grandmother coughing and pulled at the girl's dress. "Auntie, help me down now. Grandmother's awake," he said softly. He had climbed the steps by himself, but he didn't quite know how to get down.

When Yuemin had taken the child down the steps, she noticed the maid washing clothes in the courtyard. Yuemin squatted down beside the basin herself and scrubbed at a couple of things, but she didn't find it much fun.

"Cuiyun, you're awful busy. I'll go hang the clothes up on

the porch for you." She took some damp clothes that had already been wrung out and went back up onto the porch. In a short while she had hung the clothes on bamboo poles.

Since the bridge over the river was far away, there was for public convenience a ferry boat, one about as wide as a wooden bench. It was lying there lazily, up on the bank. The ferry did not connect with a road, so often half the day might pass without a passenger, except for men from the dye works drying cloth and a few laborers carrying earth. At the moment, the ferryman was napping on a big stone in the field. The boat was gray and worn, as though thoroughly bored and fatigued with being rocked in the water by the gentle breezes.

"Why is it so quiet?" Yuemin wondered. Far in the distance boat builders were hammering away on the sides of a boat, while in the little village on the other side of the river a peddler selling needles and thread was rattling his clapper. The sounds floating on the air simply intensified the feeling of unusual quiet.

Out from the convent with the peach trees in its courtyard came a young nun in a gray robe and black skullcap, carrying a new bamboo basket as she strode across the open field toward the riverbank. She came up to the shore a little above the ferry and squatted down on a stone before slowly rolling up her sleeves. She looked around. Then she looked up at the kites in the sky. Casually and unhurriedly, she took big bunches of vegetables from the basket, set them in front of her one by one, and swished them around in the water. The river water rippled and glistened in response.

Soon a country woman came out on the city-side bank and called over to the ferryman. The ferryman got into his boat, picked up his long pole, and pushed his boat for some time before he was across the river and could ferry the woman back. He seemed upset about something and spoke in a loud voice, but the woman went away without saying a word. Not long after, three men carrying empty baskets called to the ferryman from the city-side bank and, as before, the ferryman slowly pushed the boat across. This time it was the three men who were arguing with each other and the ferryman who said not a word. When the boat reached the bank, the ferryman stuck his pole into the sand. Before long, the six baskets had formed into a line and disappeared off the far end of the field.

The little nun finished washing her vegetables and began beating a piece of cloth with a wooden mallet. After pounding it several times, she rinsed it in the water and then began pounding it again. The sound of the mallet echoed from the city wall. Perhaps fascinated by the sound, the nun stopped pounding and shouted, "Silin! Silin!" and the wall answered, "Silin! Silin!" Soon there came another woman's voice, from the convent, also sharply calling out, "Silin, Silin," and saying something else as well, probably asking if her work was finished. So it was the young nun who was named Silin! Her work was finished, and she was tired of playing in the water, so she picked up her basket and walked back to the convent, intentionally cutting across the white cloth, stepping in the empty places.

When the young nun had gone, Yuemin watched vegetable leaves float down the river. As they slowly moved closer to the ferry, she thought of how happy the nun had seemed a moment before. "Now she must be in the convent, hanging up the clothes to dry on bamboo poles – or under the peach trees, pounding on an old nun's back – or reciting sutras and playing with a kitten – " She thought of many things that seemed amusing. She smiled and imitated the little nun in a whisper, "Silin, Silin."

More time passed. Thinking of the little nun's joy, the river water, the faraway flowers, the clouds in the sky, and her mother's illness, the girl unwittingly began to feel a little lonely. She remembered that in the morning a magpie had sung for a very long time on the porch, and then she remembered that every day at about this time the mailman came. Perhaps she should go downstairs to see if there was a letter from Shanghai. She went to the stairs and saw Beisheng climbing up onto the bottom step on his hands and knees, having a second go at it. The boy was lonely, too.

"Beisheng, you little scamp, you're naughty. Your mother will be home soon, so don't you go up there again."

She went down the steps. Beisheng tugged at her, asking her to bend down and put her ear next to his mouth. "Auntie," he whispered, "Grandmother spit again."

When she got inside the house, she saw her mother lying on the bed, quiet as death, breathing very weakly and softly; her thin narrow face was marked with fatigue and anxiety. Her mother seemed to have been awake for a while, and she opened her eyes when she heard footsteps in the room.

"Minmin, come look and tell me how much water is left in the thermos."

As the girl mixed medicine into the hot water, she looked at her mother's face, which was growing thinner by the day, and at her tiny nose.

"The weather is nice, Mama," Yuemin said. "And from the porch we could see the peach blossoms in the convent on the other side of the river. They're in full bloom now."

The invalid smiled weakly without speaking. She thought of the blood she had just spit up and stretched out her thin hand to rub her forehead.

"I don't have a fever," she mumbled. She looked at the girl and faintly smiled as she spoke. The smile was so touchingly pitiful that the girl let out a soft sigh.

"Is your cough a little better?"

"Yes, it's better. No matter, it's not that bad. I was careless enough to eat fish this morning. My throat burns a little, but it's not important."

During this exchange the girl tried to look into the little spit bowl next to her mother's pillow, but the invalid anticipated her and repeated, "It's nothing." Then she added, "Minmin, stand there and don't move. I want to have a look at you. You've grown taller this month. You look just like a grown-up."

The girl smiled in embarrassment. "I don't look like a bamboo, do I, Mama? I'm worried. It doesn't look good to be so tall at my age. If you're too tall, people laugh at you."

It was quiet for a moment. Then the mother remembered something. "Minmin, I had a good dream. I dreamed that we were already on the boat. The third-class cabins were terribly crowded. I was worried, but I thought to myself that in just three or four days we'd be there and could rest for a couple of weeks."

The invalid had made up the dream herself. Her mind was confused, and this was the second time she had related it.

Yuemin looked at her mother's waxy face and forced a smile.

"Last night I really did dream that we were on the boat. And Cousin Sanmao was a steward at the Fulu Hotel. He came to meet us, and he gave each of us a guidebook. A magpie sang for a long time this morning, so let's just see if a letter doesn't come today."

"If it doesn't come today, it should tomorrow."

"Maybe he'll come in person!"

"Didn't the paper say that the Thirteenth Division in Yichang was being transferred?"

"Perhaps Papa has already started out."

"If he's coming, he would send a telegram first."

They chattered on optimistically, each deceiving the other. Though she joined the game, Yuemin thought to herself, "Mama, what are we going to do about your illness?" And the mother thought, "If this illness continues, it will be terrible."

Back from the fortuneteller's in the north part of the city, Elder Sister and Sister-in-Law stood in the yard talking in whispers. Yuemin went to the door and feigned a happy voice. "Elder Sister, Sister-in-Law, a while ago a kite broke its string. The end of the string dragged across the tiles, and that woman next door tried to catch it with a bamboo pole. Instead she broke a lot of tiles. It was really funny!"

"Beisheng, you've been up on the porch again with Auntie," Elder Sister said. "If you're not careful, you'll break a leg and become a cripple. Then you'll have to become a beggar."

Beisheng squatted beside Cuiyun, who was washing vegetables. He heard his mother speak to him but didn't bother to answer. He just looked slyly at his aunt and smiled.

Smiling at Beisheng, Yuemin walked across the yard and pulled her elder sister toward the kitchen. "Sister, it looks like mother has spit up blood again," she said in a low voice.

"What are we going to do?" Elder Sister said. "A letter from Peking has just got to arrive."

"What lot did you draw?"

Elder Sister took out a copy to give to the girl, then beckoned to Beisheng, who was still squatting on the ground. The child came to her side and put his arms around her.

"Mama, Grandmother spit again. She put it under the pillow."

"Beisheng," Elder Sister said, "I've told you not to go into Grandmother's room and disturb her, do you hear?"

"Yes," said the child, as if he understood. Then he asked, "Mama, the peach blossoms on the other side of the river are all open. Can Auntie take me up on the porch to play for a while? I won't make any noise."

Elder Sister pretended to be angry. "You're not to go up there. It's rained a lot, and it's very slippery. You go to your room and play. If you go up on the porch, Grandmother will scold Little Auntie."

The child went over to his aunt, squeezed her hand, and then obediently went to his room.

Cuiyun had finished washing the clothes and was rinsing them. As she was wringing them out, Yuemin said, "Cuiyun, let's take them to the river next time. It's lots easier. We can take the ferry to the other side. There's no one there, so we don't have to be afraid of anything."

Cuiyun said nothing, but her face reddened, and she bowed her head with a smile.

The invalid had a fit of coughing; Elder Sister and Sister-in-Law went inside. Cuiyun finished wringing out the clothes and prepared to take them up onto the terrace. Yuemin stood in the yard looking at the shadows. Then she went to the door of the sickroom and looked inside. She saw her sister-in-law cutting paper and her elder sister sitting on the edge of the bed, trying to look into the small spit bowl. At first the mother would not allow it; she covered the bowl with her hand. Finally Elder Sister managed to get a look. She shook her head. All three were forcing themselves to smile and trying to talk about other things to relieve the mournfulness of their situation. They began to speak of unrelated matters, but in the end they came back to the letters and telegrams. Yuemin didn't know why, but her heart was full of sadness. She stood in the yard, her eyes red, biting her lip as though angry with someone. Time passed, and she heard Cuiyun call down from the porch, "Miss Min, Miss Min, come up and see the new bride on her horse! She's about to cross the river."

Another while passed, and Cuiyun said, "Oh look! Hurry! A big tile-shaped kite has got away. Hurry! It's right over us. Let's catch it."

Yuemin looked up. From the yard she too could see the kite up high, weaving back and forth like a drunken policeman, and she could faintly see the long, white kite string waving about in the air.

Yuemin was not interested in seeing either the kite or the bride. She waited until Cuiyun had come down from the porch before she went up herself. She leaned against the railing and looked around. Her heart slowly calmed down. She watched the people from the dye works pick up their cloth in the big field. They folded the white sheets into strips like dried bean curd, then piled them onto the grass one by one. She saw smoke above the roof tiles of the convent. When smoke was coming out from most of the houses, she left the porch.

After coming down the steps, she looked in the door of the sickroom. All three women were asleep on the bed. Then she went to Beisheng's room. He was sound asleep on the floor, with a little stuffed dog. She went to the kitchen. There she found Cuiyun, sitting on a wooden bench by the stove and stealthily whitening her face with tooth powder and water. Afraid that the maid would be embarrassed, Yuemin quickly returned to the courtyard.

From the other side of the wall she heard knocking at the neighbor's door, then voices. Who could they be looking for, she wondered. "Could it be Papa and Brother, asking where we live?" Her heart began to pound, and she hurried to the front door. She waited for someone to knock or ring the bell. It must be someone from far away.

But after a few moments everything was quiet again.

Yuemin smiled faintly, without knowing why. The slanting rays of the sun threw a shadow from the roof and the drying pole onto a corner of the yard. It was just the shape of the little paper flag planted in a place far away, a flag on the grave of the Papa for whom they were waiting.

The Vitality of the Primitive

Meijin, Baozi, and
the White Kid

This section pulls back from the classic Shen Congwen canon to sample unique earlier works embodying the author's tribal and regional roots. The stories here contain strange tales, fantastic customs, and outlandish dialect, which he learned to tone down before writing stories like "The New and the Old" and "The Husband." To view the folk material with which Shen worked in even purer form, with less artistic processing and even fewer concessions to modern taste, see the appendix at the end of this book.

"Meijin, Baozi, and the White Kid" ("Meijin, Baozi, yu na yang"), written in the winter of 1928, is narrated as if by a traditional storyteller, as a legend of adolescent love among aborigines like the Miao and Tujia of the borderlands of West Hunan. Several tribes of Southwest China, notably the Nakhi, are famous for their elaborate oral tales about love suicides by star-crossed lovers, and the manner of the telling of Shen's story suggests an authentic legend, one he may have heard as a child; the Tujia village of Huangluozhai, home of his father, is said to have been known for its double love suicides and stories about them. A folklorist of the functionalist school will not miss the fact that Shen's story gives a legendary rationale for local romantic mores, explains the origin of strange customs such as a taboo on goat meat and the use of goats as betrothal presents, and commemorates a pair of deities: Meijin and Baozi, who are "today" worshiped in the cave where they belatedly kept their tryst. The tribal peoples are much less inhibited about sexual intercourse among young people than the Han, and extravagant, far-fetched metaphors and indirect reference to oneself are true features of Miao formal and singing discourse, as in love songs like the ones paraphrased in this story.

On the other hand, Shen Congwen also admired the works of Shakespeare, presumably including Romeo and Juliet, *and has admitted to having invented folklore for artistic purposes in the case of his famous story "Long Zhu." Asked about the authenticity* of "*Meijin, Baozi, and the White Kid*," Shen Congwen in 1980 smiled and said that he could not remember. But the story is memorable in universal terms, for its sheer mythic power, without on the other hand having become a children's fairy tale like "*Long Zhu.*"

Describe to one who has never known the taste of our pears
from Pear Market village the sweetness of songs sung by
girls of the White-faced Miao tribe, and you would be wasting your breath. Some people think the sound of sweeping
oars beautiful. Others find beauty in the sound of the wind
and the rain. Nor is there any dearth of simpletons who find
it in a baby's cries at night or the sound of reeds as they
whisper their dreams into the breeze. All these are poetry.
But the songs of the White-faced Miao girls are even more
poetic, more apt to lead you to intoxicated rapture and to
dream. Men who have heard their songs think nothing of
shedding blood for these girls, such is their magic, handed
down through history. Someone familiar with Miao legends
could tell you fifty stories about famous, handsome men
ensnared by ugly girls endowed with beautiful voices and
fifty more about handsome men driven to distraction by the
songs of girls from the White-faced tribe. And if, after all
those, the tale-teller had yet another left to tell, the one forgotten would surely be the tale of Meijin.

The story goes like this. Meijin[1] was a stunningly beautiful girl of the White-faced tribe. She and a boy from the
Phoenix tribe, who was very handsome and of exemplary
character, paired off while exchanging songs across mountain valleys. They expressed passionate love for each other in
their songs; the girl proposed that the boy meet her that
night in a cave. He who promised he would come was
named Baozi.[2] Baozi also meant to bring the girl a young
mountain goat as a present, for it was the first time; he
wanted to exchange a white kid for the red blood of her vir-
ginity. Even if their tryst was wrong, it was as if the gods
themselves had given their assent. And yet, by nighttime,

[1]"Bewitching Gold."
[2]"Leopard."

Translated by Caroline Mason

Baozi had forgotten all about it. After waiting for him all night long, Meijin froze to death in the cave for want of the warmth of a man. When Baozi, who slept at home until dawn, awoke and suddenly remembered, he hurried to the cave, only to find the girl already dead. So Baozi lay beside her and killed himself with his knife. Or, according to another version, he killed himself later on because he kept hearing Meijin singing and was unable to find her.

But all this was constructed from hearsay; what really happened was quite different. From a final poem that Baozi is said to have left before he died, written with a twig on the sandy floor of the cave, it seems to have been this way: Meijin was upset because Baozi failed to keep the appointment. She waited for him, but he did not come, and in the end, thinking she had been deceived, she killed herself. Baozi failed to keep the appointment because of the kid; when he did arrive, Meijin was already dead. That is why he pulled the knife from her chest and plunged it into his own, and he, too, fell lifeless in the cave. As to what happened afterward to the kid and why the hitherto always trustworthy Baozi became such a faithless lover, you would have to ask the kid. It was all because of the kid that what was to have been joyous turned into a tragedy. It is no wonder that even today the White-faced Miao do not eat goat meat.

But if you wanted to question the kid, where would you go? Lovers today still offer their mistresses a small white kid, and, to express their loyalty and the strength of their love, they always say that the kid is descended from the one Baozi brought for Meijin all those years ago – though in truth, even whether the original kid was male or female no one can really say now.

Just let me set down what I know. The source of my story is the robber Wu Rou, a descendant of the man who took the kid that Baozi and Meijin left behind and who also was Baozi's martial arts instructor. What has come down from him is naturally likely to be more reliable. This is the story:

With Meijin standing on the southern mountain slopes and Baozi on the northern, they sang from morning till night. It was on the slopes known today as the Mountain of Singing. In those days it was called the Mountain of Wild Chrysanthemums, for the flowers ran riot there, covering the whole hillside with a sheet of yellow in autumn. Yellow flowers cover the mountain yet today, but it has been renamed because of what happened to Meijin. In her song Meijin finally admitted defeat and that she must by rights give herself to Baozi, to do with as he wished. She sang:

> It is only by letting the autumn wind have its way
>   with them that the red leaves may fly over the
>   mountain.
> It is by you alone that I shall be made a woman.

Baozi was filled with delight to hear this song. He knew that he had won – that the heart of the most beautiful and enticing girl in all the White-faced tribe now belonged to him. And so he replied:

> You who are renowned among the Miao as the fairest
>   of all,
> Please go to Precious Stone Cave by Huang village,
> And when the great stars above gaze at one another in
>   the sky,
> That's when I'll see you, and you'll see me.

Meijin sang back to him:

> Oh my beloved wind, I shall do whatever you wish.
> All I want is that your heart should be as bright as the
>   sun.
> All I want is for your warmth to melt me, like the
>   sun's heat.
> Give no one cause to jest that the Phoenix tribe's finest
>   man is faithless,
> And forget not what it is that you have asked me to do.

Baozi sang back:

> Rest easy, greatest goddess of my heart.
> Thine own eyes have witnessed the beauty of the
> "leopard."
> And others universally bear witness to his faithfulness.
> Though the time comes that it begins to rain knives,
> I shall flinch from nothing to reach your side and kiss
> you.

It grew dark. Wild Chrysanthemum Mountain was wreathed in purple mist as it is still today at dusk. A few red clouds filled the sky, billowing to see the sun off on its downward journey, and the sun bade them farewell. This was the time for woodcutters to go home and herdsmen to return their sheep and cattle to the pens, for the day was at an end. The people who led this peaceful life had turned over another page, without any need to ask what was on the next, for this was the time to come down from the mountains, return from the rivers, and go home from the fields; it was the time to come home to the evening meal.

After whistling to wish Meijin farewell, Baozi hurried home, intending to find a newborn kid after his meal and take it to Precious Stone Cave for the meeting with his lover. Meijin too went home.

When Meijin had gone home and had something to eat, she changed into fresh undergarments, rubbed her body with sweet-smelling oils, and powdered her face. Then, in front of a bronze mirror, she did her hair up into a big coil and wound a sixteen-foot silk scarf around it. When she was quite ready, she set off for Precious Stone Cave with a long-necked gourd full of wine, an embroidered purse full of coins, and a sharp little dagger.

Precious Stone Cave was then as it is today. It was dry, with a floor of fine white sand, a bed and benches made of stone, a fireplace, and a natural hole through which you could see the stars. The only difference is that then it was a bridal chamber for Meijin and Baozi and today it has become a sacred place. The age of Meijin and Baozi has passed. Good customs, like lovely women, wither in time. This cave, safe from the chills and the heat, this wonderful place just made for young lovers, is now a place to worship gods. Though it is said that these gods are none other than those two young people who died for love, if the souls of Meijin and Baozi are with us, they must surely regret that this cave has been taken over for such a purpose. No use could be more fitting for such a beautiful place, as a memorial to the lovers who died there, than to furnish it as a meeting place especially for young men and women who have fallen in love through song. But, as I said, the good customs of this area have died out, the passions of its people have declined, and the women are slowly becoming more like Chinese women. Their affections have shifted to empty and meaningless things like cattle and sheep, gold and silver, so that the importance of love has clearly deteriorated. Beautiful songs and beautiful bodies alike have been supplanted by material things and are no longer valued. Meijin and Baozi probably could not tolerate such false warmth and empty love, even in this fine place. Better, then, to let it be a place of worship after all than have it sullied by the "love" of modern times.

But let me tell you what it was like when Meijin went to Precious Stone Cave.

She came early, to wait for Baozi. Once in the cave, she sat on the edge of the bed, which was hewn from a great blue rock. This was to be her bridal bed. It was spread with straw, and there was a bundle of straw for a pillow. The vaulted cave roof, with its dry, crisp air, was like a canopy, so that this bed seemed much better than most real ones.

She hung the calabash of wine from a wall hook and put the embroidered purse beside the pillow (she had prepared them both for Baozi), and then she waited in the darkness for her young and handsome lover. The mouth of the cave was faintly illuminated from outside; she sat there gazing at the light, waiting for the time when Baozi's massive shadow would appear.

To amuse herself, she softly sang to herself all the songs she knew. With them she praised the valor of the leopard in the mountains and the beauty of *her* leopard among men. She described her feelings at this time and how Baozi must be feeling. She ran her hands over every part of her body and smelled herself just as thoroughly. Everywhere she touched was rounded and smooth as silk and butter, and all the fragrances she smelled were sweet. She unfurled her turban and undid the coil of her hair, letting it fall free and spread, blacker than the night, down to the very ground. She was the most beautiful girl in her tribe. Of all men, only Baozi was fit to possess her body.

Her body was round and filled out, with curves everywhere, yet it was also very slender and well proportioned. Her perfect round face was set with a tiny mouth, a fine, straight nose, a pointed chin, and long, long eyebrows. It was as though her mother had molded her along the lines of the Fairy Lady He, for among mortals there could never be such a model of perfection. Just think how moving was this scene: in an hour or two she would take off all her clothes and become a bride – a girl like her, in a place like this, and yet a little shy to think of this momentous event, when she would take up all the passion and all the strength of a fiery young male.

Even a writer born in the twentieth century and plying his trade in Shanghai, 1928, an expert at digging up dirt about his friends and spreading rumors – an acclaimed littérateur with a gilded tongue, of acknowledged intelligence and wit – even he would be hard pressed to imagine the beauty of Meijin that night.

The elegance and purity of the girls of the White-faced Miao are long gone since the time of Meijin. We can all believe that. The girls you see today are far, far inferior, yet even so they turn the heads of countless males and make self-respecting Han Chinese hang their heads; from this, you may get some idea of Meijin's beauty.

Long sullied now by many vile and false desires, the word *love* can never regain the purity of a prior age. We shall not use the currently fashionable words to try to elaborate on Meijin's feelings at the time; we shall say only that her heart was pounding as she waited for Baozi to come and lie with her: she did not sigh or soliloquize, as your average literary genius might imagine!

She hoped only that Baozi would come soon, and, though she knew that leopards bite, she was quite happy to be devoured.

But where was her leopard?

There was no kid in Baozi's home, so he went to buy one from the old chieftain in the village. Bringing with him four strings of copper cash for the purchase of a young female kid with a white coat, Baozi explained what it was he needed the moment he entered the chieftain's gate.

When he heard that Baozi had come for a kid, and realized that a happy event was imminent, the chieftain asked, "Whose bridegroom will you be tonight, my fine young fellow?"

Baozi said, "*Your* eyes, Uncle, can see who is to be Baozi's bride this night."

"No one but the camellia goddess is fit to share Baozi's home. None but the fairy of Big Ghost Cave is fit to love and be loved by him. Which mortal woman could it be? I do not know."

"Uncle, though all call Baozi of the Phoenix tribe handsome, he is unworthy to be the footrest of this bride."

"Do not be so modest, young man. When he surrenders to a woman, a man always sees himself as worthless by comparison to her."

"How true, Uncle! When I am with her, I cannot talk about myself. I beg your pardon, Uncle, but tonight I shall become a man, and I simply cannot express what my heart feels about her. I have come here to see if you could spare a kid that I might take and give to this goddess in return for her blood."

The chieftain was an old man who could see the future and read a person's fortune in his face. He gave a start when Baozi mentioned blood in connection with the happy event to come, sensing that it did not augur well. He said, "Young man, there is something wrong about the way you look."

"Of course I would not look the same today as I usually do, Uncle!"

"Come into the light, and let me look at you."

Baozi turned his face toward the big tung-oil lamp as the old man commanded. The chieftain looked at Baozi, and nodded his head, but said nothing.

Baozi said, "Uncle, you can see things so clearly – can you tell whether the omens are good or bad?"

"Young man, knowledge is just a kind of pastime for old people; it is of no use to you! Now, if you want a kid, go to the pen, and choose one that you like. No need to give me any money, and no need for any thanks. Tomorrow I would like to see you and your bride – "

He stopped talking and led Baozi round to the pen behind the house. The chieftain held the lamp while Baozi searched among the goats for the one he wanted. There were close to fifty goats in the pen, of which half were kids, but, search as he might, there was not one he liked. The pure white ones were too big, and the smaller ones looked rather mottled. A big one would naturally be unsuitable, and one with an impure coat would not make a fitting present for Meijin, either.

"Any of them will do, young man; just pick one."

"I am trying."

"Are none of them suitable?"

"Uncle, I simply cannot compare my bride's spotless virtue to a kid with a patchy coat."

"Take any one at all, and go quickly to your bride."

"I cannot go empty handed, and I cannot take any of your kids, Uncle, so I had better go look elsewhere."

"Please, simply pick one."

"Thank you, Uncle, but this is the first time I have ever made a promise to a woman; I cannot make do with an ordinary kid."

"But I tell you, it will be all right even if you bring nothing. It is not good to make your bride wait. What she wants is not the kid."

"I know you mean well, Uncle, but I have made a promise to my bride."

Baozi thanked the chieftain and set off to look for a kid elsewhere.

The chieftain saw Baozi off at the gate and sighed as he watched the boy vanish rapidly into the darkness. The seer could do nothing, for what was to happen had been predetermined. He could only close the gate and wait for news. Baozi went to five houses, but none of them had a suitable kid – either they were too big, or their coats were not pure white. A good kid was as hard to find in this place as a good woman, and it would only be by chance that he might find one that he liked.

By the time Baozi emerged from the fifth house where goats were raised, the sky was full of stars, and all was quiet. He thought, if I cannot keep my very first promise to my girl, how will I ever win her trust? If I go empty handed, saying it is because I searched the whole village but could not find a kid I liked, she will know that I am lying. So he decided that he must search the whole village.

He went and knocked at the gates of all the families he knew, and, when the gates were opened, he quietly told them that he wanted a kid. He was known to all the villagers for his strength and good looks, and, when they heard that he wanted a kid to give to his girl, they were all very keen to help. They led him to their pens to look at their goats, just as kindly and patiently as had the chieftain, for

Baozi was a fellow villager. But he looked at them all, and strangely enough not a single kid was to his liking.

He had not forgotten that Meijin would be anxiously awaiting him in the cave. Her request to him as he left, that he should come when the stars came out, still rang in his ears. But, having promised his sweetheart a little kid, he was now very anxious that he had not found one, and, in the search, he had forgotten the time.

He decided that, since he could not find a pure white kid in this village, if he really wanted one, he must go to another village a mile away and look there. He gazed up at the sky and judged that there was still time. Thus, to keep his word, Baozi went straight to the other village to buy the kid.

The way to the village was very familiar to him. He had gone but a few hundred yards when he heard the sound of a kid bleating in the grass beside the road. The sound was very low and faint, but he knew at once that it came from a kid. Baozi stopped. He listened carefully, and the kid bleated again, very softly. He realized it must have fallen into a deep pit by the roadside. Having been there all day by itself, it was crying miserably in the dark, missing its mother and feeling homesick.

Parting the grass by starlight, Baozi saw an opening in the ground. The kid bleated again on hearing the grass stir; its feeble sound rose up through the hole. Baozi was delighted. Knowing that the weather had been fair lately and that the pit must be dry, he slid down into the hole. It was only as deep as his waist, with a bottom that was indeed solid and dry. In a moment Baozi saw the kid, which started bleating all the more piteously, though it did not approach him. It was newborn, not ten days old, with a foreleg broken from the fall, probably caused by a goatherd who had carelessly driven his flock across the pit.

Baozi cradled the injured kid in his arms as he climbed out of the pit. Thinking that he would have to use this one in any case, he set out toward Precious Stone Cave and his tryst with Meijin. But the kid kept bleating softly as they went. Realizing that it was in pain, Baozi felt he must carry it to the home of the village chieftain and ask him to dress it with some ointment before he took it to the cave. So he turned back and went to the chieftain's house.

Baozi knocked at the door. The old man, unable to sleep for worrying about the boy, thought that the bad news about him had arrived. He asked who it was, through the door.

"It is your nephew, Uncle. I have found a kid, but the poor little thing is hurt; it has a broken leg. I have come to ask you to heal it."

"Have you not gone to your bride yet, young man? It is already midnight. Leave the kid here, and do not delay a second longer."

"Uncle, I am certain my bride will love this kid. I cannot see the color of its coat properly, but, when I was carrying it, I felt sure it must be pure white! It is as gentle and soft as my bride, and its – "

The chieftain was alarmed to hear the young fellow waxing so lyrical about an injured kid he had just happened to pick up. He drew back the bolt with a thud and opened the door. A ray of light from his lamp fell on the kid in Baozi's arms, and Baozi could see the color of its coat.

It was as white as the snow on Dali. Baozi quickly lifted it up and kissed it.

"Young man, what are you doing? Have you forgotten that tonight you are to be a bridegroom?"

"I have not forgotten, Uncle! This kid is a gift from heaven. Please, quickly rub some ointment on its leg so that I may carry it to my bride."

Shaking his head, the chieftain took the kid in his arms and examined it by the light of the lamp. The kid stopped bleating when it saw the lamplight. It only closed its eyes and snorted.

Soon after, Baozi was on his way to Precious Stone Cave, the kid sleeping peacefully in his arms. He longed to see his Meijin there and to tell how heaven had sent this kid. Taking long strides without ever resting, he ascended the hill, crossing countless high cliffs and ravines as he went, until he came to Precious Stone Cave. By the time he reached the mouth of the cave, the eastern sky was getting light. The heavens were full of stars, and their light shone on the entrance to the cave. It was cold and desolate inside. He could see no one.

He called out softly, "Meijin, Meijin, Meijin!"

He walked a little way inside and was met not by a voice but by a smell from the interior of the cave. He recognized it at once as the stench of blood. Stunned, he stood there for a moment like an idiot, then flung the kid to the ground and ran inside.

He went to the bed. In a few moments, with the faint gleam of starlight coming through the open roof, he made out the shape of Meijin lying on the bed. The smell of blood was coming from her. He rushed over and felt her forehead, her face, her mouth: her mouth and nose were still slightly warm.

"Meijin! Meijin!"

He called her name several times before she managed a faint response.

"What have you done?"

He listened to her breathing, which seemed to come not from her mouth but from her belly. At last she turned toward him, wanting to raise herself but not having the strength.

She said, quietly and haltingly, "You who call out to me, are you the one who sang to me in the daytime?"

"Yes, my love! The one who always sang so sadly during the day and was so alone in bed at night; but now, today, that boy has come to be your bridegroom. – What has happened? Why are you like this?"

"Why?"

"Yes, who has done this to you?"

"It is that faithless boy from the Phoenix tribe; he lied to me. Even the most handsome, perfect boy must have a fault, so the gods made him capable of lying. I did not want to be deceived by a liar. And now it is over for me."

"No, no! You are wrong! It was all because the boy from the Phoenix tribe did not wish to break his first promise to the girl. He went and searched the whole night, until by chance he came upon the promised kid. Now he has found the kid but lost the girl. Oh heaven, tell me how I should have kept my word!"

When the dying Meijin heard this, she realized that Baozi was late because he had searched for the kid, not because he had broken his vow. She realized that she had been wrong to give up hope and plunge the knife into her breast. She asked Baozi to take her up and lay her head against his chest so that he might kiss her on the forehead.

She said, "I am dying. . . . When it grew light and still you had not come, I thought myself deceived. . . . And so I stabbed myself with this knife. You wanted my blood, and here it is. I do not hate you. . . . Pull out the knife, and let me die. . . . Run, escape beyond the mountains before it gets completely light, for you are innocent of my death."

Baozi wept silently as he listened to her speak in fits and starts about her death. He thought a moment and touched her gently. Her breasts were wet with blood, and between them was the bloody handle of the knife. His heart went cold. He shuddered.

She said, "Baozi, why do you not do as I ask? You told me that the whole of you belonged to me. So do as I say, and pull the knife out, to save me from suffering any more."

Still Baozi said nothing.

In a little while she spoke again.

"Baozi, I understand now. Do not be sad. Bring the kid, and let me see it."

He laid her down again very carefully and left the cave to get the kid. He had unthinkingly hurled the poor thing on the ground. It lay there panting, half dead.

Baozi looked up at the sky, which was now completely light. Far away, a cock crowed. He heard waterwheels in the distance – sounds he usually sensed while dreaming.

He carried the kid into the cave and put it near Meijin's breast.

"Lift me up, Baozi; let me kiss the kid you have brought."

With his arm around her shoulders he raised her up and put her hand on the kid. "How sad that it has been hurt, too. Take it away now. . . . Pull out the knife, my love. Do not cry. . . . I know you love me, and I do not hate you for what you have done. Run away now with the kid; make your getaway. . . . Oh, you fool, what are you doing?"

Baozi had bared his own breast and was pulling at the knife. It was lodged so deep inside her that he had to use great force to remove it. Her blood gushed out and spattered him all over. Then he thrust the bloody knife into his own chest. Meijin saw this. She died with a smile on her face.

After it got light, the chieftain led some villagers to Precious Stone Cave to look for the couple. They found the two dead bodies, the half-dead kid that the old man had earlier anointed with his own hands, and a song that Baozi must have written with a twig in the sand just before he died. The chieftain committed the song to memory and carried the kid home with him.

Nowadays, the women of the White-faced Miao are no longer filled with such passion. They can still forgive men, they can still sacrifice themselves for them, and they can still sing songs to stir the soul. But they cannot do as Meijin did.

Ah Jin

Shen Congwen's sinicized Miao hero Ah Jin is something of a comic type, yet he is not the sort of caricature that an urban intellectual would create. In fact, he comes from within the rural culture, for the plot, humor, and characters of "Ah Jin," written by Shen in December 1928, are derived from a folk story. In 1980, it was still known to some Miao people of Yala Camp who, because of Shen's unhappy fate under communism, had never heard of Shen Congwen. It was some years later, after his rehabilitation, that Shen suddenly became a local hero – "China's great Miao author."

In this case, the folk material has been reshaped into a well-made story with every sentence in its place. The tale is told in the voice of a storyteller, one inclined to cut to the chase, although he cannot resist slyly commenting on human nature. Hence the funny dialogue that communicates Ah Jin's burgeoning frustration. There is a surprise ending, as in Shen Congwen's nineteenth-century European and American short-story models. And many turns of speech can be taken two ways, particularly those that are overstressed: "Everyone regarded the headman of the Yala Camp district as a good man. Just because he loved to talk didn't make a man bad." Yet, whether from the folk origins of the tale or Shen Congwen's own predilections in delineating character, the insufferable bully of the piece is hard not to like. After all, his motive is to make Ah Jin his relative! So even this simple, well-plotted story in Shen Congwen's classic oeuvre turns out to be rich with ambiguities and ironies as it goes about exploring rural "friendship" and kinship. Foolish Ah Jin himself looks less like a fool than a victim of fate – a West Hunanese kind of fate, which has a sense of humor.

The fifteenth of the month was market day in the village of Yellow Cow Stockade, and the *baojia* head from Yala Camp was there in a dog meat stall at the entrance. With a catty of richly marbled dog meat and a half catty of fiery corn liquor in his stomach, he was especially ardent and voluble today as he spoke his mind to a certain Ah Jin who was about to marry a young widow. This headman was as good at talking as he was at eating dog meat: he could keep it up all day without having his fill. And his big appetite just seemed to make him all the more talkative.

"Proprietor Ah Jin, I'll give it to you straight as an onion; it's up to you whether you listen. Let me lay it out before you clear as I can. It's right there in front of you, and you'll have to decide for yourself whether you want to go ahead or not. You're not a child any more. You know many things other people don't know – like how to use an abacus – and that makes folks respect you. You have a clear head, and you're not a drunk. If you want to get married, that's your business; nobody else has to put you up to it. But I just want to say that women aren't easy to figure out. We've seen lots of men who can figure out accounts but can't figure out a woman. They have a pretty wife at home but can't enjoy her, so their feet get itchy, and, before you know it, they've run off with a drumsinger. And we have to admit that many noble officers are able and firm, even rather peremptory and imposing when they command soldiers, but as soon as they run up against a woman they go to pieces. Why else does everybody here know the joke about how his honor the brigade commander was brought to his knees by his scolding wife? And why do people go on about our henpecked magistrate and even act out the story in plays? And why should Ah Jin, this nice fellow from Yala Camp, one day have to go down on his knees before a woman, too? But if such gossip doesn't bother you, I guess it can't very well bother me, can it?"

Translated by William MacDonald

With the very best of intentions, and a little help from admonitions both classical and modern, the headman was telling Ah Jin that some people just shouldn't get married. It was as hard to ignore as a gong going off in your ear. The one called Ah Jin seemed a little tired of listening, so he stood up and was about to slip away.

The headman's eyes were sharp, and his hands were quick. He reached across the table to grab Ah Jin and wouldn't let go. Ah Jin couldn't leave. The headman was strong, and he knew his martial arts. He was more than a match for two Ah Jins.

"Don't be in such hurry, my friend! Hear me out, I won't make you late! I'm not afraid if people say I'm selfish and want this good fellow Ah Jin from Yala Camp to marry my own niece. Let the rumors fly; let them come down from heaven itself. I'm not after money or fame. I just want you to think it over for another day or two. Why the hurry? If you can't hear *me* out, how long will you be able to put up with *her?*"

"Brother, let me go! I'll listen to you," pleaded Ah Jin, as if begging for mercy.

The headman smiled, knowing full well that persuasion through force never changed any minds. He also smiled to think that Ah Jin could be so fascinated with a woman that he would bring her into his home without another thought, as if someone had slipped him a love potion. And he smiled at himself for acting the old friend, even though he wasn't altogether sure why he was taking such an interest in Ah Jin today and just had to speak his piece. Ah Jin looked as if he were pleading for a pardon, and this, too, began to look very funny to the headman. Today, as always in the past, the headman had nothing but the best of intentions toward Ah Jin.

Except that he was talkative and loved to gossip, everyone regarded the headman of the Yala Camp district as a good man. Just because he loved to talk didn't make a man bad. And his talkativeness was no crime as far as he was concerned. How could you show you were headman if you acted like a dummy – if you didn't like to talk and spend all day going here and there drinking and holding meetings? According to the local people, the magistrate's duty was to make his bearers really sweat when carrying his stout, 162-pound body on all his rounds in a sedan chair. And not much else. If a headman wasn't long on talk, he wasn't much of a headman!

The headman watched Ah Jin sit down again. Using the same right hand that had pulled Ah Jin back, he picked up a knife from the table, cut off a slice of dog meat, and popped it into his mouth. He made smacking noises as he chewed the fatty morsel. Narrowing his eyes a moment, he opened them up again and went back to discussing the pros and cons of Ah Jin's marriage.

To make a long story short, he wanted Ah Jin to think it over one more day. Just one more day. Advice from an old friend wasn't something you could ignore! Since he couldn't say that he didn't approve of the marriage, the headman finally came up with this solution. They would wait until tomorrow and *then* talk about it. It was as though this one day were of great consequence. As soon as tomorrow came, just like in the "revolution," everything under creation would change, and the world would be at peace. Ah Jin had been ready to settle the marriage tonight. The bundle of bills in his pocket was for the bride-price and betrothal gifts. This country fellow was thirty-three. His hands had fondled those banknotes and silver coins until he was sick of them; now he was ready to fondle a woman. He didn't think this was such an unreasonable desire! But with the headman advising him as an old friend, and saying that it was only one day – just think about it for one more day, and it's up to you whether you go ahead – it really did seem unfair not to let this good man have his way. So in the end Ah Jin had to go along with him.

To make the headman believe him – and it seemed that the only way he could get away was to make the headman believe him – Proprietor Ah Jin picked up his cup, drank the wine down, and swore by heaven that he wouldn't go to the matchmaker's today. He'd go home without fail and think it over, reconsider all the pros and cons. This oath was the promise the headman had been waiting for. At last he smiled with satisfaction and released Ah Jin, almost as though he were liberating him.

Ah Jin walked around the market for a while. Miao women were there in unusually large numbers. Everywhere was the air of youth, the sound of youth, the flavor of youth, so Ah Jin found it harder than ever to forget that young widow from Baba Stockade. Girls of the Wupo tribe were fairies, goddesses. They could get a man drunk faster than wine, there was no denying it. The woman that Ah Jin planned to take into his house had the firmest body, the whitest skin of all the Wupo women.

Other places, when a man had some savings, there were a lot of things he could do with them – maybe spend five hundred silver pieces for a wolf-dog named Napoléon or a thousand on a rare book printed in the Song dynasty. There were always things to spend money on, and they could be decorous as well as amusing. And there were army officers who made a lot of money killing a lot of people and blew it all on gambling and whoring, as if spending bad money on bad things were the natural order of things. But Ah Jin was a Miao. He had grown up in Miao territory and didn't know about these things of the city people. He only hoped, as the ordinary man hopes, to have the chance to use his energy on a woman. Elegant things are just for the enjoyment of the rich; this is accepted throughout all the world where money circulates. This woman was worth five oxen, and anyone who had the price was qualified to become her husband. Ah Jin was up to it, so naturally he thought to make this sturdy and handsome woman his wife.

She was newly widowed and locally famous as a beauty. It was probably her beauty that had stirred up so much resentment. A good many men who could never even get near her passed on rumors of the sort that only men can, and, as Ah Jin's old friend, the headman naturally felt a sense of responsibility toward him. The headman advised Ah Jin not because he had a niece who had taken a fancy to Ah Jin or because he liked the woman himself. And Ah Jin understood his intentions. Since he did understand his old friend, Ah Jin really felt that it wouldn't be right to go to the matchmaker's on this day.

A lot of people knew that Ah Jin was soon to become this beauty's bridegroom. Today they were all at the Yellow Cow Stockade market, and, when they saw Ah Jin, they would ask, "Proprietor Ah Jin, when will you be inviting us to drink at your wedding?" And this honest villager, feeling good inside, would answer, "Soon, within a month I guess." Ah Jin was evidently very happy to be answering in such a fashion because, according to local custom, treating people to wine meant receiving presents and congratulations in return. Now it had just entered the tenth month, and the tenth month was a good time anywhere for playing trumpets and getting married.

As for the woman, it seemed to Ah Jin that squeezing her white leg or pinching her cheek would bring with it an inexpressible excitement. His body was walking around the market, but his mind was at the matchmaker's. And the folks over there were just waiting for Ah Jin's word to settle the matter.

Although he had promised to think it over one more day, in the end he couldn't keep his promise. His "go-ahead star" was already on the move. Involuntarily he started for the matchmaker's again. But, when he'd got as far as the dog meat stall at the end of the street, he ran into the good-hearted headman, who stuck out his hand to stop him.

"Proprietor Ah Jin, this is your business, and I've got no right to meddle, but you promised to think it over another day."

The headman was devilishly clever, and he'd been waiting for him all along. He knew that Ah Jin would break his promise. As soon as Ah Jin saw that big nose ruddy from wine, he turned around without even stopping to listen.

The headman's only thought was to do him a good turn, so he had waited there on the road to the matchmaker's ready to stop Ah Jin, his concern was that deep. Ah Jin knew of this concern, and his only recourse was to go back at once.

As he headed back he walked about the market. He went over to the cow and sheep grounds, to watch other people deal in livestock. Those who knew Ah Jin asked him if he wanted any cows or sheep. He wanted only a woman. He was ready to swap enough money for six bulls for a plump, fair-skinned woman, twenty-two years of age. Watching the others exchange cows and sheep, he felt a little sad and, without being aware of it, started walking toward the matchmaker's again. From far away he heard the voice of the headman talking to someone and knew that the busybody was still standing guard like a watchdog. He turned back for the second time.

The third time he had already slipped past the headman when someone else stopped him to talk. The headman spotted him, and once again Ah Jin failed to make it to the matchmaker's.

When he got the urge a fourth time, another acquaintance came along and informed him that the headman was still sitting up straight and tall at the dog meat stall, jabbering away as ever. They were talking about Ah Jin's promise, so he was too ashamed to risk going past.

The headman's kindness was only for Ah Jin's benefit, of course. He didn't want to get anything out of it, nor did he want to keep the happy pair apart. But why he would not let the money in Ah Jin's pocket get to the matchmaker's was hard to understand. He had his reasons. The headman had a busybody's temperament, usually not very much, but as it happened today he'd drunk a half catty of "knock-your-socks-off" and downed a catty of "bowwow," and he was especially concerned about Ah Jin's marriage. Why, then? Because the woman was too beautiful, like a woman who was "inimical to husband," as they say in the fortune-telling books. His old friend didn't want all the wealth and enterprise Ah Jin had accumulated over so many years and with so much labor to be wasted on a woman who was sure to bring about his demise.

To avoid any trouble, Ah Jin planned to give in to the headman until the headman went home for supper; then he'd go to the matchmaker's to place his deposit. Unthinkingly, Ah Jin went into the gambling booth. A man with something on his mind, of course, doesn't gamble carefully. As soon as Ah Jin got into the game, like so many others, he played with such enthusiasm that it was already dusk when he came out. Surely the headman must have gone home to eat his stewed pig's feet by now. But Ah Jin's pocket was empty, even the second time he checked it. He had gambled away all his money, and there no longer seemed to be any need to go to the matchmaker's to discuss the wedding. It would save him a lot of effort, and he didn't need to worry about an old superstition after all.

Several days later, the honest and ardent headman of Yala Camp met Ah Jin's matchmaker on the road and began to ask how Ah Jin's wedding was coming along. The matchmaker said that Proprietor Ah Jin hadn't been able to pay the money, so the woman had been taken by a silk merchant from far away. The headman, who had seen with his own eyes the bundle of notes in Ah Jin's pocket, assumed that his good friend had taken his warning to heart and decided that a beautiful woman wouldn't make a good wife. He must have given up his plans and pretended to be broke so as to call it off. Thinking that he had done his friend a good turn, the headman immediately set off for Yellow Cow Stockade with a big gourd of wine, to congratulate Ah Jin for his resolve.

The Inn

*"The Inn" ("Lüdian"), which has a postscript reading "10 January
1929, while sick," is one of Shen Congwen's most fluent and guileless
celebrations of the vitality of supposedly primitive people and their passions. The heroine, Black Cat, is a sinicized Miao woman who runs
an inn; among the Han there were many jokes and tales about the
romantic availability of such women, not unlike the jokes in our culture about farmers' daughters. But this story is sensual without being
ribald. It may even be called a love story, a fairy tale from a faraway
place, told in the abstracted voice of an old-style storyteller. Black Cat
is a foil for urban hypocrisy, much as the hunchback is a foil for Black
Cat. "Little Black Cat," incidentally, was the nickname for the genuinely beautiful, dark-skinned college student Zhang Zhaohe. Shen
Congwen was wooing her in 1929, quite unsuccessfully. This story
might not have helped his cause with a well-bred Chinese woman like
her, but she did become his wife four years later.*

*From the subliminal hints in the characters' conversations, the big
nose of the guest who reinitiates Black Cat into sexuality, and the references to wild animals devouring people, one can see that this is a post-
Freudian story. Besides Freudian symbolism, which he put into many
of his works, Shen Congwen was intrigued by the theory that sexual
repression is psychologically harmful. It seemed to justify the uninhib-
ited mores of the Miao.*

Only one who is awake can find something significant in watching another sleep.

They had come from far away, a distance of eighty or a hundred miles, and they were bone tired, sound asleep: snoring and open mouthed they lay, dead to the world on a hard, straw-covered kang.[1] They dreamed of nothing but fighting, thirsting, gambling, and burning off mountain brush. During the day they lived in the simple fashion that had become their habit: eating, drinking, hiking, cursing. They felt that these were enough, and, when their chance came to stretch out, they were asleep within moments of hitting the floor.

There are such people everywhere, but city folk, even those of talent, could never imagine that they actually live in the same world with them. Men with doctorates – those upper-class people who understand so many things – could never know that such people exist. Maxim Gorky, Bernard Shaw, all the great writers of China, not to mention its poets, and all its college professors – the critic Li Changhong, who has been abroad, all those important people in the Party and government who talk about People's Livelihood, men like Zhao Jingshen who are so familiar with the literary scene, male authors whose works find their way into a journal's "special women writers issue" – none of these people could know. Revolutionary writers ought to know, but most of them are so obsessed with finding love in revolutionary sentiments that they, too, seem vague about it.

Most people in China live under conditions that are not only forgotten by the average person but beyond the writer's imagination. The country is so big that just waging civil war is a problem, let alone finding out about these people. But this is probably inevitable. As a case in point, if you go a thousand miles south from the center at Nanjing, you will

[1] A rustic brick platform bed, heated by a stove underneath.

Translated by William MacDonald

come to a place in the interior where there dwells a foreign tribe, a place called the cauldron of the Miao people. This is a story about what happened there one day.

It would soon be light.

Four travelers were sleeping and dreaming on a large wooden bed in a little inn run by a woman called Black Cat. They had come from beyond Zhenyuan, where paper was manufactured, and each of them carried a load of paper destined for the old district of Chenyang in Hunan, where the ancient poet Qu Yuan had moored his boat on his travels upstream. They were almost halfway there. In another eleven days they would sell their paper and start back. The men in this profession were like mendicant monks. They spent long years on the road for the sake of their families. After each trip they could rest for ten days, so three-quarters of their nights were spent in small inns. Custom made these men able to endure more hard work than other merchants; the inns where they lodged felt like home to them.

This particular inn was at the foot of a mountain that must be crossed to pass from the Hunan border down to Chenzhou. Long-distance travelers generally stopped here to rest their tired bodies and gather strength to make the climb. The proprietor of the inn was a twenty-six-year-old woman of the Flowery Foot Miao. The reason for her name, Black Cat, was hard to trace. Probably it was because of her dark skin and winning disposition. The name seemed to have come from her husband. Though the husband who had thought it up had died before his time, he left this good name behind for all the passing travelers to call her by. The name itself was one thing and not so important; ever since her husband's death, Black Cat's body was not nearly so easily taken by the ordinary passerby.

Miao people do not get as excited about white skin as the Han, but then the men of the White Ear Miao know more about dark skin than any Chinese does. Since her husband's death, Black Cat had continued to run the inn, selling food and wine and caring for the passing travelers from far away, but there was never any talk about someone having found out what was inside Black Cat's skin. People who travel for a living have eyes that can spot a pretty face as well as a business deal, but Black Cat really seemed to be a cat, uninterested in relations between men and women, as if she were not meant for love. This wasn't surprising, for she was no ordinary woman of the Flowery Foot tribe. She lacked none of the charm and beauty of the Wupo women, and she possessed a great deal of the passion of the Flowery Foot women, but at the same time she had the self-respect and shrewdness of a Luoluo. As for her husband's death, well, let it be. She continued to live as a widow by choice.

She had been a widow three years without seeing one single man who could move her. The looks of the White Ear men no longer attracted her, and the singing of the Buyi men could not conquer the fortress of her heart either. She did not want a tribal chieftain's wealth, and the extravagance of the opium dealers only made her laugh. She had hired a hunchback man in his forties to help her with odd jobs around the inn and to serve as her guard. Those who came here with designs on her could not achieve their desires, yet it was just as impossible to stay away. Black Cat attracted business all by herself, and there were those who also thought that her cooking was especially delicious.

This being the case, Black Cat lived on in the spotlight, with her full share of joys and sorrows. Although she succeeded in business, she suffered, too. Since neither singing nor wealth could win her over, some decided to use force as a last resort. Thanks to Black Cat's alertness, things never reached the point where anyone had his way, and there had been many attempts. Such had been the case up until now.

When the sky grew light, Black Cat usually got up at the same time as the hunchback to heat water for the guests and warm their wine. Then she let them don their sandals by the fire and opened the door to see them on their way. Early on a winter's morning, once the guests were gone, she could snuggle down in the blankets to sleep a while longer. Between the third and the ninth months it was usually very foggy in the early morning, and she would go to the well by the road to draw water until the great water vat was full. Drawing water was something Black Cat did herself.

Today Black Cat woke up earlier than usual. She hung up the linen mosquito net and pushed open the tiny window by her bed. The sky was full of stars, and the yard was filled with the sounds of insects. The chilly breeze made her feel that the weather would be clear today for sure. The sound of the insects seemed wet with dew, and even the starlight seemed damp. The weather was just too lovely. At times like these there was no way of knowing how many young girls were singing softly to their lovers as they saw them out the door and beyond the bamboo groves. There was no telling how many young men heard the crowing of roosters as they sent home from the caves the girl who had given them a night of delight. Nor was there any way of knowing how many young people wept and made vows at the moment of parting. Black Cat thought of these things and seemed a little surprised at herself. It was as though she had no part of the things that other people did. The mistresses of other inns had the right at such times to listen to the faithless oaths sworn by ungrateful men, but she could not. Other women had the right at such times to leave a cave draped in a man's grass rain cape while he saw her home, but she had no part of this.

What else was a woman in her twenties with a firm, glistening body, long arms, and a sensitive heart made for if not for a man at night? But the man with the right to enjoy all this had been peacefully sleeping in his grave for four years and so had forfeited it. As for the other men, they were not good enough.

Today Black Cat really did seem a little out of the ordinary. What ran through her mind as she stood beneath the starlight were the intimacies between men and women that normally never crossed her mind. Ordinarily she judged her guests in the course of her business, but now some other, inexplicable reason made her think about the guests who had spent the night in her inn. The four men showed up fifteen or sixteen times a year; they had been spending their nights here exclusively for a number of years now. She was well-enough acquainted with them to know all about their home situations; she had known for some time that each had a family. But, if they had wanted to, they could have forgotten their families and enjoyed all the intimacies of husband and wife without any formality, for that would not have done any harm. Mountains, rivers, and time separated them from their wives, and for this reason it might have been more interesting. Some other time, this might have occurred to her, but the fact that it did not was because she had no desire for any of them. Not one of the paper merchants seemed to be the kind of man she could weep over or swear oaths with. And, even if she had been willing to choose one of these four dishes for the night, it would hardly have occurred to them to give vent to their desires for a woman so well known for her chastity.

The strange thing was that today Black Cat's mood had radically changed.

A sudden and compelling desire had grown within her. She began to wonder which one she would like to be naked with her. She yearned for a strong, a healthy, a persistent assault on her and the kind of release that follows such clumsiness and violence. The good times she had enjoyed with the man now sleeping underground had made her think back on her own lost rights and produced in her a revulsion against her ordinary prudishness. She felt she ought to grab one of the men, any of them, and have him satisfy her desires by letting him do all those wild things to her. As these thoughts ran through her head, she thought she heard people going up the mountain.

She looked out the window again at the countless stars, the largest of them radiating a white light. The outline of the temple on the hill made it clear that it would soon be light.

She could hear roosters crowing, the creaking of a mill far away, and the yapping of dogs. They were probably barking because someone had set out early to take advantage of the morning cool. At this time on any other day she would have gotten out of bed, but today it seemed to her that the barking of the dogs expressed some of her anger at the loveless guests. She lazily closed the window again.

The hunchback was quite an accurate clock. He was getting along in years and felt a need to rise with the sun. Now he was already in the kitchen by the stove, lighting a lamp with his flint. Black Cat could hear him.

As she lay in bed, Black Cat seemed a little angry. "Hunchback, what are you doing up so early?"

"It's not so early. And the weather will be fine today. The Buddha is really taking care of us this summer month!"

As usual, when the hunchback had lit the lamp, he took it to the guest room to awaken the boarders.

One of the guests asked the hunchback how the weather was.

"Fine! Weather like this is for getting girls up into the hills with you to sleep with. It's much too good for traveling."

The hunchback's words brought a laugh to three of the men. The other was yawning at that moment and so busy with his yawn that he missed the joke. The hunchback seemed to have something else to say, so he went on, "Things have changed; they're not like they used to be. Nowadays people always get up early to work, but twenty years ago young folks had lots to do. They got up even earlier to climb out of their lover's bed and go home or to see a girlfriend off. When they parted and couldn't see each other across the valley because of the fog, they would whistle and sing to each other. That's all over now. Not many girls have strong affections and pure hearts any more."

Black Cat, in the back room, heard what the hunchback had said. "Heat the water, Hunchback, and let's have less foolishness!" she shouted.

"Huh!" the hunchback replied, with a knowing glance at the guests to show that he knew what he was talking about – that the mistress was a woman who wasn't getting her share of satisfaction. As he left the room he mumbled, "The world has changed; the woman no longer sings and drinks as she did when she was young. Instead she runs an inn. Mistress of an inn, but not of – " He didn't finish because he had reached the stove, the domain of the god of the hearth.[2] Perhaps it was because of the weather that today he felt it was wrong for the mistress to be satisfied with her widowhood.

Black Cat, who had heard the hunchback's grumbling, had already gotten up, slipped on her shoes, and gone into the guests' quarters. Her dress was not yet fastened, and her hair was casually coiled on top of her head like a bird's nest, making one think of Meijin lying on her wolf skin rug in the cave just before she committed suicide as she tired of waiting for her tardy lover. One of the guests took note of the hunchback's unusual comment, and, when he saw Black Cat's feline body and the swell of her breasts, a provocative thought occurred to him.

"Did you sleep well, Madam?"

"Yes, I always do," she replied.

"You'd sleep even better if you had a Mister with you."

Usually when Black Cat heard something like this she would suddenly become stern, but now she only cast a side-

---

[2]The god of the hearth files annual "reports" on the household with heaven. See the last paragraph of Shen's story "The Company Commander."

long glance at the author of this jest. She sized up his strong arms, his shoulders, his waist and thighs, and finally she looked at his nose: it was big and long.

The guests were already out of bed and variously dressing, fastening their belts, or putting on their straw sandals by the stove. Only the man who had made the jest was left. With the others gone, Black Cat looked at her big-nosed guest and had a secret urge to bite off his nose. She pressed her hands to her breasts and swayed back and forth as though she wanted to say something to him.

The man had only been joking with Black Cat and never imagined that she would become aroused. With his companions gone and Black Cat at his side, he had nothing left to say. Slowly he tied his leggings and went out of the room. Ordinarily, Black Cat would have made the beds, but now she bent over the bed and sniffed at it, as though she were drunk.

When one of the guests came back into the room looking for the tobacco pouch he had hung at the head of the bed, Black Cat quickly straightened up and held the lamp while he found his tobacco. He went out again without seeming to notice the great change in her behavior.

Black Cat followed him out with the lamp, placed it on the stove, and then went to inspect the water vat. Not much water was left; she would have to draw some more. She picked up the yoke and dragged the water buckets out from underneath the table.

She opened the door, but two or three dogs ran by in the street, and she quickly closed it again.

"Hunchback, why are there so many wild dogs around these days?"

"They come every fall. I said a long time ago that I'd get a bow and poisoned arrows, but somehow I never have the time. I've heard that a wild dog skin sells in Chenzhou for three or four taels of silver. If I could only get a couple of fox-dogs, I'd be rich."

"Why just three or four taels?" said the man with the big nose. "With my own eyes I've seen people spend ten dollars for a spotted-tail badger."

"I can't believe that!" One of the other guests was doubtful; if this were true, he would quit the paper business and start hunting.

"Would I lie? They sell otters for twenty taels of silver. I've seen it with my own eyes. I'll swear to it."

"What have you seen with your own eyes?" Black Cat laughed. "There are lots of things you can't see with your eyes. If you had eyes – "

They did not understand what was behind what she had said, nor did they understand why she laughed, but the big-nosed guest seemed to understand, and, in a convenient moment when the others were not looking, he touched Black Cat's waist. She made no sound, but she looked at his nose as though it were capable of doing strange and marvelous things.

Though there were wild dogs outside, they were not the sort of beasts that could eat grown-ups. Since there was no need to be afraid of them, Black Cat soon opened the door again and went out to draw some water. A pipe in his mouth, the big-nosed guest followed her out to drive off the dogs, or perhaps urinate; he must have had a reason. It seemed as though this time the water had to be brought back from over half a mile away. When Black Cat returned, she did not speak; she just sat by the stove to warm herself. The hunchback noticed that the big-nosed guest returned much later and said he thought he must have been eaten by a dog. Whether it was a dog or a cat, there are places with cats and dogs that really can eat people. Some people are frightened of dogs, but, as for cats, they're not such frightening things. If someone had asked the big-nosed guest, he could have explained.

The mistress finished washing her face and for some reason boiled eggs for the guests. The guests ate the eggs dipped in crystallized honey, then paid their money. It was already getting very light, so the men shouldered their loads and went over the mountain. Black Cat stood silently by the gate for a long time, then stayed by the stove without speaking to the hunchback.

About a month later the same men stayed at the inn again, but the one with the big nose wasn't with them. When she asked why, Black Cat learned that he had died on the road of a sudden illness. Eight months passed, and there was a Little Black Cat in the inn. Some people said it was the hunchback's offspring, so to stop the rumors the hunchback became Black Cat's husband.

Black Cat had indeed responded to the words of the unfortunate big-nosed guest: it was better to have a Mister. The other three paper merchants still often spend the night in the inn, and as soon as they arrive and see the hunchback they are amazed. They cannot understand how the man can make Black Cat happy. Who can understand such things? For instance, before there had been four, but now there were three. This is something that no one can really understand.

My Education

"My Education" ("Wo de jiaoyu"), a diary story written in the summer of 1929, treats torture and execution so lightly that it may be counted as one of the first Chinese stories with black humor. Clearly Shen Congwen meant to shock and titillate his upper-class readers with visions of barbarism and amorality at the bottom of the Chinese soul. He would show them how little they really knew about China and, by implication, themselves. Another "educative" aim, however, must have been to show urban readers that soldiers were no more immoral, stupid, or unaware of the times than other Chinese. Besides the boredom, mindless fatalism, and unquestioning identification with the codes of the higher-ups, there are hints of pride in the military life and intimations of innocence in its camaraderie and horseplay. In this respect, "My Education" fits the international genre of war literature; the story might have been more meaningful to First World War veterans in Europe than to Shen's fellow Chinese intellectuals.

In 1980, Shen Congwen said that he never kept a diary when he was a young soldier – that this work is fictitious. But it is highly autobiographical. It depicts the locale, people, and episodes that Shen observed in Huaihua when he was stationed there about 1918–1919 and that he was later to describe in his autobiography. Gory naturalism and gallows humor aside, the diary is carefully constructed. Although the beheadings are numerous (probably Shen does not exaggerate this), they do not occur randomly but at five-day intervals, as in life. They were saved for market days, which occurred twice during the ten-day Chinese lunar week.

The literariness of this apparently dismal work can be sly. Certain diary entries achieve closure in the manner of classical Chinese poems, which are known for merging an outer "scene" with an interior "feeling" only in the last line. Thus, although Shen Congwen likes final plot twists in the Western manner, he can also imitate classical technique. In "Ox," too, he changes register at the end of some paragraphs by shifting from sordid realities to a higher plane of speculation when one least expects it.

In retrospect, Shen Congwen felt that he had learned from his days in the army. To him, soldiers were innocent common folk — country folk — and he liked to say that he preferred them to well-bred urban snobs. Despite, or perhaps because of, all the conflicting emotions and ambivalent morals running through this piece, it may really be an approximation of what Shen would have written had he kept a diary in his adolescence. No historical account equals it as an introduction to Chinese warlordism. "My Education" in fact reflects an advanced state of self-awareness, although its narrator might be the last to admit it.

I

These are my recollections of life in a little town called Huaihua. I lived upstairs at the left of the theater courtyard in an ancestral temple. There were seven of us in the room altogether.

You can tell soldiers have occupied this building before, from all the medicinal plasters hanging from the walls. The ordinary person just can't understand why these plasters are so inseparable from the military life. It's the same with a lot of *my* friends in the ranks. They love putting a plaster on their back or on their leg, and then later they stick it on the wall. They're always getting a beating, tripping when they move something heavy, or they throw their back out, particularly the older cook boys. They just can't live without these plasters.

Every two men get a cotton quilt to share, with straw for a mattress. Not wet, not cold, with a cover over us and a mattress beneath, and all our food and drink supplied, we naturally find the life here very comfortable. Everybody is very satisfied since the militia provides for all our needs. The bed boards are new, the straw is clean, and the quilts are taken right off the country people's beds.

The sergeant in command of the platoon gives his lecture three times a day, morning, noon, and night. He memorized this wonderful speech long ago, so as not to look bad when the commander comes on an inspection. There are three points: One, no messing around with other people's women outside camp. Two, no stealing things from other people. Three, no fighting and scrapping. I memorized these points a long time ago. Can't speak for the others. Some have their own vices.

Translated by Jeffrey Kinkley

2

Spent the day cleaning up my quarters. Fumigated the place by burning rice straw. The moldy smell up here is really gone now!

Today somebody found a wad of three bucks stuck in a crack in the wall. It was wrapped in red paper – no telling who put it there. When you get caught finding money without reporting it to your superior, you have to fork it over, and then they bend you over the steps and give you thirty blows. This guy deserved it. He got this money without working for it and tried to keep it from us. The sergeant said it came down from heaven so everybody should get a share. It was too little to divvy up, so this evening he bought us some pork for our supper. The guy who took the beating lay on his bed, too angry to eat. Funny thing is, you get whipped for not eating, too. You'd think that in his anger he'd eat more than anybody else.

Soldiers have to follow orders. If you don't, you're beaten. That's what our lives are all about.

A lot of the guys are too smart to get in trouble with the sarge. But that's not so strange. Often they drink with him, so how could he get off beating and cursing them?

The fumigation smelled up the place, so I invited the guys into town with me to take a look around. I really can't figure out why we're garrisoned in this particular place. There's only one street. Unless it's a market day, you can't even buy a bowl of *tangyuan* dumplings. The street is filthy, covered with dirty waste water coming from the bean curd shop, slathered with white foam here, black foam there. You see a lot of dirty gray ducks sticking their pink beaks into it, sucking up particles to eat. The whole town has got just one medicine shop and two general stores, "southern goods" stores we call them. They hung out flags to welcome us. They're makeshift flags, like those everywhere else in China. Two weeks ago we stuck up bulletins that we were coming in to pacify the countryside. And the militia sent people around beating a gong to notify everybody. Everyone knows this pacification is in their interest. That's why all the flags.

When I went out on the street today, I saw a man blowing on his *suona*.[1] He sat there in the sun for warmth, playing his *suona,* with a bunch of children circled around him. It sounded good – he was pretty skilled. I thought he wanted money. Feeling I ought to show some generosity, I threw him a coin, and everybody laughed. Turned out he was just amusing the kids, not playing for money. Since it was free, I stuck around longer than I usually have patience for. All the children here look scrawny, like they're sick. No surprise there. None of the kids in any of these places I've been to look very well fed.

Later things got to be pretty slow. Luckily, I heard about a place where you can get a drink. Things might be more interesting on market day. We have to wait till then just to eat meat. The pork we got yesterday came from several miles away.

3

The sergeant told us the first day here that soldiers are supposed to get up early, so I got up real early today.

Anybody caught in bed during roll call today was punished by being made to kneel. There were nineteen of them altogether. They had to kneel all in a row in the corridor of the main temple hall, until nine o'clock. They looked pretty funny, with the sun beating down on their broad shoulders. Sarge laughed, too, when he saw this pack of midgets. Their punishment was up at breakfast time, so they came and ate with us.

It'll probably be a few days before we begin drilling

[1] Brass-belled Chinese oboe.

because we still don't have any orders. So what do you do when you get up early, anyway? There was frost today, like it was November, so we put on our new uniforms and went up into the hills out back. It was fun. We had no idea how nice it is up there, lots of fields and not many people – no wonder it attracts the bandits, but we've never seen any. They were probably scared when they heard so many soldiers were coming, us with our shiny bayonets, and went and hid deep in the mountains. I expect after a while we'll be sent out all over the place to fight them, which of course would be a lot of fun. If we don't run into any bandits, at least we'll run into the militia captain. He's good for entertaining us troops, not much more.

Saw a man fishing over by the stream. I asked how many he could catch in a day, and he just laughed. I asked him again before I figured out that he had nothing to do and was just fishing for fun because often he doesn't catch any all day. It'll be winter soon, so the fish aren't biting. I had no idea there were still such free spirits in the countryside. Made me want to fish, too.

The air is good and fresh up there in the morning.

I went back to camp and ate breakfast. There was nothing to do, so the squad leader said we ought to clean our rifles in this good weather. We each took our gun down from the rack, removed the breechblock, unscrewed the screw, threaded a cloth through the barrel using twine, and then ran it through back and forth. I was afraid to wear down the rifling in my barrel, though, so I just polished the breechblock and bayonet. We've actually had fewer occasions to fire our rifles the last six months than to clean them. It's as if we were issued our weapons just to keep them shiny.

It's nice to clean your gun out in the sun, and the sun gets gentler and gentler as the autumn days go by.

Some guys stayed out there to pick lice. When you're tired, you take a nap. You can do what you want.

We were cleaning our guns, so somebody asked the sarge, "Sergeant, when are we going to fight the bandits?" He just smiled and said, "There don't seem to be any bandits here any more."

If there are no bandits around, being stationed here all winter long is enough to make you curse. We're ready to practice all those orders we learned at Chenzhou,[2] like "March!" "On your stomachs!" "Prepare to fire!" and "Charge!" Who're we going to practice them on if there are no bandits around?

4

Market day today. Had no idea this place could come to life like this.

There was meat today! We dipped our little enamel bowls, the ones issued to us by the commissariat during our free period, into the meat soup, and did that set us all to smiling!

We got a speech this morning. We were told not to take things from civilians without paying. If we disobey and are found out, we'll be beaten – five hundred blows. When the speech was over and the troops were dismissed, everybody went into town to have a good time. We were all on our best behavior, bearing in mind that five hundred figure. Some guys cursed under their breath during the lecture, but I figure they'll bear those five hundred blows in mind and won't dare act up. Still, when you see something you want and ask how much, these country people are careful to quote you a price that's just half the real value. You shake your head, refusing on account of that five hundred. In the end, you give them the whole amount, but then they give you double the goods. But you can't blame this on us soldiers.

Everything is for sale at the market. Cloth, beef, mutton,

[2]"XX" in the original. Name supplied by the translator.

cooking oil, salt, and other necessities, Jiahu-style pastries, red ribbons, imitation jade bracelets, the *Three Character Classic* and the *Hundred Surnames,* just about everything. And they sell dog meat, a whole leg at a time, and much cheaper than at Chenzhou. We each got us twenty sous' worth of candy and sucked on it as we checked out everything that was going on.

They have good chickens here. All the soldiers buy little chicks to raise as fighting cocks, and hens to lay eggs and hatch more chicks.

The medicine seller at the market had a lot of trade, too. I stood outside the door for a long time and saw a lot of people go in. When the shopkeeper saw us hanging around outside, he asked us if we were interested in plasters, saying he had some samples just made up to give away. He must think all soldiers wear plasters on their legs for fun – he doesn't know which ones need them and why.

While we were just walking around at the market, we saw a lot of young women, with big boobs, fair complexions, and long eyebrows, the kind it's easy to look at.

We heard someone was running a gaming table at the market, too. But we were afraid of running into the commander there, so we didn't dare to even go look. Only this evening did we learn that it's run by the adjutant's office, which taxes it. They take in three strings of cash a table, more than forty strings total, nine of which are shared with us. But it wouldn't come to anything after being divvied up, so instead they wait until the next market day and use it to buy meat for our mess.

5

No market today, so it wasn't worth going to town.

A lot of people slept during the day up here in the theater boxes.

Instead of going out, I went to the front of the stage with a pal to count the stories told by the carvings. Then I borrowed a pen from the quartermaster to draw a picture of Zhao Zilong riding off alone to save his lord.[3] My copy of the carving really caught the spirit of it, so I hung it on the wall. When the others saw it, they all asked me to draw one for them. Naturally I couldn't refuse. I could paint a portrait of Zhang Fei on a crummy candy wrapper if I had to.

Everybody says there are ghosts in this ancestral temple. And they talk about how many there are, all over the place. If you ask me, these people have nothing better to talk about, and that's why they jabber about these things. Not one of us is really afraid of ghosts. A lot of people have eaten human livers and hearts – fried them up with hot peppers and washed them down with wine. I was privileged just to hear about it, not to partake. How could people like us find the time to fear ghosts? But the cook and the bugle boy like to hear stories, so we often talk about ghosts.

In the few days since we've come to live here in this temple, our activities can be listed as follows: (1) Roll call (if you're not there, they make you kneel as punishment). (2) Eating (mostly hot peppers as vegetables). (3) Cleaning our guns and singing army songs. (4) Looking for fun wherever we can find it, maybe getting a little rowdy (like hitting someone else's dog or rolling over on someone's chicken). No one knows how long these days will last. Not a one of us knows what we came here to do, either. I wanted to know, so I went with some others to see the provost marshal, the head judge advocate, and he didn't know. He said, "Do I know what they mean by pacifying the countryside? All I know is how to judge cases and use the bamboo rod to get confessions out of people." This provost marshal is the officer we know best, and that's all he could tell us.

[3]From the *Romance of the Three Kingdoms,* chap. 41. Zhao Yun (Zilong) saved Liu Bei's son from Cao Cao's forces.

Because the militia sends over our daily provisions and the adjutant distributes them, we're unusually blessed here, not having to listen to the quartermaster wrangle over the cost of provisions every evening like at Chenzhou. With no provisions accounts to keep, the quartermaster lies drunk all day on the stairs. Once a soldier kicked him in the shoulder and wasn't even punished for it the day after, which was really peculiar.

6

Our headquarters is in the rear hall of the temple. Soldiers can't go in except on business. Today, for some reason, six soldiers were assigned to duty inside. Since I'm friends with the provost marshal, I followed them in. Only then did I find out that the militia was sending over a bandit to be tried, so these guys were assigned to bailiff duty.

We found out that the men bringing in the bandit were here. When he was first brought over and taken to the guardhouse, everybody fought to see what a bandit looked like. What a disappointment, though. Just like ordinary people – head shaved, blue clothes. Wore a sandal on his left foot only. Probably they beat him on the right foot when they took him, 'cause it was slightly swollen. They tied his hands behind his back and then tied the rope ends to a pillar in the guardhouse. He sat there on a stool with his head lowered and didn't say a word. Didn't move. Even when someone pressed him down with his hand, he just shied away a little. We had no idea what was going on in his mind.

Soon it was time for the trial. First they read the petition from the militia, then asked the man his name and age. The judge advocate sat in the center wearing his sunglasses, all high and mighty. Sitting at his side was a stenographer, keeping his head down as he recorded the confession. After a few questions, the judge advocate got angry for some reason and yelled at him, "Confess, or you'll be beaten!" The criminal then crept over and looked up the steps at the judge, loudly pleading that this Great Infallible One spare his life. They grabbed him in the middle of his shouts and gave him a hundred blows of the bamboo rod. After the beating, the judge advocate calmed down a little.

The judge advocate said, "They say you're a bandit. If you don't own up, I'll beat you to death."

"This is an injustice," said the man. "They're out to get me."

"Why haven't they done anything to *me?*" asked the judge advocate.

"Master, you can see through them. This is a frame-up," the man said.

"Frame-up, frame-up, you look like a thief to me. I'll beat you again if you don't confess!"

Then the guy kowtowed and said, "Spare me, Master! I'm a good man. The militia are against me."

The judge advocate read the petition, mulled it over a little, then ordered the soldiers to drag him down the steps for another hundred lashes.

Later, when they adjourned, the man was brought to a newly made prison right below where I live. They gave him five hundred blows in all. But he was a healthy, sturdy peasant, able to take all the suffering they inflicted on him. He still didn't admit to any crime. I imagine they'll kill him tomorrow, for the militia say he's a bandit. Other powerful people around here hate him, too, so he ought to be a goner. Since we're here to clean up the countryside, of course it'd be improper not to kill him. Everybody's saying he's committed a capital offense, but they don't seem to feel any enmity toward him. Talk about enmity and taking reprisals, I know full well that a lot of people would like to kill their superior officer. No, they simply feel that bandits should be killed, and some are discussing who'd be the best executioner for him, talking up their friends and relatives of course since the executioner will get a reward.

An awful lot of soldiers look forward to the execution tomorrow as an amusement. Their lives are just too plain and boring. For excitement, there's nothing like an execution to stir up this tough bunch of guys.

In the evening when I went to the guardhouse, I saw men splitting thick bamboo logs, then smoothing them down with knives. They said the adjutant wanted them to prepare big *mao* bamboo planks, for the bandits here are very sly and this is the only way of dealing with them. The ordinary rods used to whip soldiers aren't enough for these bastards. Yeah, that's absolutely right. The people from these parts are very sturdy, in no ways weaker than us soldiers. If you want them to confess to things they don't even admit to be crimes, how can you succeed without beating them over and over? Sometimes they don't even cry out in pain. Real barbarians!

7

I went to see some more of the trial. Everything went the same as yesterday, except for the number of blows during the beatings. It was in the morning, and they really brought out the new bamboo rods. When they called the court into session, a soldier dropped a bunch of these giant bamboo rods on the ground with a clatter. It was enough to scare you, all right. It took only another three hundred blows to get the criminal to confess. The judge advocate told him what to say, and he said it. Just what they wanted to hear. They recorded his confession that very day, took his fingerprint in lieu of a signature, then threw him into jail again.

We thought there'd be an execution today, so we were all excited.

But they didn't kill him. It was boring as hell up there in

the balcony, so I took the afternoon off and went up into the hills.

Today some soldiers were given a lashing, too, because they'd gotten into a fight. They have nothing to do all day, so fights are really unavoidable. But it's not too important if it's just regular scrapping and wrangling – if no bayonets are involved, and there's no bloodletting. These men can be fighting today and make up tomorrow. That's how soldiers are. The two men were punished by being made to stand at attention facing each other for an hour. That made them wish they'd controlled themselves a little more!

Still, some get discharged for fighting. I dreamed that I'd been expelled. First I dreamed that I went to —— and got into a fight, and then the company commander expelled us.

8

I spent the morning at the ordnance repair shop, watching them work and taking turns myself at the furnace bellows.

Their hands and faces are completely black, as if they've never found the time to dab a little soap on their faces and necks. There are six of them, children really, working in the same place. And a director, who tells them when to work and rest. The kids put their heart into the work, and they're constantly at it. You'd never guess that these little devils, arms skinny as sugar cane, could bring those big iron hammers down on the anvil as hard as any blacksmith. They're very good with the furnace and handy with hacksaws and drills. And they can sharpen blades. They joke with each other while performing all these operations, as if very happy with their work, and like they've been at it for ten years or more.

What we envy about them there at the repair shop is their good director. Every day he cooks up dog meat or beef in his big stew pot, and all his workers get a share. Ordinary new recruits like us aren't so lucky. The battalion and company commanders can drink with the best of them, but they never invite us.

These guys invited me to eat dog meat with them next time. I accepted.

Today we cleaned our guns again.

Later in the day I left the repair shop and went out on the street, where I saw soldiers bringing human heads in to headquarters from around Shimen. They had bags of heads hanging from either end of their shoulder poles, two bags per person. They'd tied rope into crisscrossing net bags to cradle the heads, which evidently were very heavy, well over three hundred pounds the load of them. To get a better look at the heads I followed this procession of them into camp, where I learned that they'd been cut off by the bandit exterminators garrisoned at Shimen. We didn't know if they really were the heads of bandits or not.

When they deposited these things at the adjutant's, a lot of people stood around gaping at them. Later the adjutant said they ought to be hung up at the front of the marketplace. Tomorrow's market day, so they can be displayed as a warning, to let everybody know that we troops have already wiped out some bandits for them. So I went along for a look, even watched them balance the things on the incinerator smokestack before I returned to camp.

9

Market day again – what a lift to the spirits.

I had an appointment early in the morning with some soldiers who didn't get to see the heads yesterday, to go and enjoy these strange things. When we got there, other soldiers were already standing around looking at them. The heads were hung up real high, but someone had climbed up the smokestack and poked out their eyes with his fingers, till finally one of the heads fell down on the ground. Everybody fought to pick it up, and then to throw the thing at somebody else, just for fun. Out of curiosity I kicked it myself. Stubbed my toe.

Today at noon, they dragged the "bandit" out of jail over to the big bridge at the head of the street and killed him. Chopped his head off, leaving blood all over the ground. We followed behind the guards out to the execution ground and saw the headsman bring the sword down on the guy's neck with a whack. We saw everything, including how he used the sword to saw the head completely off from the body after it fell on the ground. This victim didn't sing or curse at the end, but nobody was disappointed anyway because of the hale and hearty way he stalked out to the execution ground. When he got there, someone asked if he had any last words. He just stammered, "I'll be one to reckon with twenty years later."[4] That's all he said. Then he stuck his neck right out to take his punishment.

If I could figure out why it is these people speak these macho words to the crowd and show their fearlessness in the face of death, then kneel on the ground and stick out their necks to convenience the executioner, I wouldn't bother to go see such a thing again.

This fellow probably wasn't that upset to be killed because all of them seem to believe in fate. True enough, we ought to believe in it, too. Today their fate wasn't so good, so this is how they ended up. But our fate is quite the opposite, so tonight we'll be feasting on meat.

All we talked about on the way back to camp was that man who'd lost his head. We went on about it for a long while, leaning against the haystacks, everybody referring to other stories of beheadings he knew about. Hardly any of these soldiers was as poorly informed about executions as I.

---

[4]After he'd been reincarnated and grown to maturity again.

They could even tell from the way the unfortunate man knelt today that he didn't know much about being a bandit. Longtime bandits know all the tricks of the procedure – to crook one leg while kneeling, or sit down with their legs coiled up if they're badly injured, because that way, when the head falls off, the body faces up. They go to heaven sleeping on their back, which helps their reincarnation. For him to have spoken those brave words of resistance, "I'll be one to reckon with twenty years later," and at the end not known even that little trick, meant he hadn't fully played his role. Every soldier has a lot of chances to see people killed, and not a one of them doubts this business about making the body face upward. When soldiers watch an execution, they know how it's supposed to go. Even if they don't, their buddies can fill them in when the time comes.

10

A militia captain and twenty of his men came in, escorting a batch of bandits and criminals under guard. Six bastards "just lookin' to get killed" in all. During interrogation, three of them admitted they deserved punishment. Bail was taken from them, and they were released. The other three admitted their guilt, too, after some sound beatings, so they were also released after posting bail. I understand they were fined four thousand altogether. The militia captain who brought in the criminals went to headquarters and settled in at the adjutant's for some serious drinking. He greeted us soldiers as he left, all smiles, as if we were his sworn brothers.

I heard a soldier say this was the most convenient way for us to support ourselves. His uncle is the provost marshal, so he ought to know. When I heard this, it occurred to me how handy it really is. There are over a thousand people living within a ten-mile radius of where we're camped. The militia usually supply us only with rice and firewood, no pay, so how can we celebrate New Year's? Everybody says that the garrisoning of troops in the countryside is a chance for them to get rich, and now our chance has come. And now that we have this opportunity, there's nothing to do but celebrate and make merry. But sometimes I think these people must hate us soldiers. Still, all they can do is hate us. They have no recourse. If they're not willing to pay their fines, we arrest them and kill them, and that's the end of that.

It rained today, making everything muddy underfoot. I went to visit the ordnance repair shop. Worked the bellows some more, and watched those workers who're even younger than I am do their smithing. It's an interesting process. I asked them to tell me how they tempered the iron and made it into steel 'cause I'd bummed a steel spear off them and planned to learn how to do martial arts moves with it in my spare time. No need to hide my wish: I'd like to rise from a soldier to become a knight-errant. I have no reason to deny my wish to progress and be somebody.

I went to bed very late because a soldier got five hundred blows for disobeying rule number one in the sergeant's lecture. He got caught, and they punished him. Soldiers ought to obey orders. When they do something wrong, they're beaten. When this guy was done being beaten, he just lay prostrate on his bed board and moaned, while his friends looked all over for herbal medicines to rub on his thighs. Then the sergeant angrily stalked off to see the battalion commander. It got boring after that, and soon everybody fell asleep. The soldier who was beaten seems to have slept too, but I couldn't sleep right. I kept thinking that a soldier should obey orders, and remembering that soldier's groans.

11

We were assigned to go down to the stream by squads to wash our clothes. We actually gave them a quick wash in the barracks, then cursed and splashed water at each other when we got to the river. The weather was good again, unexpectedly sunny, and fine weather makes everybody a lot more childish. Everybody had a great time pushing this cook boy from the squad right into the drink. He crawled up out of the water, his clothes wringing wet, and cried all the way back to the camp. They punished us by making us return to camp, but not a soul thought it wasn't worth it.

When I'd done my laundry, I got three other soldiers to go with me to look at the place where they killed that man. The head and corpse were gone, and so was the blood, washed away by the rain yesterday. We sat for a long time on the stone balustrade of the bridge, staring into the clear river water without being able to say anything. I felt a little lonely. If I hadn't seen him killed there with my own eyes, there'd be no way now to tell that a man had stuck his neck out at this very place and lost his head under the powerful chop of a big sword.

They seemed to have immediately forgotten that they'd killed a man, and the surviving family of the man executed also seemed to have immediately forgotten that one of their own had been killed. That's how we all proceed with our lives. I was a little troubled by the idea. But I knew the whole thing was fixed and unalterable. After he'd returned to camp and whetted his sword again, the executioner bought a hundred dollars' worth of spirit money and went that night to burn it for the deceased. But it was just a formality. Outside the formalities, no one is given the duty of remembering another person's pain and terror.

There seem to be educated people in these parts. Gentry, too. But when a scholar encounters a soldier and the soldier hits him in the mouth, he has no recourse. (Gentry usually make their living by bullying and cheating the common people. We fine them, and they have to pay it without saying a word.) Educated people don't get beat up at this place because we don't have it in for anybody. Our lives are very dull and ordinary, and we're not at war, so we're not out of temper. I believe that, in a stupid society, intelligence is useless.

12

Last evening someone asked the squad leader to go to the battalion commander's to ask if we could be allowed to gamble a little. With nothing else to do, we're having a tough time getting through the days. The battalion commander said, All right, you have yourselves some fun; just don't let your wagers get out of hand. Also, no fighting and no cheating. Each of us in turn gave our word to the commander. So from now on we'll have one more pastime.

He said no big bets, but some of the cook boys lost a half year's savings – a few dollars – this very first day. There's this cook who particularly loves plasters. Whenever I see him, he's always got one of those things on his chest. We asked him how his chest was after he lost all that money, meaning to joke about whether he was sick at heart. But he didn't get mad. He laughed and said he lost because he wasn't lucky. These men are forty years old and over. That stupid look they have is funny and at the same time makes you feel pity. They're like little children.

Cooks get a salary of three dollars a month. Subtract a dollar and a half for board, and that leaves them with a dollar and a half. They lose a half year's savings in one evening of *paijiu*[5] – get wiped out clean – and still are up the next day at dawn, carrying their buckets to the well to bring

[5]Dominoes.

back water. Only our camp has so many of them, and as a rule they lose when they gamble. In fact, they give a lot of other soldiers the opportunity to practice their cheating.

I watch them carrying water, sulkily bumping their buckets into each other on purpose, and something comes over me I can't express.

I don't gamble, though I think it's real interesting to watch. I used to be quite a sharpie, but once I got taught a lesson, so I gave it up.

I buy twenty sous' worth of candy every day to suck on. Lately it's almost become a habit.

Today two more criminals were brought over. I saw them while I was out buying candy. I asked the candy seller if they'd done any robbing around here. He shook his head and told me that there are times when bandits are everywhere because sometimes there are more opportunities for them to be highwaymen than regular citizens. I didn't understand what he meant by *opportunities,* but he looked like he couldn't tell a lie, so I took it for what it was worth.

I didn't go to watch the interrogation of the bandits at night. Later I heard that one of them, who was pretty young, had both his feet broken with the iron bar. I knew he was fodder for the day after tomorrow. They kill a person on each market day, so those country people will see that we're here to wipe out their bandits, that we're not just getting our provisions from them for nothing.

13

Today they brought over seven more.

Everybody seems very happy about it because these bandits were arrested by the militia for us to slaughter or fine as we will. And the militia know all about the prisoners' financial circumstances – they don't make mistakes or miss anything, so it saves us a lot of trouble.

But me, I don't care. That's for the judges to worry about. They're busier than usual because of it. Even these men of knowledge and status have to lay off the opium when the trial's coming up. Me, I go off by myself to the repair shop to do some smithing, try the lathe, and drill some holes in iron bars. I'm interested in those sorts of things. Admittedly, when there's an execution, I follow along and see it. I always get in on the action, but I'm not interested in seeing bandits tortured, and I don't have the eagerness to see people executed that the others do. Whenever bandits are brought over for interrogation, everybody competes to see who can bring out the bamboo rods. When they hear there's going to be an execution, they fight to be the ones guarding the victims. Mighty strange. They really do have nothing to do. They have to *find* something to do.

Today one of the kids working at the repair shop took me someplace new, an iron foundry. It was in the hills, back from the road. The great furnace there, twenty feet high with gleaming white molten iron pouring out of its mouth, is a really formidable sight. That worker knew a lot more about it than I did. He could tell an iron mine when he saw it, he knew how and why to make wrought iron, and he could wield the hammer by himself. He gets a monthly wage of four dollars and sixty cents and even has the director mail his savings home, where his mother sells dry goods. He's younger than I am, only twelve. In two years, when he's my age, he can earn eight dollars a month.

The iron works is really a good place. I've learned a lot there. Xinshou is a good fellow, fine in every way – Xinshou is the name of the little boy who works at the repair shop.

Today they killed four of them. The bodies were all lying on the bridge, blocking the way of travelers. People out walking all had to wade across the stream. It was interesting to watch them shake their heads when they saw all the blood. These people were killed at market to take advantage of the crowds and everything going on. Blood dripped down through a crack in the stones into the stream below. The water there is stagnant. It completely turned the color of blood. Everybody tried to get a spot on the balustrade so he could lean over and see it.

The adjutant, head secretary, and judge advocate all came over from headquarters to see the executions today. They must really have nothing to do at all. Must be so idle that they're bored. So they came over to the bridge via the rear gate for a look. The judge advocate even ran part of the way in his long gown, carrying his hookah.

Everybody admired the executioner's way with the sword, for he severed the heads of each of them with one chop. He really is wonderfully skilled. He's a soldier in the bodyguard squad. After performing the executions, he strode with his sword over to the pork butchers' tables at market since custom allows him to slice off some meat for himself from each table. He collected almost a hundred pounds, and two soldiers carried it back to camp. Before today I'd only heard of this custom – thought it belonged to the past, maybe two hundred years ago. Probably they've done it on previous market days, but today I got to see it with my own eyes. The meat ought to have gone to the executioner alone, but there was too much of it, so later it was divvied up. Some of it naturally went to headquarters staff. We each got a share.

At supper we each got a big piece of meat, about four ounces. Needless to say it was the meat that had been cut with that same sword that killed human beings. As we ate we couldn't help discussing the executions some more. The talk came around to the executioner's technique. We didn't stint in our praise of the condemned man who stuck his head so far out, either. That got us back to the locals' regional character, for people from other places lack the courage to draw near to death. Even a good, fast chop won't have the proper effect on a softy, shrinking-necked turtle. Bandits from Zhijiang and parts east are truly admirable in that regard. They don't give you any cause to snicker.

We were issued wine to go along with the meat. Someone who got a little drunk couldn't keep from suddenly standing up and bringing his palm down on the back of a squatting drinker's neck, like it was a sword. The one "beheaded" swore and started scrapping with him. Then everybody got tangled up in one big ball and wouldn't let go. Our squad leader had no way of controlling it because he wanted to try it out himself on a cook boy.

They'd killed a man, and they all acted like it was a holiday. Drunk and filled with meat, they were exquisitely happy.

15

Unable to understand, I went again by myself, early in the morning, to the bridge where the men were executed. I saw the four corpses still there. Soldiers had already cast the heads into the muddy fields. Somebody had stolen in during the wee hours to burn some paper money next to one of the corpses. The ashes looked like the common blue wildflowers you see by the road, a dreary, blue-gray contrast with the bloodstains, which had already congealed into a black ooze.

I stared at the corpses for a time. Then I looked under the bridge and went back.

By my calculations, there'll be at least another four for the next market. We get about four bandits in during a five-day period, and there are already four in the brig now. I heard them say that two were originally intended to be executed yesterday, but they were worried there'd be nobody to kill on the next market day, so they're holding them over until then.

The sergeant assembled us at ten o'clock to give us a lot of talk about how we're supposed to "be patriotic to the nation and protect the people." We also joined hands in a circle to sing some new army songs, with the message "Compatriots, compatriots, love and help one another. Hand in hand, forward we go." Our platoon really did clasp hands and play games for an hour. Everybody was tickled to death because it's been twenty days now, not since we left Chenzhou, that we've had any sports. Although a lot of the men are already old enough to be fathers, play is still quite necessary because they're very childlike at heart.

The song lyrics got me sentimental. In our company we really do love and take care of each other. When one of us is beaten, we get him medicine. When one gambles away his money, we lend him some. When there's wine, we all share equal glasses. And when there's work, we all vie to be the one to do it. We don't concern ourselves with anything else outside. Often we don't even have any reason to worry about the other battalions. Nobody knows why, and nobody even thinks we have to know.

Today the adjutant of the day punished someone by making him kneel in front of the temple hall with a bowl of water on his head. If he spilled any water, the time elapsed wouldn't count. Everybody thought this was particularly amusing. It got us in a cheery mood – everybody was grateful to the adjutant for thinking up such a good idea. This is about the only place where the adjutant's intelligence can show itself because apart from that he just eats and sleeps along with the rest of us.

We're all just about that innocent and simpleminded.

16

Went to the ordnance repair shop today to eat dog meat. When we got our dog, we put him on the furnace to roast. After the fur and skin were burned off, Xinshou and I took it to the stream for scraping and cleaning. When we had him all scraped clean, we cut him into little pieces, added seasoning, and put the whole thing into the stew pot to simmer. We hung it up over the blacksmiths' furnace so the boys could keep on working. By afternoon it was ready for all seven of us to enjoy. These little workers may be young, but, under the good training of the director, practically each and every one of them knows how to squat down next to the stew pot of dog meat and down four ounces of strong spirits. Then, when they're all liquored up, they'll toss off a few wild promises like, "Today I've just got to – !" or, "I'm gonna fight a water buffalo!" Very resolute words. Also, we all tease each other about getting some ass. They don't really have any need for it – they're too young. But they get tipsy and want to get things off their chest, and that's why they bring up these extraneous matters. Everybody also gets to explaining the usage of idiomatic words with double meanings, most of which they heard from a cook or a groom. So, in the end, we all take our utensils back to the kitchen to wash, singing the army song "The General on His Southern Campaign."

The director is a good sort. He practically lets me be one of his workers.

If I were a smith, I wouldn't have trouble using any of the tools or equipment. Like the kids, I could get interested in the work. I'd be a superior worker, and ten years later you'd still find me there at this job.

17

I got in line for roll call particularly early this morning and my uniform was neat, so I got a commendation. Made me very happy. Then I went with the others for an hour to drill on the parade grounds. We all need something of a little weight to be put on our shoulders if we want to get through the day. I'm not necessarily one of these people, but some of the other dumb clucks can't keep in line without any work. And the weather's so good.

We wanted something to do, so today we finally went to see the company commander. Everybody pleaded to be sent out on patrol, to see if there were any bandits raising a disturbance in the neighborhood. This officer is a relative of mine, and he's often bummed some rock candy off me in the name of our kinship. He said, "Patrol duty is assigned, not requested."

"Then we're requesting that it be assigned to us."

"Pack of idiots, what would you do if you *were* assigned to it? If there are any bandits, the militia will tie them up and bring them over to us. Would we be able to catch any if we tried?"

"Then what can we do?"

"Go clean your rifles. Look how wonderful the weather is! A commissioner will soon be here for an inspection. If he sees that your bayonets aren't shiny, won't that be a bad joke?"

"When's he coming?"

"Soon. I heard them say soon. After we've pacified the countryside for a while, he'll come to see how we've done."

"But I've already polished my rifle so much that I've worn down the unloading pin. I'm fed up with such stupid stuff."

"If you think it's stupid, you're the only one."

"I wouldn't clean my gun even if it weren't stupid."

"Then go out and have yourself some fun; just don't make trouble outside camp."

He walked off, sucking on a piece of my candy. Well, if I can't go out on patrol, then all I can do is go out and enjoy myself, as the company commander ordered. Today seven of us went up into the hills out back to cut firewood. Besides hacking off dead limbs, we cut some pieces of thin bamboo to make vertical flutes when we got back to camp. We also picked flowers and stuck them on top of our bundles of firewood, singing army songs all the way back to camp.

Our joy was something no laws could restrain. We kept singing as we came into the camp, as if returning victorious from a faraway campaign. We stuck the wildflowers in a foreign wine bottle, then placed it squarely on the rice bucket where the quartermaster-sergeant figures out his provisions accounts. In the faint light from the Standard Oil kerosene lamp, the shadow of the flowers that evening was quite beautiful.

At night the camp had a major crisis, a desertion from the unit stationed in the rear left courtyard. He was caught and brought back to camp the first time he made off, taking his firearm, but he wasn't executed by firing squad as the law on desertion requires because he promised to ransom himself by handing over three rifles. For the sake of getting those guns, he was allowed to live in the camp. But now he's absconded again. I've often seen this criminal before. He's tall and light skinned, far more handsome than your ordinary soldier, wearing foot fetters that clank when he walks. Sometimes when we'd be cleaning our weapons he'd be given the privilege of coming out onto the parade grounds to get some sun. He'd sit down next to the stone balustrade and look up at the clouds going by. But his mind was on deserting again. He asked to go to the latrine during the night. A cook from his squad went with him to the vegetable garden outside the ordnance repair shop so he could take his crap. After waiting at the door for a long time without hearing anything, the cook got suspicious and called out his name. When there was no answer after several shouts, the cook searched all over, but the guy was gone. Frightened stiff, the cook yelled at the top of his voice, "Runaway mule! Runaway mule!" all the way from the repair shop to the temple. That cook was a Miao, with an extraordinarily broad, resonant voice that shook up the whole camp. Everyone groped for his rifle and assembled outside.

I was down at the repair shop, making an iron crossbow with Xinshou by putting a rifle spring in a little bamboo tube. I figured that, by fixing an arrowhead on the compressed spring, I could shoot at a passing tiger or wildcat and get him right in the eye. Having discovered a little of Bai Yutang's[6] prowess in myself, thanks to lessons from others, I took great interest in this dart-shooting crossbow.

I heard someone pass by outside, which was quite normal. I thought someone who couldn't control his eating was coming to take a crap. Then when I heard the shouts of "runaway mule," I ran out to where the Miao was. That Miao cook was given a chuck behind the ears by the deputy battalion commander to wise him up. That brought him to his senses a little, and he said Corporal Luo had deserted. When we realized that it was just the same old deserter who'd stolen off again, we calmed down. Someone said, "Let's go chase him." A lot of the men wanted to grab their rifles and march on out. Some drunks came teetering down the stairs with their bayonets, leading to still more disgraceful confusion.

We went out back to check the garden. The guy had crawled over the earthen wall, even left tracks, so there was no doubt he was already hiding in the hills. Not long after, we were individually issued torches and weapons to go out

[6]Legendary tiger-hunting folk hero who appears as a knight-errant in the Qing popular novel *Three Heroes and Five Gallants.*

back to the hills to pursue him. We stuck long spears into all the haystacks, and someone or other climbed every single tree in the course of the search. Still no trace of that tall, fair-skinned fellow. Since this criminal is already sentenced – he was just being kept in the camp under guard until he brought in the guns – the battalion commander posted a reward forthwith: three hundred if you bring him in alive, two hundred dead. Even the secretaries, who ordinarily just shuffle papers, sign forms, and compile statistics, were inspired to go all over with lanterns and long spears to search for the deserter. But, however much we searched for him, the guy clearly was about to escape our jurisdiction.

We were assigned to twenty-man search parties. We fanned out to set up roadblocks on the post roads because we figured that, even if he'd made a clean getaway, he'd have to take one to go anywhere. So 140 of us were formed into seven teams to stop this one man. I was ordered with the rest of my squad down a little path past a place called Jiangkou, one of the lines of escape that for various reasons we figured he'd have to take. We got out our sandals, shouldered our rifles and ammunition on the double, then set out in our assigned direction. Of the seven roads, we were to take Route 4. We were on our way in no time. No more sleep for us under those new quilts tonight. The only thing that interested us in this operation was that three hundred dollars. We felt no need to cut his head off. We weren't friends with him, but on the other hand he wasn't our enemy, either. We didn't know in what direction he'd taken off, and we couldn't know in advance if they were serious about the amount of the reward, but we did feel that it would be pretty exciting if we could find this deserter ourselves. Realizing that this guy wore foot fetters and couldn't get very far, and secure in the knowledge that we had the numbers and were each armed with weapons that could send him to his death, it never crossed our minds that this was a senseless or dangerous mission.

It did occur to me along the way that three hundred dollars is equivalent to five years' pay for a soldier – ten years' for a cook. If I'm lucky, might I not get it, just by slashing my bayonet into the right spot or poking around in the right thicket? The sweet dreams of all of us are on this one man.

It was tonight that I learned some things about human life that lie on the dark side.

18

The deserter was captured and brought back. He'd circled around, like we figured, taking Route 4. No luck for us, though. He was even cleverer than we thought. At first he'd meant to pass through Jiangkou on his way to ——, but then he evidently thought he'd go do a favor for the other search parties. He would have run right into us, but he said he changed his mind and went to Dazhai instead. So he was captured and brought back by the group that took the road to Dazhai, which returned to camp four hours after we did. His swollen face was whiter than ever, but he still stood on the field, taking up the sun for warmth. His fetters had been broken. I heard that he'd broken the chain with a hammer in camp, then wrapped his shins in cloth to hide the manacles. We stared at him, and he stared at us. He probably noticed our sorry condition after chasing him all night long, because when he saw the captain, he apologized to him and all the brothers in the ranks. Later, when the battalion commander interrogated him, the guy apologized to him, too, saying he'd acted shamefully toward him.

"Luo," the commander said, "so here you are, back again. I thought you were smarter than to make me have to see you again."

The fellow paused to think and said, "No doubt about that."

"I wanted to save you," the battalion commander said, "so I agreed not to cut off your head if you handed over the rifles. You're too clever for your own good. You saw I was easy on you, so you thought you'd take off. Well, you've deserted, something you obviously enjoy, but you probably don't enjoy being beaten. I'm going to give you a dose of it, and we'll see."

The man really was given a beating. When that was over, they threw him into the jail for bandits. As he hobbled over to the door, he still knew enough to walk in backward. I asked other people and learned that he'd been an elder brother, a secret society member.

After eating, everybody, exhausted from the events of the night, had just hit the hay and was in dreamland when suddenly the bugler blew the call to assemble. The platoon stood in ranks by squad to hear the battalion commander give a lecture. He said that headquarters had issued an order that Corporal Luo was to be executed. Soon the man was hustled off by his campmates to the bridge that we used for killing, and his head was duly cut off.

"He stole a firearm and should have been shot. But we didn't do that, and still he deserted. There's no choice but to decapitate him." Those were the battalion commander's words.

The man's armed escort to the execution were his campmates, the soldiers he ate and drilled with. Everybody just chalked it up to military law, so, when the time came, they had no trouble finding an executioner for him. After the man was killed, all who'd come to get in on the action talked about how heroic he was: "He sang as he went out the gate," "His face didn't change expression," "He never cursed the officers," and, "At the point of death his neck was firm and sturdy." Everybody said he knew exactly how he was supposed to act. Such fellows are rare indeed.

Come evening, the battalion commander brought the reward money over from headquarters. The way it was distributed was a bit unusual. The team of soldiers that caught the deserter got one third, and the other two-thirds went to all those who had worked for his capture. Nobody could argue with that. The quartermaster-sergeant became the currency exchange shop for a while, and immediately a lot of the men went nonchalantly about their business, gambling at dominoes on their straw beds. These men all seem happy about last night's mishap.

I can't understand why they had to bring that fellow back and were willing to shell out three hundred dollars (such a large amount!) for him. When they got the man back, they killed him, and the three hundred dollars given to those of us who searched for him were promptly gambled away. Exactly why it was necessary for them to do that the battalion commander never clearly explained. In his lecture he never explained why it was "necessary."

It all seemed so inevitable. That's the way it's always been, in other people's worlds, and in ours, too.

19

There was another incident today. Three soldiers were interrogated from Company 14 (the company that guarded Corporal Luo). Each man was given five hundred blows and sent to the guardhouse, for they'd helped the criminal escape and been found out. They did it since they were his friends. It was because we didn't know the man that we'd been able to gamble all day. Those three men owed a debt of thanks to the superior officers, for according to regulations they had committed a capital offense, too. Call that fate as well. In the army, we trust fate more than we do ourselves. It's not even worth doubting all those things that have been arranged by fate. Cooks are often twice as strong as us soldiers. They eat twice as much and get twice as much done as we do, too. That's the beauty of being ignorant. Even if we do have to know other things, like "singing," "drilling," "shouting slogans," and "saluting," we don't have to be troubled with anything else. If we could see it for what it is, we'd really call ourselves lucky.

There must have been people within the three soldiers' company who wanted them beaten to death. The ones who wouldn't have thought this excessive would be those who bore them some petty grudge, who'd fought with them over a pole to hang laundry on or been cursed by one of them and then nursed the grievance till it became a matter of life and death. It's really true. We had such an incident while stationed at ——. A soldier climbed out of bed in the dead of night and gave a fellow in the same squad seven blows with a cleaver. The guy's face was a mass of gashes. When the interrogator asked the murderer why he'd acted so viciously and impulsively, he said it was because his companion had cursed him with a filthy word. Was this an honest confession? You bet, anyone familiar with our circumstances would say so, and the judge advocate believed him, too. He was found guilty. If nothing else, these little incidents tell you the local people's regional character. Whenever dirty words are directed at someone, it's inevitable that the debt will be washed away with blood.

But let me say something else. Our superiors can make up the most exquisite curses and fling them at us soldiers any old time they want, without cause. And all of them have a genius for it, from the young officers who've had some schooling to the ones who learned their foul language only after being commissioned. The soldier who's cursed has to take it in silence. But soon, at the first opportunity, he'll try out the superiors' clever inventions on a cook boy. The cooks can only curse each other – or their rice buckets. Of course buckets usually don't curse you back.

The battalion commander put up the money for Corporal

Luo's burial, and some of those who got the reward also went over to the dead man to burn spirit money for his soul. They didn't put him into his coffin until this evening.

Today two soldiers who'd got into a fight gambling were given beatings by the captain. I expected that tonight there'd be another of those murders like I just described, that somebody would get up in the middle of the night, go for a cleaver, and leave behind a bloody mess. But I was completely wrong. They were going at it again with their game of dominoes tonight and talking on and on about their beating, as if it were a joke. They're really blessed. No need to worry about them.

20

It rained today. The card players got up their games inside camp. There was lots of excitement.

21

Rained again. The card players are still at it.

22

Still raining.

23

The whole courtyard is muddy from three straight days of rain. The cooks made their early morning run for water barefoot in the mud, humming all the way. Before breakfast a lot of us leaned over the upstairs railing in our bored way, looking at what the rain had done to the courtyard. When the rain stopped, a healer we addressed as "Teacher, Sir," a tall man, pulled up a bench in the walkway and began to paint an amulet on yellow paper. At the end he chewed on a chicken head and spread blood from it over the amulet. He planned to use it to heal the wounds of the three soldiers who got the beating yesterday. We can't get along without such people in the army. He has to paint such a talisman every time a soldier gets a knife wound in a fight, or the battalion commander's wife comes down sick, or one of their children cries at night because its spirit's wandered. He'd never have got his position if he weren't good at predicting the future. This is probably the kind who become "military counselors." Their talent is half inherited and half from the good geomantic properties of their locality because three of them all seem to have come from Chenzhou. When you look at how the teacher casts his spells, it's like you're seeing Zhuge Liang reincarnated.[7]

I watched the teacher paint his amulet so I could learn how to do it myself. I bummed some paper used to copy documents from the secretarial office, splashed some ink on it to suit me, then hung it up at the head of my bed to keep away evil spirits. That's what I did today while it rained.

Later I sneaked up on a cook boy and stuck my charm on his back. We play practical jokes on this cook whenever we can, like painting a beard on him while he's asleep or giving him a turnip to eat with something filthy inside. When he really feels hurt or can't take it any longer, he starts sobbing, very loud. Everybody thinks it great fun to see his predicament and hear him cry. He's thirty-seven. He'd be a grandpa by now if he were married. His crying brings the sergeant over. The sarge either comes up with an unusual curse or makes one of us soldiers pay the cook off. Soon after that,

[7]Legendarily successful mystical adviser and strategist to Liu Bei in the *Romance of the Three Kingdoms*.

you see him wipe away the tears with those big, hairy hands of his, and the crying stops. People like him may seem very pitiful, but, if we still have any of this thing, "pity," in us, we'd better save it up for more important matters.

Often, when they get the chance, after a bit to drink, cooks will go up to women washing clothes in the stream and whisper dirty words or even try to get physical with them! Like most people in life, they have no need for anyone else's pity. Cooks are the kind of people who, if they see somebody outside camp they can bully, are never slow to trade in on their grey uniform. They're capable of skimming money when they're sent out to buy vegetables, of lying, and then swearing an irresponsible oath to the gods as proof of their honesty. They work a lot, but they eat an awful lot, too. Their behavior is quite unforgivable, so they're always beaten a lot more than other people. The cook boys aren't the only ones who are emotionally like children, though. The head messenger, who's a little older, is the same way. He does something wrong and cries about getting beaten for it, then wipes away his tears and chuckles like a clown when you give him a little money. It's not hard to find people around here with the heart of a child at the age of fifty – people who lose at gambling and still welsh on their debts.

The weather was dispiriting. I couldn't go out. I just went to the repair shop to spell the workers operating the furnace. They put the pig iron into the furnace's charcoal fire, and I talked with them as I worked the bellows. You quickly bring your two arms backward until they get to a certain angle, then lean forward, fanning the fire. That makes it give off a strong smell and a blaze of red. When the iron is red hot, one of the kids draws the iron out with tongs and places it on the crane-bill anvil, while two others pound it with their thin little hammers. They lift those hammers above their heads and behind their backs before bringing them crashing down. That sends sparks flying off everywhere.

The director sat on a pile of old rifle barrels to supervise us from above. While watching the children work, he brought out his book of lyrics to the story of Lady Mengjiang and her husband Wan Xiliang and sang it for all to hear. He's been doing that for days, and the kids can recite the story backward and forward, but he just keeps on reading and singing, not letting a single character get past him. From time to time someone comes to the repair shop to talk business with the director. He answers them in the same cadences as his songs. He seems to be able to drink all day without getting drunk, but he gets drunk quite easily on the sound of his own voice.

When I tire of working the bellows, I often climb up on the scrap heap to amuse myself. I love this roomful of people covered with soot and rust, and I particularly like those things we make: wedges, bars, rods, and so forth. And that earthenware crock. It gives off the sweet smell of dog meat when it's filled. When you fry dried bean curd in it, it still smells like dog meat. I can always find it, wherever it's hidden.

Xinshou and his pals aren't as upset as the soldiers about the weather. The colder it is, the happier they are – they get to eat more meat, and it's easier to work. On really cold days, when the cooks in our camp are bundled up in padded uniforms till they look like bears, the thin and dirty arms and shoulders of Xinshou and company are still working bare. They eat dog meat all the time without putting on any weight, yet they're each so healthy that you could give them a good meal and stand them out in the rain for two hours till they got soaking wet and they still wouldn't catch cold.

Market day tomorrow, so I'd better go to sleep early. Everybody who isn't gambling tonight will be doing the same.

The Company Commander

Quite opposite to "My Education" in tone, characterization, and theme (romance with native women rather than beheadings!) is "The Company Commander" ("Lianzhang"), an idyll that only a West Hunanese with fond memories of his days in the service could have written, at least in the 1920s, when China was racked by warlordism. Here we see Shen Congwen in a romantic mood, in both senses of the term, yet he is writing in 1927, closer in time to his actual military experience than "My Education." Was Shen's reaction to his demobilization nostalgic, with disillusion coming only later? The main point in common between the two works seems to be a sense that the local armies were not noteworthy for their discipline. And both are regionalistic works full of local color.

In fact Shen Congwen wrote far more stories about the joys of army life than he did naturalistic works like "My Education" or send-ups of martial corruption like "Staff Adviser," the piece that follows. One need not read "The Company Commander" simply as an army story, however, or as a "Miao romance" tale. The intimate emotional exchange between the company commander and his lover is touching and subdued. Shen Congwen was developing skills in dialogue and characterization that would serve him in his classic works of the 1930s. One can see from his occasionally jocular tone that he was practicing his irony, too.

I

In summertime the bugle call for lights up from the army barracks carried far enough for even the grazing horses to soon recognize it as the signal to return to the stockade, but with the coming of winter it was no more than companion to the howling of the wind and died dejectedly away into the woods that covered the surrounding hillsides.

The bugle call was even more subdued when snow fell, so much so that it was inaudible to those living at a distance, and many children in country cottages were deprived of an interest in their lives.

However, the grown-ups who had seen some military service could tell the time without the aid of a bugle call. If they had relied on the bugle call to alert them, they would not have been able to stray very far from the barracks. Not every soldier was equipped with a means of time keeping like a clock or watch, nor even every officer. Yet for those stationed in this or that stockade in this neck of the woods a certain amount of wassailing was only to be expected; swapping yarns or playing a hand of cards with old comrades when the opportunity offered was also a permitted form of recreation in the ranks. Besides that, if the men had their own ways and means of taking a lover on the sly, their officers were inclined to turn a blind eye if they found out. So some went to other villages to play their drinking games, some sought to copy Pigsy[1] in his domestic arrangements or to re-create the battle of wits between Jiang Ziya and Shen Gongbao,[2] while others wooed the ladies with saucy songs. If

[1]The lecherous pig monster in the sixteenth-century novel *Journey to the West* who, banished to the mortal plane, shacked up with a farmer's daughter.
[2]Two characters in the sixteenth-century novel *Investiture of the Gods,* who contend militarily.

Translated by David Pollard

all of them had been totally inept at estimating the hour, they would have missed roll call time and time again, which would have been too embarrassing. The important thing for the soldiers in these barracks was to get back from wherever they were in good time for the evening roll call and be standing in the square for the deputy company commander to call out their name so that they could answer with a resounding "Sir!" Only thus could camp rules be satisfied.

The countryside where they were stationed was peaceful and law abiding, meaning that there were no bandits or thieves for them to put down; naturally there was no need there for the rigid discipline of the regular troops, with all their drills and lectures. However, if they fell down even on the thrice-daily roll calls, then to get a dressing down or be punished by having to stand at attention for an hour was thought in all conscience deserved and indeed necessary by all the officers and common soldiers.

In ordinary camps, roll call was held morning, noon, and evening. The evening one was about nine o'clock, that is, not long before the bugle for lights out, but here nine o'clock did not accord with the romantic interests of the generality, so the company commander and the deputy commanders consulted together and moved the roll call forward to near the time of the first watch, about seven o'clock. Given this concession, it would have been letting oneself down to miss it. Thus the soldiers hereabouts were very well informed about the time for lights up.

The hour had come round again for a red-faced bugler dressed in an ill-fitting gray greatcoat to stand on the stone slab at the foot of the flagpole and blow the call for first watch of which he was so proud. All the soldiers, that is to say, the company stationed in this old temple, were already paraded as usual in the snow-covered square. They stood in single lines with their squad leader behind them. Each man remembered his place in the line and took it up out of habit. Owing to men being on leave or on outside duties, some gaps were left; on the squad leader's order to close up, the lines shortened. After the men had fallen in but before the bugle call had finished, the deputy company commander on duty emerged hurriedly, his hastily donned hat somewhat askew, from a new unpainted door whose lattice window was pasted over with protective paper.[3] Everybody liked to take a drop to drink to keep the cold out, and the deputy commander was no exception – he indeed had just absented himself from his place beside the lamb hot pot to attend to his duties.

The deputy company commander having appeared with roll in hand, the first squad leader brought his men to attention, whereupon the men who were huddled in their heavy padded coats shook off their lethargy and snapped themselves up ramrod straight. The snow, indifferent to their discomfort, promptly fell down their necks. When they were stood at ease, the smarter soldiers, those who realized they could stop the snow getting into their collar by tilting their head back, pretended to rub an itching neck or to adjust their belt in order to obtain relief.

When a name was called, someone in the ranks jumped to attention and responded, whereupon the deputy company commander made a mark against his name. If no one responded after a name had been called twice, the squad leader went forward to explain. The roll call completed, the customary brief address was given, during which everyone had to stand rigidly at attention, with no talking in the ranks. Finally they were stood at ease, brought to attention again, and dismissed.

After the parade was over, the deputy company commander and the squad leaders crowded round the stove to resume consumption of the lamb hot pot and the liquor, the rank and file went their separate ways, and the snow fell

[3]A kind of paper made from bamboo and grasses, typically used to line buckets for carrying tung oil.

unabated on the square. The difference was, there was no longer anyone offering his neck to receive it.

According to camp rules, the roll call marked the end of duties for the day, and everybody was left to his own devices until morning roll call the next day. Hence the local inhabitants who had friends or lovers in the camp could calculate their arrival pretty accurately from the time of the bugle call, depending on the distance from camp to house. How different was the significance of the bugle here from on the battlefield!

2

The squad leaders were in charge of these hundred volunteer soldiers, each having ten men under him, like the fingers of his hands. Over the squad leaders were three deputy company commanders, one being a first lieutenant, the other two being second lieutenants. Over the deputy company commanders was the company commander. Under army regulations, this company commander was to take command of his century for exercises and in warfare and direct their advance or withdrawal, but, being billeted in this place, what operations were there for him to command? Besides finger guessing games, the only work he had was to hunt wild boar in the hills at the invitation of the captain of the local militia. But that was his private affair. The company commander was idler than a monk in a temple. If he had not had the initiative to find ways of passing the time, he would long since have taken to his sickbed.

So what exactly did the company commander do to pass the time? Well, there were some things he could attend to. Experience tells us that a commanding officer has twice, or several times, the chance of earning the respect or abomination of the population where he is stationed than his subordinates. This company commander is precisely a case in point. For example, when a company commander first brings his troops to a certain place and finds a billet in a local home, the owner might just turn out to be a young widow; now this young widow might take it into her head to choose from among these swaggering heroes a favorite to replace her dead husband, in the hope of getting all the love and other gratifications that fortune will allow her. In that case she will always offer herself first to the exalted commander.

And in fact, just as we have postulated, this company commander, thanks to his youth and position, did receive the favor of a woman commended by local swains and became the dedicated purveyor of physical and spiritual love to this woman. With the decrease in his responsibilities in the camp came an increase in his awareness of his multiple duties in his newfound occupation. The woman's home was all of a mile from the base, yet from the onset of winter the company commander was duty bound to come and go twice daily practically every day! If he hadn't needed to settle the provisions accounts regularly with the quartermaster, there would have been hardly any reason for him to put in an appearance at all. As a squad leader put it, the company commander was so infatuated with the woman that he was willing to hand all his responsibilities over to his first lieutenant; he might as well give up his pretension of being an officer in command of a hundred men and devote himself solely to the service of that woman for the rest of his life, letting her command him.

Even if that were truly the case, would it have been the company commander's fault?

Judging by the company commander's age and looks, he was eminently suited to get involved with a woman. Fate had deposited him in this backwater and arranged for a mature woman to be here; however resolved the company commander might have been to lock up his passions, clearly the gods had other plans for him.

Still, for a young officer – a captain who had received the best military training – to forget his purpose in life and be bewitched by a woman into casting aside all other considerations like some lovesick fool was not really possible. Besides which, if we admit that brief separations are no obstacle to love, and indeed can be a relief from the weariness of day-long embraces, then it was no great matter that he could manage to stay the night with the woman only about twice a week. Nevertheless, youth would not have been youth if all the time he was detained at the camp he had not longed to be elsewhere!

Because he was not able to divide his body and mind between two places, the company commander sometimes quietly slipped away at night to the woman's house or pretended to go and inspect the sentries and ended up in the same place. In this respect the company commander was playing out the roles of poet and hero. When, recognizing the company commander's voice, the woman opened the door to his quiet knock, attired in a thin white shift, then her hair streaming loose, her heavy limbs, and her languorous state were to him the sacred stuff of poetry. It often happens that someone unable to express his inspiration through the written word is able to express it doubly in his behavior; just so the company commander divested himself utterly of the bellicosity of the camp in this woman's presence and became the soul of gentleness.

As for the woman, she was swept away by the company commander's tenderness and found herself dreaming dreams without measure, like those any young woman weaves round her lover. She had given her heart, it seems, to this man and would thereafter follow him, to the ends of the earth if need be. When the company commander was unable to spend a promised night at the woman's because of camp business and arranged to come instead the next morning after the breakfast bugle call, that call seemed to be blown for her, the commander's mistress, and for her alone. The woman was also young; what made people think of her as still young can be inferred from that example.

The company commander regarded the woman in the same light as the major, his superior officer, whose word was his command. The woman regarded the company commander as her future husband and gave herself to him completely. Love does not neglect anyone because of their kind or their walk in life. The shoots that might germinate at nice young people's parties in the city may here too grow, flower, and bear fruit.

If one thinks of the company commander as the governor hereabouts, then in the soldiers' minds the position of the governor's lady was unanimously accorded to his woman.

3

It was snowing and so cold that the water in the stream froze over. Nowadays only one old deputy company commander and a few soldiers had any interest in the sport of hunting hares in the snow with dogs or shooting pigeons in the wood camouflaged with snow-covered straw capes. The majority of the soldiers sat around the log fires drinking. A minority went to homes in the village to play mah-jongg or chat up women. Needless to say, our company commander was detained at the side of his mistress.

The two of them sat beside the open hearth, eating chestnuts to go with the local liquor. The company commander was drawing on his military experience to tell her of strange practices he had encountered in the places he had been stationed. When she filled the wine cup from the jug, the woman would drink only a fifth of it; the rest went down the company commander's throat. The two-catty jug they had started after the noonday roll call was now almost finished.

"You've really been knocking it back today!"

Indeed he had drunk more than usual: the spirits that were meant to last two meals were nearly used up after one. With some disbelief the woman shook the long-handled wine vessel with the black markings.

The company commander did not reply. He just passed the empty cup to the woman, who could do nothing but refill it, making the excuse as she did so that it was all right to drink a little more than usual when the weather was so cold.

The company commander downed the cup in two mouthfuls, still without a word.

The woman shot him a worried glance. "That's the end of the drink. You don't look too good; why not take a nap if you're feeling tipsy?"

"No." That monosyllable meant, no, he wasn't tipsy, no, he didn't want to sleep, and no, there was nothing wrong with him whatsoever.

But the fact was, the company commander *had* drunk more than was good for him, and the drink had affected his temper.

"I'm going back to the barracks. Would you mind taking my cape down off the hook?"

"Don't go back. It's not as if there is anything for you to do at the barracks."

"I've got to go back. If you wouldn't mind!"

This wasn't the first time that such a situation had arisen. The woman was now familiar with this mood that would take him. He would suddenly decide he would go back to the barracks, as if he had remembered some urgent matter awaiting his attention; but after some persuasion he would stay, though he would not erase from his face that look of unease.

So, when she heard him say he had to go back, the woman used the tactic that had proved successful in the past and affected an injured tone: "Are you tired of me again?"

The question only succeeded in putting the company commander even more out of humor. The woman immediately realized she had gotten off on the wrong foot. She changed her tune: it was so cold, and it would soon be dark; whatever needed to be done could be fitted in the next day if he made an early start.

"In any case, I'm going back. You wouldn't understand even if I explained. I'll be off now, while it's still light enough for me to see my way."

The woman was taken aback. But, from what she had learned of his character, the company commander would not hold out till the very end, so she still said in a bantering way that she couldn't think of any business more vital than checking the provisions accounts with the quartermaster.

"I said I'm going!" The company commander's tone was meant to convey that he wasn't drunk and that the woman had better believe he was in earnest.

The woman asked, "Why?"

"Why? In this weather who's to say we won't suddenly get an order from our brigade commander to break camp and set out for the frontier. We've got to be prepared for a long trek."

"You're not serious?"

"I'm not serious?"

The repeated question seemed to set off a deafening explosion in the woman's ears.

Seeing how the woman froze, the company commander realized that the way he had couched his reply was too close to affirming that they really had got their marching orders, so he hastened to add that this was his speculation about what possibly might happen.

Though "possibly might happen" sufficed to explain that "it really is the case" was still a very long way off, yet he had inadvertently implanted the notion of moving on in her passionate breast, and it would be no quick and easy operation to remove this thorn.

"All right, I'll stay," the company commander said, and pushed the wine cup across to her. "Please pour me another cup."

The woman most dejectedly poured a cup of liquor from the jug. The company commander took the proffered cup but did not immediately raise it to his lips. He too had been hurt by his own words.

The company commander turned his head to avoid the woman's eyes. It was windy outside, and as he watched the snowflakes through the window they floated so lightly that he could imagine they were cotton wool scattered from up above. They did not seem to be falling at all; some indeed were actually rising. The window bars were already encrusted with snow, while fresh flakes that touched the glass dissolved without a trace. Because of the warmth indoors, on the lowest pane of glass had gathered a patch of condensation, about as big as the imprints of a child's hands, as if a layer of fine gauze had been pasted on it.

Were it not for the snow, it would have been dark by now. Because of the snow that blanketed the ground and the roofs, reflecting a silent and subdued light, the time of day appeared earlier than normal. The features of the two people facing each other could still be seen distinctly, but the corners of the room and the vessels and crockery under the table were already lost in the stealthy embrace of darkness.

Now that they had fallen silent, the two could hear the very faint, very regular sound of the snow falling on the ground outside. They also heard the bamboos in the back garden spring upright as great wedges of snow slid down from their crests. Otherwise all was still. No dog barked, no voice was heard, there were no gongs or trumpets; everything in the village seemed asleep or dead.

By and by the sky grew darker. The colors indoors imperceptibly faded, but the charcoal in the open hearth burned with a more fiery glow.

Each of them knew the other was mulling over the implications of that reference to moving on and carefully weighing the distress it would cause them, if indeed it happened.

The company commander looked at the woman in the

light of the fire at their feet. His gaze was drawn to her white hands, dangling lifelessly. He took her hands and held them in his. The woman did not speak. The wine jug was placed on the table; he straightway withdrew one hand to pour some liquor. The woman snatched it from him with her free hand.

The company commander said plaintively, "Let me drink my fill!"

The woman was unmoved by his pleas; she was determined that he should drink no more.

"Let me have my way," the company commander said. "It will make things more bearable."

"The liquor is finished."

"There's plenty left."

"You can't drink any more." The woman moved the wine jug out of the company commander's reach and touched his chin. "Look, your cheeks are on fire; won't you be sorry if you get drunk?"

"When one meets one's own kind, a thousand cups are too few": in other circumstances, this saying had meant something quite different from what it did now to the company commander. On many occasions in the past he had appreciated the force of "a thousand cups are too few," but today he really felt like draining cups without number. Normally drink was called for to celebrate success and happy encounters or to dispel life's frustrations, and then it was a life-giving water; now, because of this woman, the company commander was inclined to get drowned in it.

4

If we look on the devotion of a soft and yielding female as a net, then none of the world's sinners can boast that it was easy to escape after falling into such a net. The Musty Rice immortal who had mastered the supernatural arts and could ride the clouds, harness the wind, and sail through the air as he pleased had only to catch a glimpse of a bare ankle to lose his magical powers. How much less could it be said of us ordinary mortals, successors to a potent heritage of sexual desire, that any one kind of person could be free from such entanglement? There is no great difference between saints and sinners in the torment they suffer from being snared in these toils once they have set out with wavering steps along the way of All for Love. An emperor and a soldier are palpably different in their standing, but, having once fallen in love, both feel with equal anguish the emotional stresses and strains natural to a relationship with a woman. Neither would the empire's greatest scholar differ from a village schoolmaster in this respect. A doctor of philosophy and an errand boy would suffer the same headaches. Given the position of the company commander, therefore, there is no need for any elaborate explanation of why he was now so bent on hitting the bottle.

What could be more natural than that, precisely because of the precarious stability of their relationship, a couple brought together in a love tryst should be wrapped up in their private thoughts, feeling passive, helpless, possessive!

Deprived of drink, the company commander regarded the outline of the woman, now turned away from him, by the light of the faint blue flames of the brazier beside him; he still uttered no word. Then out of boredom he swept together the husks of the peanuts and chestnuts on his lap, on the table, and from beside the brazier and strewed them on top of the burning charcoal. First they smoked and crackled, then burst all together into roaring flames. In this blaze the company commander could see that the woman's face was streaked with tears. Nodding his head, close shaven in army style, he said huskily he would obey her order and not go back to the barracks.

With a bitter smile the woman poured out the last of the liquor from the jug and downed it herself in one go.

"I thought you said there was no more left!" the company commander exclaimed, as if to rebuke the woman.

"I didn't want you to go on drinking."

"Then don't you either!"

The woman agreed not to, but as she spoke she swilled the remaining drops round in the jug and poured them into the cup. The company commander snatched it from her grasp and dashed it onto the fire. This dribble of liquor turned into a leaping flame when it came into contact with the fire. The woman covered her face with her hands. The braided silver bracelet on her wrist glowed like gold. After covering her face, the woman began to cry softly, though not because she was angry at the company commander for snatching the liquor away from her.

"I agreed to stay, but still you cry."

She went on crying, though she had heard what the company commander said all right. She realized that, if she went on crying, her crying would itself drive him away, yet, despite his promise not to leave this time, in the end there would come a time when he *would* leave! The thought of this future circumstance, remote enough not actually to trouble her yet, could not but make her pain more acute. Like it or not, they would break up; the bonds of affection that united them would be shuffled off. This prospect of being left desolate made her forget the arts she knew of shackling the company commander to her. If he really drowned himself in drink, then the woman would be obliged to dissolve herself in tears.

On his part, the company commander felt, strangely enough, that the woman's crying absolved him from having to write her a bothersome blank check for the future, and he was actually relieved. He was nonplussed by the woman's sobbing and, being unable to cope with it, got to his feet. Though her hands were over her face, the woman heard him move.

"Leave if you want to; in any case the performance has got to come to an end!"

"I said I was staying!" His intention in getting up had been to stretch himself, but to avoid misunderstanding he had not done so. The reason why he had reiterated that he was staying was to correct the misunderstanding caused by the sound of his standing up.

Nonetheless, the woman gave herself up to wailing, discomposed by her own utterance.

To cut someone down with a saber would have caused the company commander less distress than the situation in which he now found himself.

The liquor spilled on the fire was consumed in one tongue of flame, and the husks had no lasting power: the room was soon reclaimed by darkness. The sudden reversion to darkness obliterated the outline of the person opposite, and in the darkness it seemed to the woman that the company commander had already really left her, which made her cry even more pathetically.

A military man's skills in coaxing a woman are about as adequate to the task as rabbits harnessed to pull a cart. Before long the company commander was wiping the sweat from his brow with the back of his hand and was half sober.

The company commander resorted to that hand to caress the woman, who pulled it to her mouth and sunk her teeth into it.

"Doesn't that hurt you more than it hurts me?" the company commander asked the woman.

"You feel the pain in your hand; have you thought how long you have gnawed at my heart?"

The company commander brushed the tears on the woman's cheek with his lips, and the two fell into an ungainly embrace.

5

On the twenty-third of the last month of the year, when every household prepared a figurine and sweets so as to send off the god of the hearth on his journey to report to heaven, the company commander changed his place of work. Thenceforth the quartermaster had to make a daily trip to the company commander's home to go through the provisions accounts. The bugle for roll call was still blown three times a day, but it was no longer able to make the company commander's wife's heart miss a beat at its sound.

Staff Adviser

In utter contrast to the story just preceding is "Staff Adviser" ("Guwenguan"), a ten-barreled satire of warlord decadence and moral corruption that ought to have been the envy of Shen's colleagues on the Left. Yet the rather venal protagonist is comic and has claims to our sympathy. Shen Congwen attributed this aspect of his creativity to the influence of Chekhov. Even when exposing the blackest of human and social conditions, he could rarely bring himself to create a truly evil character.

The interesting details about army life, institutions, and social manners are told from the point of view of an insider and drawn from Shen Congwen's experience in the armies of his native place, with which he actually did invade and occupy eastern Sichuan in the early 1920s. Perhaps the lateness of this work in Shen's oeuvre (it is about the last "army story" he ever wrote, finished 26 April 1935) explains why here the author was finally able to speak unflatteringly about the profession he had always before been able to excuse and even romanticize. However, he does not identify the origins of the troops at issue, thus sparing his old Zhen'ganese comrades the criticism. In fact one could infer that the venal troops depicted here are the hated Sichuanese, for it was chiefly Sichuan that collected an "indolence tax." In his Communist-era revision, perhaps feeling less of a need to protect the reputation of his fellow provincials, Shen Congwen altered the story, specifying the adviser's army as the Thirty-fourth Division, as the Zhen'gan army was renamed by Chiang Kai-shek's Nanjing regime in the 1930s. But that is anachronistic and not necessarily in keeping with the spirit in which the piece was conceived. This translation follows the original text.

The —ese Army stationed in eastern Sichuan boasted twenty thousand rifles and was a force some thirty thousand strong – counting all the officers and subs, foot soldiers, cooks, porters, and other flunkies, *and* the assorted dependents, legal and otherwise. But, when it came time to close the register and sign for the provincial pay subsidy at the end of the month, there was only forty thousand yuan in it for them. To make up the rest of their support they had to rely on the duty from opium coming into the province and the county government's taxes on households doing the planting and inhaling, respectively. There were the land tax, the indolence tax on farmers too lazy to plant opium, the assessment on opium poppies – and on opium lamps – plus all the various and sundry taxes on brothels and anyone in the flesh trade. Yet these sources of provisions had run particularly dry, leaving pay in arrears of outlays, till all expenses had to be gouged from the peasants. But that particular well, too, had been drained almost dry, and still the pay for both officers and men was minuscule; just getting by was no joke. Many soldiers would be lacking a cotton-padded uniform during the cold months.

Not a single month went by in which any of the staff got their full regulation pay. Most were single and could cope, but those with children were quite angry. It was just a favored few of the headquarters staff who, though titularly paid about the same as everybody else, could get an extraordinary allowance on the side, besides some no-show official positions at various revenue stations that paid a monthly allowance. Those who "had their ways" could also ask the opium merchants to buy three or four loads of the merchandise for them on credit and then sell it; they "went along for the ride" free, earning sure profits without putting any of their own capital at risk. For these reasons they found themselves idle day after day – they could play cards with their

Translated by Jeffrey Kinkley

superior and win or lose four or five hundred dollars without a second thought. The guys who were left out of all this were in pretty tough circumstances, even if they were a senior staff officer or colonel in rank.

A game of cards was going on every day in the reception room at army headquarters, with high-ranking officers as players and kibitzers, all as carefree and leisured as the Eight Immortals. At the sound of the noon cannon shot, they would lay down their cards to savor the many delicacies specially prepared in the army commander's great kitchen. The officers feasted on all varieties of dimsum in succession: round ones, long ones, sweet ones, bland ones; now southern dishes, now northern fare. Without these talented bureaucrats, many a thing would never get done, as will become apparent in the story below.

Just now four men were sitting around the card table on tiny little stools: the head of the opium suppression bureau, the provost marshal, the quartermaster general, and the army commander himself, all fidgeting with their cards in a game of *paohe*.[1] The quartermaster general, sitting across from the commander, had won a hand with a straight in reds and a joker. The commander, the one in "dreamland," as they called the dummy, got to turn over the last card. It was a big red ten, and there was money riding on it. That meant he got sixteen dollars from both losers just as the dummy. The commander was chuckling and making ready to gather those thirty-two dollar earnings into his kitty when suddenly a scrawny little hand, dark yellow like turmeric, reached out from behind him and snatched five dollars. As it seemed about to retract, there came a hoarse shout that bore a slightly fawning tone:

[1]"Picking up tricks." A local game played with a special deck of eighty-one paper cards shaped like ladyfingers: four cards each of "big numbers" from one to ten, four each of "small numbers" from one to ten, and a joker.

"The commander's luck has come in! Let me cash in on five dollars' worth."

The one taking the money was Adviser Zhao Songsan, whose affectations were not in earnest; a longtime subordinate of the commander, he often got in a little joke. Just now an opportunity seemed to be flowing his way, moving downstream full speed ahead, so he'd taken advantage of it. If he didn't succeed, he could make like it was a joke and pretend it was uproarious; if he made a catch, then instead of the *zhajiang* noodles served in the commander's mess, he could leave the yamen behind him to go feast and drink at Butcher Wang's. He'd been standing behind the commander forever, looking at his cards and waiting for his chance, and that was just how the commander knew without ever turning his head who it was who'd grabbed his earnings.

Tilting his head and covering the money with his hand, the commander laughed and roared, "What do you mean by this? So you're going to claim a piece of the winnings of the very man who's sitting it out in dreamland? Tell me, provost marshal, is that utterly lawless or what? Do your duty!"

The provost marshal was obese – his weight had long since soared way out of bounds – and often he fell asleep in the middle of game. This time he'd lost nearly two hundred dollars, and it had just occurred to him that his luck had been compromised by this string-puller standing behind him. He wasn't in a good mood.

He said, sarcastically, "Commander, he's your lucky star – let him have five dollars of your winnings. This guy has given you quite a bit of help!"

Thereupon the skinny hand clutched the money and quickly drew back. He kept standing there, turning the coins over in his hand, clinkety-clink.

"The commander's star is that of a grand marshal, and I'm his lucky star. You won seven hands with me standing behind you. Count it up, you've won almost three hundred dollars!"

The commander said, "All right, all right, lucky star, hurry up and make off with it. Stop standing in back of me. I don't want you as my lucky star. I know you have a lot of important business to attend to. They're waiting for you, so get going!"

The adviser himself had meant to leave immediately, but that exchange left him too embarrassed, so for the nonce he declined to "deploy and move out." Mumbling an excuse, he went behind the provost marshal to look at his cards.

The provost marshal turned around and eyed him wearily: "Third Elder Brother, if you want to play, I'll let you take my place. All right?"

An invisible barb was apparent in these words, but the adviser extracted it with a sly and slippery smile.

"No, provost marshal," he responded, "I'll let you enrich yourself this time – *you* rake it in. Ha, I see from your temples that your luck hasn't been so good. You can count yourself lucky if you don't lose this belt that keeps your trousers up!"

Chuckling as he spoke, and letting the five dollar coins clink as he turned them over in his hand, he strode off with a smug and cocky air.

Once out of the army headquarters yamen, the adviser hastened to Butcher Wang's outside the East Gate. By the time he arrived, the noon cannon shot had just sounded. Two bull penises stewed in a big earthenware pot were already tender and coming apart; the meat and the wine bowls were laid out on the ground and surrounded by a crowd of men squatting down low. The adviser had made it there just in time; no sooner had he joined this gluttonous mob than he found himself drinking one cup after another of imported whiskey, "the red beards' firewater." He also rolled up his sleeves and bellowed out three rounds of the guess-fingers game with the proprietor of the medicine shop, the penalty being to drink a big cup each time one lost. His only title in camp was "military adviser," but the local merchants thought of him as a real "commercial adviser." Everybody ate and drank, speaking freely as they dined, and he had to answer all their questions.

The man from the medicine store said, "Third Elder Brother, you told us not to buy mercury this year, and we didn't, on your instructions. As a result, all the profit went to the Good Health store in town."

"The trusty old *Shenbao* informed me that the government had issued an order prohibiting the sale of mercury to the Jap devils, and who would dare be a Qin Kui and sell out his country?[2] Then that traitor who'd sell his own asshole, ——, turned on us. He lifted the ban. Is that my fault?"

The merchant who ran a general store went on, "Third Elder Brother, didn't you tell us that the price of tung oil was going to go up?"

"Of course. It was posted as fifteen taels five in Hankou – how could it help but rise? A dispatch from Washington, D.C., in the old *Shenbao* said that America was rushing to build 170 warships, getting ready for a big war with the Jap devils. So naturally the Japs will have to build 170 more of their own. Tung oil is what it takes to waterproof ships! He who gets his tips from me, the undiscovered prophet Zhuge Liang, will get the pot of gold."

"Gold, huh? This telegram from Hankou says the price has gone down to twelve taels eight!"

The adviser was embarrassed to learn that the price of tung oil had dropped.

"It's got to be that the foreigners have invented electric oil. You don't understand about science or realize how powerful the foreigners' science really is. They invent something

[2]The *Shenbao* was a well-established daily newspaper in Shanghai with a national circulation; Qin Kui was a famous traitor of the Song dynasty.

new every day. Whoever invents it gets a patent. Believe it or not, the papers say that they're even preparing to mine seawater for gold. They must have invented electric oil. Only that could make Chinese tung oil go down."

Butcher Wang cut in, "Pastor Huai of the Protestant church is very particular about sanitation. He buys beef and eats it rare so he'll live to a ripe old age. It was the middle of summer; when he saw these green-headed flies on my table, he said, 'Butcher, this won't do. It won't do at all! People can get sick from this. You mustn't eat it!' (Butcher Wang mimicked the foreigner's accent.) Then he gave me some gauze to use as a cover. Fuck his ancestors! I'll sick the flies onto his favorite cuts. We'll see if his Lord Jesus protects him!"

An apprentice butcher who'd been a soldier in the "Mission to Rescue Hubei" recalled a hymn he'd heard there from a low-class prostitute, a girl in the Jingzhou town of Shashi. He broke out in laughs and imitated her in a falsetto voice: "Jesus loves me, yes I know, for the Bible tells me so; and He loves my face so sunny, I love Jesus' handout money – "

That got everybody to telling their own stories about whores and rice Christians. And they got to talking about the Burlap Garment School of physiognomy of the ancient Daoists. Someone said that the temples of the adviser's head gave off a glow – he seemed to have an auspicious physiognomy and was bound to become a county magistrate in no time. Laughing and talking as they feasted, their spirits were really soaring, when suddenly a scab-headed boy came in from the butcher's block outside and gestured at them.

"Third Uncle, Third Uncle, your family has been looking for you everywhere. It's something urgent. They want you right away!"

When the adviser saw that it was the scab-headed boy from the family of cotton fluffers next door to his own home, he realized that this was genuine. Picking up a piece of bull penis with his chopsticks and dipping it into the sauce, he raised it and lowered it, as if teasing a dog: "Hey,

Little Scabby, would you like to eat a bull prick? It's good!" Too embarrassed to eat it, Little Scabby just shook his head. Stuffing it into his own mouth, the adviser clinked another glass with Butcher Wang, downed another in honor of the man from the medicine shop, and still another with old man Daring Wang. He drank a half bowl of bull penis and pickled cabbage soup, then wiped the grease from his lips with his sleeve. Admonishing the party to "please go on without me," he took his leave and hurried on home.

Now, during the former Qing dynasty, this adviser had passed the lowest-level examinations and become a *xiucai*. He was a past expounder of the emperor's Sacred Edict and a teacher in private family schools. Again, under the Republic, he'd been a clerk in the county government offices and a copyist for the police department (going on to help people write out their suits as a petty lawyer, after being relieved of his position). Then, by some means yet unclear, he'd entered the ranks of the military and been able to follow the troops everywhere they went on tour. Since the army had wholly controlled eastern Sichuan's many counties for the past twenty years, he, like a lot of other literati, had fastened onto it for his living. He'd run one of their tiny tax bureaus, collected their slaughter tax for a term, been sent to the neighboring district as a representative, and then served as opium suppression commissioner for a spell. He had also been investigated and thrown in jail for short periods, when found derelict in his duties or when his accounts didn't balance. Therefore he'd experienced short terms of unemployment, too.

Business went smoothly some years, when he picked up serious money off the books; he ate a little better, dressed a little more flashily, and his complexion was inevitably a bit ruddier. He'd bring along a little retinue during excursions down to the countryside or up to the yamens and put on airs like a VIP. And everybody would treat him as someone rather important. Then his luck would run out for a year or two. Either his take would be wiped out at the gambling table, or he'd spend it all on medicine as he lay in bed with malaria. Or business might be bad, providing him with no income at all. Then he'd be on the prowl with nothing to do, cadging and welshing on his debts everywhere, without any regard for face, just like a good-for-nothing – to the point that even his old cronies and acquaintances would keep their distance.

He'd been pretty down on his luck for the last two years. His title was military adviser to headquarters, but, apart from writing out his pay receipt and going to the quarter-master-finance section every month to draw his twenty-four-dollar salary, he seemed to have nothing better to do than go to the yamen reception room and stand behind the headquarters favorites to watch them play their cards. While gawking he'd smoke high-class cigarettes like State Express. Otherwise, he'd sit in a corner of the room and flip through the newspapers. But he read carefully, learning the names of the firms in Shanghai and Hankou, tidbits about all sorts of new commodities and their prices, and any other information he could pick up. So, although he couldn't be considered a "capitalist," the local merchants looked up to him as an "intellectual."

Besides that, he was good at guessing and good at talking even when he was in the dark. And in fact he was an honest and forgiving man. Sometimes, when levies on the locality were just too extortionate and the tax collector wasn't averse to bending the rules, people might ask the adviser to help them out of a tight spot. He'd put in a word or two on behalf of the petty merchants affected. And that was why he was seen everywhere, eating and drinking every day of the week, and why everybody let him buy and sell on credit. His monthly salary was twenty-four dollars and didn't cover expenses, but he maneuvered here and there and found ways to get by.

At home he had a wife who was seven months pregnant

and a three-and-a-half-year-old daughter. The wife was short and slovenly but quite pure at heart. The baby daughter, suffering from malnutrition, looked jaundiced and skinny as a pile of bones. Her eyes bulged out of their sockets, and she was forever crying, like a shrieking cat. But he loved his wife and child.

On five occasions his wife had been about to bear him a son, but each time she miscarried. So this pregnancy had the adviser constantly worried about another miscarriage.

When he got home and saw his wife looking out into the street from the threshold, a baby on her back and her stomach still distended, he knew it wasn't that. He calmed down.

His wife saw him panting, red in the face. She asked why he was such an awful color.

"Why do you suppose! When Little Scabby told me there was an emergency at home, I thought you'd gone and done *that* again!" The adviser stroked his own belly and bent over in a comical way. "I thought, kerplunk, it was all over again. I was anxious to know why you wanted me!"

The woman said, "Bureau Chief Yang from Dayong county came into town to hand in the taxes. He had other business to attend to and has to return to the —— temple tonight. He said he hadn't seen you, his Third Elder Brother Zhao, for six months, so he stopped by anyway. And he brought us three pounds of rutabagas. He asked if you wanted to come see him in Dayong and have some fun – "

"And he left just like that?"

"He kept waiting, and you didn't come, so I had Little Scabby go to Big Miao's place and buy the bureau chief a bowl of noodles, on credit. I sent the groom to look for you at the martial arts practice hall in the temple of the Heavenly King, but you weren't there, either. Or at the yamen. The bureau chief said it was a pity he couldn't see you, but he had to hurry off to spend the night at Corn Cake Hollow, and he was afraid he wouldn't make it. So he rode off on his horse."

The adviser went over for a look at the rutabagas. While tearing off a leaf for his baby girl to eat, he thought to himself how peculiar this was. Bureau Chief Yang was related by marriage to the chief of staff, and his ears always picked up things before anybody else. Could he have caught wind of news that the superiors mean to take care of their adviser, maybe make me tax collector in Dayong? Is this in answer to my dream, a dream from two nights before, about picking up a handful of horse manure?[3] Or might there be a vacancy next door, in Yongshun county?

Agitated and carried away by his imagination, the adviser suddenly made up his mind. He put down the rutabagas and dashed madly down the street, bumping into people as he went. Not knowing what was up, some of the townsfolk even ran with him part of the way. Once outside of town, he went straight off down the road to Pengshui. He finally ran into the bureau chief at Wulipai. The chief was under a big walnut tree, changing his horse's saddle girth.

Beside himself with joy, the adviser hailed him from a distance: "Bureau Chief, Bureau Chief, so you came to see me. How come you had to rush off without even stopping for a drink?"

When he saw it was the adviser, the bureau chief appeared elated, too.

"Ha, Third Elder Brother! Aren't you something! I looked for you in every nook and cranny, behind every outhouse door in town, and still couldn't find you! Son of a gun!"

"Aw, Bureau Chief, sure, you looked for me everywhere, everywhere but out back of Butcher Wang's! I was back there with the other guys, enjoying bull prick and *maotai* liquor."

[3]Folk belief holds that this is a sign of good things to come, horse manure being the color of gold.

"Tch, tch, aren't you something!"

As the two sat under the walnut tree and got to talking, the adviser learned that this long-eared bureau chief had indeed picked up something in town: it had been decided that this year's November tax in opium poppies would be collected in advance, in August. To the adviser, this was joyous news beyond all expectation.

Regular pay in the army was pretty scanty; officers who didn't have an inside track were hard up. So, when it came time to dun for taxes, as a rule headquarters would temporarily appoint some of those officers to tax-collecting positions, letting them roam all over with the local troops to press for payment. In name they were pressing for payment of taxes, but in reality they were taking care of themselves – you could call it a meld of the public and the private. If one of these commissioners was lucky and got assigned to a good area – and "had his own methods" – he could rake in eighteen hundred. If he was unlucky and sent to some lesser place, he could still make four or five hundred. So, during the many tax-collecting seasons, headquarters staff hoped to be sent out on assignment. Still, there was a limit to how many commissioners could be appointed. Everyone wanted this work, to satisfy their own needs, so, as the time approached, they all went around lobbying for it. When word got out, the local pubs and more notorious brothels would begin to get real busy.

Once you were a commissioner, it was easy to rake in the dough. If apprised herewith to inspect assessments and given no fixed quota to fill, you underreported what you took in. If advised to collect a percentage or taxes in advance, then you just added any surcharge you pleased. You held a meeting in the home of each township head and gave each one a time limit for getting the amount together; the township heads then went to the various *baojia* offices, giving them so many days to make good on their sum. Finally, the *baojia* officers went with the heads of the *pai,* the basic-level ten-household units, into the villages to extort the money from the peasants. As the sum passed through the hands of the *baojia* office, they'd set aside a little for themselves. When the remainder passed through the hands of the township head, he'd take a little cut of his own, leaving the rest for the commissioner. (If the commissioner knew the right means of approach and was personally formidable, he could get a few more dollars out of the purses of the township and *baojia* heads; if the commissioner was stupid or incompetent, the township and *baojia* heads could make use of the confusion and take a little more for themselves.) A fortnight later, when it was time to deliver the taxes to headquarters, these commissioners would take a portion of their illicit gains out of their own waist purses to grease the palms of such comrades as the paymaster, the chief of staff, and his deputy. Then their work in the countryside would be officially wrapped up.

Having heard now that the opium tax would be collected in advance, the adviser was beside himself with joy, even though at headquarters an hour earlier he had heard the commander say that every cent of the November levies had to go to the military government this year and that anyone who embezzled so much as a dollar would have his head cut off.

The provost marshal had put in a good word for the adviser, but he hadn't given him wind of anything yet, so the adviser asked, "Bureau Chief, is this news reliable?"

"Elder Brother of mine," he replied, "how could you of all people, a seer like Zhuge Liang, be in the dark about such a simple thing as this? The personnel have been assigned for some time. The commander's venerable brother-in-law is going to Huayuan, his honorable cousin is headed for Longshan, and even that sissy, 'Lady Cricket,' has an assignment. Here you are the mastermind at headquarters, like Wu Yong up on Mount Liang, yet they've got you waving your goosefeather fan in a box, completely cut off from the action."[4]

"That fatso stuffed-headed provost marshal deceived me! The dummkopf pighead," said the adviser, in the manner of a Shanghainese, "just now told the commander, right in front of me, that I could go to Qiancheng in November."

"The addle-brained lard head wants to send his younger brother-in-law up to my territory. Hurry up, lobby for it; seize the corn cakes while they're still hot! You can't delay, Elder Brother. Step to it!"

"Won't you stay in town an extra day, Bureau Chief? You're a man of broad influence – help me work on the chief of staff. In any case I'll have to do it right, meet the going rate – "

"Go find him and say what has to be said. Everything will work out all right."

"Naturally – of course – I'll remind him how we've always been just like brothers. I get it. I understand."

The two men talked a little longer, and then the bureau chief, who had to be on his way, mounted his horse and galloped off. The adviser ran back to town with wings on his feet. That night he went looking for the chief of staff. He cozied up to him by the opium lamp and talked things over. He said on his word of honor that he'd do it all up proper.

The adviser rushed about for three days. He really did get those orders to serve as tax commissioner at Dayong, all fixed with the proper big red seal. On the fourth day, he was on his way, riding in a palanquin, two carriers in front and one in back.

[4]A goosefeather fan symbolized omniscience for Wu Yong, grand strategist of the *Water Margin* bandits, but here there seems to be a double entendre, for the phrase *wu yong* means "good-for-nothing."

Twenty-one days later, by which time the adviser had sent his tax moneys back to headquarters under escort, he had already become a capitalist worth two thousand dollars. After greasing some palms to the tune of four hundred dollars and showing his filial respect for the chief of staff's wife with another five hundred,[5] he still had a good eleven hundred dollars in his treasure chest. Seeing the rising price of housing in town and how everybody was vying to build new dwellings, his wife persuaded him to buy some land and build thatched-roofed houses on it. They wouldn't have to pay for their own dwelling, and they could rent out the others for ten or twenty dollars' pocket money a month. The adviser was quick to agree. He said he'd have the medicine shop proprietor buy them a good site, one that would bring them prosperity. But in the back of his mind he remembered the old *Shenbao.* It had said that a certain export item was still going up in price. He thought he'd buy some, keeping the secret to himself. It was mercury. He planned to turn all twenty-two packets of banknotes in his chest into that runaway liquid substance.

He went to the yamen to read the papers, study the situation in Europe, and speculate on the price of mercury. In the commander's reception room the provost marshal had got a headache from drinking too much and had to drop out of the card game. Someone was needed to make up a foursome. The quartermaster general, who knew just how much the adviser had made during his recent mission, proposed him as the substitute.

"It would be a sin to make him play, this man of learning, a real sin," said the commander. But, in the end, he had the adviser fill in anyway. So the camp had to get by with one less "intellectual" for a while.

---

[5] A gift to the chief of staff's wife is preferable to an outright payment, which might be construed as a bribe.

Black Night

"Black Night" ("Hei ye") is a story of military heroism in actual combat, one of only a few that Shen Congwen ever wrote; his revulsion against violence grew throughout his career as a writer, and by the Second World War he was a pacifist, although still anxious for the restoration of Chinese sovereignty and the defeat of Japanese militarism. The story features gritty realism, lively dialogue, an intimate understanding of human relationships, including "love" – which Shen understood as a very abstract and all-encompassing emotion, not just as romance – and suspense.

The postscript of "Black Night" reads "24 September 1932, Qingdao, in memory of Zheng Zican." The story seems to be about China after the warlord period, but the situation is sufficiently abstract that the heroes could be either Nationalist or Communist, fighting Chinese of another political persuasion or likely the Japanese (during the heroic Chinese resistance to the January–May 1932 Japanese attack on Shanghai). Scholars in the People's Republic have looked into the political affiliation of Shen Congwen's childhood friend, the dedicatee, and from that proclaimed the story patriotic. But it has enduring value precisely because its heroism transcends any topical political incident or cause.

Two men on a bamboo raft floated down the river with the current. They had managed to get past four sentry posts on the riverbank, but, only two miles from their destination, the raft came to a stop by the marshy, rush-covered bank. The men could hear gurgling water flowing beneath their raft and the rustling of rushes in the wind. It was dark.

Luo Yi, the unit communications liaison, cursed his companion in a low hiss: "Damn you, Pingping, what happened? This is all a game to you. Do you want us to stop here and become sitting ducks so they can fill us full of holes?"

The other man was silent. He had been squatting down, and now he stood up, his stooped figure becoming a faint silhouette against the dim light from the river. He walked to the other end of the raft.

"We're aground. Something's holding us." It was clear from his voice that he was still just a child.

The young man pulled in the oar from under his friend. Then he picked up the bamboo pole and tried to push the raft, first one way and then the other. The water did seem very shallow, but from its gurgling they knew it must still be flowing here. They should not have run aground. The other man stood up now, and they pushed both their bamboo poles to one side as hard as they could, hoping to get this raft of theirs back out into the stream. The poles sank deeply into the soft mud of the riverbank, and, though the raft creaked when they pushed, still it didn't move. Then they stuck their poles into the water on all four sides to see if something was holding them. All around was clear: water was present on all sides and flowing underneath, too – it couldn't be anything else; they had run aground.

This really was no place to stop. The worried Luo Yi blamed his young companion: "We still have almost two miles to go, damn it! You've got to know how dangerous

Translated by William MacDonald

this place is – if anyone shines a light on us, it'll be all over!"

Apparently oblivious to fear and anxiety, the young man listened quietly to this grumbling as he took off his cartridge belt and rolled up his pant legs, getting ready to check.

He nimbly jumped into the water on the side toward the bank. When he had a firm footing, he pushed hard on the raft, silently but joyously. The raft creaked like a stiff joint as it moved. It seemed to be struggling too, as if wanting to get free as soon as possible, but something underneath appeared to be detaining it, restraining it, holding it back; it moved a little but did not float free.

"Easy," said the man on the raft. "I know you're strong. Take off your shirt and run your hand under the raft, along the chinks between the poles, and see what sort of ghost is holding us. It's got to be a ghost, gotta be!"

The young man laughed. "Gotta be. All right, let me see – "

He made a circuit around the entire raft, stretching out his hands in the cold water. When he came to the places where vines bound it together, he submerged his whole torso. Both arms and shoulders reached out beneath the raft. His chin touched the water.

The stream wasn't very deep, but there were many deep mud holes; it took great effort to pull his feet out of them. Slowly he worked his way to the other end of the raft, where there were other vine lashings. Suddenly his hand touched something – something round and hard – a millstone. And something else – a piece of rope, some clothing – a body, ice cold. The young man called out softly in a voice filled with surprise and delight, "Hey, damn it all, there *is* a ghost here. So he's what this is all about!"

"What is it?"

The young man didn't answer right away; he just reached out and felt all over. He found himself touching hair, a face, then an arm. The corpse was tied to the millstone with rope, and the rope was caught underneath the raft. There was also a post in the water that had got stuck in one of the chinks between the raft's bamboo poles. That was why the raft wouldn't move. "This poor stiff has been causing our trouble," the young man called out softly. "He was tied to a millstone and sent to the bottom here."

"Pull him free," the man on the raft ordered. He heard a rooster crow in the distance and cursed anxiously, "Damned thing. You were useless alive, and now they've gone and drowned you, and you're still causing trouble."

He'd waited interminably without the man in the water being able to get them free yet, so he pulled out his knife and tapped it on the edge of the raft.

"Pingping, hold out your hand. Take this knife, and hack him loose. If that ghost has us by the hand, chop it off. We can't wait any longer. We still have two miles to go, and this is a dangerous place. Hurry up! Make it snappy!"

The young man laughed at his companion's impatience – "if he has us by the hand," indeed.

A faint splash of the knife in the water, and the raft moved. Soon after, the man in the water tried to lift it by pushing up under one end with his shoulders. But he was too young, not strong enough yet, so the raft only turned on its axis.

The raft could move, but it wouldn't float free. The post in the river was still stuck in the chinks between the raft's bamboo logs. It was too much to cut with a knife. To get away, they would have to take the raft apart and put it back together again.

Time did not afford them the leisure to carry out such a plan. When the raft got down near the floating bridge, they would have to abandon it anyway, for they wouldn't be able to get it past. The man on the raft was worried; he let loose a stream of curses and threats, as if it were all the fault of the one in the water and he would be reported to the executive board and punished for his negligence once they got back to base. But the man in the water simply said, "We can get there by daybreak only if we walk along the bank."

"If we walk along the bank, the devils will hang a millstone around *our* necks."

"You mean fear of that is what's holding you back?"

The younger man won out in the end. They picked up their two Mauser pistols, their knives, and their other gear and went up onto the bank from the deep mud of the marsh. Slowly they felt their way up the high embankment in the dark. When they reached the top, they sat down in the tall grass by the road to figure the distance to their destination. They had traveled this river twice, but both times had been in darkness, so the road along the river was very unfamiliar. They did not know how many streams and bogs they had to cross or how many sentry posts or houses they'd have to pass. The sky was so black they couldn't even see any familiar stars or landmarks to get their bearings. They had a flashlight to light the road, but in the enveloping darkness it felt like there were eyes and muzzles everywhere. If they showed the slightest light, bullets would come flying. Once they were discovered, it would be difficult to get through. It would be a fight to the death, and a second party would have to risk their lives carrying out this mission.

The two men stopped for a moment. It was too dangerous to walk along the dike, but they knew there must be a path below along the river, and, since the water had receded a good deal in the past few days, it would be easy to walk along it. They might even come across a small boat. So they went back down the embankment to the riverside. They could afford to delay no longer, so they set off without further hesitation.

After walking along the muddy shore for some time, they drew near a marshy area and breathed a little easier, for the path was surrounded by rushes. It was slippery and wet underfoot. And there was a sickening smell that became more unpleasant the farther they went.

"There must be someone lying on the road up there. Be careful you don't trip over him."

"I forgot to check the body under the raft. Maybe it was one of ours."

"Who would it be, if not one of ours?"

"I know that the Seventy-fourth's messages are sewn into the collar, and the Thirteenth's are hidden in a cigarette. Then there's the – "

"Careful! We're still surrounded, and we could rot here, too. Watch where you step."

Luo Yi thought the corpse must be five or so feet away. He was about to turn on the flashlight to check.

His young and cheerful companion suddenly stopped him. Listening intently, the two men heard the faint and steady splashing of oars nearby. They were only fifty feet from the river, but they were screened by a stretch of dense rushes. They knew this was a very dangerous situation, for the boat was clearly not from their side; obviously it was patrolling the river to cut off contact between two friendly bases. If the boat went upriver a little farther, the men on it would discover the raft, and, when they inspected it, they would find footprints in the mud by the embankment – and, if they followed them right away, heaven only knew what might happen.

Fortunately the two companions were on shore. If they had been on the water, their lives would certainly have been at risk.

Just then, a very large water bird, startled by the two men or by the sound of their oars, flapped its wings in the rushes and flew up out of the darkness. It made a big circle for no apparent reason and then flew off across the river. They heard the men on the boat talking as though suspicious of this stretch of rushes and about to come ashore. But soon they went on in the direction the bird had flown, still rowing up the river at an even and leisurely pace.

When the two companions heard the boat come near the rushes, they lay down on the damp ground, took out their Mausers, and aimed in the direction of the sound of the oars. Their minds were very calm. At last the boat drew away, and the danger passed. The two men reached out to each other in the darkness and firmly clasped hands.

Not daring to lose a moment, they immediately began to move forward again.

They walked ahead a little, and the smell of the corpse became stronger. But a few steps more, and suddenly it appeared that they had passed it. Evidently the body hadn't fallen onto the path but into the reeds to the left.

Luo Yi's companion tugged at him.

"What is it?"

"Wait a minute. I'll bet it's one of our comrades from the Seventy-fourth. I want to go check. It'll just take a minute, half a minute."

The man didn't care how unhappy this made his superior. Bending over in pursuit of the smell, he bravely wound his way into the thick rushes. It wasn't thirty seconds before he'd turned and come out again. "I said it was him, and so it was. That stench has his character in it too. When this guy was living, he was very brave. And now that he's fallen and rotting away, he's still very brave!"

"What did you find?"

"A handful of maggots."

"How did you know it was him?"

"I pulled on his collar, and as soon as I touched it I knew it was him."

"You're good lads, all of you."

The two men started on their way again, silently and uncertainly. They seemed to have forgotten all about fate and responsibility, having taken that infinitely long step into the darkness.

When they came out of the rushes they faced a new danger.

Ahead of them was a mountain spur they would have to pass. They could go around the hill, but they would have to pass by the ferry, and far away they could see a small fire. Someone must be on guard. They could go over the hill, but the path was unfamiliar. It might be too dangerous. They couldn't decide whether to take the upper road or the lower road; both were dangerous. They didn't know which one would get them through.

With every second of hesitation they lost another opportunity. They decided to go straight ahead because it was easier for them to see the fire from the darkness than it was for the enemy to see into the darkness from the fire. And this road was more familiar. If all else failed, they could always swim across the river. As they got closer, they saw that it wasn't a beacon fire and noticed that it was almost out. The alert young man meant to go ahead boldly and without hesitation, figuring that there would be no one there. The older man grabbed him.

"Are you crazy, Pingping? Where are you going? You can't!"

"Don't worry. The devils stationed on the hill must have made the fire when they went down to their boat. We heard oars a while ago, didn't we? Even if they did build it as a beacon fire, it's only for show."

Once again the young man won out, and they went closer to the fire. Fearing a trick, they carefully lay down on the embankment and waited before climbing up on all fours. There was nothing there, nothing at all! They knew that once they got around the spur there was a long stretch of level road. On the side next to the mountain was forest, and on the side by the river there was thick grass. Only when they were almost to their base would there be any new dangers. They felt more courageous. The two men walked in the grass beside the road.

A little further down the road, the sharp ears of the young man heard hoofbeats on the highway. Then the other man heard them too. They knew it must be a mounted devil courier traveling along the road. Afraid he might have a dog able to pick up their scent, they scrambled up the hillside, taking advantage of what little shadow there was. On and on they climbed, not knowing where they were going. Soon the sound of the hoofbeats drew nearer, clopping on the uneven gravel road. The horse's shoes sent off sparks from the stones, and steam puffed from its mouth. The horse galloped past quickly, with a dark shadow lying across its back.

As the two men walked down the hill back to the road, Luo Yi twisted his ankle.

Yet they knew they must get to the last dangerous section of road soon. They were almost running.

When they drew near the dangerous point, they heard a village rooster crow for the second time. The sound floated out over the water.

They should have gone down to the bank, buried their guns in the reeds, and floated down the river with the current. Just a quarter mile past the floating bridge, they would be safe. But Luo Yi had sprained his ankle and could no longer swim. If they didn't swim down the river, they would have to climb over the mountain. The mountain road was unfamiliar, and on the other side were steep cliffs. One stumble, and there'd be no hope. Even if they didn't fall, they would have little chance of getting away if discovered by the mountain sentry. Still, they had to pick one route or the other.

Realizing how close they were to their goal, the older man said angrily to his companion, "Pingping, this is the devil's work. I ought to rot here too, so you can come and feel *my* collar next time you pass. My foot is pretty bad; it won't do any good to try to go by water. Let's each of us go a different way, all right? Give me your gun, and you go by water. I'll take my time and make my way over the mountain."

"That's no good. Your foot hurts, so I ought to go with you. Let's go over the hill right now. If we're going to rot, we'll rot together."

The older man suddenly scolded him, as if angry: "Do you have the right to die? You little devil! We can't both rot here! Obey my orders; give me your gun. We can't waste any more time. Understand?"

The young man kept still, so Luo Yi asked him again before he said, in a low voice, "I understand."

"How can he climb over that mountain on one foot?" thought the young man as he took off his belt. He wanted to obey, but still he hesitated. Luo Yi knew what was on his companion's mind: they had been through danger together so many times that they were terribly close. Aware of the danger in crossing the mountain, the boy didn't want to let his old friend go over it alone. But it had to be this way, so he mellowed his tone to comfort the boy.

"Comrade Pingping, don't worry; you just go on down the river. Don't worry about me. I've got two guns, so I'll get some of the bastards. You'd be risking it taking this road. Your way is dangerous enough. If there's barbed wire in the water under the floating bridge, you'll have to go over the bridge itself, and that's pretty difficult. I'll go up this way. I can feel my way along the road. When I get to the other side, I'll give you back your gun. I promise. We'll be there in a little while. I'll see you there. In just a little while."

They both knew that "just a little while" was an empty phrase.

As he spoke, he took his companion's pistol and cartridge belt and put them on. Then he clapped his young friend on the shoulder and made a joke. He wanted to see his companion get into the water with his own eyes before he started on the road. His old comrade had been firm and to the point, so the young man was forced by his strict Party discipline and friendship to slide down the bank and get into the water. There was nothing he could say.

The water was cold.

When the young man had swum silently to the middle of the river, he signaled to his old comrade, who was still standing on the bank, by imitating a water bird. A rock thrown from the bank immediately hit the water near him. Each man now had his go-ahead, so they parted and went their separate ways.

The young man cautiously swam down the river. He could not forget his companion. When he was almost to the floating bridge, he could see beacon fires burning brightly in the distance at both ends of the bridge. The firelight reflected in the water. The devils had made their floating bridge by binding small fishing boats together with heavy wire. There were guards at both ends and no doubt a sentry patrolling on the bridge, too. With only his face breaking the water, the boy drifted with the current. Shortly before he reached the bridge, he began to worry about what to do if there was barbed wire in the water. Just as he was considering this, he heard a gunshot on the ridge and another right after it. He knew from the sound of the shots that they were from a rifle on the other side. But he didn't hear his friend's Mauser reply. Clearly his friend had been discovered and become a target. In the faint firelight coming from the two banks, he could see that he had already floated to within twenty feet of the bridge and had better keep his head under water until he was under the bridge. Luckily, there were no obstacles in the river of the sort rumored about. Thirty feet the other side of the bridge, as he raised his head out of the water to catch his breath, he heard the Mauser ring out seven times. The rifle fell silent. But almost immediately he heard another rifle fire. The Mauser returned the salute four times.

Then he heard the rifle crack three times more. After a long pause, there was one shot from the Mauser. He heard a whistle from one of the beacon fires, and from the bridge the beam of a flashlight shone nearby on the water. The young man put his head under water again and swam for all he was worth.

The next time he pulled his head out, all the gunfire had stopped.

Beneath the young man's body was the silently moving river, and all around was the darkness, limitless darkness. Darkness filled up all space and seemed to penetrate the young man's body like the coldness of the water. He knew that in another half mile he would be able to see their own beacon fires. With all his strength he swam toward the light and the warmth.

. . . .

"Password."

"Nineteen. Bind feet with turbans."

"Just one of you? Why only one?"

"Go ask your ancestors!"

"Lost?"

There was no answer. There was just the sound of the young man's hands and feet slapping the water as he came up on shore.

Ox

This section of the anthology features Shen Congwen's country-folk characters. His dedication to them and their counterparts in life is one of the few intellectual or ideological commitments he was ever willing to make explicit. The heroes and heroines whom we encounter below are not necessarily fully rounded characters, yet they are not the "typical" figures of peasants that intellectuals of Shen's and later generations were used to drawing, generally for purposes of ridicule or sympathy. In the current Hegelian jargon, Shen Congwen's country folk are subjects, not objects. Even their foolishness belongs to them; it is not inherent in rusticity.

Uncle Ox is one of Shen Congwen's more memorable, even if somewhat opaque, country-fellow characters. His draft animal, too, may be understood allegorically as a country "fellow." Silence, stoicism, impenetrability, even a hint of enigma – and a touch of stubbornness, a point beyond which they will not be pressed – characterize country folk as Shen Congwen understood them. If country-folk characters are types, used by the author to make a point, they are not, however, perfect. They have weaknesses like anyone else: fits of anger, impatience, sullenness, greed, and unwillingness honestly to recognize their own motivations.

Still, why all the fuss about an ox? Why does he become a character in his own right, with interior monologues and even dreams? Debates about proletarian literature were raging when Shen wrote this story, in the summer of 1929; the owner-ox relationship could be an allegory of the master-slave or capitalist-worker relationship. Far from conveying Hegelian or Marxist optimism, however, "Ox" ("Niu") has a dramatic and equivocal plot twist at the end. While this story is didactic however interpreted, Shen Congwen's main interest is still in the psychology of its "human" relationships.

It happened like this. The day before, the man they called Uncle Ox, who lived in the Mulberry Creek marsh, got angry with his plow ox over something very trivial while they were out in his buckwheat field. He actually struck it on the hind leg with a wooden mallet. Normally he treated this plow ox like his own son. Though he was used to swearing at it, a good deal of tenderness would be mixed in with the curses, as if he were swearing at his own child. But, once his temper was up, he lost all self-control and lashed out, and that was why this unusual event had occurred. He did not notice anything at the time, but the next day, when he went to get the ox so they could plow the rest of the buckwheat field, the ox was unable to walk from its pen as easily as usual. There was something wrong with one of its hind legs, and it was all due to the master's thoughtless mallet blow in his rage of the previous day.

When he saw that the ox was not going to be of any use, Uncle Ox was uncertain what to do. Leading it into the yard and tethering it to a stake, he squatted down under the ox's belly and lifted its leg for a look. He examined the little ox so gently that the animal seemed to realize that he was inwardly acknowledging his mistake. Remembering how close they had been in the past, the ox turned its head to look at him, its eyes full of tears, as if it felt very sorry for him and wanted to say the sort of thing a slave might say to his master: "I'm not holding it against you, Papa. You usually treat me very well, and, though you did hit me and hurt my leg, that happened yesterday, and now we've made up again. It hurts a little, that's all. It'll get better in a couple of days."

But, when Uncle Ox caught its meaning, he slyly resumed his habitual expression and closed his left eye. He stopped rubbing its leg, stood up, and gave it a punch on the hindquarters.

Translated by Caroline Mason

Clapping his hands, he said, "I know what you're up to, you wicked animal. You're good at putting me on – really smart of you! Where did you learn that? Pretending you can't move! You must have heard some tale or other that made you think you could get the boss sorry for you – yes, very smart! One look at your eyes, and I can see your heart getting blacker all the time. You never did want to work properly, and you're choosy about what you eat – did you ever see *me* get so bad tempered?"

After making quite a lot of these clever remarks, the master walked up to the ox's head and, facing it squarely, jabbed his finger into its forehead.

"If you don't do as I say, I'll hit you here, too, on the right side. And then on the left. When the village children skip school, Teacher's rule is that he smacks them on the hand. They have to bow to Confucius and then to him. And they aren't allowed to cry. Are *you* going to cry? Wretched creature! Don't you realize how good the weather has been the past few days? Can't you see that the rains came five days ago because heaven took pity on us, knowing that we should be planting our buckwheat? The ground was made damp for us, to save *you* from having to make so much effort."

Uncle Ox kept one eye on the weather as he lectured his ox. It really was a very fine day, so he shouldered his plow and led the ox off to work in the fields after giving it this dressing-down for being spoiled and lazy. Although it had been wanting to make up with its master, and he seemed to be aware of this, the weather was just too good; not to work would have been out of the question. So, in the end, the ox did hobble along, pulling the plow in the level field and turning the rain-wet soil.

Uncle Ox had disciplined his young ox as if it were a schoolchild and put the yoke on its back. Yet, when he saw it limping along in front of him without a murmur of complaint, he couldn't help feeling a little compassion. It occurred to him that maybe he had been a bit headstrong and should not have struck it as he had. His mood was like that of a father who, having done something wrong, to all appearances refuses to admit that he is at fault but still feels very sorry in his heart. So he put in more effort than usual, working together with the ox until the sweat was pouring down his face. He shouted at the animal a lot less, too, though normally he would have made up innumerable weird and wonderful words with which to curse it, for the ox liked to turn its head from time to time, slowing down to gaze at the scenery and passersby.

That's the way it usually is: nothing surpasses silence in leading people toward understanding. Some people think that heaven gave us mouths for talking, that if you have something on your mind you can tell other people and they will understand. But if that's the case, and mouths are meant only for speaking, since large oxen and tiny birds also have mouths, and the big ones have mouths large enough to "talk big," why don't they go and get jobs as officials or lecturers? And, where "small talk" is concerned, little birds will never be a match for humans. As Uncle Ox saw it, there could be no mistake about this.

They could only understand each other in silence – that much was certain, and for the moment the friendship between Uncle Ox and his little ox was founded on this absence of words. The ox said nothing; it did not moan or groan, nor did it ask, "Papa, would you be good enough to give me some medicine or a little money to buy it?" (Had it been human, it would definitely have made such a legitimate request for itself.) And neither did the ox say things like, "I want revenge; I must have revenge," to scare its master; it was not the sort to gnash its teeth in resentment. It just meekly carried on as usual, pulling the plow as hard as it could and turning over the clods of earth. It could smell the delicate scent of the newly turned soil. But its efforts caught the master's attention in other ways. It was panting, for its foot hurt when it walked and was not as supple as usual. The ox did not utter a sound – it was panting, definitely not sighing. Eventually, Uncle Ox's heart melted completely. He knew all – he understood the ox completely, having no need to depend on words, which are clever people's means of dressing themselves up.

But, even after the melting of his heart, Uncle Ox was unable to say anything. If he said, "Friend, I was wrong," the ox might still suspect him of dissembling – of trying to use words to wipe away his fault and meanwhile tricking it into working much harder. Humans often behave like this with one another, and it is not only oxen who can be so suspicious. Or suppose he were to say, "There's nothing to be done – I did hit you, but I'm your master, and although I may have been a bit hasty, it was mostly because you weren't putting enough effort into your work for me. Now we're even, so let's try to get on with life, shall we?" If the ox could understand all that, it would be displeased, for it was ever confident of having put every bit of its strength into its work, never daring to slacken even for a moment.

As for getting even, there were no two ways about it: if the master had been human hearted, the ox would never have had to suffer that blow from the mallet in the first place. What's more, the use of words to soothe wounds created by a solid object proved, if nothing else, that humans were unfit lords and masters. With the power of speech, they used words to make themselves appear more virtuous and kind and to do you favors that cost them nothing. But this ox understood its master's mood precisely because he said nothing – he neither took the blame nor defended himself, and he didn't push it off onto the pretext of drunkenness, either. Some folks are always using words like *drunkenness* to cover up all the terrible things they have done.

He said not a word but crossed the field back and forth with his ox, hissing at it as usual to make the turns, and still hitting it on the back with his whip. Yet he felt very ashamed of what he had done the day before, so he pushed the plow extra hard, and expressed his feelings above all in the way he handled the whip. Saying nothing about wanting to sort out whose fault it was, he saw how much the ox was in pain, though at the same time he kept an eye on the weather. "I would have liked to let you have a rest, but we *have* to work to see that we have enough to live on for the second half of the year" – this was clear to the ox, even though its master had said nothing aloud. But they really had already made up.

Only when he and the ox had plowed a section and come to a halt together, and the yoke was lifted from the ox's back, did he speak.

"I'm old," he said. "When people get old, they do stupid things. I figure that, if you have half a day off and rest a bit, you'll be fine – don't you think?"

The young ox had no view to give. It looked up at the sky. A magpie flew by over its head.

So he let the ox go off into a ditch full of waterweeds to enjoy itself, to have its fill of grass and water, while he sat himself down on the plow to think. He honestly did believe that his ox would be all better by the next day. Without even having sown his buckwheat yet, he was already calculating how much the new crop would fetch at market. And he was calculating other things too, all pretty run-of-the-mill. He struck his flint and had a smoke, looking up at the sky all the while. It was so blue it was scary, high and limitless, with white clouds scattered all over and the white sun beating down on people's backs as though it were spring. But this was the ninth month – still a long way off from the real spring.

The ox stood a while beside the stream. The water was cold and clear, the grass withered. The ox's leg was very painful, and the faithful beast was worn out after its labors. Finally it lay down on the flats at the bottom of a slope and went to sleep. Bathed in sunshine, it could dream in comfort. It dreamed of Papa, wearing a new outfit, and of itself, with red cloth wound around its horns. The two of them were striding out from the village at New Year's, ready to go home. This was the most glorious dream an ox could have, and needless to say it meant that the ox had forgotten not only all that had passed but also the pain in its leg.

At noon, a cock crowed in the hilltop village, and Uncle Ox led his ox home.

When they got there, the ox noticed that its master seemed worried and realized that this must be because it was walking with a limp. It had walked very carefully and obediently, hoping its leg would soon get better. It was even willing to have it massaged by that fierce veterinarian you just couldn't reason with.

Its master was indeed rather concerned because, when the ox had lain down on its side in the meadow to rest, he noticed that the leg he'd hit with the mallet was still having spasms. It did not look as if it would get better by itself in a couple of days. He also looked at the newly turned earth in the field that he and the ox had plowed together, damp and fragrant as flowers in bloom. Thoughts of something that might happen in the future, something he hardly dared contemplate, scared him stiff: "What if, by some chance – ?" In that case, the price of buckwheat would be of no concern to him – nothing would be of concern to him any longer.

On the way home, he noticed how the little ox was walking, and all his thoughts had to do with things other than the price of grain, though even he couldn't be certain just what they *were* about. In a word, if by some chance it did turn out like that, he and his whole future would be ruined. It was like losing money when you gambled: you make a bet with heaven, but good luck lies with heaven itself; men have no part in it. So, if you lose, you're completely done for. If you looked at it like that, then if the ox went lame because of a chance blow from a mallet and could not be cured – so that it was useful only in cooked dishes, or as beef jerky, or cut up into joints six or ten pounds in weight and hung up on ropes over the fire to smoke, to be taken down when needed for frying and chopping up with hot peppers – then Uncle Ox would also have to. . . . Because once the animal was dead, it would be all over for Uncle Ox.

As he tied the ox to a wooden stake in the yard and went to the big basket to fetch sweet potatoes to cook with his rice, the shadow over Uncle Ox's heart was still there.

Later, when he took a handful of rice hulls to scatter in the yard for the chickens and saw the ox pulling up its leg again as it slept, the shadow over his heart grew darker.

After the midday meal, he went to the marketplace a mile down the road to see the headman, a minor local official under the *baojia* system who also served as the local cattle doctor. In common with many famous medical men, the headman gave the impression of being extremely busy, though in reality he had nothing to do. The two men had known one another for a long time.

Uncle Ox spoke first. "Headman, there's something wrong with the leg of my ox."

The headman said, "That would be an ulcerated hoof. Just rub in some ointment, and it'll be fine."

"No, it's not that," he said.

"How do you know it's not? There's a lot of it going around these days – two people came in today from Mulberry Creek, and both their oxen had it."

"It's not an illness; it's an injury."

"I've got some medication for injuries." By this, the headman meant that on the whole there was only one kind of leg injury – knocking against a rock – and that was what his medication was for.

It was only then that Uncle Ox told him that the injury had come from his striking the animal with a mallet.

He went on, "I'm afraid I may have hit it too hard because this morning the creature wept in front of me, as if it wanted me to give it the day off. But how could I do that?

This rain is meant to make things easier for us. When the sun comes out, that's to help us too, and if we don't finish plowing in the next few days, how much time will be left? So I dragged it along anyway. I put in a lot more effort in the morning than it did, but it wasn't well, and it went to sleep on the grass looking very unhappy. It seems to be afraid I'll get rid of it, so it shuts up when it sees me, looking all sad. But I know what those big eyes are trying to say and what's going through its mind."

The headman agreed to go with him to the village for a look at the ox, but, just as they were about to step through the door, there came an official dispatch saying that troops had crossed over into the county. They wanted to hold a fund-raising dinner; the headman was summoned to attend a meeting at once.

Cursing with the self-importance of a country squire as he changed into his rich, green satin jacket, he called for his horse, shouted that the man from the yamen should be given a snack, and was generally as busy as could be. Uncle Ox heaved a sigh and went home on his own.

When he got back, he looked at the ox, and the ox looked at him. The two really had made it up between them, just as both seemed to realize that the leg would not be better in a day or two. In an admission that he had done wrong, Uncle Ox carefully pulled up the ox's leg again, looked at the injured place, and put on some ointment made from herbs dug up on the fifth day of the fifth lunar month – the kind that human beings typically use when they have fractures and sprains. Then he bound up the leg with a piece of cloth. The ox, being very sensible, meekly let the master treat it, and just as meekly went back into the pen to sleep.

Hearing the ox munching on its hay that evening, Uncle Ox got up to shine his lantern on it several times. The ox realized that its master was going to bed late on account of it and stared at him with wide open eyes every time Uncle

Ox's big round head and his tung-oil lantern stretched round the corner of the pen.

He never asked, "Better now?" or, "Is it very bad?" and the ox never said to him, "It's not serious," or, "Please don't worry." Their understanding did not lie in words, but it was very real nonetheless.

That night the ox too had many things on its mind, for it understood their relationship very clearly. Its master needed its help, so they lived together, but, as soon as he saw that he could not use the ox any more, he would have it led away by someone different. The ox wasn't too clear yet about what it would be used for after that, but every now and then it heard its master angrily saying strange things like, "Pesky brute!" or, "Use it for a sacrifice," or, "Off to the butcher's with it!" and it would have a vague feeling that things would not go well once away from its master; it would have to put up with more than just a little swearing and beating. There was no way of knowing what the future held, but, like many stupid people, it thought long and hard about the question – should it run away from the butcher, or jab the evil fellow with its horns and fight him, or should it – ? Only vow making was beyond its powers, for humans alone knew about such things, and, what was more, it was often said that, when people make a vow to heaven in return for help and protection, once the disaster has passed and good fortune arrives, they slaughter an ox, a pig, or a sheep – a chicken at the very least. If they have nothing to offer (like this ox, with nothing to call its own save its physical exertions, which did not count for much), heaven will not help them.

The ox grew sleepy and began to dream. It dreamed that it was able to race along, pulling a triple plow. Wherever the plow passed, the earth turned over like waves, leaving the master standing up to his knees in loose soil, shouting with laughter. While such happy visions filled the poor ox's head, Uncle Ox was dreaming much the same thing. He dreamed that he had four big grain-drying mats spread out on the drying ground, all piled high with mounds of new buckwheat, and when he took a handful of the brown grain and held it up to the sun, it gleamed dark gold in his hand. The buckwheat was this year's harvest, put on the ground to be weighed and stored. He had borrowed bamboo tallies from the headman, and a big bundle of them fell to the ground with a clatter. The valiant fellow who had helped with this harvest – the little ox – was standing beside him, decked out in red ribbons, and Uncle Ox was talking to it as if to an old friend. He said, "We'll be all right this year, partner. We can build a new wall around the place; we can get some new gates; we can plant some grapes along the dike; we – " He kept saying "we," as if the ox too had had a part in the rise of the family's fortunes, sharing in both the glory and the work that led up to it. He gazed solemnly at the ox, which looked just the same as usual. Its bright eyes shone with the words, "I agree with all of that."

Happy dreams are the enemies of life, a joke played on men by God, and so, when Uncle Ox awakened, he was much more disgruntled than if he had not dreamed at all. First he realized that the buckwheat was not yet in the storehouse, and then he remembered that the ox, who with its eyes had said, "I agree with all of that," was still suffering in the pen. He lit the lantern again – for it was not yet light – and went to the pen for a look at his "partner." As if still dreaming, he hailed the ox, calling it "partner," and asked if the ointment had made it any better. The ox made no sound, for it had no way of expressing what it had just been dreaming. It gazed sorrowfully at its master. Remembering the normal daily routine, it wanted to stand up and follow him out of the pen.

It rose to its feet and took a couple of steps. Seeing that it was still lame, Uncle Ox sighed and blew out the lantern, then walked into the house and lay down on the bed.

Each of them wept, separately. They both realized that what they had been dreaming about was a miracle such as they could never hope for, and in their hearts they grieved deeply over the realities of existence.

In the morning, at the time when they usually went to the fields, Uncle Ox was out on the main road headed for the village of Taking-the-Tiger Battalion three miles away, where he had heard there was a practitioner skilled at healing cattle. Uncle Ox had specially changed his jacket and wrapped two hundred cash in red paper in preparation for asking the cattle doctor of that stockade village to make a house call to see his "partner." A dog scared him just as he got there. As luck would have it, the doctor had gone out. Hearing that he would be back soon, Uncle Ox could think of nothing better to do than sit down and wait for him under a big shade tree outside the stockade. From under the tree he could see fields of twelve or fifteen acres that had been plowed by other people, proudly displayed before his eyes. He had to wait a long time for the doctor to come home. When they had introduced themselves and the doctor had questioned him, he, too, pronounced with great certainty that it was an ulcerated hoof.

Uncle Ox said, "No, I know it's because I hit it a bit too hard and maybe broke a tendon."

"Then it's an infection that developed from the wound. Take this medicine along with you, and it'll be fine."

Uncle Ox thought to himself, "Don't I have plenty of such medication at home? Did I really need to trek three miles just for this?" But he kept his mouth shut tight, which made him look rather comical.

It was odd because he had always said very firmly that he would never walk such a distance for something so minor. Finally it suddenly dawned on him that his money packet was not heavy enough; he promised to enclose another whole string of cash for the doctor's pains, and at that the wheels in the doctor's mind began to turn. Before long he was hurrying along the road with Uncle Ox back to Mulberry Creek.

This famous doctor behaved as grandly as any renowned physician from the city. When he reached Uncle Ox's home, he first of all had a drink and a good meal. Only after he'd eaten, picked his teeth, and had himself a smoke, did he ask Uncle Ox to lead the ox into the yard. Rolling up his sleeves to the elbow, he took a needle and gently pressed the wound with his hand while his assistant raised the ox's leg. Then he inspected the ox's tongue and ears. Because he felt he had to say something, he criticized its master for having been so rash, as he always did in such cases. He said that it was not good to strike the creature so cruelly. And he reckoned that, in future, Uncle Ox should think more carefully before casually treating its leg with ointment meant for human use. After all that, the doctor gave the ox two injections in its leg, chewed some medicinal herbs to a pulp and spread them on the area he had injected, then bound it up with fir bark and pronounced that it would be better in three days. He instructed his assistant to shoulder the strings of coins that had been promised him and swaggered off like a wandering monk.

While Uncle Ox was standing outside the gate after seeing the doctor off, a local man selling candy passed by on the main road. Seeing Uncle Ox there at the threshold, he said to him, in a friendly way, "Uncle Ox, Uncle Ox! There's some nice tender beef at the market today, have you heard?"

"Go to hell!" Uncle Ox said under his breath in response to this news. He walked back through the gate, slamming it behind him.

He had wanted to believe the doctor and remembered how, when he had asked him for the cash, he had not begrudged giving it to him at all. But now, watching his back as he hurried off along the road, and especially the strings of cash slung over the assistant's shoulder, he began to have his doubts. He felt as if he had done something else wrong, something just as bad as hitting the ox with his mallet, and he began to regret it. He felt that, even if those two rather slapdash injections were worth two hundred cash and a good meal, it was obviously a trick of some kind; he must have been cheated. Angry to begin with, and now even more upset by the candy seller's invitation to buy beef, he swore loudly at the ox while entering the gate as he caught sight of it sleeping in the yard. "Tomorrow we're going to kill you and eat you – we'll see if your leg gets better or not!"

The doctor's injections and poultice had made the pain in the ox's leg unbearable. It felt cold one moment and hot the next. Hearing its master swear at it so furiously, and observing, wide eyed, how he looked, the ox felt miserable and wanted to cry. Only the sight of this reminded Uncle Ox that he was still in the wrong and should not have spoken so angrily. He sat down on the stone roller in the yard and said nothing. His back was to the sun, but he was oblivious to its burning heat. The weather was just right for plowing. He wondered whose ox he could borrow to break up the soil on the few acres of land he still needed to plow before sowing, but he couldn't think of any family that might have an ox to lend at this season.

Soon after, unable to contain himself any longer, he began to curse again. He said to the ox, "You're just being difficult – you've still got to work, even with only three legs!"

What could the ox say? It was not doing it on purpose. It had never known a reason for an ox to rest during the busy season, much less any "mere excuse." Why ever would it not be pleased to go to the fields and enjoy itself in this lovely weather? Why ever should it not want to work a bit harder for its master, until the whole house and the whole granary were filled with grain – "all of that" it had "agreed" to, in fact? And even now, with such a painful leg, had it ever said, "I won't do it," or, "I want a rest"? It could forgive its master for his anger, for he was not like other people, who went crazy for no reason. But what could it say? Could it say things like, "I'll be fine tomorrow," or, "Let's go now, this instant"? It had never said, "I want a rest," so of course it did not need to say, "I can do without a rest."

It did all it could for Papa – this had always been its nature. If its master were to take the plow out now, it would go with him to the fields and start work without showing a trace of unhappiness or impatience.

But, although Uncle Ox had said that they must go to work come what may, in the end he went over and rubbed its ears, its eyes, and its jowls; he hadn't really meant to curse it all the way to hell; he'd just been angry for a spell, not wanting to say goodbye and hand the ox over to the butcher! And the reason why it never did speak was that it could understand its master – it knew how much it had figured in his dreams. It also knew its duty. And that, if its leg were not back to normal in three days, its master would suddenly, and as a matter of course, turn terribly irritable.

When Uncle Ox entered the house to get a sickle for trimming the wooden pegs in the plow handle, the ox stole off by itself and made a circle in the yard, just to see if it could manage as usual. Poor creature, it was like certain people in this world who've never had a day off in good weather and can't get used to it. It was only on this point that Uncle Ox failed to understand his partner's feelings. He had never imagined that the ox might feel bad about slacking, for, as a rule, the person in charge can never understand the feelings of those who work for him.

When Uncle Ox had trimmed his pegs, he struck the front of the plow, right there in the yard, as if angry. He had been thinking that, even if his partner did recover three days later, they would never be able to make up for those three days of idleness; good weather was not like borrowing money, which you pay for with interest. It's hard to come by even when you make vows to the gods. So, after worrying for a while, he set out to borrow an ox from someone else.

He reckoned there were three possible places, one rather more likely than the others, and once he had got an ox he would finish plowing that field immediately, even if it meant having to work at night.

He went to the first of the families of his friends who owned oxen and spoke to the head of the household.

"Old Number Eight, I'll give you two pecks of wheat if you can lend me your ox for two or three days."

The man said, "I wish you could think of a way for *me* to borrow an ox. I was just on my way to see you, to offer you four pecks!"

"Then I'll offer four myself."

"How's that? Isn't your ox well?"

"It's got a hoof ulcer – "

"How can that be?"

"I asked the cattle doctor to have a look at it. Cost me a string of cash."

The head of this household knew that Uncle Ox's animal was very sturdy and usually very well looked after, and that was why he asked him how come he needed one. Naturally, even though he wasn't going to be able to borrow an ox here, Uncle Ox still had to tell the whole nine yards of how his partner had suffered from a mallet blow at his own hands. He didn't stint on expressing remorse in the telling, but regrets are no compensation for mistakes, and, when he finally ran out of explanations, he went on to the next family.

On seeing Uncle Ox, the head of this household at once inquired if he had finished plowing his fields. When Uncle Ox told him that his ox was sick and couldn't work, the man said, "You're kidding, old fellow! When you're finished with your plowing, lend it to me, will you? That little ox of yours wouldn't get sick if you hit it on the back with a mallet a hundred times."

"A hundred times? That's right, even if I hit it on the back a hundred times, it would still work hard for me."

"Or a thousand, even? Yes, it could take it — I figure it would be impossible for you to hurt it even then."

"A thousand times? That's right — "

"Even two thousand wouldn't — "

"Yes, two thousand — "

At this point the two men laughed because in this sort of idle talk they could bandy about large numbers, as if they were dealing with money or big orders of barley. In the end, he told the man that he had only hit it once, and now it couldn't move properly. The man still didn't believe him, so Uncle Ox had to explain again that he hadn't hit it on the back, but on one of its hocks. He had come to borrow an ox but ended up only talking a lot of nonsense again. This man's ox wasn't sick, but that didn't mean it was free, and he, too, was trying all over the place to see if he could borrow another, to get his land plowed during the good weather.

It was already dark by the time Uncle Ox reached the third family, the one he thought the most reliable source of help, but the head of the household was out, not yet having returned from the fields. When Uncle Ox questioned his wife, he discovered that the friend had borrowed an ox for *five* pecks of wheat. He'd yoked it with his own ox to plow his fields and would not be back till late.

When he got home, Uncle Ox inspected his partner's leg and was going to undo the poultice. Had the little ox not had its own idea about that and shooed him away, the money spent that day on medication might have been entirely wasted.

Unable to borrow an ox anywhere, and with his own quite unfit for work, he went that night to a nearby village to hire laborers to pull the plow for him with their own muscle power.

After lengthy discussion, he finally had a deal. The hired hands, two of them, promised to go to his fields the next morning at the first light. Although the three of them together weren't as strong as his little ox, at least they could turn over the soil while the weather held. Uncle Ox went home feeling happy and drank a small calabash of liquor; then, playing the part of a quiet drunk who doesn't want to make a nuisance of himself, he went softly to sleep across his bed. He dreamed hazy, pleasant dreams, now that it was possible to ready his fields for sowing. His partner remained awake in the middle of the night, expecting its master to extend his big head and his oil lamp into the pen at any time. To its surprise, after dawn someone came and called his master's name before the master had even risen.

The three men plowed for a long time, with two in front and one behind, while the young ox stood on a path between the fields eating grass and looking at the view. It felt just like a child who misses school because of a toothache and only realizes how taxing it is to be a student when he sees the others reciting their lessons and having to work so hard at it. But, once its injury had healed, it would inevitably take on again all the jobs that used to fall to its lot.

As the men worked together plowing the field, Uncle Ox, pushing from behind, saw his partner standing there, lonely in the sunshine. He said something the likes of, "Come on, partner, you come and help us too!" The ox would never have refused if it hadn't been a joke. But the master, remembering that string of shiny cash he'd slung over the shoulder of the doctor the day before, felt he had to let the little ox relax.

The little ox didn't have to do a lick of work. It did as it pleased – ate grass, drank water, lay down to sleep, and enjoyed the good weather as much as it wanted. Even so, it was sick at heart, for, as the two farmhands pulled the plow, they talked of slaughtering cattle and selling the meat, all without the slightest regard for the little ox standing nearby. They spoke of why a lame ox was only good for eating and about making boots and suitcases out of cowhide.

These bad men kept on saying that only tripe from a young ox went well with liquor, of how easy it was to stew the wind-dried meat of a young ox, and how comfortable were waist purses made from the cowhide of a young animal. The little ox couldn't tell whether they were saying all this deliberately. It began to detest them, especially the younger of the two, who actually said things like, "It's only pretending to be sick," trying to destroy the friendship between the ox and its master. Although its master was unlikely to be swayed by this, there was no doubt that the man was evil.

That evening they all went home. When its master went to shine his lantern on it, the ox's bright eyes expressed how it felt. It seemed to be telling him, "I'll be all right tomorrow, Papa – why not dismiss those hands you hired with your money? I can't stand their sneers and insults. I'll work even harder to get those fields finished. And don't worry; I'll see that you don't miss out on the good luck that this fine weather has brought – it won't just go to the others."

The master understood what it meant, because shortly afterward he spoke to it and said, "Yes, partner, you'll be better very soon; the doctor said it'll take three days at most before you're well. It'll be much better if the two of us can go to the fields and help each other. We'll soon have that bit of ground turned over very nicely, and then we can sow. I got them to come and help because it was hard for you with your leg, but you can see we only plowed a very small area, and for all that money too! Of course they're not as strong as you are. Farm workers these days are allowed to get away with murder. They've got none of the good old ways, and what they do isn't half what you, an ox, can do. Yet they want money, and liquor, and now they'll feel they have rea-son to go someplace else and tell them, 'Today I plowed all day for Uncle Ox of Mulberry Creek, who treated me as if I were an ox. But we have to eat, so I had to go through with it, and now my back aches. The only difference between me and an ox is that I don't get whipped.' They're bound to say all of that, but there was no other way; I just had to have them come and help."

The ox would have liked to say, "I wish I could be better tomorrow because I don't like those fellows who ask you for money, and liquor, and food. They seem to be up to no good." But, before it could say anything, its master already understood, and as he left the pen he said loudly and firmly, "I hate them. I spent so much on them in a single day, and they still went on talking about how handy cowhide is for waist purses. It was highway robbery!"

When, in due course, the little ox did go to turn the earth with its master in a part of the field that had not yet been finished, it was four days later, and the good weather in Mulberry Creek seemed to be persisting for the sole purpose of making Uncle Ox happy. They would probably need a couple of days to finish it. Uncle Ox did not stint in his own efforts, for he was being very solicitous about his partner's bad leg; meanwhile, the little ox went pushing on ahead, working especially hard, too, because it was worrying about its master. So they plowed more than twice as much in one day as the hired hands had.

As a result, when they got home, the two of them had good reason to dream happy dreams. Uncle Ox was very surprised by his, because he dreamed there were four oxen in his cowpen, two of them spotted ones that looked even more handsome than his partner.

So, the next morning when he got up, he went to look in the pen and said loudly to his "partner," "It's only right that you should have a companion, partner. Let's think about it in the twelfth month."

His partner thought that the twelfth month was quite far off and just nodded its head, as if to say, "Okay, in the twelfth month."

When the twelfth month came around, all the oxen in the marsh were requisitioned by the yamen and sent away to some place unknown – and all Uncle Ox could do was spend the whole day at the claims office making inquiries. He happened to catch sight of his mallet, which he'd left in a corner of his house. He regretted not having hit the beast harder and broken its leg.

Sansan

Written in Qingdao from 5 August to 17 September 1931, during Shen Congwen's classic period, "Sansan" is a forerunner of the author's master work, The Frontier City *(1933–1934). Both pieces are idyllic in mood and setting, yet tinged with bittersweet passions and hints of repressed conflicts. Both focus on an archetypal adolescent girl character (a theme studied by William MacDonald) and subtle trans- formations of her psychology and relationships with people close at hand: unconsummated new friendships with males outside the family and attachments to older and more familiar adults within, which, however, become inexplicably problematic and more distant as time passes, until the denouement. Innocent and unsocialized, Sansan is a mere country mill owner's daughter until she breaks out of her restricted world and comes to understand the world of men – in both senses of the phrase.*

Sansan helps define the role of country person as not necessarily masculine or proletarian. She is rather well off, although far below the rural class of "masters" who live in fortifications left over from the eighteenth-century colony fields. The commander in this story is one of those hereditary and landed masters, addressed as "Zongye" ("His Honor the Company Commander," from qianzong, *an archaic term last officially used in the Army of the Green Standard of the Qing dynasty). Like many other small towns in this part of West Hunan, the town outside Sansan's mill is called a "fort," after the old stone* bao *forts, already in ruins by the time of the story, that anchored the towns and protected their first Han settlers from the Miao in the coun- tryside. By Shen Congwen's era, considerable melding of the aborigines and Han pioneers has made the village and small-town dwellers into "country folk" of unclear ethnic origins. The "lords" still live apart. And they have their retainers, like the commander's overseer.*

The close attention to manners, as in how flustered country women get when city folk "scold" them for not "dropping by," is by turns comic and pathetic. The story may be read socially, as a confrontation between city and country – with a relatively complex view of country folk adapting to change instead of either resisting or going under, a rare thing in Chinese literature even today. "Sansan" may even be given a feminist reading: the ailing city man is particularly dangerous to Sansan, for, were she to become a widow, even as a teenager, she might never be able to marry again. Another theme is loss of innocence; the story turns on illness and death, subliminally prophesied in this piece by the color white, the color in China of death and mourning. Passages of comic relief, such as the country women's absurd speculations about city life, accentuate the country folk's health, vigor, and constancy (constancy like the mill's turning), but also their vulnerability; and some of the other symbols appear to be of Freudian inspiration. The name "Sansan" (Three-three), incidentally, is a family nickname for Zhang Zhaohe, third born in her generation. Shen Congwen was wooing her – still unsuccessfully – as he wrote this piece.

Yang Family Mill was a few hundred yards outside town, down the road that followed the mountain spur. The "fort," as the town was called, was situated by a mountain brook in a crook of the range. Flowing placidly past the foothills, the stream suddenly grew turbulent while making the turn at the spur, and this the settlers had turned to advantage long ago by building a stone mill over the racing waters. It had taken the name Yang Family Mill for as long as anyone could remember.

Looking up at the fort from the mill, you saw the rooftops and the walls of the houses all huddling up one against the other and shaded over with the verdure of great trees, a spectacle of abundance and vitality. Down below, you saw countless hillside terraces cuddling in on the stream from both sides, like steamed cakes in layers. The tillers of the land had made use of the water power. Lashing thick bamboos together into wheels, with toon wood serving for cross axles and support braces, they had dotted the riverbanks with myriad waterwheels of every size, all perfectly round like gongs. This gang of waterwheels, like a gang of streetside loafers, kept chanting their unintelligible songs all the day and all the night long, never tiring: Eeeee, eeeee, yaaaa, yaaaa.

There was just this one mill in the neighborhood; it hulled and ground rice for the whole fort. People came in turns all day long with their shoulder poles, bearing sacks of rice from the granary. Once the grain was emptied into the stone trough, a sluice gate was opened, and water would course down a bamboo tube toward a wheel hidden underneath. Then came the gratifying sound of the millstone, which began at once to rotate. Setting out his winnowing basket and sieve without any need to interrupt the conversation, the mill owner would wrap his head in a white turban and follow the millstone round and round, using a

Translated by Jeffrey Kinkley

long-handled brush to sweep out the milled rice as it brimmed over the trough. And that was how field grain became white rice.

When the grain was all ground and sifted and both the rice and the chaff had been borne away in bags on shoulder poles, the mill owner was often covered in white dust, just like a boiled dumpling rolled in bean flour. Yet this clearly made for a better life than that of most people in the fort, and they envied it.

Anyone who had ever gone to the Yang Family Mill to hull rice knew about Sansan, the young lady of the Yang family. Her mother had married Old Yang, the mill owner, ten years before. Then one day, when Sansan was four years old, he passed away without a word, abandoning his mill, his wife, and his daughter. With the father dead, the mother became the master, the mistress of the mill. Sansan remained at the mill house, eating good meals of rice with leafy vegetables, fish, and eggs. Nothing had changed. But she was used to seeing her papa covered in rice chaff all the day long. Now that he was gone, her mother was the one permanently covered in rice chaff – and so Sansan grew up, in her own good time, amid laughter and amid tears.

Sansan's mother followed the roller round and round with a little bottle of oil to grease the millstone's iron shaft. Or she stood in a corner and vigorously shook the sieves. Meantime Sansan would quietly play by herself in another corner. In hot weather, she sat in a breezy spot and made little baskets from corn stalks; in winter, she squatted inside the square brazier barrel, warming herself and the cat over the charcoal while eating chestnuts roasted in the ashes. Sometimes, when a customer gave her a homemade hollow-reed *suona,* she would march all around the yard like the Daoist priests she had seen officiate at the year-end Great Nuo exorcism, tootling on it endlessly as if she would never tire.

The roof and outer walls of the mill house were smothered in vines, while sunflowers and Chinese date trees grew all around; the green of Sansan's outfit could often be seen darting through that stand of trees. Tired of playing by herself indoors, she would go sit on the old cracked stone trough outside and throw rice for the chickens to peck at. When one fowl took grain meant for another, Sansan chased the barbarous ingrate, until even her mama on the other side of the house heard the ruckus and begged that it be spared.

There was a little pond above the mill race, shaded over on all four sides with tall trees, so that the summer sun never fell on the water. The mistress of the mill kept a few white ducks here, and the pond held more fish than the waters either upstream or downstream. It was the custom that the water in front of your own house belonged to you; the dam was built expressly for the mill, and putting stun poison into the waters, while setting up a net downstream, was not allowed in these parts. So this little stream was really teeming. When a stranger approached, drawn by the tranquillity of the pond, and squatted down with his fishing pole, Sansan was sure to warn him, "Not here! My family raised the fish here. You go downstream to do your fishing." If the man had a mischievous streak and threw out his line anyway, as if he hadn't heard, and smiled at the young lady while nonchalantly smoking his pipe, Sansan would get upset and call out to her mother, "Mama, Mama, look, a trespasser, someone who won't mind his own business. He's catching our fish. Come here and break his pole, hurry!" But of course her mother never did.

Instead of coming out to break the fishing rod as her daughter commanded, Mother typically said, "Sansan, we've got plenty; let him fish. Fish can walk, you know. The fish upstream at the commander's pond have all run off to visit us. They like our water."

This would remind Sansan of her dream about a great fish that leapt out of the water and ate a duck. After her mother's rejoinder there was nothing more she could say.

She just looked on quietly, watching to see how many fish the trespasser hooked, so that she could tell Mama afterward.

Once, when a fish got hooked but was too big to pull in, the man's rod broke. Sansan was delighted; maybe her mother wasn't on her side, but the fish was. Now it was Sansan's turn to laugh gleefully at the fisherman. But when Sansan ran home in a hurry to tell her mother, mother and daughter had a good laugh together.

There were other times when it was someone she knew who wanted to fish. Catching sight of Sansan, and knowing her temper, he'd remember to say, "Sansan, let me fish please." And Sansan would say, "Fish go wherever they please, and we don't feed them, so of course you may."

Often Sansan would pull over a little wooden stool and sit down beside him to watch his angling and also tell him the story of the man who got his pole broken. Before leaving, the friend would stop by the house and share the larger fish from his catch with Sansan's family. Sansan watched her mother clean the fish and cut out their white bladders. Then Sansan put the bladders on the floor and stomped on them. To her great delight, they popped like little firecrackers. When the fish had at last been cleaned and rolled in salt, Sansan hastened to string them through with a hempen rope, for hanging out in the sun. While frying up the dried fish with hot peppers for a guest, Mother would add, as if remembering the man with the broken rod, "These are Sansan's fish." Sansan smiled, thinking, "And why not? If I weren't here to guard the fish, the cowherd boys would have eaten them all up long ago."

And so Sansan grew up, like other children: through several new outfits of clothing, several rounds of seasonal festivals, and several trips to see the lion dances and dragon lanterns. Friends all said they'd seen her mature through a cloud of chaff and milling dust. And everyone in the fort wanted this girl who'd grown up in the chaff for a daughter-in-law, for they knew her dowry would be a mill built of stone. According to custom, fourteen-year-old Sansan had come of age. But her mama had her own ideas, for she believed a fortune-teller more than the matchmakers. And so the mill had but two masters.

Sansan was a big girl now, yet she clung to her mama like a child. After supper mother and daughter would go to the flowing stream, wash their faces, and watch the sun set on yet another day. Occasionally they heard the sound of gongs and drums from the fort; there was either a wedding or a funeral. "Ma, take me there," Sansan would say, both commanding and pleading. And her ma would agree, if she could think of no reason against it. They would stay a while or stop at a friend's house for a cup of sweet tea. Their money pouches stuffed full of hazelnuts and walnuts, they'd have no trouble walking home on a moonlit night; and when it was dark and gloomy, they lit a torch. With the torch crackling and popping, there was nothing to fear. If they went to have a good time at the commander's estate, "the stockade," one of his laborers would escort them back with a lantern, all the way to the mill. The most fun of all was going out on a rainy night by lantern light, an opportunity Sansan seldom got to enjoy. So she often dreamed of walking alone by the stream, a little red paper lantern in her hand, and only the fish seemed to know.

To tell the truth, it was quite natural that the fish knew more about Sansan's affairs than her mother did. With her mother, Sansan had to use words that her mother understood. All those things that were beyond her mother's comprehension were left to be said at the brookside. There were only fish there, apart from the ducks, and the ducks kept up their quacking all day long – what ears had they for anyone else's problems?

This summer, every evening between supper and sunset, mother and daughter were in the habit of coming to the fort to chat with a young woman due to be married off in a faraway village. They also went to hear a singer who had come in from Xiaozhai. One day, while they were visiting at the fort as usual, the women got to talking about embroidery. Sansan raced back to the mill alone to retrieve a pattern. When she was almost at the house, there in the twilight she saw the dim figures of two people by the stream. One, under a tree, held a rod and looked about ready to cast his line. Thinking him to be another poacher, Sansan approached to see who it was, yelling out as usual, "You can't fish here. These fish are private property!"

"You're saying that even fish in a stream belong to people? Who ever heard of fish farming in running waters?"

"It's just the young lady of the mill, kidding with you," said the other.

At that, the one who had first spoken laughed.

Then she heard the second man say, "Come here, Sansan; your pond is all fished out!"

Sansan was upset to be made light of, and the voice seemed familiar. She charged forward to see who was responsible for this effrontery so that she could report it to her mother. But then she recognized the second speaker as the overseer of the commander's estate, accompanied by a young man she'd never seen before. And the rod he held was a walking stick, not a fishing pole at all.

The overseer was an important man in these parts. He had met Sansan, and Sansan knew him, so he teased her when she came within range: "So your family raised these fish, eh, Sansan? How many head of fish do you keep?"

Seeing as it was Mr. Overseer from the commander's, Sansan kept quiet and smiled as she bowed her head. Head lowered, she still looked at the white trousers and white shoes of the other man, who seemed to be from the city. And she heard him say, "This girl's very intelligent and beautiful. Not bad at all." "The local beauty," put in the overseer. The young man laughed as they went on like this.

She sensed that he was laughing at her. "What's so funny

about me?" she thought to herself. And then it occurred to her, "You city people are afraid of dogs, any old dog, and here you are laughing at me. You've got a nerve!" Then she felt as if she'd said it out loud and been overheard, and she wanted to run away. Realizing that she was about to run away, out of shyness, Mr. Overseer said, "Don't go, Sansan. We came to visit your mill. Is your mother in?"

"No, she's out."

"I'll bet she's at the fort, listening to the singer from Xiaozhai, isn't she?"

"Right."

"Don't you enjoy that sort of thing?"

"What makes you think I don't?"

"Here you came home alone; I thought you must be tired of the songs and worried that all the fish in your pond had been stolen, so – " Mr. Overseer said, laughing.

While conversing with the overseer, Sansan slowly raised her head to look at the stranger's face. His pale white face seemed somehow familiar; mightn't he be one of those opera singers, playing the role of a young male – a scholar perhaps – still white because he'd forgotten to wash the powder from his face?

Seeing that Sansan had overcome her timidity, the man asked her, "Is this your house?"

"And why not?" Sansan retorted.

Amused by her reply, he asked again, "Aren't you afraid of being carried away in a flash flood, living so close to a ravine?"

"Hmhm!" Sansan said as she pursed her pretty lips, glaring at this stranger and thinking, "Look, dogs are coming, dogs are coming. They'll scare you and back you into the stream, and then the water will carry *you* away." Picturing how funny it would be if he really were washed away, she ran off laughing, deciding to pay no more heed to these two men.

Sansan retrieved the embroidery pattern and started back upstream toward the fort. A short distance past the pond she could see the white outlines of the two men up ahead. Not wanting to get involved with the overseer again, she purposely followed at a distance behind them, walking ever so slowly. She overheard them talking about city people and city things, about constructing a canal, and about how the education bureau wanted the commander to set up a school. They had no idea they were being followed. To Sansan, this was great fun. Then she heard the overseer mention the mill and what a good person her mother was, and now she was really happy.

After that she heard the city man say, "She's really cute. I suppose, according to your custom out here in the country, it's about time for her to be sent off?"

The overseer smiled and said, "If Young Master is fond of her and wants the commander to make a match, we can go talk to him. But running the mill goes with the girl."

"Phmph!" Sansan sputtered to herself, stopping long enough to plug her ears with her fingers. But she could still hear the two men laughing, and she wanted to know what this city man who looked like an opera singer would say next, so after a moment she continued following them.

She couldn't quite make out what this boy actor was saying, just Mr. Overseer's part: "If Young Master becomes the mill owner, you'll have fresh eggs whenever you want them, not to mention all the other good things. It would be quite a bargain!" At that, both men burst out laughing.

Unable to follow them any longer, Sansan sat on a rock by the stream bed, her face burning with anger. "You may want to marry me, but I won't let you! And even if our hen laid two dozen eggs a day, I wouldn't give you a single one." But, after a spell of sitting with the cool breeze in her face, the gurgling of the brook water reminded her of the man falling into the stream for fear of the dog, and she was her happy self again. She looked into the depths of the stream and murmured to herself, "Pretty helpless, huh? The overseer will save you; why don't you call for him?"

When she got to the Song household, Auntie Song had been holding forth for some time. Sansan heard her say, "They've got a funny way of convalescing – that's what they call it, convalescing – he sleeps all day out on the porch, all exposed to the wind. . . . His face is as white as a young girl's, and he's always smiling at you. . . . A relative of the commander? Nah, you haven't seen how respectfully the commander treats him. Even the foreigners at the Protestant church are afraid of him. Brides – that man can have as many as he wants."

"Well, then, what illness does he have?" asked Sansan's mother.

"Who knows? He lies in bed all day, doing nothing but taking that sickly sweet medicine. He has it as easy out here in the country as in the city. My fellow birthyear mate says it's some 'disease in the third stage'; others call it consumption – they can't explain it in plain language. Who can be sure of all those names for diseases city folk have? If you ask me, city people like to get sick – that's why they have all those names for diseases. Out here we can't stop working just on account of illness, so apart from malaria we just get fevers and the runs. All those diseases with the fancy names haven't ever come to the countryside."

Another woman, who had suffered from scrofula, was slightly put off by the Song woman's pronouncements: "I'm not a city woman, and I got one of those diseases."

"Your aunt is a city woman!"

"What's that got to do with me?"

"You're as refined as city folk, and that's how you got your infection!"

That put everybody in a laughing mood.

On the way home Sansan asked her mother, "Who's that

white-faced man?" Repeating what she'd just heard from others, Sansan's mother told her about how a sick man from the city had come to the fort to live with the commander. She stressed that he was handsome and strange in temperament. Her descriptions betrayed just how little a country woman understood city folk; they were of course quite hilarious. Ordinarily, Sansan would have taken the little criticisms and exaggerations in her mother's account to be right on the mark and quite fascinating, but for some reason she didn't exactly believe her this time.

When they'd been on the road a while, Sansan asked, "Ma . . . , Ma . . . , have you actually seen that pale-faced man from the city?"

And Mama said, "No, how could I? I haven't been to the commander's house for days."

"Then why do you run on so much about him if you've never even seen him?" Sansan thought.

Sansan realized that she'd already seen what her mother hadn't. She kept this a secret, quite elated to think that only she understood such things and that none of the others' talk about city folk was very reliable.

When they reached the pond, Sansan asked again, "Ma, have you seen Mr. Overseer, from the commander's estate?"

If her mother hadn't and answered Sansan with a question of her own, Sansan was ready to tell her all about her meeting with those two men from the commander's house. But her mother was preoccupied with another matter and ignored what Sansan had said, so Sansan kept it all from her mother, saying not a word.

The next day, on her way to the fort, Sansan's mother encountered the white-faced guest from the city and the overseer, in front of the commander's estate. They were by the corral, watching horses roll over on the ground. The overseer said that they'd gone for a stroll down by the mill the day before and come upon Sansan. He also told Sansan's mother that the guest had come from the city to convalesce.

Then he said to the guest that this was Aunt Yang, the owner of the mill. The man marveled at her resemblance to Miss Sansan, adding how pretty her daughter was, how quick witted, and how fortunate she was to have a little girl like this. Such talk delighted the old lady and put ideas into her head, though she caught herself right away for being so foolish. She hurried back to the mill and gaped at Sansan with a silly grin.

Having no idea why her mother was in such good spirits, Sansan asked where she'd been and whom she'd seen.

Her mother weighed her words carefully before finally saying, "Sansan, did *you* see anyone yesterday?"

"Me? No," Sansan replied.

"Try to remember, Sansan," her mother chuckled. "Yesterday at dusk, didn't you see two men?"

"Oh, yes," Sansan hastened to say, thinking that her mother knew everything. "There were two of them. One was the commander's overseer, the other was a stranger. Why?"

"No reason. Except that the stranger was that very man from town. When I ran into them today, they said they'd already met you. We talked for quite a while. The Young Master looks like a girl." When she got to this point, the mother recalled something funny.

Thinking that her mama was laughing at her, Sansan tried to ignore her by looking down at the ground at the "kitchen horses," crickets attracted by grain, instead.

"They asked for eggs," her mother said, "so will you take two dozen over to them this afternoon?"

When she heard about the eggs, Sansan figured that her mother knew all about the men's joke from the day before, and she was angry. "*Who's* taking those eggs over to them? Ma . . . Ma . . . listen – those are bad men."

"Why?" asked her mother, completely at a loss. "How are they bad?"

When Sansan blushed and didn't respond, her mother said, "Sansan, what's the matter?"

After a very long pause, Sansan finally said, "They're secretly making plans to get the commander to be match-maker and marry me to that white-faced man."

Instead of answering, Sansan's mother had herself a good long laugh simply to hear her daughter's naïveté. But, just as Sansan was about to run away, her mother pulled her toward her and said, "My little penance, Mr. Overseer and his friend were only kidding; you're not angry at that, are you? Who would dare take advantage of you? The commander is master of the whole fort, and he's scolded them *for* you."

In the end, even Sansan was amused enough to laugh.

When she told her ma how much the city people feared dogs, her mother listened in silence, finally saying, "Sansan, when it comes down to it, you're just a little girl. You don't understand anything."

The next day, Mama wanted Sansan to take the eggs to the stockade, but Sansan refused, just shaking her head in silence. Having given her word, Mama had to take them herself. When her mother had gone, Sansan played by herself in the mill house. Tired of that, she went to the pond to watch the white ducks. When she'd played with them a while and still her mother didn't return, she began to wonder if she'd gotten into an argument with the overseer or suffered a heatstroke out on the road. Feeling upset, she went back inside the house.

Finally her mother returned home. She was all smiles as she entered the mill house, striding right in like a man, and she sat on a little stool to tell Sansan that she'd seen the gentleman – and how he'd asked her to sit down in a plush chair that rocked back and forth like a cradle. It was oh so comfortable and yet so uncomfortable. The city man had also asked why Sansan wasn't in school, for all the city girls were. And so forth.

Sansan was already upset by her mother's long absence; she couldn't make any sense of what her mother was saying, and she wasn't in the mood to hear any more, so she walked off while her mother was still talking. Going to the stream, and gazing into its clear waters, she remembered what someone had once told her, that the water flowed downward, straight down the mountains a hundred miles, until it reached the city. She imagined that someday – she couldn't possibly let anybody know in advance just when – she would flow with the waters down into the city, too, and never return. Yet she wanted the mill, the fish, the ducks, and her spotted cat all to come with her. Not only that, she wanted her mother to be at her side always, for only then could she go peacefully to sleep.

Sansan was not to be seen, so her mother stood in the mill house doorway and shouted, "Sansan, Sansan, it's hot out there – your face will get all oily. Don't go far, and come home soon."

On her way back, Sansan whispered to herself, "Sansan is never coming home!"

It was hotter than ever in the afternoon, enough to tire one out. Sansan lay on a bamboo mat bed in the corner of the room. As the lazy drone of faraway waterwheels filled her ears and she squinted up at the bun on top of her mother's head, it began to look like a face – a haggard face, more and more alive – and she drifted off to sleep.

Yet she thought she saw her mother in a white turban, following the millstone with her brush, going round and round and round the room, and then she heard a voice from outside, someone who spoke her name.

She caught the words, "Where has Sansan gone? Why doesn't she come out?"

Puzzled that this voice was so familiar and yet not quite recognizable, she rushed to the doorway to look, only to find that it was the white-faced man. He was fishing, minding his own business. Going up for a closer look, she saw that his fishing pole was really the long tobacco pipe used by the commander's overseer. Smoke was coming out the end of it.

Fishing with a pipe was quite an interesting thing, but by his side she could see how many fish he'd already taken, and that seemed very strange indeed. Sansan was about to go tell her mother when suddenly the overseer came up.

It was just like the other day. The sky was aglow with the rosy sunset, and Mama was not at home. Sansan had returned because she'd forgotten to lock the chickens in their coop; now she was chasing around to catch them. Presently she encountered those two men, Mr. Overseer and the pale-faced city man, standing on top of a block of stone, whispering about something. Their voices were very low, but Sansan could make them out. It was something bad for her. This talk made Sansan very anxious, for she couldn't make the men go away, and she couldn't tear herself away. She felt her face grow as crimson as the sunset.

Pretending that he was serious, the overseer said, "We've come to buy eggs. However much money you ask for them, we'll pay it."

With a gesture like an opera singer, the city man said, "That's not it. However much *gold* you ask for them, we'll give it."

Because they were trying to scare her with this talk of gold, Sansan said, "I won't sell them to you. I don't want your money. You can bring all your gold bars from home and take them to market and buy crows' eggs."

Whereupon the overseer said, "Would that do? I wouldn't even take phoenix eggs if they were from someone else. If you won't give up a few chicken eggs to help me out, how do you think your mama will get along, without Mr. Overseer to write out her daughter's horoscope for her betrothal?"

And the city man added, "Why deal with someone so stingy? Best to forget it."

"Call me stingy if you like," Sansan yelled angrily. "I'd

rather feed my eggs to the shrimp than sell them to you. We don't envy other people's gold and jewels. Offer your gold to someone else; go frighten *them*."

But the two men still refused to leave, and Sansan grew upset. She wished a dog would pounce on them. No sooner did she think it than a large hound sprang from her house, white as could be from head to tail, yapping all the way as he rushed past Sansan and pounced ferociously on the two bad men, pushing them into the water.

That raised a spray from the stream and a lot of giant bubbles. With the overseer's bald head surfacing and the city man's long hair entangled in the roots of the brookside willow trees, it made quite a spectacle.

Then everything disappeared from the water. So the men had been catching fish in their hands all along. They went ashore, shook off the water, and made away with every fish in the stream.

Sansan was about to go tell her mama when she slipped and fell.

It had all been a dream. Her mother, who must have been making lunch in the kitchen, had heard Sansan talking in her sleep and come out to wake her. Sansan had awakened, so her mother shook her and asked, "Sansan, Sansan, who were you quarreling with?"

Sansan collected herself and smiled at her mother without saying a word.

"Get up and take a look," her mother said. "I've stewed taros for you today. Look at yourself in the mirror; your face is all red from sleeping." Sansan looked at herself in the mirror as her mother had asked, but still she said not a word. She was completely awake now, but her dream remained very vivid. Then, remembering that her mother had asked with whom she'd quarreled, Sansan asked her just what she'd heard. Her mama, of course, hadn't paid much attention, so she said she hadn't been able to make it out very clearly. Sansan didn't ask again.

Not until it was time to eat, when her mother said again that her face was red from sleeping, did Sansan tell her the dream. Her mother found it amusing and had a good laugh.

When she went to take the eggs the next day, Sansan went, too. It was in the afternoon, after lunch, when the two entered the great courtyard of the commander's mansion. In the eastern courtyard, they caught sight of the guest from the city, lying in a rattan chair on the porch and looking up at the doves circling in the air. The overseer was away. Although Sansan recognized the other man, she was too shy to go up to him, so she had her mother go on ahead while she waited by the circular cutout archway, the "moon door." As her mother was about to proceed, Sansan got another idea. She wanted her mama to stand by the arch and get his attention by shouting, "I've come with the eggs, sir." The mother of course did everything Sansan asked. Hearing her mother rouse the white-faced city man only after calling out the third time, Sansan was both anxious and amused.

Sansan was standing outside the moon door and looking in through a crack. She saw the pale-faced man get up and sit down again, just as in her dream. She could hear the conversation with her mother. While they talked about the weather and other things, Mama kept looking back to where Sansan stood.

Thinking that she wanted to leave, the white-faced man said, "Sit a while, old lady, I like talking with you."

So Mama sat down. But now the pale-faced city man noticed that someone was waiting at the gate. "Who's that? Could it be the young lady of the family?"

The jig was up; Sansan wanted to run away. But when she turned around, there was Mr. Overseer; perhaps he'd been there quite a while. Escape was impossible. He pulled her into the courtyard by the sleeve.

She heard the man ask her to sit down; he told her mother all about how he'd seen Sansan that day by the stream. Sansan kept close to her mother, looking away from them and saying not a word. She was anxious to get away immediately but couldn't think how.

They'd been sitting just a while when out came a woman, curiously dressed in a white robe and cap. At first Sansan thought it was a man and didn't dare look too closely. But then she heard this person speak and saw her go up to the city man. She stuffed a tiny white pipette into the mouth of his white face and took his hand – touched it for quite some time – then took something that appeared to be a kind of writing brush and wrote some numbers on a piece of paper. When the gentleman asked, "How many d' geese?" the figure in white was heard to reply, "The same as yesterday." It was only when she laughed, at another query, that Sansan knew for sure it was a woman. Mama seemed just now to have come to the same conclusion; puzzled at this talk of "geese," mother and daughter looked at each other and suppressed a smile.

The woman in the white robe, who was in turn amused that all this was so new to them, didn't leave immediately.

"Mademoiselle Zhou," said the pale-faced city man, "you haven't made a friend since you've come here; why not start with this young lady? Her family has a good mill, downstream, with quite a fetching waterwheel and a nice little dam in back of it. Make her acquaintance, and you can go there for some fun, maybe catch a few fish for us. Why don't you take her outside for a walk in the woods? She can tell you the names of all the plants and flowers."

This Mlle Zhou came over with a smile on her face and took Sansan's hand to lead her away. Sansan didn't much want to go, but when she looked at her mother, and saw that she was pursing her lips that way to encourage her, she couldn't very well refuse.

When they got outside, though, the two quickly warmed to each other. The nurse asked Sansan every little thing about the countryside. Sansan answered her, all the while wanting to ask some things of the woman, herself, but unable to think of how to phrase her questions. So she just kept smiling and giving that white cap a curious stare. She couldn't for the life of her understand how it kept from falling off.

When at last Sansan heard her mother call her name from the house, she had no idea what kind of words to use to say goodbye to a new friend, so she simply said that her mother was calling her and she had to go, then ran off by herself to her mother's side and departed.

On the way back to the road, mother and daughter traversed a stand of bamboo. It was flooded with the golden glow of late afternoon. Balancing a basket on her head like an old fisherman, Sansan was thinking about the woman in the white cap who nursed the sick man at the commander's home. She asked her mother, "Ma, did you like that woman?"

"Which one?" asked her mother.

Sansan marched out in front, seemingly just a bit put off at the thought that her mother was purposely playing dumb.

"Who do you mean, Sansan?" her mother asked again.

"I'll tell you who. The woman we just saw, that's who. Who do I mean!"

"How did I know who you meant? The young woman with the white skin and rosy cheeks? Is that the one?"

Sansan slowed down so her mother could catch up and chuckled at her own impishness. Her mother drew abreast and gave Sansan a little shove. "Sansan, that young woman looked very nice, don't you think?"

Sansan thought she looked very nice indeed, but, because her mother had said it, she deliberately answered, "How can you say that, when she's tall as a cucumber? You call that nice?"

"She's been to school, Sansan. Didn't you notice that she could write?"

"All right, Ma, then tomorrow why don't you invite her

into the family as your goddaughter? She's educated, and that's the only kind of people my ma seems to care for anymore."

"Hmmh, just look at you. I praise education, and you get angry. Still – surely you respect schooling yourself."

"It's all right for men. For women, it's disgusting."

"If you find it disgusting, then that's what we'll call her, end of subject."

"Not at all. How can we call her disgusting when you don't find her disgusting at all?"

"All right, then, you find her disgusting."

"Not me!"

"Then who is it that does? Answer me that, Sansan."

"Nobody, I tell you."

This exchange made her mother laugh, and pretty soon Sansan did, too.

Sansan began to hurry on ahead again. But because the sunset was just too beautiful, she stopped again by a maple tree and asked her mother to sit down so they could watch that cloud up there go by and send it on its way. Naturally her mother couldn't refuse. The two sat on a stone slab, Sansan removing the basket from her head and straightening her hair. She was reminded again of the woman with the short hair, hair as short as a man's. "Sansan," her mother said, "take your apron and wipe your face; you're sweating." Sansan looked away as if she hadn't heard. She puzzled over why so many people had faces as white as camellias. When she unwittingly said this out loud to her mother, the mother answered that this was precisely why they were called city people: they were all very white to begin with, even without powder.

"That's not very pretty," Sansan said. "No, of course not," her mother agreed. "But that dusky girl in the Song household is the ugliest of all," Sansan added. Her mother didn't know what Sansan was driving at or where she was going with it, so instead of saying anything more she just pretended to be absorbed with what Sansan had said, so that her daughter could explain it.

Sansan's point was simply that she wasn't going to agree with anything her mother said. So if her mother didn't say anything, Sansan didn't need to, either. She, too, fell silent.

One day a man and a woman came to the mill from the big stockade with a load of grain to mill. The man went on his way, leaving behind the woman to tend to business. She was a talkative sort; having just come from a wedding at a village twenty miles away, she was full of stories and local gossip that just had to be told, so she duly poured it all out before the millerwoman and her daughter. Having this daughter of her own, Sansan's mother was curious to know all about where the wedding had been held, how the bride had looked, and the state of her dowry. And she knew that Sansan was usually interested in all these things, too, so she asked the woman to tell all about it, not leaving out anything.

Sansan sat through it quietly in a corner, soaking it all up, but saying nothing. When the woman lowered her voice at the parts she thought unsuitable for a maiden's ears, Sansan would pretend not to be paying attention and go on with her play, tying ropes into nooses. Really she was still getting every word. She couldn't help smiling at some of those funny words, but she turned her head to do it on the sly so that the gossipy woman couldn't see.

Finally the two old women got around to the commander's guest and that woman in the white cap and gown. The woman doing her milling said she'd heard that the woman in white had been hired to come out here, hired to take care of the gentleman – for several ounces of silver a day. But she didn't consider this information entirely reliable; she felt sure that this woman must be the city man's wife and mistress of his household or at least his concubine.

Sansan's mother couldn't disagree more. She couldn't believe that the woman in white was married to him.

"How do you know she's not?" said the other woman.

"How could she be?" Sansan's ma insisted.

"Give me a reason."

"I have my reasons for thinking so; I just can't put them into words."

"How would you know? You haven't even seen her."

"What do you mean, I haven't seen her?"

The argument went on, without resolution. Neither could come up with a conclusive case, and Sansan's mother forgot to enter into evidence the fact she'd heard the girl addressed as Mlle Zhou. Sansan remembered everything she'd heard, but she didn't want to tell that woman, so she thought of another way of ending the two women's inconclusive conversation.

"Ma," Sansan said, "don't argue about this anymore. Help me wash my hair. I'll go heat the water."

The woman went on her way with the rice. When the water was hot, Sansan sat on a little stool. As she undid her braids, she said disapprovingly to her mother, "Ma, what's wrong with you, talking all that nonsense with an old woman?"

"What nonsense did I say?"

"What's it got to do with you whether she's married to him or not?"

. . . .

Her mother seemed to have been struck by some thought. She puckered her lips and stared into space a long time before finally letting out a soft sigh.

A few days later the woman in the white cap and gown came to the mill to visit, accompanied by a little girl from the commander's house. She stayed quite a while and talked about all sorts of things. Never having had a guest like this before, Mama bustled about nervously, thinking she ought to kill a fat mother hen and invite the guest to dinner, but afraid to be so presumptuous as to suggest it, and so completely discomfited.

Sansan took the guest downstream to see the waterwheels, which they enjoyed for a good while, meantime picking lots of day lilies along the stream bank. On the way back Sansan took up a fishing pole and brought over a couple of stools, then went with her to the stream so that the woman in the white cap could fish.

The fish in the stream seemed ready to play their part; in no time the woman had pulled in four big carp. This made her ecstatic. When finally it was time for her to go home, she didn't want to take the fish with her, but Sansan's mother insisted. And, having heard the woman in the white cap say that she liked pumpkin seeds, she brought out a bag of raw ones, which she had the woman's little girl companion take back for her.

A few days after that, the white-faced man and the commander's overseer came again to fish, bringing with them many presents.

And, a few days yet after that, the sick man came again, with the nurse. This time he gave them candy in a jar and some other things that really left the old woman at a loss for words. She couldn't presume to keep these two noble guests here for dinner, so when they were preparing to go, Sansan's mother grabbed two live chickens, insisting that the guests take them back. The guests said they should be spared to go on laying eggs, but Sansan's mother wouldn't have it. She wasn't about to spare them until the guests promised to eat them for dinner next time they visited.

Ever after that, things at the mill were not quite the same. Mention of how things were "in the city" gradually cropped up more and more in the conversations between mother and daughter. Neither really knew what it was like there or what it had to recommend it. Letting their imaginations fly, from the airs of the commander and what they could see of the white-faced man and the woman in white, to the usual run of stories country folk told, together they conjured up a vision of what the place must be like. There would be a great wall built of stone and behind it many fine houses, each the home of an old lord, a troop of young gentlemen, and many ladies, all made up like brides and wearing embroidered gowns from dawn till dusk while they sat at home all day doing nothing. And each person would have rooms full of footmen and maidservants, the footmen sitting outside the main gate to take visitors' calling cards, and the maidservants peeling lotus seeds and taking feathers out of bird's nests for the lord's soup. Broad avenues must crisscross the city everywhere and still be full of horses and carriages. Those stiff-legged foreigners would be pacing the streets, too. There would be a great yamen, full of judges as awe inspiring as the ancient Judge Bao, holding court from morning until night, and at night too, passing down judgments by lamplight. And the city would be filled with shops, selling all sorts of strange and marvelous things. There were sure to be lots of temples big and small, with people singing operas in them all the livelong day, and big audiences to enjoy them. The playgoers would be seated on long benches, enjoying melon seeds as they listened. There'd be bad women with wandering eyes trying to seduce men and roly-poly butchers selling their wares by the city gate. And needless to say there'd be Wang of the Iron-Clad Predictions, who read faces and divination sticks for people there at the city gate.

And of course it was all real to them. Inspiring as a fairy tale, this imaginary city that mother and daughter kept within their hearts could never do them any harm. Fortunate in the life to which they were accustomed, they drew happiness from their fantasies; however happy their past lives, there was the hope of even better ones in the future.

And yet another kind of memory would press in on Sansan's mama, sometimes causing her suddenly to clam up in the midst of their conversations about the city. When Sansan asked for an explanation, her mother would only grin, as if breaking out into a smile were a motivation unto itself.

Sansan could see that something lay behind her mother's smile, but she could never figure it out. Perhaps her mother meant to move them to the city or had journeyed there in a dream. Or perhaps she was startled to see how Sansan had matured. From a distance, she could pass for a bride. So many things were hidden away in this old woman's heart. Sansan would often break into a smile herself, without letting her mother know the reason why. Every time she heard her mother call out, "Come home, Sansan," when she went to play by the stream, Sansan would obey and yet say to herself in a soft voice, "Sansan is not coming home. Sansan is never coming home." She never squarely faced the question of why she wasn't coming home or where she might go instead.

The two would be discussing the city they had seen in their dreams the night before and what the great yamens and temples had looked like, and it would occur to Sansan that her mother always traveled to a city that was different from her own. There must of course be as many kinds of cities as villages. Sansan had realized this for some time. The city to which Sansan journeyed must be somewhat farther away than her mother's, for her mother's was about the same as the commander's estate, only a little bigger, though not a lot. The city Sansan dreamed of was home to a couple hundred and more women in white caps, for that was what her friend had told her.

Every time Mama went to take eggs over to the stockade, she brought back word that the people there had asked after Sansan and invited her over for a visit. Sansan just scolded her mother for not helping her put up her hair. But sometimes her braids would be just fine.[1] Then she would say

[1]Marriage is marked by a woman giving up her pigtails for another kind of hairdo.

that she needed a change of clothes before she could go. When no such excuse was possible, as the time drew near Sansan would simply refuse to go. Naturally Sansan's mother didn't force her. But sometimes she would express annoyance; Sansan would change her mind and end up going. Both would be in very high spirits by the time they got there.

Even when she didn't go to the big stockade herself, Sansan was anxious to hear all about it when her mother got back. The old woman looked Sansan in the face while she spoke; she knew her daughter's thoughts. She thought she understood her so well that in some parts she went into detail. Speaking tenderly of how the woman in the white cap nursed the white-faced man, she would look into Sansan's eyes and see the same sort of tenderness. At that point, something far, far away would suddenly occur to the mother, and likewise to Sansan, rendering further talk unnecessary. Mother and daughter became silent.

Sometimes folks from the stockade would come to visit the mill and find that Sansan had already gone downstream by the waterwheels to pick day lilies. When Sansan got back to the mill, she would find her mother talking with the overseer as if they had something serious to discuss. Catching sight of Sansan, the overseer would smile and say nothing. Sansan could see that something funny was going on from the expression on her mother's face.

Mr. Overseer looked at Sansan and said, "Let me ask you, Sansan, why do you so seldom visit the stockade? We've been expecting you."

"Nobody's expecting me there," Sansan said, looking at her yellow flowers and not daring to raise her head.

"Your friends are," said the overseer.

"I don't have any friends."

"Sure you do! Think a moment. One, at least."

"Must be, if you say so."

"How old are you this year? Were you born in the year of the dragon?"

This was a strange conversation, Sansan thought. She looked at her mother in silent perplexity.

"In fact, I already know," said the overseer, "because your mother just told me. Your birthday's the seventeenth of the fourth month; isn't that so?"

It's none of your business if it's the seventeenth of the fourth month or the eighteenth of the fifth, Sansan thought to herself; I'm not asking you for any birthday presents. What she couldn't figure out was why her mother would talk about such things with an outsider. Pouting at her mother with those tiny lips to show her dismay, Sansan in her pique put the flowers she'd picked just for her mother down on the resting millstone and ran out to the stream. She gathered up some stones and started skipping them across the water.

Not long after, she heard her mother escort the overseer outside the house. Sansan quickly turned her back to the road, pretending to be watching cows that were fighting on the opposite bank of the stream, until the overseer went away. But when he caught sight of her, he stopped and called out to Miss Sansan – called her name several times – and still Sansan paid no attention, though in the end she heard him chuckle as he left.

When the overseer had gone, her mother said, "Sansan, come in. I'd like to talk to you." Still pretending not to hear, Sansan didn't turn her head and didn't answer. For, as he was about to go, she thought she'd heard the overseer say, "Sansan, you'll be having to invite me to feast and drink." She knew what that meant. So, for some reason, she was quite displeased with him this day. And, because this man had undoubtedly discussed a lot of things with her mother, she seemed to feel angry at her mother just now, too.

That evening her mother noticed that Sansan wasn't herself and wouldn't talk to her. "Sansan," she asked, "what's the matter? Are you angry at someone?"

"No," whispered Sansan, though really she felt like crying.

Two days later, Sansan appeared to have forgotten all that and made up with her mother, but no more did she speak of going to the stockade for a visit, nor did she ever suggest that her mother take eggs to them. Her mother, who seemed to have caught on, didn't speak much about the city with Sansan any more, nor did she mention taking eggs to the big stockade, either.

The days slowly passed. Thanks to good sun and favorable rains, the rice plants bent down low in the fields, heavy with their ears of grain. In some families, the new grain was in the granary, while others had already picked the early ripening rice and hulled it for distribution to friends and family, so that they could savor the new harvest.

The joyous day was almost here for the bride-to-be in the village; word came that Sansan and her mother should come keep her company before the wedding. Sansan's mother, who had just sewn her daughter a leek-green apron, suggested that they go for a two-day visit. Sansan could raise no objection, so the two of them set out for the fort with their gifts. It was the local custom that a bride display her dowry before the wedding, for all the village women to see, so, when they got to the bride's home, Sansan and her mother encountered the woman in the white cap. Because there was little else she could do here in the countryside apart from caring for the sick person, she had been visiting with the country women day in and day out for the past month and thus had come with them to view the dowry.

City woman that she was, the woman in white at once chided Sansan's mother for not coming to visit them more often at the commander's home. And she asked Sansan why she'd forgotten her friend. This of course put both mother and daughter at a loss for words. Country women that they were, they just looked at the woman, now grown thinner and darker, and smiled. Then the woman in the white cap told Sansan's mama that the patient wasn't doing very well. A doctor had been summoned from the city. He felt that the white-faced man needed a change of air for the autumn. He was getting ready to move him back to the city in the eighth month, en route to a seaside getaway far, far away. Because he would be leaving soon, the two of them had been thinking a lot about Sansan and her mother and their little mill.

The woman in the white cap added that she'd sent word inviting them to visit; why hadn't they come? She also said she'd wanted very much to come again to fish in the little pond by the mill but had found the weather a little too hot for going out.

Noticing Sansan's new apron, with its embroidered flowers and lovely pattern, the woman in the white cap asked, "Sansan, this is really a beautiful apron. Did your mama make it?"

Sansan, however, was amused at how tanned the woman's face had become in the last month and laughed. It was the sincere laugh of a friend.

"We country folk," her mother said, "aren't very discriminating. We'll wear anything that fits."

These words of her mother's were pretty far off the mark, so Sansan added, softly, "But she altered it three times."

The woman in the white cap smiled at them when she heard this and said, "You're a lucky mother. And you're lucky to be her daughter."

"Us, lucky? We country folk don't have it nearly as good as you city folk."

A pair of men were just then carrying off a pile of gifts on a litter. The woman in the white cap gestured at the figure of Sansan as she hurried over for a look. "When your daughter marries, her dowry will be even richer than this."

Sansan's mother followed her gaze and said, "We're poor folk; maybe no one will want her."

Having overheard every word, Sansan lingered before coming back, though she had already had her look at the gifts.

The woman in the white cap invited mother and daughter to the stockade to see the sick man, but Sansan's mother could see that her daughter was displeased, and she also remembered that she was empty handed. Country folk were usually embarrassed to visit someone at their home without a gift. She said they'd come some other time, in a couple of days.

It was a few days later, while mother and daughter were at the mill, talking about the cosmetics worn by the bride, that they thought of how much redder the white-capped woman's face had become since she moved to the countryside. Sansan's mother remembered her promise to the woman. She asked Sansan when exactly she'd like to go to the stockade, to see the "city person." At first Sansan said she didn't want to go, but then, deciding there was no harm in it, she agreed to go any day her mother liked. That, of course, meant that she'd be ready the next day.

Remembering that the woman in the white cap had wanted to visit the mill, Sansan asked her mother if they couldn't set off in the morning, the better to invite the guests back to the mill. Sansan could escort them home in the evening. Her mother, remembering that she'd wanted to give them the two hens the time before and how the guests had agreed to eat them the next time, decided that they would return early, to kill the chickens and prepare the feast.

Mother and daughter set out for the big stockade early in the morning with a basket of eggs. As they passed over a bridge, through a bamboo grove, and over a hillock, the roadside was still damp with dew. "Golden bell" crickets made their ding-dong sounds in the grass, and magpies flew overhead, chattering away. Walking behind Sansan, who was flailing the grass by the roadside with a stick as she went, her mother couldn't help noticing that her figure was slender as a bamboo shoot. She remembered how the overseer had asked Sansan a question at the commander's house and how she hadn't quite caught his drift. She also remembered what the woman in the white cap had talked about a few days before and thought of all the things she'd be having to do now that Sansan was growing up so fast and her day was approaching.

She remembered bits and pieces of things that had happened to other people. A string of pearls that made a phoenix bridal tiara — now who had worn that? Twenty litters full of presents, with golden locks and golden fishes — to whom did they go? Flowers scattered across the bed, with seeds of ginkgo and lotus, and dates — whose were they? Four maids waiting on her, and still not satisfied — who could that have been? Was Sansan city folk, then? . . .

If she hadn't slipped and fallen forward, her dreams might simply have run wild.

Sansan finally noticed that her mother was sputtering in back of her and turned her head. "Ma, what's the matter? What were you thinking? You almost dropped the basket of eggs. What got you so carried away?"

"I was thinking of how I've become an old lady. I'm too old now to enter the city and see the world."

"You're not saying you ever liked it anyway, are you?"

"That's where you'll be going one day, you can be sure."

"But why? I *won't* go to the city!"

"All the better, then."

They walked on, and suddenly Sansan asked, "Ma . . . , Ma . . . , why did you say I'll have to go to the city? What gave you that idea?"

"You're not going there, child," her mother hastened to explain, "and neither am I. The city is made for city folk. We have our mill. Of course we'll never leave it."

Soon they could see the gatehouse to the big stockade, with all the great elms and parasol trees in front of it.

Heading south after entering the gate, they saw a crowd of spectators gathered under the elms before the mansion. Some were busy carrying things this way and that. Something must have happened; perhaps a guest had arrived from far away, or maybe something else. Sansan and her mother weren't too surprised, so they slowly continued on their way.

"Maybe a commissioner has come here from the yamen," Sansan said. "Ma, you go ahead and see what it is; I'll wait for you here." Her mama gave a noncommittal reply, thinking that something strange must be going on. She set her basket down for Sansan to guard and went ahead alone.

Just then a woman who was returning home, carrying her baby, saw Sansan and asked, "Sansan, why so early? Do you have business here?" But just then she caught sight of the eggs in her basket. "Who's this gift for, Sansan?"

"It's just something I felt like bringing," Sansan said. She didn't want to have any more conversation with her, so she lowered her head and fidgeted with the cloth waist button on her green apron.

"Where's your mother?" asked the woman.

"Over there," said Sansan, pointing to the south, her head still bowed.

"They've had a death there," the woman said.

"Who?"

"That young master who moved here from the city last month to convalesce at the commander's home. They said he was sick, that's all. It was only a few days ago that he was always coming out to get some air. But he just up and died."

Sansan's heart skipped a beat. This couldn't be true! she thought.

At just that moment her mother rushed back, her heart pounding and her face white as ash, for she had heard the news, too. She looked at Sansan without saying a word and led her away, muttering either to her daughter or to herself, "Dead – dead. Who would have predicted?"

But Sansan halted and asked her, "Ma, did the white-faced gentleman die?"

"That's what everyone says."

"We can't just go home, can we?"

No indeed, puzzled her mother, we can't just go back.

After a short discussion, mother and daughter decided to stay and find out what really happened. Sansan wanted to see the woman in the white cap. If they could find her, they'd understand everything. But as soon as they were back at the gate, which was wide open even with all the people standing around, they were afraid people would know they had come bearing gifts, so they dared not enter. They heard people saying all sorts of things about the white-faced man, and about the woman in the white cap, whom they called his wife, and so on, all of which proved how little they really knew these two people from the city.

Her face white as could be, Sansan tugged at her mama's clothes and whispered, "Ma, let's go." And they left.

Back at the mill, Sansan's mother hurried in with her basket of eggs, for there was a customer waiting to have his rice hulled. Sansan stood by the stream gazing into its blue-green currents, feeling as if she had lost something. She struggled to remember what it was called, but she could not.

Remembering that Sansan was outside, her mother called her name. "Ma," she answered, "I'm watching the shrimps."

"Come put the eggs in this jug. The shrimps will be there all day for you to see." Sansan had to obey her mother and come inside.

The sluice gate was up, and the millstone was already starting to turn. The millwheel shaft needed lubrication; Sansan's mother hunted everywhere for the oil. Sansan knew that the bottle was hanging up behind the door, but she kept still while her mother continued the search. Sansan stared at the basket, then knelt and counted out the eggs on the floor. She counted them over and over, until finally the person who had brought the grain to mill asked why she'd been out with her eggs so early in the morning and for whom they were intended. As if she hadn't heard a word, Sansan stood up and ran out the door.

Life

"Life" ("Sheng") is in every sense a Peking story; its postscript reads "Peking, 3 September 1933" – six days before Shen Congwen married, as it happens. The capital had long been his beloved second home. From the day he arrived he was devoted to the ancient palaces, the food stands, the sidewalk antique stalls that made Peking an outdoor museum – and no doubt also to the activities at Shisha Lakes, an old district in the north of the city near the Drum Tower, where acrobats and jugglers performed. (Qianhai, the "Front Lake," is one of a series of linked ponds that includes the more famous Beihai and Zhongnanhai to the south.)

The nameless old man of the story would be a person who knows the city, possibly a native. But Shen Congwen's "city man" is a moral construct: one who is rude and thoughtless, benumbed by complexity, and preferably a selfish or neurotic member of the monied classes. The hero of this story, who is consciously depicted as a member of the lumpenproletariat, rates as an "honorary country fellow" in Shen's scheme of things. Unspoiled and not self-centered, the old man shares the country fellow's enigmatic pathos and above all his sense of life as drama, for he eternally puts on shows reenacting, and amending, the great tragedy of his life.

With economical means Shen Congwen has recreated the world of those who live on the edge. And then, in the last two paragraphs, as C. T. Hsia notes, the scene is invested with an entirely new meaning – "lifted to a high level of poetry."

In the Shisha Lakes district of Peking there was a landfill area at the southern end of the Qianhai where residents dumped cinders from their stoves. A band of people with time on their hands had gathered there in the sun to see what was going on, for the least bit of commotion was enough to collect a crowd.

Sssss. . . .

The sound was like the ripping of silk or a firecracker going off. A toy with wings of brightly colored paper spiraled into the air, lofted on a wire held by the vendor. All the different faces turned skyward to watch. It was a tiny airplane, flying up and coming down. In the air it caught the attention of those standing farther away. For this little plane had especially bright colors, characteristic of toys made in Peking.

After reaching a certain height, the toy plane would slowly descend, like a parachute. Usually it landed somewhere on the field, where it could be collected and sent up on another mission. But, if the angle of the launch was askew, it would land elsewhere; sometimes a breeze would get it entangled in the tops of the willow trees, or land it on the white awning of one of the many stalls, or even on the straw hat of an innocent bystander. It was so light that the person could be unaware of it and continue walking. A group of noisy children would then follow him like a pack of dogs, laughing and yelling until he finally caught on. And then he would snatch the object from his hat and throw it on the ground, whereupon the children would fight over it and forget the passerby completely.

It cost three cents to send this little airplane into the air. Anyone willing to pay the price could do it and could do it over and over again until the little plane was lost.

As more people reached into their pockets for coins to fly the plane, a smile appeared on the toy vendor's face. He soon

Translated by Peter Li

disappeared, counting his money, into the Lake View Teahouse, a place to drink tea and listen to Peking opera. The crowd disappeared as quickly as it had gathered. Soon only lotus pods littered the site. The pods were normally light green on the outside and pale green on the inside, but some were also brown on the outside.

An old man past sixty walked onto the grounds carrying two large puppets, half life size and joined to each other. He looked around at the empty site and knew that this was not a good place to put on his show. But he had little choice.

Laying his puppets down under the bright sun, he picked up a lotus pod and felt its contents, then coughed a little to test his voice. He didn't have a gong or drum. He had only those two joined puppet bodies, crudely made and stiff as boards, one with a black face, the other with a white face. That was all. Nor did he have an audience.

The old man looked around the landfill with his blood-shot little eyes. It was so hot and the location so bad, he knew that, without a few tricks to attract an audience, he could never hope to get anyone to watch his show. The old man looked at the white face and spoke to it gently in a low voice, as if comforting himself.

"Wang Jiu,[1] don't you worry. People will come. Look at these lotus pods; they're signs that our honored guests are on their way. We'll wait a while and then perform for them. If we do a good job, there's no need to worry that these gentlemen won't spare us a few coppers. If the show is good, the gentlemen will go home and tell their children, Hey, Wang Jiu and Zhao Si[2] are really good wrestlers. They grapple with each other, trip each other up, and throw each other around, all under the hot July sun, and they don't even sweat."

"It's true, you don't sweat," he said, mumbling to Wang

[1] Wang the Ninth.
[2] Zhao the Fourth.

Jiu. "Hot as all get out, and still you don't sweat, or even get tired. Good fellow!"

Finally a single person came over, looking like he was testing the waters before a dive. He wore a striped shirt with his shirttails hanging out, like he was one of those sloppy college students from the city. And he had that frail, sickly look of a scholar from bygone days.

The old man gave the Peking student the once-over and smiled at him, thinking that his savior had arrived. His whole body came alive, like a young person's. He moved his arms up and down while the college student stood there looking the puppets in the face, as if studying them. The old man started muttering again, speaking to the white-faced character as devotedly as a father to his son.

"Look, Wang Jiu, the honored young masters and mistresses haven't arrived yet, but this gentleman is here. All right, let's begin, for I'm sure this gentleman won't leave. You better be careful; don't let Zhao Si get the better of you. This gentleman will be on your side, watching you trip up bad old Zhao Si. This gentleman won't go away."

The old man stood the puppet body up and smoothed its tattered old gown. Next, he took out two wooden puppet legs and tied them so they hung down from his own belt. When everything was set, he lifted up the puppet torso, hunched over, and crawled inside its outfit. Hidden under the puppets' clothing, he then put his arms into the false legs, one for each character, adjusted their position, and began to act out the part of two men wrestling there in the ash field. He jumped, he slid, and used his own feet to try to trip the false legs of the other puppet. Though he could not see the puppet outfit he was wearing or even his audience, the result was extremely lifelike.

The college student flashed a sad smile. And, quite a distance away, someone else noticed what was going on here.

He came over out of curiosity. The second member of the audience had arrived.

Soon the third had rushed over, and so on, up to thirteen.

The crowd of people come to watch the puppets fight grew bigger, until the performers were surrounded on all four sides.

The crowd was roaring with laughter. From under his clothing the old man could barely make out the feet and legs of the people who had gathered around to watch. Then he used Wang Jiu's real leg and tripped up Zhao Si. The outer puppet and the old man who was acting out the other puppet by hiding under his clothes both fell into a heap on the dusty ground. There was a burst of laughter on the field, and this comic little scene came to an end.

The old man slowly crawled out of the dirty, tattered clothing, revealing a head of graying hair. His face was all red and sweating, but there was a smile written across it, a tired smile.

After he was out of the puppets' clothing, he stood the puppets up again and mumbled to himself, "Good work, Wang Jiu! You did it. Look, I told you that honored guests were on their way over to watch you, and don't you see them all before you now. Now that you have played your part so well and thrown Zhao Si, our honored guests are sure to favor us with fistfuls of their spare change, and we'll be able to satisfy ourselves with some *wowotou*.[3] Look at your face — you look like a young lady. Are you tired? Is the sun too hot for you?"

Wiping his brow with a corner of his shirt as he spoke, he said, "Come on, how about another round if you're so good. Some day we'll go to Nanjing for the national boxing competition and show those Southerners a thing or two."

The crowd burst into laughter again.

[3]Cornmeal muffins of the coarsest grade.

As he was about to step into the puppet suit again, a pock-faced policeman responsible for assessing sideshow concession fees pushed his way up from behind.

The policeman thought this act of one man wrestling with himself was interesting, so he kept quiet and watched from the front row. But, as the old man turned around in his hunched-over position, he saw those thick leather boots and quickly assessed the position and importance of this member of the audience. The old man immediately pretended that Zhao Si was out of breath. He went limp and slid to the ground in a pile.

The old man quickly stepped out of his suit and smiled ingratiatingly at the policeman, as if to say, "Sir, how do you do, how do you do, *nin hao, nin hao.*" He took his hands out of the false legs and said softly to Wang Jiu, with self-deprecating humor, "See, our honored guest has indeed come. He wears a brown uniform and holds a pad of receipts for collecting his four-cent fees on floating concessions. He knows very well that we can't afford a simple wheatcake to fill our stomachs."

Looking at the people, he continued, "These people have come to watch us wrestle. It's really hot. But our honored guests are just standing there. Wait just one moment, and we'll begin."

He eyed the policeman, but he didn't have a cent on him, so, after a moment, he looked at the sizable crowd that had gathered and began to bow and solicit money. "Honored guests, my apologies for the delay in this hot weather. Those who have some change on you, please spare us a little. Those whose wallets are empty, please stay around and give us moral support."

Some in the crowd threw him a coin or two, but the others just stood still and looked on. Then a young army officer tossed a handful of coins before walking away with a frown on his face. The old man had to walk to the edge of the crowd to pick them up. Because he still had the legs of the puppet tied to his waist, they moved this way and that as he walked, which the crowd found uproarious.

The policeman had already made a mark on the piece of paper and was preparing to give it to the old man. The puppeteer looked it over, quickly counted out four coins in his hand, and gave them to the policeman. Murmuring, "Wang Jiu, Wang Jiu," the policeman went away with a smirk on his face. When he had left, the old man rolled up the receipt and stuck it behind his ear. He said to the puppet, "Wang Jiu, four cents isn't much, is it? You're hot, are you? You aren't even sweating. But look at the poor policeman. He sweats a lot because he has to walk all over the place!" At this point, he thought about the sweat on his own head. He crouched down and used Wang Jiu's shirt to wipe his own sweat, hoping to elicit a laugh from his audience. But no one laughed.

The old man belonged to that class of people in society that performed for others. They acted and sang, not because they were especially good, but because people came to watch them, out of curiosity and pity. When it came time to pay, those who could afford it paid without hesitation, but in every case, as soon something new began elsewhere, the crowd would suddenly dissolve and move on.

At a concession selling lotus fruits under the shade of the willows, a person had fallen down unconscious from heat stroke. No one knew what had happened, but, because someone had run over there, a crowd of people followed. In a moment, half the crowd that was watching the puppet show disappeared. Those remaining also seemed to notice the hot sun beating down on their heads. They, too, began to leave.

The college student who looked as if he were testing the waters before a dive also seemed to remember that he had something to do. He disappeared into the crowd along the road.

Now there were only seven people left.

The old man looked around and smiled. Without a word, he clasped his hands together and crouched down again to pick up his puppet. He put the puppet clothing over his head, placed his arms through the puppet's legs, then shook his shoulders and began the same act all over again. His strange motions attracted four more people, but soon five others left. When a real fight broke out elsewhere, the rest of the people all left in a hurry.

The old man continued with his act. He lifted up the false legs, making it look as if Wang Jiu had lifted Zhao Si's entire body. He energetically tipped his shoulders to the right and to the left, as if the two puppets were viciously attacking each other. Finally, after the fierce struggle, he would fall down, always in the same way. It was, of course, Wang Jiu who had defeated Zhao Si.

When the old man emerged from the heap of old, tattered clothing, there was only one observer left, a short policeman who stood there with a smile on his face. But he loomed especially large and appeared particularly happy, for he was the only one there.

The old man went up to him, bowed, and felt for the receipt he had stuck behind his ear. It had disappeared. Searching for it in the pile of clothing where the puppets were, he found it on the ground. Instead of inspecting at it, the policeman just looked with a silly grin at the pair of false legs tied to the old man's waist and walked away, shaking his head.

The old man sat down on the ground in the same posture as the puppets and counted the money in his can. He smiled at the white-faced puppet, Wang Jiu, speaking to him in the same tone of voice he had used to capture his audience, and with the same self-deprecating humor. His voice was affectionate and tender. He did not want people to know that he had had a son named Wang Jiu, a son who died in a fight with Zhao Si. He never told anyone. He only let the people see the fight between them. Although he kept Wang Jiu at a disadvantage, giving Zhao Si the upper hand at first, it was Wang Jiu who always won in the end.

Wang Jiu had been dead for ten years now, and the old man had been performing this act all over Peking for about as long. As to the real Zhao Si, he had died of hepatitis in Baoding prefecture five long years ago.

Guisheng

"Guisheng," written in March 1937, is virtually a summation of country folk as a moral type. It is one of the last times Shen treated them in the abstract, as timeless beings innocent of the tides of history. Amah Wang and Qiaoxiu in the stories that bear their names below are affected by war and civil war. In those stories, one cannot escape the possibility that the character of the Chinese people may some day change.

Guisheng is a poor hired laborer who wears cast-off clothing and addresses his master in terms that may seem servile. But he has dignity, freedom, and joy, and he never accepts a gift from the master without giving country things in return. He does not dwell on his poverty and in fact makes a good living from the fecund natural surroundings. He is socially "backward," bad at conversation, and in some situations apparently dumb. But he has his own skills, aspirations, and, surprisingly, as we see from the ending of the story, a fair amount of slow-burning resolve and ability to take drastic action. Both superstitious and practical, he is not fatalistic, for unwillingness to accept fate is his ultimate undoing. What he really thinks is enigmatic, as in so many of Shen Congwen's stories. But there is no doubt that he does think and that his thoughts are complex.

The setting, of course, is West Hunan, evidently near the village of Xikou just down the Chen River from Gaocun (today called Mayang). Socially, Shen Congwen would no doubt include the kitchen hands and Uncle Duck Feathers with Guisheng in the class of country folk, even the shopkeeper's daughter and her well-to-do father, who exchanges her for the highest bride-price – and certainly her stolid, now deceased mother, who fits the image of the country woman as described in "Mountain Spirit," "Snow," and many other stories, including "Amah Wang" and "Qiaoxiu and Dongsheng." This is not a view of country society that Marxists could condone. Income gaps are quite irrelevant to the story. Evil is not; it unites the classes. "Guisheng" may even be called a parable about the harmfulness of supersti-

tion to all social classes. In that regard it is a typical "May Fourth" story, as also in its self-conscious use of rustic language for cameo effect. Its view of country virtues is what sets it apart. Yet the final evil deed in the story seems to rest with Guisheng. Or can he be excused for being driven by society – not so much by class oppression as by an environment of "feudal superstition"? This story shows the soul of the country person to have a dark side. Where ultimate responsibility for that lies, whether in the individual who does not accept fate or in society, remains moot.

Guisheng[1] whetted his sickle by the brook, grinding away at the blade until it glistened. He ran his hand over the edge to test its sharpness, then made a few practice jabs into the water. The brook waters had been running brisk and utterly transparent since the coming of autumn. Myriad tiny shrimp clung with their legs to the water weeds, bobbing up and down in the shallows and occasionally curling up their little bodies to spring away, as if for joy. Guisheng felt joy just to see them. The weather was wonderful, the season just what refined city people called "the clear skies and crisp air of autumn." If Guisheng used his sickle well, he could get through the winter without wanting for fish or meat. The cogongrass blanketing the hills and hollows had blossomed with the fall, its white flowers swaying in the breeze and beckoning him, "Come, cut me, my strong big brother, now that you've honed your blade in the fine weather; quickly, come cut me, carry me into town, eight hundred cash the load, good for half a catty of salt, or a whole catty of pork, whatever suits your pleasure!"

Guisheng knew its worth. He knew that for ten loads he could buy a boar's head. Rubbed in four ounces of salt and cured for a fortnight, the ears would last him two or three drinking bouts. During the rice harvest the month before, when everyone else was letting the water out of their terraced fields and using chicken coops to pounce on the fat carp stranded there, Guisheng had honed his sickle, lit a torch, and gone alone to the stream in the middle of the night to stab a dozen big fish that slipped by. He'd salted them down and hung them above his kitchen stove to smoke till they were dry as a bone. This time he was whetting his sickle to cut cogongrass. He would carry the bundles into town on a shoulder pole to exchange for things he

[1]"Nobly Born."

Translated by Jeffrey Kinkley

needed for New Year's. There was a saying for it: "With strong arms and a good bod', you can be as happy as a little god." Since everything sold in town had got so expensive these last few years, villagers couldn't live nearly as well as they used to. But a bachelor in the prime of life who wasn't afraid of work and didn't usually go on a toot after sundown could get by easily enough.

Guisheng lived about seven miles from town and a mile from Fifth Master Zhang's stockaded estate. Fifth Master was the richest man around; he owned most of the hills and fields in these parts, so those who did the farming all had to deal with him one way or another. Fifth Master had wanted Guisheng to work for him on long-term contract, but Guisheng knew that meant either living on his estate or looking after his preserves in the hills. That would be too restrictive, so he turned it down.

Moving stones to a piece of Fifth Master's land at the foot of a slope not far from the brook, and felling bamboos and stripping tree bark with his own sickle, Guisheng built himself a little shack near the hillsides that Fifth Master had had planted with tung-oil trees, which he could guard in lieu of rent. He earned his daily expenses cutting firewood and grass. In the agricultural busy seasons of spring and autumn, when short-term laborers were in demand, there wasn't a farm two miles around that didn't ask him to help out (he ate enough for two, but then he had the strength of two men).

To greet the New Year, villagers went around getting contributions to make dragon lanterns for the competition in town, and during the dragon dance it was Guisheng who went ahead of the dragon to tease it with the magic pearl, an orb of embroidered red cloth that he brandished like a ball of fire, to cheers from the crowd. During the spring and autumn offerings to the tutelary gods, when the villagers got together to act out their own operas, he played the comic part of Mother Wang, the cauldron mender, and that of Cheng Yaojin, the general who had begun as a firewood seller. He liked a drink now and then, but he didn't get drunk with the pack and get into fights. He enjoyed chess, without being obsessed with the game. And sometimes he'd tell a joke, but never at the expense of others. He could be a little dense, but not to the point of making a fool of himself. And though he was a poor man, he had strength and self-respect. When he went to the estate, Fifth Master would sometimes give him a jacket, a pair of trousers, or half a catty of salt. Feeling uneasy about taking things for nothing, he would bring Fifth Master something in return another time.

He went into town often, to sell firewood and grasses and buy his provisions with the money. He had a fifty-year-old uncle in town who cooked for a rich family. Guisheng didn't see much of him, but the two were on good terms. When Guisheng called on his uncle, he always brought a gift; if not a sack of walnuts or chestnuts, then a weasel or a pheasant he had trapped in the hills. Sometimes he stayed with his uncle while in town. When free of an evening, the uncle would take him up the riverbank to the Tianhou temple to take in a night opera and afterward treat him to a bowl of noodles with beef.

Guisheng was known and liked in all the country villages for miles around. But he liked to hang around at a little store not far from home, at the foot of the bridge in the village of Xikou. It was a general store; the proprietor, a man named Du from Pushi, a town in the middle reaches of the River Yuan, had started out as a traveling peddler. He had made his rounds to each village monthly, selling every sort of condiment and utensil to the country folk, until later that bridge caught his eye. Seeing so much highway traffic there, he decided it would be better to settle down by the bridge than to bear his city goods all over creation. He could do business with all the villages and build a pavilion where passersby could rest their weary bones while he did business with them. So he set up shop at the foot of the bridge. That settled, he moved in his wife and his young daughter, thirteen years old.

People from Pushi are kind and gentle folk to start with, and he'd been coming to all the villages and stockades around for some years, so naturally his business prospered once he had that shop by the bridge. His wife still made herself up like a Pushi matron, wearing a long, black crepe turban all year round, and plucking her eyebrows very thin. She waited on people attentively and spoke most ingratiatingly, addressing men as "Elder Brother" and women as "Elder Sister-in-Law." It wasn't six months before the shop by the bridge had become, not just a place for country folk to shop, but a favorite gathering place. Three great shade trees at the foot of the bridge made it particularly cool and comfortable. When you had a spare moment, you could lie down for a nap under the trees, and breezes would refresh you from head to foot. In winter, they burned big logs and cakes of pressed oil on the earthen floor of the shop, which made a very bright fire. It couldn't have been better.

Guisheng got on well with the shopkeeper family, young and old alike, and he was very handy. So the proprietor's wife had treated him very well the last few years, and he was good to her daughter, too. The hills were teeming with wild melons and fruit, and it wasn't unusual to find chestnuts and hazelnuts up there. In the third month he picked strawberries for her. In the sixth month he brought loquats. In the eighth and ninth months he took her the banana-shaped akebia fruit for which the area was famous, their pulp shaped like sea slugs and jade white like the driven snow. She liked them especially. The girl's name was Jinfeng, or Golden Phoenix.

The year before, the proprietress had died of a heart attack at a wedding feast in Pushi, so a young fellow had taken her place at the store. They called him "Scabby" – not because of any physical defect, but because he was jumpy, fidgeting and scratching all the time like a person with ringworm.

For some indefinable reason Guisheng didn't particularly like Scabby. They took opposite sides in most every conversation. But Scabby always smiled and tittered back at him. Guisheng said, "Scabby, if you lived in town, you'd be a hoodlum, and if you were in a book, you'd be a scheming official." Scabby kept smiling at him. Nobody could guess why Guisheng disliked Scabby – but the proprietor, he knew. Guisheng feared that Scabby would become the proprietor's son-in-law – that he might rise from subordinate to equal.

In fact, just as Guisheng was down by the creek, puzzling over whether Scabby might become an "oil peddler" like the lad in the old story[2] who married above himself just through patience and solicitousness, Fifth Master's estate sent word that Guisheng was to take a look to see if the tung-oil nuts were ripe on the south slopes, then report back to the master.

Guisheng set out at once to inspect.

The soil up there was soft and crumbly underfoot, the tree roots and undergrowth noisy with the sounds of autumn insects. Crickets – big black ones and the "golden bell" singing variety with tiny heads and pointed tails – leaped out in all directions wherever he trod. He surveyed several hilltops. There they were, the boughs of every tree bent low from an overload of robust tung nuts. Many had already dropped to the ground; they littered the undergrowth at the foot of the hillsides. A long vine that lay across one of the ridges had come to fruit and was covered with ebony-black balls; a flock of mountain magpies was chattering nearby. Realizing that the akebia fruits must be ripe, Guisheng hurried over, sending the magpies flying. He picked every one of them off the vine, half filling his

[2]By Feng Menglong.

broad-brimmed rain hat, to take to Jinfeng at the foot of the bridge.

By the time Guisheng returned home, it was still early in the afternoon, so he went to the estate respectfully to inform Fifth Master.

When he got there, he saw a palanquin parked in the courtyard and several bearers squatting on a stone roller, smoking dry tobacco in their long bamboo pipes and resting with their eyes closed. Guisheng realized at once that a visitor had come in from town; he went around to the storage barn to find Uncle Duck Feathers, a hired worker of Fifth Master's who sat out there every day to weave straw sandals. No one was there, so Guisheng went out to the cookhouse. Uncle Duck Feathers had seated some young fellows from town at his little table for a feast. With his bucket dipper he was scooping up wine from a great black earthen cask and frying up fish to help it go down. When Guisheng showed up, he was invited to join in. It was Fourth Master who had come to visit, Fifth Master's older brother. Just back in town from his official post in Henan, he had hastened to call on Fifth Master so they could spend a few days together before he returned to Henan. The fellows in the cookhouse were swapping all sorts of interesting stories about their respective employers.

A short, bald-headed man with the rough air of an old soldier sniggered, "They say our Fourth Master womanized his way right out of a cavalry brigade commission. When a man likes to play around, his losses are credited to him in the account book of fate. Even if he doesn't dissipate his wealth during his lifetime, he can't cheat the king of hell; he'll have to lose it after he dies, in the next life. Last year, while our unit was camped in Runan county, Henan, he had himself eight women in one month – worked his way through all the best ass the place had to offer and still complained, 'What the devil kind of place is this? The sweetbreads on the menu here are down in the bladder category!

Pale as dough about to go bad and all flabby – no fun at all, yet they act like they're really something!' Can you guess how much he spent on them? Forty yuan in one night, and that's not even counting the tip to the pimp. You may say that young fellows away from home can't run wild like that, but I ask you, friends, could we ever get the chance? Seven yuan sixty a month – what's left, after they deduct three yuan thirty for our rations? If you went without shaves and laundry for a year, you couldn't save enough for one fling! Even if you gave me permission, Uncle, where would I get the wherewithal?"

Another tall, army veteran type said, "*Fifth* Master's all right. He's not as reckless that way with his money as Fourth Master. When he fools around with women, he does so in moderation; sure, he'll blow eighty here, a hundred there, but there's always a limit to it in the end."

Uncle Duck Feathers said, "Some like leeks, and some like meat; it all depends on what's your treat. It's not painted ladies that shake money out of our Fifth Master; it's those painted dice. When he lived in town with his old mother, he dropped twenty-eight thousand in a single night, and the operator of the joint came to Fifth Master's home to collect. The old woman was concerned with face. Afraid that Fifth Master would be so disgraced he couldn't face people in public, she had us dig up her silver from beneath the cellar floor. We unearthed one pair of ingots after another, and she counted them out before the proprietor. Having cleared his debt, she smiled at Fifth Master and said, 'Let this swindle be a lesson to you. Let's not do it again. When you're not on a lucky streak, don't put down stakes so others can nibble away at you like you were a live bar of silver yourself and go around saying that the Zhang family is paying its retribution.' "

"I heard tell that the old lady choked to death on her anger."

"Isn't that the truth. Such a lot of face, thirty thousand

worth – she'd have had to be distressed, however refined she was. It was clear as could be that Fifth Master was cheated, but she couldn't say it, any more than a dumb person can complain after he's eaten bitter medicine. How could she keep from being apoplectic? She bottled up her anger in bed for forty days, then the jig was up – she was dead."

"But Fifth Master was a filial son. When the old lady died, he saw to it that she got the whole seven-week, forty-nine-day Daoist rite for her funeral. Spent sixteen thousand yuan in the process – it was the talk of the town. Everybody had to admit the old lady had a good heart and good fortune to match. She enjoyed her luxuries to the fullest while alive and still took with her thousands of paper silver ingots and forty effigies of maids and serving girls to see to her trunks and wait on her all the way up to the Western Paradise. The turnout and excitement were even greater than at Old Lady Duan's funeral – the funeral banners and memorial scrolls stretched a mile long. When your son does his filial duty, you can die without regret."

Uncle Duck Feathers said, "Fifth Master feared people would laugh at him, that's why he wanted such conspicuous face – because the old lady had always been worried about face, and he was really her nephew, a son she adopted because she was heirless. Yet he got such a tremendous inheritance out of it. With the old lady gone, Fifth Master just couldn't spend too much on her, and that was only right. It wasn't just face for her but for him, too. Everybody thought him a fool, but not a chance! If he just wasn't addicted to gambling, what other cares would he have?"

"I heard that he lost another five thousand in town not so long ago. Then, to wash away his bad luck, he decided to 'hang up his clothes' with a virgin at the Chez Lin Daiyu bordello who called herself the Southern Flower Consort of Chu. Six hundred bucks to do anything he wanted – Fourth Master helped him negotiate it with the madam. But for some reason Fifth Master changed his mind at the last moment and went off to play cards in the back room of that foreign outfit, the American Standard Oil firm. They 'took him for a ride on a sedan chair,' three 'chair bearers' hoisting the one of him, and that night he lost another eight hundred. Six hundred here to a 'Flower Queen' he didn't even deflower, eight hundred there that didn't get him anywhere, a whole night carried around on a palanquin lifted by three shills – when it was all over, people were mocking Fifth Master, thanking him for his 'philanthropy.' That really made him see red."

"A spotted-leg dog's not a white-faced cat. Each has his own temper. When a fortune comes to you, you spend it, jingly jangly jing. How can you not? These people are rich without a lick of work; their fortune's in their fate. If your fate tells the money to come, even a door plank won't block it. If your fate tells that money to go, you can't keep it tied up, not with a rope, not even with a chain. If Shoemaker Wang finds a bar of silver, he can take it to bed with him, clutch it real tight, but, when he wakes up, it'll have turned to mud. Strange, you say? We folk are poor folk; nothing at all is in our cards – except maybe liquor, now and then. After this bowl, let's have another! Join us, Guisheng. We're all brothers here; don't stand on ceremony."

Not wanting to drink, Guisheng carried a big bag of chestnuts over to the stove and put them in the hot embers to roast. He told Uncle Duck Feathers that he'd been up in the hills to inspect the tung-oil trees for Fifth Master and that there was a bumper crop this year. In three days it would be the season of White Dew,[3] just right for beating the nuts off the trees. Whatever date was picked for the harvest, he would be there to help. Did Fifth Master have any further instructions? If not, he would be on his way home.

Uncle Duck Feathers went to Fifth Master and respectfully reported, "Guisheng from down by the brook has

[3]In the ninth month.

inspected the tung-oil nuts, sir. Those hills are well exposed to the sun, and the season of Frost's Descent[4] falls early this year. The nuts are ripe, so it's about time to pick them. Guisheng wonders if Fifth Master has any further instructions for him."

Fifth Master had been discussing fortune-telling and physiognomy with his citified brother, telling how a certain Half Idiot Yang in town could use his philosophical vision to tell whether the year would be lucky or unlucky for a person and the auspicious and inauspicious determinants of his fate. Fifth Master was just going into a rapture about it when he got the news that Guisheng was at hand; he asked Duck Feathers to call him in for a word.

As Guisheng entered the courtyard, he quickly removed his straw sandals, lest he dirty Fifth Master's floor. He went before the master barefoot.

"Guisheng, have you seen the tung nuts on our southern hills?" said Fifth Master. "They're very good this year, and the tung-oil firms in town have raised their prices. Twenty-two taels, three cents a barrel is the price they've hung out on their boards. Foreign companies in Shanghai and Hankou are buying like crazy. The newspapers say Europe is getting its navies in shape for a world war. They're buying tung oil to coat their ships, buying it in quantity. Those hairy, fur-ball foreigners go in for face – even if their country is poor, they can't stand to let their armaments be second to others'. I say let 'em fight! We Chinese can get *fur*-ociously rich off it."

Guisheng didn't have a clue what Fifth Master was saying; he just stood there in a corner of the great hall, with a mixture of awe and dread.

"Fifth Master, when shall we gather the tung nuts?" Uncle Duck Feathers said, to break the impasse.

"To corner the supply, better make the fur fly," chuckled

[4]At the beginning of the eleventh month.

Fifth Master. "If the foreigners are waiting for our Chinese tung oil to coat their ships so they can go to war, dare we slack off? Tomorrow or the next day, either one. I'm going myself, to inspect, and Fourth Master and I can hunt a couple of rabbits. Are they very plentiful in the hills this year, Guisheng? The weather looks good, so let's go tomorrow."

"Fifth Master," Guisheng said, "if that's your decision, then tomorrow it is. I'll have a pot of tea on, for when Fourth Master and Fifth Master drop by to take a break. If that's all, then I'll be going."

"Go right ahead," said Fifth Master. "Duck Feathers, give him a catty of salt and a couple catties of sugar to take back."

When Guisheng had given his profuse thanks and turned to leave, Fourth Master suddenly put in, "Guisheng, have you taken a wife yet?" That was a question Guisheng didn't know how to answer. Gazing at the lecherous old ex-army officer straight in his thin face, Guisheng just shook his head with a foolish grin. The man's haggardness reminded Guisheng of a phrase that was going around: "Your wife, your wife, the bane of your life; three years' trying to meet her demands will wear you all down, till you're nothing but glands."

Duck Feathers spoke for him: "We keep urging him to get married, but he's afraid of being bewitched, too scared to take the plunge."

Fourth Master said, "What are you afraid of, Guisheng? What's so frightening about women? You're not the kind who's likely to be henpecked. I tell you, if you see someone you like, marry her. Having a wife can be useful to you, don't you see? Come on, try; no need to be afraid."

Remembering the conversation he'd just heard in the cookhouse, Guisheng simply answered, softly, "Every man has his own destiny. You can't force it." Then he followed Duck Feathers out.

Fourth Master grinned at Fifth Master and said, "Fifth

Master, Guisheng is a good-looking fellow, don't you think?"

"A big dimwit," answered Fifth Master. "I'm afraid that, even if he got a wife down on his wedding bed, he wouldn't know what to do with her!"

On his way home with the sugar and salt, Guisheng went out of his way to stop by the general store at the foot of the bridge. But, when he got there, he found that the proprietor had left for town to buy supplies, leaving behind only Jinfeng, mending shoe soles as she sat by the wine vat. She smiled affectionately at Guisheng, welcoming him in. Guisheng wasn't quite himself. Standing in front of the counter, he fumbled for his pipe and flint lighter so as to sound nonchalant, then asked, "Will the proprietor be back soon?"

"Guisheng, have you been to town, too?" she asked. "What's that you've got in your hands?"

"A catty of salt and two of sugar, gifts from Fifth Master. I went to his estate to tell him to gather the tung-oil nuts."

"Does your Fifth Master treat you well?"

"Fourth Master from town was there, too. He said he'd go into the hills tomorrow to hunt rabbits." Guisheng thought of the advice Fourth Master had given him. He began to chuckle.

Not seeing what was so funny, Jinfeng asked Guisheng, "What kind of person is this Fourth Master?"

"A high military officer. They say he's been a general, a commander. But he's loved to play around his whole life long, and in the end he lost his commission."

"Rich people always spend their time that way, whether they're officials or merchants. The owner of the Yuanchang shop in our town of Pushi floated ten timber rafts from Hongjiang downriver to Taoyuan county.[5] He lost them in a single night."

[5]A center of prostitution.

Guisheng already knew this story. When men told it, they always said that the rafts had got lost in a "cave."[6] So he slipped and said, "Blame it on women."

Flushing scarlet, Jinfeng gave Guisheng a reproachful glance. "What do you mean, blame it on women! How many women do you know? There are good ones and bad ones, just like you men; you can't generalize."

"I didn't mean you!"

"You men are awful! Fourth Master, Fifth Master – their money makes them lords. They ruin women, as if they weren't even human beings – "

Just then, three travelers, paper merchants, crossed the bridge and unloaded the goods from their shoulders. There at the thatched shed in front of the store they could smoke their pipes and see what might be on hand to eat. They each ordered a bowl of wine and shared some popped corn to go with it.

Guisheng had more to say to Jinfeng, but he didn't know how. Since the three men didn't immediately go on their way, he went down by the bridge to wash his hands and feet. He came back just as the men were preparing to leave. The youngest, who dressed like a gigolo and flirted like one, too, beamed as he cast Jinfeng a sideways glance. When he paid the bill, he lifted his jacket to display the big silver chain on his embroidered waist vest. And he said, very softly, "A heart can't be bought, even with thousands of pieces of silver. A girl can buy precious jewels easier than she can find a true love." These words were intended for Jinfeng's ears. When the three men had left, Jinfeng sat on the wine vat, silent and with her head down, her thoughts a million miles away. Guisheng wanted to continue their conversation where they'd left off, but he couldn't get started.

Finally he took a cue from the good weather and said,

[6]That is, a "vaginal cave."

"Jinfeng, if you'd like some chestnuts, they've been bursting out of their hulls up in the hills recently. A couple days ago I set a trap. When I went to check it in the morning, a squirrel was bent over it, eating a chestnut. He made off at the sight of me, completely unruffled. Really funny. Come over tomorrow to gather chestnuts. The ground is covered with them!"

Jinfeng paid no attention to him. She was still angry over the impertinent words spoken by the traveler. Not realizing this, Guisheng said, "Remember that year when you snuck some chestnuts out of that sandy grove of mine? If you hadn't run away so fast, I'd have made you sorry!"

"I remember, and I didn't run. I'm not afraid of you," Jinfeng retorted.

"I'm not afraid of you, either," Guisheng said.

"You're afraid of me now – " Jinfeng smiled at him.

Seeming to understand what she was driving at, Guisheng squinted and smiled. He kept his answer in his heart: "I couldn't possibly be."

Scabby arrived with a big load of hay. On seeing Guisheng he yelled, "Guisheng, didn't you promise to go up into the hills to cut fodder?"

Ignoring him, Guisheng told Jinfeng he had found a lot of akebia fruit up in the hills. She could come to his place and help herself if she liked because tomorrow was the day for gathering tung-oil nuts and he had to go up into the hills to help out. What with Fifth Master and Fourth Master coming, too, to hunt rabbits, he'd be too busy to bring them over.

When Guisheng was gone, the assistant said, "Jinfeng, that big lummox is as slow as he looks, really."

"You'd better watch your mouth," she retorted. "He can flatten you if you get him mad."

Scabby said, "His kind don't get mad. And I'm not a tin teapot. He can't flatten me."

The next day at dawn, Guisheng went up into the hills with his sickle. The foot of the hills was blanketed in mist, like a white rug slowly unfurling and thinning out. Far off in the distance could be seen the shady trees of the Zhang family estate, and a few old ginkgoes thrust up toward the sky, further proof of the estate's financial prosperity. They all seemed floating on top of the clouds, distant and impermanent. It occurred to him that Fifth Master and Fourth Master might still be asleep there on the estate, dreaming of the guess-fingers game and mah-jongg they played when drinking.

But soon he heard the clatter of horse bells coming from the ridges between the fields and the hubbub of voices. So Fifth Master and Fourth Master were out early after all. Guisheng hurried down the slope to lead their horses. Twelve hired hands had come in all, including women, plus four servants and several children from the estate, to help glean the nuts. They all began to work the moment they arrived, starting from the top of the hill. Some climbed up into the trees, while the others beat the branches with bamboo poles from below. Wine-colored nuts tumbled across the entire expanse of dirt and grass.

Fourth and Fifth Master looked on for a while, then took up bamboo poles of their own and took a few swats. They soon grew tired of this and asked Guisheng to take them to his house. The water was already boiling in the pot on his stove. Duck Feathers steeped tea for the two masters. When Fourth Master saw the akebia fruit in Guisheng's bamboo hat in the corner, he picked one up and chuckled.

"What does this look like to you, Fifth Master?"

"Fourth Master, you really haven't been around much – don't you know akebias when you see them?"

"Of course I do. I was just pointing out that they look like women's little – "

Having meant to give these fruits to Jinfeng, Guisheng felt uncomfortable to hear such an uncouth reference by

Fourth Master, so he said, offhandedly, "Take them home to eat, Fourth Master."

Fifth Master picked one out. After roasting it a while in the cinders, he plucked it out and peeled back the hard, black rind to get at the flesh. Fourth Master tried it and pronounced it too sickly sweet to eat, but he went on and on about the virtues of Guisheng's fishing rod.

This got him to talking about the different ways of fishing, in brooks, streams, rivers, oceans – not to mention the northern marshes. His disquisition was interrupted by the clear, crisp voice of a young girl calling for Guisheng over the fence. Guisheng hastened outside. He returned for the akebia fruit and left again.

Fourth Master's eyes didn't miss much. Peering from the doorway at the maiden's white turban[7] and her long, glossy black pigtail, he asked Duck Feathers, "Who's the girl?"

Duck Feathers said, "The daughter of a shopkeeper, the man from Pushi who has the general store by the bridge. Her mother died of a heart attack last summer when she went home to a wedding feast. She had only this one little girl. She's sixteen this very year, name of Jinfeng. They really should have named her after beautiful Guanyin, the goddess of mercy! The shopkeeper has had his eye on Guisheng for some time. Simple, strong, and a handy helper, he's one who could inherit and carry on the business. But Guisheng still can't make up his mind. It's like he's waiting for the wind to change. He's wasting time."

"Fifth Master," Fourth Master said, "you're like the last emperor of the last dynasty, luxuriously eating and drinking in your palace without a clue as to the hardships of the common people outside your estate. Why don't you get to know them? Beautiful country like this is bound to produce fertile land and good women – "

Duck Feathers put in, "The fortune-tellers say she has a

[7]Showing mourning for her mother.

bad fate, from a horoscope that's very heavy – enough to do in her parents and crush any husband – so nobody dares touch her. That must be what Guisheng is afraid of – dying before his time if he marries her – " Just then, Guisheng returned, red in the face. He wanted to say something but didn't know how, so he just rubbed his hands.

"Guisheng, what are you afraid of?" Fifth Master said.

Not at first realizing what he was talking about, Guisheng answered, with bewilderment, "I'm afraid of spirits."

Everybody laughed at that, and Guisheng couldn't help joining in.

They climbed a barren hill with two scrawny yellow dogs to hunt rabbits, but, when the day was half over, they had nothing to show for it. At noontime they returned to Guisheng's place. Fifth Master asked his hired hands how good the tung nut harvest was this year. Told that it was better than ever, he asked Duck Feathers to measure out three piculs for Guisheng, to reward him for his services. Then he and Fourth Master mounted their horses and rode back to their compound. Xikou was not on their way, but Fourth Master proposed that Fifth Master make a little detour with him and check out the bridge. They bought some food at the general store, chatting quite a while with the proprietor and getting a good, long look at Jinfeng before returning to the estate.

There Fourth Master chided Fifth Master again about being an emperor who didn't know the hardships of people outside his castle.[8] His intent was clear, and Fifth Master understood it.

"Fourth Master, you son of a gun, so you'd have me steal meat right out of the mouth of a poor mutt!"

Fourth Master clapped him on the shoulder. "Nonsense! If I were you, I wouldn't let a dog have a juicy leg of lamb in

[8]Since he could help them by marrying a commoner and sharing his wealth.

the first place. Didn't you notice those long eyebrows and bright eyes of hers? With a voice like a songbird, and spunky, too."

Fifth Master smiled without saying a thing. Each man had his own lot in life, and his was gambling. He never admitted to an error in the way he played; if he lost, it was due to bad luck, not lack of skill. He was amused that Fourth Master couldn't pass by a woman. Satiated now with all the delicate flesh served up in town, he was turning to "wild game" in the country.

Of course Guisheng knew nothing of what they were up to.

He only knew that he'd got three extra piculs of tung nuts this year and could glean two or three more. Left to ferment under his bed, they would keep his lamp filled the whole winter long.

Weeks passed. The foxtail grass surrounding his shack blossomed white and swayed in the breeze. Clusters of wild jujube dates lay by the wayside, yellow as gold. They'd turned from tart to sweet some time ago. Guisheng had made a dozen trips into town to sell his fodder and also took several baskets of the jujubes, which he sold to the medicine shop. That made it the tenth lunar month, Indian Summer. Wild peach trees by the brook had blossomed in the warm weather. During the evenings, Scabby set blazing fires with the logs where they lay outside the general store, as an invitation to the neighbors to come to the bridge and chat around the campfire. By this time of year the fodder was baled, the grain was in the storehouse, and the sweet potatoes were in the cellar; it was time for everybody to have a good rest, so people gathered there day and night. Weather permitting, it was especially animated in the evenings, when occasionally a soldier on home leave or a cinnabar merchant from the mines of Houziping and Datongcha would turn up, bringing news from Changsha. The talk ranged all over creation and always left the listeners spellbound.

When Guisheng went there, he usually sat by the fire but didn't say much. He listened to the others talk and every so often stole a glance at Jinfeng. When his eyes met hers, his blood raced. He also helped the proprietor with his chores and Jinfeng with hers. When it rained and he was the only one in the shop, he sat quietly by the fire, smoking his long pipe and listening to the click of the proprietor's abacus as he sat by his Standard Oil lamp, settling his accounts. Guisheng was pushing the beads of a mental abacus back and forth in his mind, reckoning up his own net worth. He knew that tung oil was going for a good price in town. He could exchange twenty-five catties of it for six catties of cotton and two of Sichuan rock salt. This year he had several piculs of tung nuts – a small fortune! He'd have pork, fish, whatever he wanted for the New Year – everything but someone to share it with.

Sometimes, when the proprietor had settled his accounts and had nothing else to do, he would fish an almanac with red covers out of the wine vat and read out the predictions day by day from the "human interactions" and "divine prognostications" columns. When he got to the day of Jinfeng's birth, he'd say her horoscope was ominous, extreme, heavy: if she didn't end up with the "rich people," she'd "bewitch people" – hurt them. Bringing her mother to ruin wasn't the end of it – there was more trouble ahead. At this Jinfeng just pursed her lips into a pained smile.

Sometimes when the proprietor was speaking in this vein he would abruptly ask his guest, "Guisheng, do you mean to get married? If you want a wife, I can help you out."

Staring at the flames shooting up in front of him, Guisheng answered, "Do you really mean that, sir? Who would want to marry me?"

"If you want a wife, there's one for you."

"I don't believe it."

"Who would ordinarily believe that the Heavenly Hound

could eat the moon?[9] You might not believe it, but when the time comes, and the Heavenly Hound really does eat the moon, you won't find a doubter anywhere. I'm telling you, when the cock thrush up in the hills wants a mate, he has to sing for himself. You'd better keep an eye out and learn some serenades: 'to-wit, to-wit, to-wife!' 'go-be-tweet, go-be-tweet, go-between.' "[10]

This kind of talk got Guisheng to thinking and made his blood race. Not knowing how to respond, he made a few cuckoo calls of his own.

Occasionally the assistant would stick his nose in, causing Jinfeng to answer for Guisheng: "Guisheng, don't listen to Scabby. He's full of nonsense. He set a trap behind the shop and said he'd catch a fox or an otter, and instead what he caught was my little spotted kitten." Although Jinfeng was talking about the assistant, she was really using his words to change the subject from her father's question.

Guisheng went home after midnight, carrying a torch and thinking as he went, "The proprietor has set a trap there, too, to catch a son-in-law." He couldn't help chortling. If one person set a trap and the other was willing to walk into it, things should be fairly simple. The problem was all in his mind. Guisheng was like most country folk, a little superstitious. A woman with a pink and white face, long eyebrows, and eyes that turned up at the corners had a physiognomy boding an early demise for those around her. And if she didn't ruin other people, she'd destroy herself. She'd be in the clear only when she reached eighteen! "Jinfeng is sixteen this year." This little superstition made him back away; the proprietor's trap failed to spring, missed its prey. But all favorable winds must change direction sooner or later.

[9]The folk explanation for an eclipse.
[10]The Chinese indicates onomatopoeic renderings of the calls of the cuckoo and the cock thrush.

One rainy day, Guisheng stayed inside to twine rope from wild grasses. He uncovered the tung nuts he'd been soaking under his bed and found that they had already turned warm and black. He poured out a half basketful to peel, but his mind was on his problems. There was no telling when the wind might change, so it suddenly struck him that he was taking a risk. Jinfeng was a big girl now and knew about men and women things; the assistant might end up a member of the household at any time. And there were the merchants out on the highway, men from Pushi selling pigs and looking to link up with people from home, and those driving cows to Guizhou, bringing back mercury on the return trip. They were all smooth talkers and free with their money. They crossed the bridge and had plenty of opportunity. Who among them could pass up this lovely flower? If one of them up and made off with her, wouldn't that leave him in the lurch! She was only human; she needed someone to rely on. Once that was fixed, her whole family would have its backstop. His approach to the problem might be a little too simple, too crude, but it did yield a decision: Shape your *baba* biscuits while the rice is still hot! He must act quickly — no more delays. The winds were coming from the right direction.

He decided to go into town the next day, to talk it over with his uncle.

So Guisheng went to town and sought him out. It happened that rich family for whom his uncle worked had invited guests and was preparing a banquet. They had called in a famous cook, and Guisheng's uncle was his helper. He was at the chopping block, cutting pig kidneys into pieces that would cook up into the shape of flowers. Seeing his uncle so busy, Guisheng stayed in the kitchen to help him peel scallions and shell soybeans. It was nearly the second watch, nine o'clock, before the dishes were all cleared away; the diners went straight to bed. The next day, the master of the house kept Guisheng's uncle busy all day again, making Inlaws' Gruel: dried longans, lotus seeds, fish, and meat all boiled up in a big pot. Guisheng still couldn't get to talk to him about his problem. On the third day, the uncle fell ill from exhaustion.

Guisheng went to a stand where fortunes were told by analysis of written characters the customers drew by lots. Guisheng selected the character *shuang*[11] for his uncle and drew a *hui*[12] for himself. Said the fortune-teller, Half-Immortal Yang, "Blessed events make people feel good in spirit and can cure their illnesses." He also explained that the character *hui* made up half of the characters for *happy* and *auspicious* – but also *talk*. "There'll be a lot of gossip, so do what you have to as soon as possible; delay will mean failure." Guisheng felt that this Half-Immortal Yang was really making good sense.

Back at his uncle's bedside, Guisheng told him he wanted to marry. The daughter of the shopkeeper by the bridge at Xikou was virtuous, and she came from good stock. She'd make him a good wife. She could help him feed the pigs and cut grasses, and he could help her turn the mill to make bean curd. If he could just get up the nerve to propose, he could be pretty sure of success. If the proprietor agreed, Guisheng had enough money to get married at the end of the year. There'd be one more mouth to feed but also someone to mend his clothes and rub his feet. He'd come to ask his uncle's advice about all the pros and cons.

When his uncle heard about this good prospect, he naturally was elated. He had just been struggling with what to do with the twenty yuan he'd saved up over the years – whether to buy himself a coffin for the future or purchase some piglets so someone could raise them for him. When he

[11]"Feel good."
[12]"Go back."

heard that his nephew wanted to take a wife, indeed, marry into a proprietor's family, he of course made up his mind on the spot, deciding to invest his money in this.

"If you need money for the feast, you needn't go to a revolving credit circle to borrow it. I'll help you out." The cook got up and placed all his savings in Guisheng's hands, after fishing them out from beneath the brick under one of his bedposts. "If you need it, take it all. Later, when you have children, let me count one of your sons as my little grandson, to burn three hundred yuan of spirit money for me each New Year after I'm dead, and I'll be happy."

"Uncle, I don't need so much money," stammered Guisheng. "I'm sure the shopkeeper won't accept any money or presents from me."

"Why not? You give it to him whether he wants it or not. It's not like you'll be a poor bachelor at loose ends any more, able to just skip a meal and tighten your belt whenever the pantry's bare. You can survive by roughing it when you're alone, but it won't work when there are two of you. You have to mind the question of face. When you take a wife, you've got to be able to keep her and raise your children. You can't live off Proprietor Du and let people say you're being kept by your wife. Take the money. What belongs to your uncle belongs to you."

When the two had talked it all over, Guisheng went out to shop. He bought seven yards of machine-woven blue cloth and seven of white, three catties of vermicelli made from beans, and a boar's head. Candles, paper, and incense, too, for a total of almost five yuan. When he had everything, Guisheng left for home with his purchases, walking on air.

Outside the city wall he ran into two hired hands from Fifth Master's estate, bearing baskets of goods into town on shoulder poles. Guisheng asked why they were in such a hurry.

One of them answered, "I don't know what's got into Fifth Master that's made him send us to town, to the Righteousness Conquers store. He made out a whole long list of things for us to get; it looks like he may be preparing for his son's wedding."

Guisheng said, "That's Fifth Master for you, big hearted and free with his money. He's not the kind to itemize everything before giving the go-ahead."

"Isn't that the truth. He rushes into a lot of things without thinking."

"A man of his power, when he does good, can become a Buddha in heaven; when he does bad, other people had better run for cover."

Noticing that Guisheng had bought quite a lot of things himself, one of the workers joked, "Guisheng, you're loaded down like you're getting ready to redeem a pledge to the gods. Could it be that you'll soon be inviting us to drink at your wedding?"

The other added, "Guisheng, you must have made a fortune in town to buy such a big boar's head. Twelve catties, am I right?"

Realizing that they were joshing him, Guisheng answered half in earnest and half in jest, "Three catties and a half, no more, no less. I'm planning to stew it and invite you over for a drink!"

As they parted, one of the workers said, "Guisheng, I can tell from your glowing face that you're overjoyed about something. You're holding out on us! That won't do among friends; you've got to come clean!"

This kind of talk made Guisheng glow the more. "Get off it," he guffawed, "I wouldn't keep a secret from you!"

That evening Guisheng made up his mind to go to the bridge at Xikou and have his talk with the proprietor of the general store. But, when he arrived, he learned that Proprietor Du was out on business. Guisheng asked Jinfeng where her father had gone and when he'd be back. She just said, lackadaisically, that she didn't know. When asked, the assistant said his master had gone to the estate, for what reason he didn't know. The atmosphere struck Guisheng as a bit strange; he wondered if father and daughter had quarreled, with the old man going off in a huff, leaving Jinfeng upset, too. Guisheng sat on his stool as usual, rolling an ember out of the baking pit with his foot and taking out his pipe.

Suddenly the assistant couldn't hold his tongue any longer. "Guisheng," he blurted out, "Jinfeng is about to ride in the wedding palanquin!"

Thinking that Scabby must know about his own plans, Guisheng looked at Jinfeng and asked, "Is this true?"

Jinfeng glared at the assistant: "Scabby, you're full of nonsense. I'll sew your lips together!"

The assistant leaned over and flashed Guisheng a silly grin: "If she does that, there'll be no one to play the *suona* at her wedding a few days from now."

Still thinking that Jinfeng was embarrassed in his presence, Guisheng changed the subject. "I went into town, Jinfeng, and spent three days at my uncle's."

Jinfeng hung her head and said, despondently, "You can have fun in town."

"I went for a purpose, to talk something over with my uncle – " Not knowing what to say next, he turned to the assistant: "Fifth Master is buying up supplies to entertain guests, too – must be a big shindig!"

"He's not just entertaining – "

The assistant meant to go on, but Jinfeng made him check to see if the gate to the duck run was closed.

As Guisheng sat there, she seemed as cold to him as a wok long removed from the burner. Proprietor Du still hadn't returned, and Jinfeng didn't seem to be paying attention to what Guisheng said. He could see that something was amiss and that he wasn't going to have much of a conversation with her. He'd smoked a few pipes, so it was time to leave.

Back home, he built a fire with some straw and a log from behind his house, then took out half a basket of tung nuts and by the firelight started peeling off the rinds with a paring knife. He sat up working until the wee hours. Something seemed to be gnawing away at his heart, but he couldn't quite say what.

The next day, just as he was about to set off for his talk with the proprietor, word came from Fifth Master's estate that feasting was going on there. Fifth Master had taken a concubine: the daughter of the man from Pushi who lived by the bridge. They'd already named the date, and she was to cross the threshold this very evening. Everybody was to come over before dark to help out, to carry the palanquin and receive the bride. This news struck Guisheng like a heavy blow from behind. He was stunned for a long time, unable to catch his breath.

When the messenger left, Guisheng still couldn't believe it. He rushed off to the store by the bridge, only to find Proprietor Du bent over the counter, putting money into red envelopes to reward the chair bearers.

When the shopkeeper saw it was Guisheng, he squinted his eyes into a smile and hailed him, "Guisheng, where have you been? We haven't seen you for days – thought maybe you'd done a Xue Rengui and run away to join the army!"[13]

"It's the bandits I'll be joining," thought Guisheng.

"Did you see any operas during all those days in town?"

Standing in the road outside the shop, Guisheng stammered at him, "Mister proprietor, mister proprietor, I have to talk to you. They say you're planning a wedding in your family – is it true?"

"Just look at these," said Proprietor Du, holding up the ceremonial red envelopes. He was beaming from ear to ear. He didn't need to say any more.

Hearing the sound of someone beating clothes under the bridge, Guisheng realized that Jinfeng must be doing the

[13]Tang dynasty general whose original enlistment is celebrated in a Peking opera, *Toujun bieyao* (Leaving the hearth to enlist).

laundry there. He went straight over to the railing to find her. Jinfeng had removed the white turban of mourning and was bending over to pound the laundry, a tiny red bridal flower pinned onto her long, ebony pigtail. "Jinfeng," Guisheng called out, "so you're getting married. Congratulations!" Jinfeng stopped her pounding but did not raise her head. She stood there silent. Guisheng could see from her expression that it was all true – that his own plans were completely dashed, forever. Everything was over. Unable to speak any more, he returned to the shop, glared at the proprietor, and marched off.

That afternoon, Guisheng went to Fifth Master's estate all the same.

There he found Fifth Master in the courtyard, wearing a turquoise-embroidered satin jacket over a light silk gown and ebulliently supervising the workers as they decked out the palanquin for the bride. Catching sight of Guisheng, Fifth Master said, "Guisheng, good to have you here. Have you eaten? Go have a drink in the cookhouse." "Which of the twelve animals matches your horoscope?" he added. "Those born in the year of the dragon can help me carry the palanquin tonight to the foot of the bridge at Xikou to receive the bride. Those born in the year of the tiger or the cat shouldn't go. They should hide when she gets here so as not to bring bad luck."[14]

Guisheng could barely get out the words, "I was born in the year of the tiger, the fifteenth of the eighth month, in the wee morning *hour* of the tiger. That makes me a tiger twice over." Then he stood there grinning foolishly and fidgeting with his hands and feet, the way he always did when he was at a loss for words. Seeing that the men Fifth Master had asked to fit out the sedan chair were making a mess of the carrying poles, he went over to give them a hand. Fifth Master asked him again if he'd had a drink, but

[14]Since the bride was born in the year of the rat.

Guisheng didn't answer. Uncle Duck Feathers, wearing a new blue cotton short gown, hurried over to look at the palanquin. He caught sight of Guisheng and took him off to the cookhouse.

There he found five or six workers sitting on stools by the fire, drinking and joking. They were the ones assigned to go to Xikou to receive the bride. The *suona* player, red in the face and running off at the mouth from drinking, said, "Proprietor Du is a real generous guy. When we get there, he's bound to give us some of those delicate Jiahu-style cakes he bought in town, and there're those red envelopes coming to us, too."

Another said, "I still owe him two hundred cash, and he's got it written down on his little blackboard. I'm afraid to run into him."

"Aw, he'll call off all your debts," Uncle Duck Feathers added, poking fun at the man. "Just be careful how you carry his daughter."

A bearded fellow said, "As you carry her, see how far down the road she keeps up her crying. If she's still mewling like a cat by the time you pass the big hollow and you want her to stop, tell her, 'Sister, if you cry any more, we'll take you back.' She won't dare keep it up after that."

"But what if she does?"

"Then we'll carry her back."

"And then what?"

"We'll bring her to the estate, but only if she doesn't cry. We'll insist that she laugh up a storm."

"And if she doesn't?"

"Doesn't laugh? I'll bet you one of my fingers she will." That made everybody roar with laughter.

The *suona* player was quite a card. He broke in with a dirty joke about a bride on her first trip back home to her parents' on the customary third day after the wedding. He raised his voice like a girl complaining to her mother: "Mama, I thought once I married that all I'd have to do was wait on my in-laws and bear them an heir. Mama, you can't believe how horrible my man is; he won't let me pee all night!" That set off an even bigger howl of laughter.

Guisheng didn't say a word. Biting his lower lip and repeatedly clenching his knuckles, he stared at the long nose on that red face, wanting to smash it in. But, when his hand went out, it was to lift an earthenware bowl. He drained it of half its wine in one noisy gulp.

The farmhands started betting on whether Jinfeng would cry when she was borne away from home. Some thought she wouldn't; others said she would, adding that her liquid eyes indicated a weeper. Things were getting pretty rowdy when the men fixing the palanquin joined them in the cookhouse. That really threw the place into an uproar.

The place was getting crowded and noisy. Guisheng went by himself to a shed by the storehouse. Finding an unfinished straw sandal there, he sat down and twisted some straws together to finish it. His mind was reeling; he didn't know what to do. He still had sixteen yuan weighing down his tightly laced belt purse. His thoughts went all over the place. Three catties of vermicelli, seven yards of blue cloth, a boar's head – of what use were they now? He'd taken a couple of piculs of tung nuts to the Yao family oil press to have the oil extracted, which was needed by the foreign ships with their big guns, so they could fight a war at sea. What was it that flirtatious merchant had said? "A girl can buy precious jewels easier than she can find a true love." Well, she'd found him. Old man Fourth Master had had his pleasure with eight girls still in pigtails[15] in a month and still said they were pale as dough, no fun at all. You government officials are always bringing ruin to other people!

It was getting dark.

A clamor of voices came from the courtyard. The *suona* player, pretty soused by now, had been blowing on his

[15]Virgins.

instrument inside the cookhouse and continued it on into the courtyard. Guisheng could hear people shout to light the torches, set off firecrackers, and get a move on. Two bronze gongs were resonating, as if to say, "Let's go, let's go, hurry up!" Indeed, within moments a troupe of men and horses left the compound and started south. One could hear the faint weeping voice of the *suona* far into the distance, as the procession made its way to the hills. Guisheng looked in on the cookhouse. There he saw some women who had come in to prepare refreshments of fruit in syrup. Spotting Guisheng, Uncle Duck Feathers asked him, "Guisheng, I thought you'd left. Help me out, will you? Carry some water. We'll need it later."

In utter silence, Guisheng carried the buckets outside on a shoulder pole. Fires had been made from kindling in the courtyard and candles lit in the central hall, which was hung with red cloth from the families of the bride and groom. Women and children of tenant families on the estate had gathered in the courtyard to get a look at the bride and enjoy the excitement. The shortest path to the well was through the main gate, but Guisheng went out the back gate, taking the long way. Only after seven trips, when the water vats were full, did Guisheng let up. He went to the stove to dry his sandals.

The yin and the yang and the bride's date of birth had put her in the year of the rat,[16] so it was best she enter her new household after it was completely dark. To avoid inauspicious conflicts with others in the house, anyone born in the year of the big cat[17] or little cat had to hide when she entered the compound. Ordinarily it would have fallen to Uncle Duck Feathers to dispatch and receive the palanquin, but since he was one of those who had to avoid contact with her, and figured that she would soon be arriving at the

---

[16]Which is nocturnal.
[17]Tiger.

estate, he took Guisheng to the bamboo grove out back to see the cabbages and turnips. He talked along the way.

"Everything that happens is fated, Guisheng, you can't fight it. When a physiognomist said that Deng Tong had the face of someone who would starve to death, the emperor tried to prevent it by granting him a copper mine, so he could mint his own money. Still he starved to death. Rich man Wang in town used to make his living selling dumplings from a little stand that he carried across his shoulders. Then his luck came in, while he was homeless, living in a little tutelary temple. It rained for two weeks on end. The foundations eroded, and the temple walls collapsed, nearly crushing Wang and his wife. But when they clawed their way through the mud, they found two tubs of silver that had been hidden in the walls. That's how he got his start. What was that if not fate? Who would have guessed that the little girl from the store by the bridge would be joining us here on the estate?

"Fifth Master is a learned man. He understands science, puts no stock in any belief, except that he goes to a foreign-devil doctor and lets them shoot him with 'hex' rays or something. Nothing else. It was when he lost another two thousand yuan during his last trip into town that Fourth Master put this idea into his head. 'Fifth Master,' he said, 'you're on a losing streak, and it shows no signs of stopping. Why don't you try getting a virgin to wash away your bad luck – then you'll win for sure. Those feathery hens[18] in town try to make you think they're virgins by splattering chicken blood from a pig's intestine during penetration. Their eyes are on getting your money coming and on deceiving you going. What good are they? But there are plenty of fresh girls in the countryside. Why don't you investigate?' Just as Fifth Master was beginning to get serious about it, that storekeeper's daughter came along, and he

[18]Prostitutes.

took a liking to her. Her father agreed at once. What's that, if not fate?"

Guisheng stepped on a rotten winter squash and slipped. He swore at himself under his breath, "Blinded by ghosts! Didn't see what was right there."

Uncle Duck Feathers thought he was cursing Proprietor Du's daughter, so he said, "Good things they can see fine; it's good people they're blind to."

"Guisheng," Uncle Duck Feathers continued, "to tell the truth, I could see early on that Proprietor Du and that little girl of his had their minds set on you. Outsiders have a clearer view than those involved. You didn't catch on. If only you'd had the gumption to speak for yourself, you could have done a great thing. Wild ducks fill the sky; reach up anywhere, and you can pull down a tasty morsel for yourself. When two sides are contending, the one that strikes first wins; remember the twenty-eight legendary figures who turned things upside down in Kunyang. He who holds back suffers disaster. You didn't make your move while you could, so you've no one to blame."

"You're joking, Uncle Duck Feathers," said Guisheng.

"Not at all! Fate decides all – the doings of men, a little, maybe. A fortnight ago I was sure that girl expected to have you at the bridge by her side, turning the mill while she made the bean curd. But you couldn't make up your mind, so you can't blame her." He was not really joking, but at this point Uncle Duck Feathers couldn't help laughing to think of the unpredictability of life.

The two walked up the ridge toward the bamboo grove. From there they could already hear the sad sound of the *suona* in the distance and the explosion of firecrackers. They knew the palanquin would soon be arriving with the bride. Suddenly the estate compound was in commotion, too. Torches were lit, and voices were raised. Some farmhands who were supposed to stay away came rollicking out back to the bamboo grove, and some even shimmied up the bamboo like monkeys to get a better view — to see if the procession had entered the compound yet.

As the sound of the *suona* drew near and the uproar in the courtyard grew wilder, they realized that the bridal palanquin had entered the main gate. Some who had feared to break the taboo now could stand it no longer and hurried inside to get in on the excitement.

Big, triple-shot firecrackers were set off, and the *suona* played a wedding song, "Heaven and Earth Unite." The bride and groom bowed to heaven and to earth, to the ancestors, and then to each other. The *suona* stopped playing, and the torches were extinguished one by one. Uncle Duck Feathers knew that the bride had been led inside and that the ceremonies were over. He took Guisheng back to the cookhouse, telling the torch bearers along the way to watch out not to cause a house fire. In the cookhouse, the men were opening red envelopes and counting their money or jostling to pour hot water into a wooden tub to soak their feet. They joked about how flustered Proprietor Du had been when he sent off the bride. And they said Proprietor Du and Scabby must be dead drunk by now so as not to have to think about how bad the girl felt on her wedding night. Uncle Duck Feathers poured more wine for the young people and set the table. When the young hired hands sat down to eat — a dozen or more, all told — they discovered that Guisheng had slipped away.

Deep in the night as Fifth Master dreamed with his arms around his bride, under a delicately woven canopy in a wooden bed with flowers carved into it, the dogs of the compound started barking wildly. Uncle Duck Feathers got up to see what was going on. There was a rosy glow on the horizon from a fire in the distance. Judging by the direction, it had to be by the brook. Before long, people were hurrying back to the estate with news of it. The general store was burning, and Guisheng's shack had caught fire, too. It was an extraordinary coincidence that two places were on fire at the same time. Nobody knew the facts.

Uncle Duck Feathers rushed to the scene of the fires, first to the bridge. The blaze raged fiercely. Even the big leafy trees by the bridge had caught fire. He could only look on from a distance. It wasn't yet known if Proprietor Du and Scabby had perished in the blaze or got out. Then he went to Guisheng's place. As he drew near, he found a crowd gathered to watch the fire, but no one had seen Guisheng. No one knew if he'd burned to death or escaped. Uncle Duck Feathers stirred the fire with a bamboo pole and tried to sniff, but there wasn't a clue whether he'd gone down in the flames. At heart, he understood. There was a reason for the fires. He met Fifth Master and his new concubine on the way back to the estate.

"Did anyone die?" asked Fifth Master.

"It was fated, Fifth Master," stammered Uncle Duck Feathers. "It was fated."

Looking back and seeing Jinfeng in tears, he thought, "Well, little girl, not happy to be a concubine? Go back and hang yourself. What are you crying for?"

People still rushed toward the flames.

The Vegetable Garden

Transplanted to the city, which thenceforth would be his home until he died, Shen Congwen began to cast his artist's eye on urban China, with all its change, foreign influences, and revolution. His fiction examined foibles of the gentry and the bourgeoisie: their love affairs and political activities, their psychological hang-ups, their complicated social loyalties and betrayals. A college teacher himself as of 1929, when he wrote "The Vegetable Garden," Shen Congwen began to write "problem" stories full of modern ideas, although not, typically, full-blown ideologies.

"The Vegetable Garden" ("Caiyuan") helped lead the "Shen Congwen craze" on Taiwan when the ban on him was finally lifted there in 1987. The story betrays a jaundiced view of revolution, but its popularity must be more complicated than that. The victims of the story are Manchus, the Inner Asian people who gave China its emperors during the last dynasty, only to become casualties in the 1911 revolution, the event supplying the founding myth for the old Sun Yat-sen/Chiang Kai-shek Nationalist regime that still rules the island. Taiwan was fast outgrowing that and more strident myths about the absolute correctness of the Chiang family's insistence, from the late 1920s when Shen wrote this story until the lifting of martial law on Taiwan in 1987, of suspending civil rights whenever necessary to combat communism. The young people executed in this story seem innocent, and one might infer that they are innocent and *Communist.*

"The Vegetable Garden" also has a feel for the culture of old China that is so valued on Taiwan – for the role of poetry and art when China was ruled by literati, the sacredness of marriage, and the nostalgia of old Peking. The symbol of it all (and potentially of Taiwan itself) is the garden, an oasis of culture amid turmoil, of stillness amid change. All this even though the story extols new-style marriage and the "new culture" of post-May Fourth Peking. Shen Congwen indeed paints a rosy picture of the capacity of the old ruling class to adapt itself to these new ideas – until the "unfortunate intrusion of politics."

"The Vegetable Garden" has many layers of meaning. One can read it as a story that does not ignore but frontally addresses China's quickly developing generation gap, showing two ways in which the gap can be resolved: with love or with executions. The story is rich in symbols. Yu, the name of the protagonists, means "jade," which typically is green, the color of life and of cabbages — or white, the color of death. In Chinese, the word for cabbage is "white leafy vegetable." Heaped into piles and covered with snow, they look to the Yu family like grave mounds. Although not as round as ours, Chinese cabbages are harvested with a sickle, which suggests decapitation. One of Shen Congwen's most vivid boyhood memories, from the defeat in 1911 of a local anti-imperial revolutionary putsch, was of human heads stacked in piles like a mountain. The images in this story must come from deep in the author's subconscious. But they can be looked at another way, too. In the days before refrigeration, the cabbage was the rock (sometimes literally) of stability and survival for the Peking poor, their chief vegetable for getting through the winter.

Not to overstress the story's significance for Nationalist China, note that, as commentary on revolutionary aftermaths, "The Vegetable Garden" is prophetic of Mao's Cultural Revolution, when Chinese intellectuals often repeated the words of Mrs. Yu: "For people like us, more knowledge means more trouble!"

The Yu[1] family was known for its leafy white cabbages. Their seeds were special; no one else in town could raise cabbages with such big hearts. For the Yus were a bannerman family of Manchus who had come here from Peking, bringing the seeds with them. And Peking, after all, was famous for its cabbages.

Yu Huichen,[2] Old Master Yu, had come to this little town as an expectant officeholder before the Republican Revolution of 1911. He brought his family and the cabbage seeds with him at the time, most likely just for his own use. But, soon after his death, the revolution followed, and the Manchus were overthrown. Although the Manchu noblemen had enjoyed great power and authority, they were all suddenly stripped of their position and privilege. Reduced to poverty, the bannermen scattered throughout the country and had to fend for themselves. Fortunately, the cabbage seeds the Yus brought with them from Peking were to save them from disaster. From that time forward, the family raised cabbages for a living, and their cabbage patch became a landmark for the whole district.

The mistress of the estate, Mrs. Yu, aged fifty, had been a beauty in her time. Even now you could tell that she was a beauty from the way she carried herself. She had a son, aged twenty-one, who was tall and pale skinned. Tutored at home, he was brought up with the urbanity of an aristocrat. But the other big families around, the newly arisen gentry, looked down on Manchus out of hatred for their past sins against the Chinese. And these days he was merely the son of a vegetable tender. But he was not like the sons of other vegetable growers. Though he had no close friends, he was still respected.

[1]"Jade."
[2]"Tabooed Treasure."

Translated by Peter Li

As the Yu family garden expanded, mother and son could handle the work by themselves no longer, so they took on several hired hands. Every autumn, the mother had the men dig a cellar. Come the snows of winter, the big white-leafed cabbages all went into storage, and thus the vegetable was on hand for the townsfolk all year long. Besides cabbage, the Yus planted other vegetables on their three or four acres. With their keen business sense, the Yu family was soon able to supply the town with all kinds of hard-to-get vegetables the year round. In ten years' time, they were rather well off.

It seemed as if their ethnic background caused very few people to associate with the Yus. Aside from the fact that they raised vegetables and were well-to-do, nobody seemed to know very much about them.

On summer evenings, this middle-aged woman, cultured and enjoying the "breath of the forest," the easy self-posses- sion of a woman – and earning her own living, too – stood unprepossessingly, fanning herself by the cool of the stream that ran just outside her garden. She was clad in a simple old-style dress of fine white linen. Her son was at her side, in a short-sleeved shirt and pants of silk. The two of them often stood there quietly, listening as the cicadas sang in the willow trees, or taking in the flow of water in the stream. The stream circled the garden and then flowed eastward. Its water was so clear that you could see through to the tiny shrimp and minnows at the bottom. But the fish were too small to be good for anything but looking. At that time of the day, most of them were at rest, too.

Evening breezes brought with them the fragrance of orchids and jasmine. There were many flowers and trees still in the garden, and they swayed gently in the breeze. Gazing up between the willow branches at the stars that had just come out in the night sky, the mother thought of poems written by the ancients. But she could not remember who had written those wonderful lines about the lonely goose that flew across the rosy evening sky. Turning to her son, she said, "The beauty of this scene must have inspired the ancients as it inspires us today. We should write a few verses."

"The ancients must have written something to that very effect, but I can't remember who."

"That's what I think. Maybe it was Xie Lingyun or Wang Wei. But I can't remember. I'm really getting old."

"Mother, why don't you try a verse, and I'll match your rhyme."

"All right. Let me think."

And the mother went at it for some time, softly intoning the words under her breath, but no words were capable of expressing the beauty of that scene. She was a little rusty, and, besides, it really was beyond words. As the Buddhists say, it could be apprehended in the mind, but not expressed in words. She smiled and said, "It's no good. I'm not a poet."

"Shaochen,"[3] she said after a moment, "how about you?"

The youth chuckled and said that it was a sacrilege even to speak before a scene such as this. To versify was to destroy it. The mother smiled when she heard this, and they crossed the bridge. Their shadows blended into the bamboo groves behind the white wall of the garden and disappeared from view.

But on other cool summer evenings mother and son would go into the garden to watch their workers build trellises for the melons and water the plants. They talked over what seeds to plant in the autumn and discussed the price of turnips. Sometimes they went into the garden themselves to look after the seedlings or dig irrigation ditches with their own hands. It was all so natural – poles apart from the idyllic poets who composed pastoral verse in the ancient style after one hour under a melon trellis or extolled the beauty of any old rustic bridge the moment they stepped foot outside the city.

[3]"Younger Treasure."

When the Yus' cabbages were on the market during the winter months, everyone in town feasted on them. They would think about the Yus as they ate, praising the cabbages and expressing gratitude to mother and son at the same time. The townspeople knew very little about the Yus, but what they did they admired.

Like any other town, this one had ten times as many ignorant people as smart ones. Soon there was a nasty rumor going around that the cabbages were so big and juicy because each head had been fondled by the mistress. *And this was the absolute truth.* From such dull-witted talk as this, one could see that the townspeople harbored jealousy of the Yu family on account of their comfortable circumstances.

The mother knew all kinds of ways of pickling the different parts of the cabbage – roots, leaves, and hearts – until they had all sorts of different tastes. But the young man's knowledge of these matters couldn't match his knowledge of literature. Even so, he spent more of the day tending the garden than reading and writing. His heart was pure and fine as the white feather of a dove; he needed study, and he needed play, and the vegetable garden had become part of his recreation. He wasn't able to haggle with people over small amounts of money, but this very weakness made him all the more personable.

The young man was not the sort to give up working with his hands because he knew how to read or to become haughty on account of his wealth. He slighted no one with whom he had dealings, not even the small vendors. Though he rightfully belonged to the educated elite, he did not feel it necessary that scholars such as he be put on a pedestal. He was sincere to others and expected the same treatment in return. He regarded sincerity as foremost in one's personal conduct. This young man's character and conduct were wholly the result of his mother's influence.

The time finally came for the young man to think about marriage, yet he had no one in mind. It was already the custom in this town for young people to marry of their own free will, on the basis of love. Still, many marriage brokers came to the Yus' home. These matchmakers made their rounds everywhere with professional dedication, thinking only of doing a good deed for two young people and procuring a very modest gift for themselves. Exaggeration had of course become one of the tricks of their trade, for they were zealous. When at last they realized that all their efforts were in vain with the Yus, the matchmakers finally gave up on going to see them.

Yet, thanks to the matchmakers' machinations, and for other reasons besides, many girls in town secretly wanted to become the Yu family bride.

On the son's twenty-second birthday, his mother prepared a special birthday banquet. After the feast that evening, mother and son sat across from each other sipping wine. It was the twelfth lunar month, and it had just snowed. From the window on the garden they saw white all the way to the horizon. Piles of cabbages stood in the garden, harvested but not yet stored underground. Covered with snow, they looked like a series of burial mounds. Then there were the unharvested cabbages, looking like row upon row of little snowmen standing in formation. After a few cups of wine, mother and son were holding forth on snow and on vegetables, claiming that turnips and cabbages needed a heavy snow to become truly flavorful. They pushed open the window, and the whole garden came into view.

The snow had stopped. It was very quiet and windless. The crows that had been pecking there for food earlier in the day had already flown away. "What a beautiful snow this year!" the mother said.

"It's just the beginning of the twelfth month. Who knows how many more snows we'll have this winter."

"People here consider even a light snow like this unusual. It's not even very cold. In Peking, a little snow like this is hardly worth mentioning."

"I hear that Peking has changed a lot lately."

"Even here, things have changed a good deal in the past ten years!"

As the mother spoke, she remembered all that had taken place in the last twenty years. She took another sip of wine.

"You're all of twenty-two today. It's eighteen years since your father passed away and fifteen years since the revolution. The world has changed. So has our family. I'm fifty this year, and I'm getting old. I've raised you all the way to adulthood, to keep the Yu family line from dying out. If only your father were alive today, how wonderful it would be."

The only impression that the son had of his father was of a dignified man smoking a "Capital" cigarette. At that time it was very stylish to smoke a Western brand. Today, of course, even workers can buy the "My Dear" brand,[4] and they no longer use flints and long-stemmed pipes. How difficult it had been for his mother to struggle through those twenty long years can be imagined. Now her son had finally reached adulthood. If fortune smiled on her, she would soon have a grandson. When Shaochen heard his mother say "I'm getting old," he suddenly recalled something that had lain dormant in his heart a long time. Now he finally had the chance to say it out loud. He wanted to go to Peking.

It happened that the mother had a brother in Peking who had been a minor official in the palace before the last emperor was dethroned. They understood that he now ran a little shop off Qizhang Lane where he sold ice and foreign delicacies and that his business was flourishing.

The mother was taken aback to hear her son speak thus. And he had anticipated this, which was why he hadn't spoken to her about it before. But she, too, missed her brother.

---

[4]Satirical reference to the Meili (lit., "Beautiful") brand, which ran full-page ads in literary magazines with the incongruous figure of a pretty Chinese woman with a cigarette hanging out of her mouth.

"Do you just want to visit your Third Uncle in Peking, or do you have other plans?" she asked.

"I want to study."

"What good is it for a family like ours to study? The world is changing every day. It frightens me."

"Then let's go together."

"Do you think I can get away from here?"

"I'll just be gone for three months and then perhaps come back."

"Once you go, more likely it will be four or five years. Still, I won't stand in your way. If you want to go, then go. But study isn't so important. To be a good person, one doesn't need a lot of bookish learning. For people like us, more knowledge means more trouble!"

The woman spoke with sadness. Then, having her son drink to her toast, she asked if he intended to leave after the New Year, or would he spend it in Peking?

The son said he wanted to sit for the examinations, so he must leave soon. The roads would be less congested, he added.

Although his mother agreed to these plans, she couldn't see why he had to leave so early. It was finally decided that he would leave after the fifteenth of the first lunar month. This settled, they returned to the subject of the snow. The mother remembered that she wanted to give a jug of wine to their workers, for this was a special day.

Soon New Year's Day had passed, and the date for Shao-chen's departure arrived. The mother had written to his Peking uncle well in advance; her son took the little steamer up the river to Changsha, the bus to Wuhan, and then the train for Peking.

Three years passed. During this time, the Yu family garden remained the Yu family garden. But gradually it came to be known that the young master of the Yu family was studying at Peking University. This news caused a bit of a sensation in the town. How that came about is a complicated story with many twists and turns. But, as far as the cabbages were concerned, the Yu family still had the best.

There were a few changes in the Yu family. The son would often send home newspapers and books with the new ideas. His mother still oversaw work in the garden and now took on the task of raising a brood of white hens. Every day when she could spare the time, as she fed corn to her chickens and played with the little chicks, she would read the books and magazines from Peking. Though she was over fifty now, she was inspired by the same news and events that were stimulating the young people in Peking.

A lot of changes were occurring locally. There was the Revolution and the Northern Expedition[5] – whereupon many young men died in the fields, left to rot with no one to claim their corpses – although in the process many heroes and martyrs were created, as well as bureaucrats, of both the old and new schools. – Whereupon party[6] branches and labor unions appeared – whereupon a lot of young people were killed, on the Day of Horse,[7] and labor unions were disbanded, and the people in the party branch changed – and whereupon Peking,[8] the Northern Capital, changed to Beiping, the Northern Peace, while the capital shifted to Nanjing.

After the name change, North China became tranquil. It seemed as if a real Son of Heaven had emerged and that peace all under heaven was near at hand. The son in Beiping still wrote home frequently, but he sent fewer books and newspapers.

[5]The Kuomintang's Nationalist Revolution and conquest of the north, 1926–1927, led by Chiang Kai-shek.
[6]Kuomintang.
[7]21 March 1927, the day of a Kuomintang massacre of Communists and peasant leaders in Changsha that marked a turn toward the full-scale purge of leftists in China. Until then, Communists had joined the Kuomintang with the common aim of overthrowing the warlords.
[8]*Beijing,* in Mandarin.

The woman at home sent her son sixty dollars every month. Besides inquiring after his health, she would ask whether he had met any suitable girls. She was getting older and naturally was concerned about such matters. During the three years that her son had been away, she remained as much at ease with herself as before. Inside, she had learned a lot about current affairs on account of her son, yet without having lost any of the traditional family virtues on the outside. Through her help, two of her workers had gotten married. When she wrote her son about it, he wrote back to say that she had done the right thing.

The son had also written suggesting that his mother come to Beiping for a visit and let the workers take care of the garden. She didn't find the idea inconceivable, but neither did she ever really seriously take it up.

The mother was overjoyed finally to receive news that her son was coming home for a month at the end of the semester. The letter came in April. From that day on, she began making preparations. She thought of everything that might please him. When July came around, she looked forward to her son's arrival day by day, sending a servant all the way to Changsha to meet him and spending a lot of money on new things for the house, as if she were expecting a new bride.

Finally the son arrived. More exciting yet, he really had brought a bride with him, though his mother learned of this only as the young woman stepped across the threshold. The mother mumbled some complaints under her breath, but she showed the "guest" into her own room just the same. Suddenly the old woman seemed ten years younger.

Looking on as her son, somewhat leaner now, introduced his wife to the two workers and their wives, with a "Please meet our friends," the mother was overwhelmed with joy.

The news soon spread throughout the neighborhood that the son had returned, and so did word of his pretty bride. Because the town was small and there were not many arrivals from Beiping, the sons of the local gentry came to visit the Yus, though their fathers had seldom come around. Even the local educational board invited the young Beiping couple to join them when they held a meeting. Total strangers, concerned about the future of China, knew the name of Yu Shaochen from other sources and got together in small groups to come visit the young man out of admiration.

From the mother's point of view, her son was exactly the same as before. He had become deeply involved in the social issues of the day, but he was as naive and idealistic about many things as ever. He retained all his former virtues; all the new knowledge that he had gained was fully integrated into his life so that no one could tell that he was educated in Peking. Except for being too pretty for a wife, the young woman provided no grounds for complaint, either.

As the weather was still hot, the family would gather together by the little stream outside the garden to listen to the flowing water or the singing of the cicadas. Or they would chat under the melon trellises while watching the evening clouds. It was just the same as five years before, except that another person had been added. The Yu family seemed to live in a different world from the ordinary people in town. They had a little more intercourse with the others now, but the townspeople mostly viewed them from a distance, with curiosity and envy.

Because the new bride loved chrysanthemums and wanted to see some before returning to Beiping, the mother had her workers set aside a special plot of land for them. She searched everywhere for the best seeds, supervised the workers as they tended the sprouts, and finally planted them in the ground herself, with her son at her side.

One day in August, after supper, mother and son were in the garden admiring the chrysanthemum plants. The son wore shorts. His sleeves were rolled up to his elbows, and his hands were soiled from digging in the ground. As the mother watched the young couple working amid the chrysanthemums, she had an innocent little daydream about becoming a grandmother some day.

While they worked in the garden, the son told his mother about raising chrysanthemums in Beiping and how they were able to get such large blossoms through grafting. In the meantime, the mother looked admiringly at the astonishingly beautiful daughter-in-law kneeling before her. Suddenly a messenger appeared from the county offices. He reported that there was a small matter for the couple to attend to at county headquarters. The young couple hardly had time to wash their hands before they were whisked away. They never returned.

Though slightly taken aback, the mother did not think too much about it. But the next day she took to her bed. Her son and daughter-in-law, with three other young people who came to the same tragic end for other reasons, had gone before the firing squad. Their bodies were on display in a corner of the town square.

On the third day several burly fellows took the five bodies to the outskirts of town and buried them in a common grave dug the day before. Because of the rain, the grave was muddy and half filled with water. The men tossed in the bodies, hastily covered them with dirt, and left them slowly to rot away. Their task finished, the men went back to the yamen to get their compensation without so much as a backward glance.

The mother, faced with such shocking news, lost consciousness several times but managed to survive. Though it was her son who had died in such a horrible fashion, she had to see to the funeral expenses, the fines, the official forms, and a lot of other things. Only three days later, from public broadsides posted in the streets, did she and the townspeople learn that her son was executed for being a Communist. It was in consideration of the townspeople's need for cabbages that the old woman was allowed to live and the vegetable garden kept from being confiscated. With a pained smile on her face, the old woman reckoned that she was supposed not to die but to go on tending the garden. Therefore she lived on, continuing to sell her cabbages.

In autumn, the chrysanthemums were all in bloom.

The old woman stared at the flowers, with nothing to say and nothing to record.

Perhaps the Yus' vegetable garden would one day become the Yus' flower garden, for beautiful chrysanthemums ran riot there. The local gentry and new aristocrats began to appropriate the place for their banquets.

The mistress suddenly turned as haggard as a seventy-year-old woman. Every day she would sit in the yard feeding her chickens and thinking about things of bygone days that were no longer of any use.

The Yu family vegetable garden did indeed become the Yu family flower garden from that time forward. The civil war was over now, and the world was at peace. During the autumn months, the powerful gentry of the region would hold banquets in the garden, eat the vegetables grown there, drink fine wines, and enjoy the chrysanthemums. And, as they admired the flowers, they would get worked up and compose poetry. There were fine specimens written in congratulation of the owner of the garden, wishing her long life and prosperity for having rendered a great service to the nation and comparing her to somebody or other in another famous poem. Other good examples wrote about her as that old peasant woman who only lamented bygone days. And these local gentry had this other peculiar habit. When pleased with a particular poem, they had to put it up on the garden wall or hire an engraver to carve it in stone for posterity. Celebrated scholars and important people would gather in the Yus' garden, make merry, and return home inebriated, where they were bound to continue dreaming of sharing wine and playing drinking games with Mr. Five Willows – the ancient wine-loving poet, Tao Qian.

The Yu family vegetable garden changed into the Yu

family flower garden three years after the son's death. The woman lived on during those three years in silence and in loneliness. Then one day, on her son's birthday – during a heavy snow – she felt that she had lived long enough; there was no need for another spring or autumn. After willing the little property she had left to her workers, she took a silk scarf, made a noose, and hanged herself.

Big Ruan and Little Ruan

Like Lao She's famous story "Black Li and White Li," "Big Ruan and Little Ruan" ("Da xiao Ruan") is about brothers (in Shen's story, first cousins once removed who honorarily call each other "uncle" and "nephew," or even "brother," they are so close in age) that take different sides in the Revolution. They illustrate a split in China's old ruling class that both authors depict as falling along generational lines. Although Shen's story, written in 1935, a year later than Lao She's, contains direct ideological debate, stronger satiric and ideological barbs come from characterization. Big Ruan, the sort of playboy littérateur that Shen loved to denigrate as a "Shanghai type" (Hai Pai), is hopelessly frivolous, selfish, and self-deceiving. Little Ruan, the Communist, is a bit more idealistic and self-sacrificing, but he, too, is arrogant and self-centered. One could conclude from this that all social impulses coming from the old gentry and from its spoiled scions are poisoned at the source. And all those impulses seem to hinge on money.

Shen's answer to "Black Li and White Li" is thus an inversion of Lao She's vision of China being served by sacrifice in both the Confucian and the revolutionary modes. In Lao She's work, the older brother has the moral virtues of the old literati (he is reserved, indirect, family oriented) and the younger the vitality of a generation ready to sacrifice self and family for the revolutionary good of all. When the younger leads the family rickshaw puller and his coworkers in a strike that could get him executed (Shen appears to have borrowed both the device of the strike and the figure of an old member of the working class — Lao Liu, i.e., "Old Liu" — as observer and measuring stick), the older brother takes the younger one's place and gets executed in his stead. In Shen Congwen's hands, both old and new value systems are found wanting. Gentry boys appear incapable of upholding their respective systems without hypocrisy, and the proletarian who watches the spectacle, the school watchman, is rewarded with an "opiate" — an ample supply of liquor.

Shen Congwen was friends with partisans of both "types," so scholars have tried to figure out whom he might have been thinking of when he wrote this story. The Chinese scholar Dong Yi posits that Little Ruan is modeled after the leftist writer Pan Mohua; Anthony Prince has suggested far earlier but equally plausible forebears: the poet Ruan Ji (210–263) and his elder brother's son, Ruan Xian. But no one ought to want to claim kinship with the Ruans, and it would not resolve opposing interpretations of the story anyway.

The school watchman, Lao Liu, quaffed his four ounces of liquor in the little watchman's shed behind the school. Knowing from long experience that it must already be twelve o'clock, he picked up his watchman's rattle and went tap-tap-tapping along the school wall, chuckling all the way to think of how the lads had given him this wine. Ten years before, a young fellow used to come running back to school every night from the warm covers of a young widow's bed in a frame shop. As the youth climbed over the school wall, the watchman would raise his lantern to help him from falling into the muddy ditch inside the wall. Lao Liu loved to drink, and his sympathy and benevolence had earned him a great deal of wine.

The world was changing every day. Warlords Yuan Shikai, Zhang Xun, Wu Peifu, and Zhang Zuolin had taken their turns occupying Peking, all wanting to sit in the imperial palace, but none able to keep his throne. Personnel at the school were also changing constantly. All but the old headmaster had been replaced over and over. Funny thing, the boy who'd climbed the wall had now come back from abroad as the dean of students. But though the world was ever in flux, one thing never changed. The old student custom of climbing over the wall had been carefully preserved, except that now the watchman used a flashlight instead of a lantern to help them. He thought to himself that each man had his own fortune. Maybe Lao Liu had another whole fifty pots of liquor coming to him in this lifetime. Only when he'd drunk his fill would he fall down and die.

The watchman walked over to the wall thinking that no one would be climbing it this evening, but when he raised his head for a look, two black shadows were just then straddling it. "Who is it?" he shouted.

One of the dark shadows said, "Lao Liu, it's me. You're

Translated by William MacDonald

really something!" From the voice he knew it was Fatty Zhang.

"Master Zhang, you gave me a start. I thought you were a couple of burglars, but here – "

The other of the two shadows said, "Burglars? At this school? We're not burglars; we're two bottles of wine. No need to be frightened. Shine your flashlight for us, but don't tell anyone. We've come back for a few things. We're going out again in a minute. Wait here for us!" This voice was very familiar, too. It was Little Ruan. The two boys jumped down from the wall and ran straight into the dormitory.

Lao Liu watched the shadows of the two lads and smiled. Then he squatted down to wait for them.

He figured that this wait would benefit him, and he had no reason to give up that benefit.

After Little Ruan and Fatty Zhang split up, Little Ruan went into Dormitory 8, where a classmate was still up reading a novel by candlelight. Little Ruan walked over to the bed of a student who was asleep, dreaming of eating pigeons' eggs, and woke him with a whisper in his ear. The two boys were uncle and nephew. The one sleeping was the other's youngest uncle; everyone called him Big Ruan.

"Seventh Uncle, help me out. Lend me that hundred dollars of yours. I've got to 'fly far and high' – I've done something, and I've got to go!"

"Why? Did you get into another scrape in school?"

"It isn't a fight at school. I've run into trouble. You'll hear about it tomorrow. Hurry and lend me that hundred dollars, will you? I need it!"

"No deal. I have other plans for my money. I've got to pay the bill for my overcoat and return twenty dollars to Shorty. A lot of things."

"Then lend me eighty at least. I'll pay you back soon. Consider the next money that comes from home yours. I need money badly. I can't leave without it! With eighty I can go to Canton and take the exams for the Whampoa Military Academy. Otherwise I'll have to go to Shanghai and wait for a turn for the better. I've got to go!"

"Take thirty, that'll be enough. Even if I don't pay the Yixing Store, I've still got to clear my account at the school co-op."

"Make it sixty. I can't stay at school, I've got to hit the road right away!

Big Ruan couldn't hold out, in part because he badly needed his sleep. With difficulty he fished around in his bed and took out his wallet. He counted out ten five-dollar bills and gave them to Little Ruan. After taking the money, Little Ruan pulled a small black object out of his pants pocket and stuffed it under Big Ruan's pillow. "Seventh Uncle," he whispered, "this belongs to Fatty Zhang in Room 15. Do me a favor and return it to him tomorrow, will you? I'll go now. Those papers of mine that I'm keeping in your trunk, burn them first thing in the morning. It won't be any fun if someone finds them." Because the schoolmate reading the novel was looking at him, Little Ruan walked over to his bed and said, "Excuse me for disturbing you, brother. Good-bye."

The nearsighted one quickly said, "Good-bye."

After Little Ruan left the dormitory, Big Ruan felt something hard under the pillow sticking into his neck. He pulled it out and looked at it. It was a small pistol. He surmised that an hour ago Little Ruan must have got into trouble with it. He might have killed someone; tomorrow morning there'd be an inspection of the dormitory. Little Ruan had said the papers he'd entrusted to him were private letters, but now he wanted them burned right away, so of course they were dangerous too. But after he had thought these two things over, Big Ruan felt a little easier. The gun was Fatty Zhang's; everyone in school knew that. Fatty Zhang was the son of the military governor. If he got mixed up in anything, there wouldn't be any questions. As for burning the papers, that was easy, and even if he didn't burn them in time they wouldn't implicate him. What really kept Big Ruan from sleeping was the fifty dollars Little Ruan had borrowed. Little Ruan could play all sorts of tricks, and usually when he wanted money he wrote home for it. He could think up all sorts of ways to get what he wanted. Perhaps this time he was putting on a show of being panicked just to swindle money out of him for something else. The terrible thing was that he'd had plans for the fifty dollars Little Ruan had taken from him, and now they were completely ruined.

When Little Ruan left the dormitory and crossed the drill field to the wall, he saw the watchman still waiting for him there. He fished out a bill and stuffed it into the watchman's hand.

"Lao Liu, take this and get yourself a drink. Don't tell anyone I came back. If you do, Master Zhang will shoot you."

"Isn't Master Zhang going out?"

"No."

"Aren't you coming back?"

"Why shouldn't I come back? I'll come back in a few years!"

When Little Ruan had climbed over the wall, the watchman shone his flashlight on the bill in his hand and discovered it was five dollars, a big bonus. He knew that he had better keep very quiet about this. This was enough to buy almost thirty catties of liquor. He hid the bill in a little pocket at the waist of his pants and said to himself, "A man really does have his fortune; you can't force it."

He felt it rather amusing. From now on he'd better keep his mouth shut about this.

At six o'clock in the morning a bell pulled all the students back from their hazy dreams to the real world.

The office clerk followed the school handyman, who was ringing the bell, to the front of each dormitory. There he stopped to tell the students that the headmaster would speak at an 8 A.M. assembly; the entire student body had to go to the drill field to hear his lecture. The old headmaster didn't address them often, so each dormitory suddenly came to life. They all guessed that something had happened at the school, but no one really knew what.

Big Ruan rolled out of bed and took the object that Little Ruan had given him the night before to Room 15; he saw Fatty Zhang still lying in bed, wrapped up in the covers. When he gave the thing to him, Fatty Zhang asked no questions, as if he already knew it was from Little Ruan. He casually stuffed it under his pillow, rolled over, and went back to sleep. Big Ruan quickly went back and burned all the papers. When he had finished, he took his towel and basin to the lavatory to wash his face. He heard his class-mates all talking about the assembly. A skinny second-year student in Big Ruan's class, a roommate of Fatty Zhang's, pulled Big Ruan into the corridor. He said in a whisper that last night when Fatty Zhang had gone out he had got into a fight, though he didn't know why. His arm was all black and blue, and he didn't get back to the dormitory until midnight. He had heard him say he was going to the south and didn't plan to study any more.

Now Big Ruan understood why Fatty Zhang hadn't questioned him when he returned the gun. Big Ruan was very upset. He ran to the gate looking for the morning edi-tion to see if he could get any news, but it was too early, and the paper had not yet come. When it arrived, at seven-thirty, he looked at the local news pages but couldn't find any related information. A seventy-year-old man had com-mitted suicide because of poverty and illness, a child bride had been scalded to death with boiling water by her mother-in-law, and a man had fallen down drunk and cursed the officials as traitors and incompetents. Little Ruan was quite obviously not responsible for this sort of news.

When the assembly met, the headmaster's lecture was the usual thing about how students should respect their teachers. Fatty Zhang wasn't at the meeting, and Little Ruan didn't show up either. After the meeting was dismissed, the dean of students called Big Ruan into his office and asked him first of all if he knew that Little Ruan had gotten into trouble. Big Ruan said he hadn't known. The dean of students then told Big Ruan that Little Ruan had left a secret organization on account of a woman, shooting and wounding a history teacher from the municipal middle school. Since he had difficulties of his own, the teacher hadn't dared say anything, but the neighbors reported it to the district officials. Investigators had interrogated the man at his house to find out why he was wounded, so maybe they would be coming to the school to search for the culprit. If Little Ruan had already left, then Big Ruan should look in his dormitory for anything that ought to be burned and burn it quickly. The dean happened to be a —— himself, and at that time the Party was half in the open. Before warning Big Ruan, he had taken care to burn his own incriminating papers. As for the young gentleman called Fatty Zhang, he just lay in bed nursing his wounds. No one could touch him, for the district director worked for his father, as the dean of students had realized from the beginning.

Big Ruan went back to the dormitory and wrote a letter to his cousin (Little Ruan's father)[1] in Hefei:

Big Brother,

Your third son, having got himself into trouble here last night and almost taken someone's life, has run away from school. Before he left he wanted some money and forced me to loan it to him. I borrowed fifty dollars from

[1]Familiarity is heightened by addressing kin as if they were closer than they really are. Big Ruan thinks of his elder paternal male first cousin as his big brother. Hence the latter's son is Big Ruan's "nephew." At times Big Ruan elevates Little Ruan further, to "Little Brother," for the full one-generation seniority deference due an uncle seems out of place when the boys are so close in age.

a classmate for him (these are funds urgently needed by someone else to pay a hospital bill, and he cannot delay payment for very long). With what I've loaned him before, he owes me about one hundred dollars. I won't count that, but please send at your earliest convenience the money to return to the other person, in order to clear the actions of yours truly, your younger brother. My classmates all stress trustworthiness, and if it isn't restored, your younger brother won't be able to face them.

This time your third son has flown far away. He said that if he had a hundred dollars he could go to Canton; lacking that, he would go to Shanghai for a time to wait for his chance. His reason for going to Canton would be to take the examination for the Whampoa Military Academy. It's said that this school has a great future, that it will equal the Baoding Officer Corps. As I see it, since Master Hulu is already studying at the Peking Army College, we already have one soldier in the family, and there's no need for any more. Furthermore, the Canton and Peking regimes are enemies and bound to fight each other in the future. If an uncle and nephew face each other across the trenches, our clan will lose, whichever side wins; it's not a good idea. So the sum I loaned him is only enough to get him to Shanghai. I presume that Elder Brother will concur with this measure that his younger brother has put into effect. The school is being understanding about this, but your third son absolutely must not risk returning to school. I think that if he could just go to Japan to study, he would have a very hopeful future. In everything he is rich in revolutionary spirit, like Mr. Sun Yat-sen. Mr. Sun once fled for his life to Japan. The history teacher talked about it in great detail in class. But your third son's nature is too violent, his spirit too untrammeled. This must be taken into consideration. What is important is that he is one of the talented men of our own clan.

Big Ruan finished writing the letter and read it over. He was satisfied. He underlined the part about the funds belonging to another individual, put the letter into an envelope, and mailed it. His main aim was to get his fifty dollars back, and in the end he was not of course disappointed. As for Little Ruan's destiny, ultimately it was indeed closely related to the sum of money he borrowed. If Little Ruan had had enough money to get him to Canton, then later on, during the Revolutionary Army's Northern Expedition, he might have been killed and become a revolutionary martyr, or he might have lived and become a major figure among the Young Turks in the military. And the rest of this story would have to be completely rewritten.

By generation Big Ruan and Little Ruan were uncle and nephew, by age more like elder and younger brother; in life they were friends, and in ideology they seemed to be opponents. But in personality they were *chabuduo,* "about the same." Both were rather clever and liked to spend money. They opposed the family elders about the same; they avoided the duties and responsibilities of the family system about the same; they were drawn to new things about the same; and they were about the same in how easily they were taken in by easily bought girls. In their studies their different roads ended them up in the same place, for their natures were just about the same. Both of them gave an impression that they were wild and boisterous; they differed only in the ways in which they let it out.

The two had passed the entrance examinations for this private senior high school in the summer of 1923.

Those who had the opportunity to study in this school were, for the most part, the sons of official families and comparatively wealthy merchants and landlords, so, besides genuine athletic, debating, literary, and artistic groups, the school had two rather strange organizations: one was called the Gentleman's Society and the other the Cudgel Club. The Gentleman's Society emphasized clothing and fostering the qualifications of the petty gentry. School regulations required all students to wear their uniforms off campus as well as on, causing these rich boys to be always complaining that they had no chance to show off, but they could still wear their shoes and socks (and even their garters) in unusual ways. Besides that, their wristwatches, fountain pens, the soap they used to wash their faces, their towels, their stationery – all were meticulously distinctive. Most of them were pale-faced youths, refined, effete, clever, and insubstantial, not so good at their lessons, but well up in their extracurricular reading. They weren't very interested in learning, yet they knew an awful lot about life.

As for the Cudgel Club, the majority of its members were sons of military families. As the name of their club implied, their main activity was looking for fights. They not only fought in school but often went outside the school to fight on its behalf. These two organizations gave the school a lot of trouble, but at the same time they added something to its reputation. For they represented a certain set, a class – one whose name we usually find ambiguous and annoying yet one that we cannot help but respect: the so-called upper crust or ruling class. It was the right man in charge of the school, and the school's lucky streak, that somehow got them an unexpected contribution of almost $500,000 from a retired warlord. The authorities used these funds to add several imposing buildings, some books for the library, and lab equipment. As time went on, the school became more and more presentable. So its social position surpassed that of all the other schools. Tuition was high, but every year the students who sat for college entrance examinations exceeded the quota ten times over.

Big Ruan and Little Ruan were scions of an old family, and they liked activities, which is a general characteristic of their kind. After passing the examinations and entering the school, they soon joined the two respective organizations.

The one they picked reflected their past environment, their present interests, and their future destinies.

The May Fourth movement had come along and fired up young people throughout the country. Dreams of youth, of breaking with all systems and customs whether they existed in name or reality, were fanned by magazines and newspapers. The demand for freedom and liberation became the sole slogan, the only aim of young people in cities large and small. Now the —— High School was in a province in the middle reaches of the Yangtze River. Most of its teachers were distinguished graduates of Peking Normal University or Peking University, and the headmaster had been an old member of the Revolutionary party in the early years of the Republic, so the school had a congenial atmosphere.

Everything was progressive and up to date, but for one thing: the headmaster was stubborn and unyielding, and because of his position and popularity at the school, and that bit of obstinacy in his personality, he would not permit it to become coeducational. The school was run for boys, he reasoned, and if girls wanted to go to school there were girls' schools they could enter. At the same time this conviction gained support from powerful authorities so that the students had no way of opposing him even if they wanted to. A few years after the May Fourth movement, when society had changed a little, the fact that the school remained closed to girls won it support from an even larger majority. This point may not seem particularly relevant, but imperceptibly it shaped the later destinies of many young people, for just at that time when these youths' bodies and minds were developing a special feeling of wonder and a physical attraction for girls, they had no opportunity to satisfy these needs at school. Their desires repressed and twisted, the group of youths having nervous temperaments produced many writers, and the group of hot-blooded ones produced many revolutionaries. Before these writers and revolutionaries ever distinguished themselves, the majority were active in one of the two special extracurricular organizations.

After Little Ruan left the school, he did indeed go to Shanghai. Just like many other young people, he changed his name and lived in a garret on a small alley and sent one registered letter after another pressing for money from his old father, who lived off his rents in the countryside. Little Ruan thought that he was initiating humankind's most sacred and glorious undertaking. If the money wasn't sent on time and in the amount needed or his father didn't recognize Little Ruan's greatness, then he said in his letters all the things that old people consider wild and muddleheaded.

The father decided that his son was a radical, so of course he didn't transfer the funds. But Little Ruan had other relatives and friends, so there were other ways. While the relatives proved to be a dead end, the friends (they were enjoying themselves in the big city the same way) were getting the benefit of mutual support from a source in common: in other words, the mutual aid of "comrades." Though materially poor, they were rich in spirit. When they had no money, they lived on air and dreams, and it seemed that this could keep them going. Finally, of course, they accepted the destinies that opportunity provided them. They became big fish – or little fish; leftists – or rightists; and went to prison – or returned home, where they married and raised sons for the sake of their ancestors and became country gentry.

The world, as the old watchman said, was "changing." Somehow Little Ruan got help from a friend and went to Japan, where he was able to enter a technical school. He studied what everyone else wanted to study: politics. Although his family had broken their connections with him, the rules said that clansmen enrolled in college at home or abroad could draw financial aid from the clan funds held in common. Little Ruan proved his student status with documents and drew on his rights for a year, but before he had been in Japan half a year, the Northern Expeditionary Army had taken Wuhan.

This news was music to his ears. Since he had helped them, they would certainly have work for him if he went home; so he did. He took the river steamer up to Hankou and looked up the dean of students from his alma mater, who was already an important man in the Party. Soon his opportunity came. He was made a member of the Hankou special Party committee. Naturally he was impressive in the performance of his duties. The redoubled enthusiasm with which he spoke at meetings made his comrades feel that he was rich in fighting spirit. He ridiculed conservatism and sneered at compromise, so the lifestyle from his days at school and in Shanghai continued developing in the new environment. He planned to strike down this, abolish that. He still wrote to Big Ruan, now a first-year student at Peking University, to make clear his own successes and self-confidence in the new enterprise. He wrote to the trustee of the clan estate, proposing that the trustee invite the participation of young people to improve the methods of financial assistance. He wrote to his father, asking him to send money. Quite simply, he wanted him to send money immediately.

When Chiang Kai-shek "purified the Party," a companion turned in Little Ruan, all but gave his life away. Quite fortunately, he escaped that bloody political maelstrom. He went down to Jiujiang and then on to Nanchang with the faction that held real power, to join in the Nanchang insurrection. After that defeat he went to Canton and did some work the nature of which is untraceable. Before long he turned up again in the Canton Commune. The Canton Commune didn't cooperate with the —th Army, and they were defeated again. The head of the labor movement (none other than his old dean of students) rode his motorcycle to a meeting of the federation of trade unions and was machine-gunned down right in front of the door. Three hundred fifty cadres had been invited to the meeting. A few who hadn't been able to come managed to escape, but the 320 other young people were detained in an old theater until they could be disposed of. Violent clashes were going on in the city, and for a time it was hard to see who would win. Everywhere there was street fighting; everywhere houses were on fire. The slaughter of young people was carried out on an ever-greater scale, amid acts of madness and retribution.

Little Ruan, who was locked up in the theater, already had plans in store. He figured all the angles. The chief had already fallen down dead, and the street fighting was continuing. Even if in a day or two his side could turn defeat into victory and take back the city center, the group that was locked up was bound to meet its end during the transition. Better to risk running away than just sit there and wait to be shot; he always believed he could snatch life from the jaws of death.

The doors to the theater were surrounded by barbed wire, and machine guns were placed everywhere, but, almost miraculously, that night Little Ruan and two companions climbed out a window onto the roof of a house, escaping behind the back of a napping rooftop sentry. They fled to the nearby home of an acquaintance. Early the next morning, their three hundred companions were taken to the dikes of the Pearl River in twelve trucks. They were formed into three groups and mowed down with machine guns.

One evening forty-one days later, at about nine o'clock, an uninvited guest came to Big Ruan's dormitory in the East Hall of Peking University. It was Little Ruan.

Big Ruan was now studying in the Peking University Department of Foreign Literatures, and he was already working for an evening newspaper as a guest editor for opera criticism and scandalous gossip. Because of his position he had become a local celebrity in the eyes of frivolous young students, brothel-goers, actresses, and prostitutes. The walls of his dormitory room and his desk were crowded with photos of actors, actresses, and starlets. The wall also sported an inscribed couplet composed by a famous actor. Big Ruan's roommate was a third-year student in history from Shandong who had nothing to do apart from studying. Since coming to live with Big Ruan, though, he had become an unadulterated "Peking opera buff."

Big Ruan was genuinely surprised at Little Ruan's sudden appearance. He had thought Little Ruan must be living in the south or perhaps had died there.

"Ah, Little Brother, so it's really you! I'm surprised that you're still among the living."

Little Ruan looked at the immaculately dressed Big Ruan and just smiled. Time had separated the two men. He didn't know why, but in his heart he had always had a little contempt for his young uncle. The ancestors had given Big Ruan an estate, he thought, but they hadn't given him a very good brain. All that cleverness was only good for wasting the small legacy the ancestors had left him. He was constantly primping and preening, just like a woman, and he always wore scent. All this effort just to please a vain and licentious girl who considered herself attractive to the opposite sex. To please a girl! His only other life's aim was to eat and drink. And so he lived in drunkenness and befuddlement. He wasn't of much consequence to the rest of the world.

Noticing the expression on Little Ruan's face, Big Ruan continued, "You didn't come from Canton, did you? You people have been busy down there!"

Little Ruan, still smiling, said softly, "It's just as busy as you say."

Little Ruan watched the tall Shandong fellow comb his hair until it was slick and then wash his face. After that he meticulously dabbed on some cologne. Little Ruan felt this particularly revolting. He indicated to Big Ruan that they should find a place to talk alone. Big Ruan understood and asked his roommate, "Monsieur Hou, aren't you going to the opera?"

The Shandong student who was so unwilling to let himself go smoothed his hair and said in an affected, nasal voice, "I just couldn't miss this performance by Yu Shuang." Then he turned around, as if he had just noticed that a guest had entered the room. "Excuse me, this guest would be – "

Just as Big Ruan was about to introduce Little Ruan to his roommate, Little Ruan cut in, "My name is Liu Shenfu; I run a small business." He paid no more attention to the Shandong student and turned to look at the contents of the bookshelves. Knowing Little Ruan's temperament, Big Ruan realized that he didn't like to talk to strangers. He was afraid his roommate would be embarrassed, so he turned and chatted with the Shandong student. They discussed some pointless question about the opera. But the Shandong student was obliging after all; after fixing his hair and face, he left, singing an opera tune in falsetto as he went. When he was gone, Little Ruan remarked, "There's a strange fish for you."

Big Ruan said, "Young man, your disposition is the same as ever; it hasn't changed a bit. Since when has your name been Liu? And what business are you in? Come, sit down, and let's talk about what you've been through. Frankly, when I heard about the purge, I thought you might long since have been taken to Wuhan, trussed up, and thrown into the river to feed the fishes. Later a letter from Sister-in-Law told me you were in Canton, just when that great upheaval took place. Even if you could fly you'd have had a hard time getting out of that one. But here you are now in Peking. You're a pretty resourceful fellow. I admire your uncompromising spirit."

Little Ruan lit a cigarette, puffed on it like a madman, and looked at Big Ruan. He said sarcastically, "Seventh Uncle, these past few years your life must have been rather interesting. You keep getting handsomer. You look like you've been getting the breaks."

Big Ruan understood only half the meaning behind these

words, and he seemed purposely to be taking in only that half. With a mixture of humility and honesty he said, "You could say that we're just fooling around; nothing we do is ever very far from that word *fooling*. I entered this school mostly so I could get my diploma by fooling around, and my job on the newspaper is fooling around to get a living. I fool around with actors and actresses, with food and drink, and with women, so you'll have to ask the fortune-teller Demigod Wang to learn what breaks I may have been getting. But I'm a man who's been baptized by science. I don't believe that a blind fortune-teller can know my affairs."

Noticing that Little Ruan was somewhat sloppily dressed, Big Ruan asked how long he'd been in Peking, where he was living, and if he'd eaten supper. Then he shifted the topic of conversation to how the financial situation at home wasn't what it used to be. Although his motive wasn't to keep his able nephew from asking for money, he did subconsciously hint to Little Ruan that, if he wanted to borrow some, there would be a limit. But his plan misfired.

Little Ruan said, "I want to stay in Peking. Is this place all right?"

"A little while ago it was terrible. The authorities were checking the apartments very carefully, so living here would have been out of the question. Now it's all right. Do you want to live in the East City or the West City?"

"I'll go anywhere available that you can vouch for. No need to see any acquaintances. I may have to go before long. I want to go to Manchuria."

Big Ruan thought about it for a while. It wasn't convenient to go looking for a room at night, so they'd wait until the next day and then see. He learned from Little Ruan that he was living at an inn outside the Main Gate. He went back there with him. The two talked all night, until they knew all the changes in each other's lives these past few years.

Big Ruan was much more at ease when he learned that

his esteemed nephew had enough money in hand. As to Little Ruan's risking his life and all his dangerous experiences, they couldn't excite his interest at all. Big Ruan said he didn't understand what *revolution* meant because of late his mind had been entirely devoted to art. He had already become an art critic and connoisseur, and if in the future he could only go abroad, he would travel to England to study art criticism. He knew many promising artists. Besides encouraging them, correcting them, and frequently writing articles on their work, he had written a few short familiar essays for a magazine in Shanghai and was preparing to publish a periodical. The sense of achievement and self-confidence with which he talked about these things were just like Little Ruan's when his nephew had written to Big Ruan years ago. Their chat removed the barrier between their mind-sets, so Little Ruan became more lively and more voluble. Eventually they even got around to the subject of sex. As formal politeness gave way to disputation, they wholly recovered the friendship of their shared days in school.

The next day, by exploiting Big Ruan's status, they found a large and quiet room in a private dormitory in the vicinity of Peking University. They moved in the luggage, bought a few necessities, and Little Ruan settled down. Uncle and nephew chatted happily all day long in the new lodgings. When it was time to part, Big Ruan's impression of Little Ruan was that he was mysterious, and he felt that this was still due to his wildness. The only change was that his behavior and ideals were different. This impression made him feel a little pessimistic about Little Ruan's future. He couldn't tell whether Little Ruan would end up a dragon or a snake, a big fish or a little one, but in any case he was dangerous. Anyway, the two lived together, and Little Ruan seemed to have enough to spend. When he went out eating and drinking and attending the theater with Big Ruan, he wasn't chintzy with his money, so Big Ruan was gradually able to pardon Little Ruan's wildness and even become accustomed to it.

Their daily verbal battles seemed to arouse Big Ruan's interest in politics slightly. It wasn't toward the Left or the Right, just toward himself.

After living there a month, Little Ruan suddenly announced that he was leaving, going to Tangshan. When Big Ruan thought about it, he could imagine Little Ruan's reason for going there. Half joking and half sincere, he offered his opinion. "My young man, you'd best stay home. That's no place for anybody, and it certainly doesn't suit you."

"Do you think that living here, talking nonsense with you, and going to the theater every day suits me?"

"I don't know what suits you. Go to Tangshan for amusement and you'll find nothing to do but burrow into a coal mine shaft and get yourself buried alive for a while. Even if you want to work, there isn't any work to do there."

"How do you know there's no work to do? A man who wants to work can find work even when he's locked up in a dungeon! If you went there, there'd certainly be nothing for you to do! The best place for you is right where you are now because it has everything you're used to. You waste fifty dollars on a bottle of perfume to send to Little Rose and write an article to boost an actress's career for ten. If you left this big city, of course there'd be nothing for you to do."

"But what kind of a world is it now, I ask you? The gentleman knows better than to stand beneath a high and dangerous wall. If you go to Tangshan, isn't that jumping into the fire?"

"Mister, if the world's to get a little better, someone must jump into the fire."

"If the world's already as thoroughly bad as you say it is, then lofty motives and ideals no longer exist. All men are dog shit – insects – and the human heart is rotten. If you jump into the fire, it still won't get any better! Just think of how many hells you've jumped into during the past few years. Has it changed the world for the better? Besides, how many men have rotted in the mud because of it, and how much good has that done the world?"

"Of course it's done some good for the majority. It hasn't done *you* any good, and it may actually make no sense to you. But, come the revolution, you'll know what meaning it has for you. The first thing will be to confiscate those five hundred acres of land under your name. We won't let you take any more blood and sweat from your tenants so you can waste it in the city. Second, people like you will have to carry sedan chairs and scrub floors. It's to reform you, to reform you completely. Then we'll see whether it still suits you or not. That day will come. It's inevitable!"

"If it's inevitable, then why do you have to see to it?"

"Seventh Uncle, you're hopeless. Just you wait."

"Little Nephew, I'm not joking. Old unsalvageable me still thinks you shouldn't go to Tangshan. The place is unsettled. —— can't understand your so-called lofty ideals at all, and he isn't too polite to your kind of people. If you fall into his clutches, you'll find it hard to escape. If you go there, I guarantee you'll find yourself in a mess. If you get into trouble here, I more or less have my ways, but they're no good in Tangshan. You could have three heads and six arms, and they still wouldn't do you any good."

This conversation was much like one they had had at another time. Neither would give in, but there had to be an end to it.

Little Ruan said, "Okay, thank you for your advice. No need for us to talk about it any more."

Little Ruan seemed to have already changed his attitude, and he specially invited Big Ruan to go out for a drink. Big Ruan was worried that it was a trick. He thought that Little Ruan knew his family had recently sent him five hundred dollars and, if they went out to drink, he'd want to borrow money from him again. So he made excuses, saying that he had another engagement. Little Ruan had to go alone. That evening, while Big Ruan was listening to an opera from a box at the Hua Le Theater, Little Ruan came looking for him. He gave Big Ruan a letter and asked him to read it. It was a notice that two thousand dollars had been sent to Little Ruan from Hong Kong.

Little Ruan said, "I've got to go right away. It wouldn't be good to have this on me, so you cash it. Keep it handy; when I need it, I'll write and tell you. If I die, or if you've had no news of me for two or three years, I hope you'll send it to my little brother in Shanghai." Then, without waiting for Big Ruan to reply, he patted him on the arm and left.

Big Ruan thought that Little Ruan really had been poisoned, poisoned by dreams of becoming a great hero.

A half month later, the Peking and Tianjin papers carried news that four thousand miners at Tangshan had gone on strike, demanding an increase in wages. Six of the people in the lead had been seized immediately and summarily executed. The striking workers were completely defeated, of course, and they called the strike to a halt. Big Ruan had no doubt that Little Ruan was among the six executed. Just as he was about to write a letter to inform his cousin, Little Ruan's father, he received a letter from the cousin saying that someone in Canton had personally seen Little Ruan die in the tumult there. With that, Big Ruan saved himself some trouble and decided not to tell his cousin about how Little Ruan had escaped to Peking and so forth.

Big Ruan felt that Little Ruan's defeat was "predestined long ago." Little Ruan had fervor but no sense. Rich in enthusiasm, he would dare to do anything, but his lack of common sense naturally brought him defeat in the end. He'd had only three chances. At Wuhan and Canton he'd been lucky enough to escape, but the third time he was bound to have met that unavoidable tragedy predestined by fate. Big Ruan felt very sad, but he thought he'd given him his sincere advice in plenty of time. Little Ruan hadn't taken it, so now he could only sigh for him. What worried him was that money in Little Ruan's name. Should he keep it or send it to Shanghai? In the end, considering all the implications, he decided not to send it.

A year passed, and still there was no news of Little Ruan. All his relatives thought that he must be long dead. Big Ruan kept the money on him. And, because he did, he was able to cover another expense: he published a small periodical.

When it was time for Big Ruan to start a family, his personality, habits, even his interests, all suggested that he couldn't help picking a mate from among the actresses and singing girls. But he wasn't a complete fool; he knew that there were more important things, and he thought of the future of his family's fortune. Years of wildness had slightly increased his knowledge of the ways of the world. He had slowly awakened to the fact that he was not willing to do anything that would lead to later "retribution." Even more influential perhaps was that in school he had been called a "writer"; the new environment forced him to abandon his erotic poetry and start writing new poetry, using the new vocabulary. And it so happened that the school accepted thirty more coeds this year, so naturally his poetic inspiration blossomed. As a result he became a poet and the sweetheart of one of the school's best-dressed girls. When the girl learned that Big Ruan was the only son of a big landlord in Hefei and Big Ruan found out that her father was a third-rank functionary in the new Nanjing government, an engagement was easily arranged.

The engagement changed Big Ruan's life completely. Although he wasn't an official, he already looked like one. And though he wasn't a member of the Kuomintang, his sympathy with the Party increased day by day.

Big Ruan graduated, and, since he was a landlord, a

writer, and the fortunate son-in-law of a man of some importance, he was welcomed back to his alma mater as dean of students. When he arrived at the school, everything seemed different. The old headmaster was a little older, the lecture halls and furniture looked a little older, and the majority of the teachers were his old classmates. Everyone talked about the changes in personnel over the past few years, and they couldn't help but feel deeply touched. The dean of students had died long before, Fatty Zhang had gone to —— as a consul, a music teacher had become a monk, and this and that were all different now. The world was changing!

Big Ruan thought that there must be *something* that hadn't changed. Just like the now-deceased dean of students, he recalled the watchman, Lao Liu. He went to the little hut behind the school to look for him, and indeed there he was, sitting in the same old way on bricks by the wall, stewing dog meat to have with his wine! When the old watchman saw Big Ruan, he expressed no surprise at all, but just said, nonchalantly, "So you've come back, Mr. Big. Are you teaching, or will you be the dean?"

Big Ruan said, "Lao Liu, everything here has changed but you."

The watchman smiled. "Sir, everything must change, everything must change. The world is not the same now. Dog meat isn't as tender as it used to be. But it's not the dog meat; it's my teeth."

Big Ruan felt that the watchman had a little of the "Dao" that the old literati were always seeking, or "philosophy," as modern scholars called it.

On 27 November 193—, in the Number Two Prison in Tianjin, a convict sentenced to eight years for agitating the army, number 48, starved to death after going on a hunger strike with another writer named Pan to demand improvements in prison conditions. The convict's arrest had come one month after the miners' strike at Tangshan some years before, and he went by the name Liu Shenfu. Near the end of the year, Big Ruan got the news in an anonymous letter forwarded from Peking University. The contents were simple but strange. Just before he died, Liu had said that Big Ruan was his relative, and he wanted this news forwarded to him. That was all. The letter writer signed himself "49"; evidently he was Little Ruan's closest fellow sufferer in prison.

When he got this strange letter, Big Ruan just couldn't imagine who this Liu fellow was or how he could be his relative. Two days later, it came to him unconsciously what Little Ruan had said to his Shandong classmate when he looked up Big Ruan in Peking. Then he realized that Liu Shenfu was Little Ruan. Little Ruan had actually died only a month ago. He believed that this time Little Ruan really was finished and that there would be no more news of him for good. The meaning of this letter to Big Ruan wasn't the news of Little Ruan's death but that it raised again the responsibility he had forgotten. His grief is beyond the scope of this story. Big Ruan wanted to do a little something to commemorate his young nephew, but try as he might he couldn't think of anything appropriate. Finally, he thought of the watchman. Big Ruan called him in and, after asking him about his capacity for drink, promised that every month for a year he would give the watchman ten catties of liquor. That was enough to satisfy Big Ruan. All of the two thousand dollars that he'd so easily come by naturally went into his own account.

Big Ruan never again talked to his friends about Little Ruan's being muddleheaded, but by his behavior he proved that his own thought and beliefs had taken another road. He still believed the reason for his success was his true and unwavering belief in man and society. Just what were his beliefs? No one asked him, and he himself never looked into them very thoroughly.

He was very happy, and that was enough. In these

strange times, many people looking for happiness fall down in silence and are gone forever. Others, among the living, tend to think that they live happily and that raising a family and being successful in everything makes them the backbone of society – indispensable to it. Especially those like Big Ruan.

Eight Steeds

"Eight Steeds" ("Ba jun tu"), written in 1935, or, according to an essay of Shen's, possibly in 1933, "analyzes" the psychology of professors among whom he lived while teaching summer school at Qingdao University in the summer of 1933. Ever since, the work has been read as a roman à clef satirizing actual personalities of the 1930s; the scholar Shao Huaqiang is convinced that the professors depicted include friends of Shen's such as Liang Shiqiu and Wen Yiduo. The characters are too vaguely drawn to permit positive identifications, however, and perhaps that is just as well. This is a comedy of manners about a whole class of people. Shen Congwen had joined it, and evidently he has not excused himself from the satire. Mr. Dashi appears to be the author's alter ego, writing love letters to his fiancée just as Shen Congwen was at the time. (The professors in the story go from A to G, omitting only F, or, in Chinese, ji, meaning "self": Mr. Zhou Dashi, whose name, incidentally, reads "Mr. All-Around Accomplished Scholar.")

Hua-ling Nieh, positing a double irony that prohibits trusting the central intelligence (a complexity of narration of which Shen was surely capable), takes literally the idea of the final paragraph, that Dashi had "contracted a very extraordinary disease himself." Dashi prescribes for the other characters a "Freudian" therapy of open sexuality so that they can recover from illness due to repression of the drive, and Nieh finds that dubious. Perhaps. But the "therapy" does represent Shen Congwen's own Freudian beliefs. He once counseled the scholar Wu Mi to have an affair to clear his mind and has explained also that the sea in this story represents "liberation of the mind." So the implication could be that, although Dashi is "ill," he is about to show an uncommon capacity to cure himself. For him, the right thing to do is to linger by the sea and accept the invitation to a tryst. Shen was too timid to practice what his stories preached, but he does seem to have asserted his right to enjoy platonic infatuations with other women. See "Gazing at Rainbows" below.

Like "Big Ruan and Little Ruan," this story refers to Shen's friend Lao She: his book Divorce, *which here suggests Dashi's subconscious fear of marriage and so foreshadows his dalliance with the other woman. The story is awash with other symbols and clues, including color imagery, and of course the delicious danger at Dashi's doorstep: the sea itself.*

"Eight Steeds" is didactic, yet it simultaneously probes modern situation ethics, presents a psychological view of the nature of man, explores a psychiatric vision of the writer as a healer of people's souls, and satirizes China's intellectual class, the author included.

"Is this your first time in Qingdao, sir, your first look here at the sea?"

"If you want to go to the beach, sir, go across that meadow and through the grove. That's the sea."

"If you want to look far out to sea, sir, look there, at the western end of the field. You go through that grove – those are Canadian aspens, and those are ginkgoes – follow the road lined with ginkgoes up the hill, and from the hill you can see the sea."

"Sir, they say that the sea at Qingdao is different from all other seas, more beautiful than any place in China. It's a hundred times better than at Beidaihe. Have you been to Beidaihe? Is the sea there clear or muddy?"

"Today is July Fifth, sir, so there are still five days until school starts. When classes start, you'll be pretty busy, so you should see the sea now."

In a bright, first-floor room of a small white house in a Qingdao residential district on the road up to Fushan, Mr. Dashi, who had arrived just fifty minutes earlier, leaned out the window to view the scenery. The porter straightened up the room for him and smoothed out the bed, chattering all the while. He obviously hoped to make a good impression on the guest. When he first opened his mouth, he saw that Mr. Dashi was smiling but not paying him any attention. A glance at the yellow steamboat labels on the small leather trunk told the porter that Mr. Dashi was a gentleman who had been abroad. That was why he had changed his tone so that the visitor would take note of the sea at Qingdao. Mr. Dashi continued to smile but said nothing. So the porter, to ease his own embarrassment, proceeded to explain how different the sea was at Qingdao than elsewhere: very mysterious, very hard to understand.

When he had finished his tasks, the porter stood in the

Translated by William MacDonald

doorway rubbing his hands. "If you want me, sir, just ring that bell. My name is Wang Dafu, but everyone calls me Lao Wang. Can you understand my speech, sir?"

Only then did Mr. Dashi speak. "Thank you, Lao Wang. I understood every word."

"Sir, I once read a book written by Mr. Zhu from the school,[1] called *Cast into the Sea;* it was very interesting." Lao Wang said this very proudly and walked out of the room smiling. Heaven knows what kind of book it was.

After the porter left, Mr. Dashi sat down at the desk by the window and began to write a letter to his beautiful fiancée seven hundred miles away.

Yuanyuan,

I've arrived in Qingdao. Everything here is just like home. Please don't worry; meals and lodging are all taken care of! There's a porter here who tends the house, and he's not a bad sort, though he likes to talk and use a lot of new words, words not too relevant to his life. You could call him a "quasi intellectual"; he just left my room. When he was here helping with my luggage, he said a lot of nice things about the Qingdao sea. I'd guess that he once was a waiter in a beach hotel; he certainly has that manner about him. He has to have heard many stories; must remember lots of them (just the sort of cow I need to milk)! I'd like to use him as a "living dictionary" for the two months that I'm here, flipping through him until I know him very well.

My window looks out toward the sea, which is really enchanting! But don't worry; I won't jump in. I might not dare say that if I were here a little longer, if I could know it, understand it. But if I should be careless, lose my footing, and fall into the sea, you can be sure that I'll

[1] Probably Zhu Guangqian.

try very hard to swim to shore. Because in my heart I'll be thinking of you. I couldn't let the sea take me away and leave you all alone.

Mr. Dashi wanted to capture in his letter part of the scene outside his window and send it far away for her to see. When he stopped writing and raised his head, the landscape outside his window was clear and bright. The meadow, the woods, the distant sea – they stood out like an exciting picture. Mr. Dashi went on writing.

My little window looks out over a meadow that seems as if it were leveled according to an exact plan; it's like a beautiful carpet, dotted with unidentifiable yellow flowers. Seen from far away, the flowers appear to be embroidered. It reminds me of that little cushion you made in the living room back home. At the far end of the field is a grove of white aspens. The porter says they're Canadian aspens. Beyond the grove is the sea. Its color seems to change constantly; when I first looked, it was a deep blue satin ribbon, but now it's like a piece of silver.

Mr. Dashi wanted to quote a couple of lines of poetry to describe the distant sea, the sky, the earth. When he raised his head, he saw a yellow dot on the meadow in just the place where a little yellow dot should be. It was the figure of a girl wearing a pale yellow dress. She was walking across the meadow toward the sea when suddenly she disappeared in the grove of aspens. It was as if she had walked into the sea.

No line of poetry could describe that exquisite, fleeting image in the sunlight.

Mr. Dashi wrote a few lines in conclusion to this first letter to his fiancée:

The school isn't far from where I'm living, less than half a mile, and when I go to class, I must walk up a small hill and follow a long road bordered by ash trees.

On the mountain road the wildflowers are just opening. Their color is clear yellow, like gold. I like that anonymous little yellow flower.

Mr. Dashi had got off the train at twenty past —— in the morning. When he had arranged things in his room and finished the letter, he went to the school office to check in and discuss with the dean how to schedule the twelve hours of lectures he'd be giving at this summer school. Things were easily arranged, so he went, all by himself, to a little restaurant on the beach. He had a good lunch there. When he returned to his room, it was already —— in the afternoon. He began another letter to his fiancée, to report what he had done this half day.

Yuanyuan,

I've just been to the office and arranged the times for my twelve lectures. They're all before ten in the morning. Eight of the lectures are on topics I've taught in Peking schools, so I'll be able to do well by them even without further preparation. I'm also responsible for four hours of modern Chinese literature and two hours of discussion on the trends represented by some modern Chinese writers.

You can imagine how much these questions will arouse their interest when I raise them for discussion in the classroom. Today is the fifth, and school begins in five days. As promised, I should be able to report to you everything I see and hear all day, apart from going to class, going to the library, or walking by the sea. That's what I'll try to do. I'll see to it that you get one of my letters every day, and I'll put myself into them. I won't withhold from you even the tiniest part of the social scene that I see here.

The building where I'm living is rather attractive from the outside. It was set up especially for us professors visiting from far away. There are eight of us living here, but I'm not acquainted with the other seven. There're physics professor A, biology professor B, ethics professor C, history professor D — an expert on the Han dynasty, literature professor E — who specializes in the literary history of the Six Dynasties period, and so forth. I haven't met these celebrities yet, but in a few days I'll be able to tell you what each is like. Tomorrow I'm going to the university president's home, and we're going to have lunch. I guess when he sees me he'll say, "How are things going? Okay — ? Should have invited your fiancée to come see the coast! I didn't ask you here to make you lovesick, just to give you a rest and let you have a look at the sea. If you look at the sea all by yourself, maybe you'll jump in and be swallowed by a big fish!"

How do you think I should answer him, Yuanyuan?

While standing around after getting off the train, I happened to see a newspaper posted on the bulletin board. It had some news about us. Said the two of us were about to come to Qingdao to get married. And there were a lot of other things we don't even know ourselves, all printed there line after line for everyone to see. While passing on these rumors about us, the editor added this eye-catching headline: "WELCOME MR. ZHOU DASHI." That's just the kind of welcome I was afraid of. I was worried that people would turn up here looking for me. I must find some way to get away from all such bother if I'm to have time to write to you. Just suppose that I'm sitting here at my desk writing a letter and someone walks into my room uninvited and asks abruptly, "Mr. Dashi, what sort of love story are you writing now? How many have you written altogether? Is every story true? Do they all mean something?" Such questions could really be embarrassing! And of course I couldn't answer them. But on the next day they'd still write many things that even I couldn't imagine. They'd say, "Mr. Dashi himself told this reporter. . . ." When in fact maybe he'd never even got to see me.

When Mr. Dash left ——, he and his fiancée, Yuanyuan, had agreed that he would write to her every day, but he wrote three letters his first day in Qingdao. When he finished the third and called Lao Wang to drop it in the school mailbox, it was almost dark.

Mr. Dashi enjoyed his first twilight in Qingdao by the window of his room. He looked at the meadow outside the window; the meadow was burned a pale purple by the evening light on the sea. The strange tint called up a memory.

He thought of another time, when the same purple seemed to be dazzling his eyes. It had been several sheets of purple stationery; he couldn't be mistaken.

He opened his trunk and from the bottom took out a thick notebook. By the fading light at the window he searched for something in the book. It preserved a part of his past life. He flipped through the pages a while and finally found it under an entry headed "July 5th."

July 5th

Everything is almost superfluous because wherever I go I am always hemmed in by recollections. What is there new that can pull me out of the mud? There's nothing "new" in this world; even vexation is a very old thing.

He finished reading this and felt vaguely distracted. Mostly, he was exhausted by the long journey. He needed rest.

But Mr. Dashi's mind was all ready for a stroll in old surroundings, and once again he read the draft of a letter he had sent on the fifth of July two years before, to X in Nanjing, asking X to go to —— to see Y for him. The letter had been written on dark purple paper and posted during just such a captivating twilight.

The relationship of these people was that X liked him but he loved Y. And Y? She was not antagonistic to X.

When Y heard that X was very much in love with Mr. Dashi, Y said, "That's really a good thing." But human affairs are often not to one's liking. What God agrees to, men do not; what men agree to, fate does not. Finally, broken hearted, X married an accountant. Having become another man's wife, she knew that Mr. Dashi still passed the time in hopelessness and helplessness. She sent him a letter asking if there was anything she could do. She wanted very much to help him because she felt that, although he didn't love her, by letting her do something for him he could still prove that he had faith in her. Her words were so roundabout, so pitiful. At the time, her hidden distress touched him, so he had written her this letter, asking her to go see Y. Not only was the letter an expression of confidence in X; it also told X not to wear herself out over dreams from the past.

X,

I've received your letter, and I understand everything. None of it is anything that humans are capable of arranging, so we shouldn't wear ourselves out. I hope that we can be a little wiser, so as to remove all bonds of love and hate.

I heard that you very submissively and modestly became someone's wife. This news makes your friends very happy. . . .

People who are dead, days that are dead, things that are dead – if they can still wear people down, then they shouldn't be kept in one's heart to make one suffer; if those who are not forgetful are anxious for "happiness," forgetfulness is the first thing they should learn. Recently I've been living in retreat, hoping to escape all the besiegements of memory. It would be better to preserve a little hope for the future than let recollections weaken me completely.

Thank you for bringing up those stories in your letter. It comes just at a time when I'm disgusted with every story ever written. One should live, not just imagine life! If the stories are really as good as you say, it only proves that although the writer *wants* very much to go amid all life and live there, because one is unable to, one turns instead and takes it out on one's hand, forcing it to write.

It's fine for you to write fiction. It's clear you're a woman who can write much better than a lot of other people. If you lack self-confidence for this, then you should listen to the loyal and honest opinions of a friend. If family life goes along in an orderly fashion, writing won't be a necessity for you. You don't have to write for your own sake, but you must write for your readers. China still needs people who can forget their own failures and successes and write a little something. I heard someone say that you were going to become a nurse for wounded soldiers, and, to be sure, your strengths could make you a nurse for the wounded souls of many men. You would feel much more at home writing than waiting on invalids. Don't you think writing more befitting than changing bandages? You need self-awareness, self-confidence.

Before long I may go to ——, to see Y, "whom I dearly love, though she ignores me." For three years I have been at an impasse. If I should go to see her and everything is just as dull as before, I would be ready to live in the countryside and never trouble her again. I ought then to keep quiet and go live in the country for ten years, wasting those most important days of my life. X, if you're so good-hearted and also have the time, would you please go see her for me? I'll wait for your letter. Just send me any little word of what went on during your visit, and I must call it my most precious news of the whole year.

Will I still be living like this two years from now?

All human affairs change in the course of time. First, X had fallen ill and died the year before. Second, Y had already become Mr. Dashi's fiancée. Third, Mr. Dashi now didn't altogether understand the emotions recorded in his diary and letter.

Man is certainly a funny animal, he thought. Who can believe in the past? Who can know the future? We forget that which is past. Yes, some people forget everything that is past yet cannot forget the shadow of a smile from some other time and place. We think that the new is correct and want to hang onto it, but who can hang onto anything in this human world?

Comparing things over time, Mr. Dashi seemed vaguely distracted. At first he just stood gaping out the window. Then he began to smile. Now everything seemed to have been arranged correctly. A man should be content, satisfied with his lot. The sky slowly grew dark. Everything was so still.

Yuanyuan,

> The summer session has begun as scheduled. The university president seemed half serious and half in jest at his welcoming banquet when he called the lecturers visiting from afar "thousand-mile steeds," steeds able to travel a thousand miles at a stretch. It's because they're all such great names, and also because they didn't mind the long journey. If we're all thousand-mile steeds, then our present lodgings must be a "stable"!

> I mean something slightly different from the dean. I think that the name of our lodgings would better match reality if it were called a "natural sanatorium." Would you believe it, from a medical point of view, the people here all seem a little sick. (Here I really become a qualified doctor!) Didn't I say that I should make every effort to escape people who might annoy me? But the result has been just the opposite. In the past three

days I've gotten acquainted with six of the seven people living with me. From time to time I've gone out walking with one or two of them, and sometimes they've come up to my room for a chat. In a very short time we've developed into rather good friends. Professors D, C, B, and E have become especially friendly with me. And because of this friendship I have diagnosed them as sick. This isn't a mistake, and it isn't a joke. At least two of these professors are quite deluded, namely Professors B and C.

I'm rather happy to have come here and met these men; I've learned many of the things one should learn from such specialists. One of them is already fifty-four; some of the others are still only about thirty. It's as if all they've ever had, all their lives, is specialized knowledge, which is inseparable from "history," or "formulas," so that they seem very serious, very sage. But this conflicts a little with life; it's not very natural. These specialists are probably inclined to class a writer under thirty as a "romanticist," on grounds of age and occupation alone. Precisely because they are "classicists," they've developed an interest in and friendship with me as their "romanticist." I believe that my chats with them can help me examine their health and relieve their "mental problems." Some of these specialists have children in their third year in college who long ago began writing love letters to their classmates and having romances, but these men are completely naive, somnolent in their own hearts. Though rich in learning, they've never enjoyed life at all. If desire ever existed in their hearts, it's been mastered, blocked. I've gotten some valuable knowledge out of this: this "freedom to love" that everyone's been calling for these last ten years has stimulated these transitional people, and many hidden tragedies have come along with it. These tragedies occur everywhere!

Yuanyuan, do you think my words excessive? I'm going to describe to you the manners of these respected friends one by one.

Dashi

Professor A invited Mr. Dashi to come to his room for tea and a chat. The arrangement of the room left the following impression in Mr. Dashi's mind:

On a small table in the middle of the room was a family portrait, of six fat children surrounding husband and wife. The wife appeared very fat.

Inside the white linen mosquito netting was a white pillow with a few blue flowers embroidered on it. Beside the pillow was an old-style bag with Chinese buttons in the form of flowers, a volume called *It Might Rain*,[2] and *Five Hundred Writers' Poetry of Seduction.* On the mosquito netting hung a cigarette poster of a half-naked girl.

On the window sill were a little bottle of red kidney pills, a vial of cod-liver oil, and a package of headache powders.

Professor B went with Mr. Dashi for a walk on the beach. Some young girls in new-style bathing suits approached and passed by. Professor B turned around and watched them from behind before saying, "Very curious, these girls, just as though by nature they needn't do anything, just go on playing, don't you think?"

. . . .

"Shanghai girls don't seem at all afraid of getting cold."

. . . .

"The nurses at the Baolong Hospital make sixteen dollars a month and clerks in the Xinxin Department Store forty a month. Unless they've chosen celibacy, the long-range

[2]A collection of erotic poetry by Wang Yanhong of the Ming dynasty.

opportunities behind a counter are much greater than in a hospital sickroom, don't you think?"

. . . .

"I don't understand the ideas of Liu Bannong. Students at the Women's Arts and Sciences College all laugh at him."

When they reached the end of the beach, the two men crossed the road to the racetrack. Someone was exercising a horse in the middle of the track. Mr. Dashi wanted to go across the course and up the hill through the public garden. Professor B said he thought it was too far; the tide was out, and it was much more interesting to walk along the wet sand. So they went back to the beach.

Mr. Dashi said, "Why didn't your wife come with you? Is your home in Henan or Peking?"

. . . .

"It must be difficult having children in school. Are all three at Nankai University?"

. . . .

"Living at home is fine when there are no bandits around. You've never returned home, have you? It wouldn't really be any trouble to bring your wife here. Why not go get her?"

. . . .

"That's all very well; you could say that living by yourself as a bachelor is free and convenient. But doesn't it get lonesome sometimes?"

. . . .

"Do you find Shanghai better than Peking? Strange. If a man over twenty wants to have a good time, I should think he'd choose Shanghai. If he wants to study, where can he go but Peking? Would you say that in Shanghai you can – "

The girls were just then walking back from the southern end of the bathing beach. One of them was wearing a red bathing suit; her body was full and tall. She was exceptionally attractive. Her bare feet had left a row of beautiful foot-prints in the wet sand. Professor B bent down and picked up a shiny shell from one of the footprints; he lightly and sensually brushed the sand off the shell with his fingers.

"Mr. Dashi, look; these things on the beach are beautiful."

Mr. Dashi said nothing. He just smiled and turned his head toward a corner of the horizon. He watched the white sails and mist on the horizon.

Ethics professor C returned to the dormitory from a stroll in the nearby hills. The porter, Lao Wang, handed him a red wedding invitation at the door. "There'll be wine to drink, sir!" Professor C noticed that the invitation was from Mr. X in Shanghai. He went to Mr. Dashi's room to chat and began to talk about Mr. X.

"You write fiction, Mr. Dashi, and I've got a story for you to write. In 1923, I was teaching at — University in Hangzhou and was one of Mr. X's colleagues. You must have heard his name a long time ago. He's one of those who's had a dramatic life in all those riotous days since the May Fourth movement. At that time Mr. X lived beside West Lake. He rented a little two-room house and lived there with his lover Y. Each occupied one room; each had their own bed. During the day, they ate together, walked together, worked, and studied together, but at night they slept apart. I've heard this called *spiritual love.* To advertise the advantages of this kind of spiritual love, Mr. X wrote a book explaining and advocating it.

"Now, an awful lot of conflicts in society are brought on by sexual behavior, and sexual morality is debated passionately by many scholars. If a rooster is put together with a hen and is unaffected, like a capon, young students will be sure to notice it. And if a macho man did this, it would naturally attract even more attention and become notorious. Our society is one where everything floats on the surface, so

Mr. X naturally had strong feelings about his life and seemed to live it to the fullest. Analytically speaking, this was just a trick played by the two devils of Buddhist chastity and Confucian moral rectitude.

"A friend asked Mr. X, 'Your life is very tranquil. Wouldn't it be more lively if you had a child?' Mr. X looked at his friend scornfully and said, 'Ah, sir, you really don't understand me. How is our love like the animal instinct of ordinary people? You're really –; you can't see the forest for the trees. Haven't you read my book?' And he gave the friend a copy of his book.

"Later on his mother-in-law came from faraway Sichuan, and the couple had to give up one room to her. They put their two beds into one room, side by side. Another friend got wind of this and asked, 'Mr. X, have your convictions changed?' Mr. X retorted, 'Hmph! You're making me out to be a beast!' And he had nothing more to do with that friend.

"A year passed. The mother-in-law felt that this life was too boring, that going on like this was a little too lonesome. She wanted to be a grandmother. She expressed this opinion at dinner, in a jesting tone – that a child in the house would be a little more trouble but would also make it a little more lively. The couple didn't wait for the old woman to finish speaking but shouted in chorus, 'Mother! What are we going to do with you! How come you haven't read our book?' The couple regarded the mother-in-law as a stubborn old thing, quite pitiful. They felt that a person without higher education, who cared only that her children have grandsons she could feed candy to and play with, could have no higher ideals to speak of!

"Later the girl fell ill; it was an illness that developed from anemia. Mr. X took her to the doctor. The doctor knew them and listed the girl's name on the bed chart as Mrs. X. The couple was very unhappy about this and insisted that the doctor fill out a new sheet listing her as Miss Y. One look at the patient, and the doctor knew right away the cause of the illness; the two idealists had harmed their bodies with ideals that went counter to human nature. The cure was very simple: let her get better naturally by developing a little animal nature! The doctor lived up to his responsibility; he gave Mr. X his honest opinion. Mr. X heard him out and said nothing; he just took the girl and left. She still didn't understand what was going on. Mr. X said, 'That fellow's nothing but a reprobate, a maniac. He isn't fit to be a doctor.' Later on he told others, 'That doctor isn't respectable, he must make his living selling aphrodisiacs and performing abortions. I ought to report him to the authorities. By rights, the government should deal with such bastards using the full force of the law and not let them out in society.'

"So the girl changed doctors and took Chinese medicines; she consumed untold doses of fritellaria and decoctions of Chinese angelica. She dragged on for half a year and finally died. Mr. X erected a memorial tablet on her grave. On the stone was carved: 'Our love was a pure, sacred love!' At the time, society was very sympathetic, so naturally it accepted the explanation. Mr. X considered any friend who disagreed to be very vulgar and dirty, unable to conceive what heights of holy purity and beauty love could attain. Never again would he have anything to do with him.

"I've just received this invitation today, so I know that Mr. X is getting married to a Shanghai playgirl in August. Very interesting. The tide has changed; he will certainly never do that again."

Mr. Dashi listened to the story. He smiled and asked Professor C, "Mr. C, let me ask you – what is your view of love?"

Professor C folded the red invitation into the shape of an old pig's head. "I have no views on love. I'm an old man now. These things should be games for girls and boys."

On the wall of Mr. Dashi's room hung a photograph of Aphrodite. Professor C looked at it with his hands behind his back, as though he wanted to find – discover – something in the marble torso's hollows and swellings. When he took his eyes away from the picture, he suddenly asked, "Mr. Dashi, isn't there a Yang Xiuqing in one of your classes?"

"Yes, there is. How do you know her? In the whole class she's the most beautiful – "

"She's my niece."

"Oh, you're related!"

"She is clever and not a bad student," he said. Professor C looked back at the photograph on the wall. He asked uneasily, "Mr. Dashi, is this a photograph of a Greek sculpture?"

The question didn't seem to need an answer; Mr. Dashi understood very well.

Mr. Dashi thought, "Mr. C has eyes after all. He does recognize beauty." He couldn't help smiling knowingly.

The impression of a slender and graceful girl lingered in the minds of the two men simultaneously.

Professor D made a date with Mr. Dashi to go to the beach for a boat ride. It was a milky white boat with a little triangular white sail. They glided along the mirror-smooth surface of the sapphire sea, blown by a gentle breeze. The weather was clear and warm. Waves lapped up lightly against the bow and sides of the boat. The boat rocked slightly, and when it glided forward, it rose and fell like a little sparrow dipping into the water. There was a pale purple cloud on the horizon, and in the sky four or five white birds were calmly flying out to sea. The scene was just like that of another situation recorded by Mr. Dashi in his diary. The boat was like this one, but with a slight difference: the person sitting opposite Mr. Dashi before had been a doctor, and now it was philosophy professor D.

The two men steered the boat around a small green island. They were discussing the same question that had not produced any conclusion when Dr. Ruomo and Mr. Dashi talked about it a year before: women, a topic that could never have a conclusion.

"Probably every individual must be restricted by something in order to be a proper human being," Professor D said. "Doesn't matter if it's God, ghosts, laws, doctors, money, fame, toothaches, or beriberi; there have to be either external or internal limits for one to be a human being. One without any restrictions may seem very unfettered on the surface, but such a one really can never succeed at anything. Because one isn't a human being. If one has no restrictions, one can't have much vitality.

"If I didn't presently have to put up with even the slightest restriction, I wouldn't suffer from any desires, and I wouldn't care about people. That wouldn't be good at all. Sometimes when I think of it I'm afraid. For being able to go on living at all I must thank society for giving me some restrictions. If I didn't have them, I'd commit suicide.

"Dr. Ruomo's former seat in this little boat and mine aren't too far apart. He wasn't married, and neither am I, but he was also fed up with women. He said, 'When a woman is beside you, she wears you down physically, and when she's away from you, she wears you down spiritually. Woman is a god imagined by a poet, a god of the prodigal instinct.' Although he said he disliked women, before long he took one of these physical-spiritual goddesses back home with him and made her his wife – earned his living at her feet. I'm the opposite in every way. Lots of girls excite my interest. Fat ones, skinny ones, the affected and the superficial – I guess I'll always like them, if only because they *are* women, with women's good points – and weaknesses. I can't sum it up as strikingly as Dr. Ruomo, but I understand women better than he does. Many men who dislike women get married to one under extremely casual circumstances. Me, I like a lot of women, I'm partial to all of them, so I could never again marry one.

"According to my philosophical nihilism, I should have

killed myself a long time ago. The fact that I've lasted until today and never committed suicide is thanks to the women in the world. I love all these women passionately. In my imaginary infatuations, I love them like a lunatic. There is one to whom I'm especially partial, but I've made every effort to restrain myself and never let her know I love her. If I should let her know, she might marry me. I'm not ready for that. I must avoid it. I just want to wait until she's forty, when she'll have lost most of her womanly assets, and then I'll tell her that what she has lost I still keep in my heart. I love her, love her passionately, so I feel that just to possess her is not enough; I'll let her marry someone obviously inferior to me so that she can finish the rest of the beautiful part of her life with that other man. When she's old, my love will still be fresh and lively.

"What do you think, Mr. Dashi?"

Mr. Dashi expressed his opinion: "Your plan is still about the same as Dr. Ruomo's. You're not creating a philosophy; you're letting a philosophy create you. Like so many other people, you make long-range plans to show your foresight and daring, thinking that in the future you're bound to double your profit. But your planning is too long range. I'm worried about you. I have no reason to oppose this sort of investment because each man has the right and freedom to squander his life, just like my plan to cast myself into the sea; if I felt like throwing myself into the sea, you wouldn't presume to intervene.

"But if I were a woman, I wouldn't have much interest in your plans. You have philosophy but no common sense. You seem to think that, when you reach that age, your brain will be as full of illusions as it is today and that, when the woman reaches forty, she'll be as amorous and full of good impulses as when she was eighteen. This is really muddled. I daresay you will have to lose on this account. If you could read a book on ——, you'd feel that your philosophy ought to be slightly revised. You love her, and you must give your love to her. This is a principle of nature. You love her but feel that even to make her yours is not enough, for time threatens your love. So you want to go against the order of human life. Yet, you say, this is all for a woman. I think that this is the same as foot binding. It is against nature, and it's a little cruel."

"You think that this is abnormal, don't you? We each of us can build a church according to our own ideas, to worship the god we believe in. I think the altar I have created is the most beautiful one in the world. You may think it a little too wasteful. But love is extravagant to begin with. It's precisely because there are too many stingy people in this world that everything is done badly. I think that stinginess borders on stupidity. A man wants to make his own character shine, to light up the sky, and dazzle people's eyes like golden stars, but a stupid man can do no such thing."

"You want to do this because you've been poisoned by the theater. If you can do this, you really do have a talent for acting. I admit your intelligence."

"You're right, I'm playacting. I've very bravely assigned myself a role. I'm waiting for the moment when the whole performance, enthralling yet logical, reaches the climax and suddenly the unexpected happens."

Mr. Dashi said, "Right. If a man really wants to live his whole life on a tense and noisy stage, live it in an aberrant, unnatural way, then through an artist's eyes there are no grounds for opposition. Art will not tolerate the ordinary. But, to continue the image of the play, if it goes on too long, do you think your leading lady can stand it? There may be many women in the world who, for a time, have divine beauty that enchants the poet and the prodigal, but they cannot keep it for long. You admit that at some point they lose the splendor of life. Try to think what is left of a woman who has lost her superficial splendor."

"What's your point, then?"

"Love her, take her. Love her, give her everything."

"If I love her, how can I have her for very long? If I give her everything, what is left of me? And without a me, how can I love her?"

Aware that Professor E had divorced one year after he married, Mr. Dashi wanted to know his opinions and thoughts about it.

Professor E replied, "Woman is a very odd creature. If you say, 'My soul, my queen, look how I worship you! Let my ardor, expressed in such Shakespearean terms, be smashed by a woman; come kiss me!' Fine words. But suppose you're not on stage but in a living room? You'll hear her answer you in a rather unnatural voice (they sound more natural when they really are performing a play), 'No, I don't love you.' Okay, it ends this way. Many men leave their lovers this way, and men, of course, consider it a love lost. Later on, if the man's business doesn't turn out well or his reputation isn't too good, then the woman will think, 'Lucky I wasn't taken in by him.'

"But comes another man who doesn't want to be a Shakespeare and isn't so eloquent. All he wants is an opportunity. When opportunity lets him be near the woman, he doesn't have to say anything; he just silently kisses her. In surprise and indecision the woman may reach out and box his ears. But the man doesn't make a sound; he just embraces her, planting a long kiss on her tiny mouth. He hasn't spoken a word at any time, hasn't explained his behavior. He knows he isn't in Parliament or teaching a class. He's just gone ahead and done it. Consequently, all is silent. The woman thinks, 'He's kissed me.' And at the same time she knows that the kiss hasn't cost her anything. Finally, she becomes his wife. They get along very nicely, and in ten years she's raised a flock of kids and turned into a fat middle-aged woman. If the man is bad, she explains it away as fate.

"Yes, women have their good points. I know what they

are. When God made woman, he wasn't completely mud-dleheaded, for he gave her a fine, soft body. He also gave her a contented and complacent disposition and, more interesting yet, at the same time he created for her a whole crowd of stupid men crazy in love. And therefore we have love stories, love poems, suicides from lost love, and – the upshot is that woman occupies a special place in society, for it seems she is indispensable for all things.

"I think there's a mistake in this arrangement. Starting with myself, I wanted to be rid of all influences and restraints coming from women, especially that most uninteresting restraint of living together. To remove these as soon as possible, I got divorced."

Mr. Dashi looked out at the meadow. "Lao Wang, what do you call those yellow flowers in the meadow?"

Lao Wang didn't hear him, so he didn't answer. His head was bent over his work.

Mr. Dashi asked again, "Lao Wang, who is that girl coming across the meadow to see Mr. G?"

Still straightening up the desk, the porter raised his eyes to look out the window. "A teacher at the —— Girls' Middle School. Very pretty, isn't she?" He pointed upstairs and said softly, "Soon, very soon now." He seemed to be saying that the two would soon be engaged or soon be married.

Mr. Dashi smiled, "Soon what?"

A novel by Lao She was on Mr. Dashi's desk. Lao Wang riffled through the pages. "Sir, this was written by Lao She. Lend it to me to read, okay? Why is it called *Divorce?*"

Mr. Dashi seemed very angry. "I ask you, Lao Wang, why shouldn't it be called *Divorce?*"

Suddenly the bell rang upstairs; probably it was Professor G. He must have seen the girl crossing the meadow to the dormitory and wanted to call the porter to make tea.

A letter to Qingdao sent from ——:

Mr. Dashi,

I've read the little portrait you sent me of the history scholar, Professor H. You must have exaggerated. His words to you as you recorded them don't sound the way he usually talks. But I believe you were sincere when you wrote it. That pen of yours can bear the accuracy of your observation. This sketch is the same as the ones you've done of the other gentlemen; each has a certain manner, a manner so vivid that on paper it's affecting. I'm elated to read them. But I hope you . . . because you should remember to whom you send these sketches. Professor H is simply crazy.

Didn't you say there were eight people in the dormitory? Why haven't you told me who the seventh is? It's funny that you haven't met him in the past half month. It seems to me there must be a reason for that. Tell me about it.

Heaven keep you,
Yuanyuan

Every time Mr. Dashi closed the door and recorded the appearance and personality of these specialists in his book, a certain feeling arose: "But for me, the doctor, would these people be mad?" Actually, these people would never be mad; that was very clear. But whether they were mad or not wasn't what interested him. He had many other things to be interested in.

He sympathized with them and pitied them because he felt himself to be healthy in body and spirit. He, who took himself to be a doctor, a healer of the souls of humankind, was ready to put these people into a play, to point out a road for them, one that all unsettled and distraught middle-aged folk could bravely walk. He made these affairs sound engrossing and sent them to his fiancée to read.

But when, feeling a sacred duty toward humankind, this

doctor discovered that six of his seven colleagues were not quite sane, it naturally aroused his interest in the health of the other man. Oddly enough, the other man seemed not to have any affinity for him at all. The man's room was just upstairs from Mr. Dashi's. He sat close to Mr. Dashi at the university welcoming banquet. A brief introduction by President X had told him that this was economics professor G. No other opportunity had arisen for the two men to become friends. There was a reason, of course, why the two could not know each other better.

Mr. Dashi had discovered long before that this man's spirit was very healthy; he alone of the seven really didn't suffer any illness. This had to be proved by someone else: a beautiful girl who came often to the dormitory to visit economist G.

Sometimes the two stayed in his room; sometimes they walked along the road lined with ginkgo trees outside Mr. Dashi's window. The visitor looked to be twenty-five or twenty-six and, at the same time, perhaps only twenty. Her figure and face were well above average. What was easiest to remember were her eyes, which, as the poet said, "could talk, could listen." And it was these eyes that made it easy for people to mistake her age.

The girl came often to the dormitory, but then they were very quiet, as though just sitting, facing each other in silence. From the look of it, they were very intimate. Mr. Dashi took notice of the two but never had the chance to make their acquaintance, so he sometimes improvidently used his special rights as a writer and, from his momentary impression of the girl, imagined her background and personality as well as her present relationship with Professor G.

Perhaps this woman has graduated from a national university in Peking. History would be her major, but she would also be interested in poetry, giving her a knowledge of rhetoric equal to her grasp of the past.

She might be the eldest daughter in the family, a wealthy gentry family to be sure. Her family education would be excellent and her middle school education likewise. After graduating from the —— University history department, she would have gone to the —— Girls' Middle School to teach – about eighteen hours a week, for a hundred dollars more or less. She would have been adored by colleagues and students alike; when she first came to the school, maybe there was a bold and reckless literature teacher from Shandong who showed her a rather improper attention. But her upright and serious manner would have stopped the man's wild ambition from developing further. Yet there was a more important reason. Every day she would get a letter from Peking, and, the way her school colleagues saw it, this was proof that she "had a master," maybe a lover or a good friend. Because of the letters, the illusions of many people had been destroyed. There had been no letters since last week because the letter writer, Professor G, was already in Qingdao and there was no longer any need for him to write.

The girl never laughed or talked in a loud voice; sometimes she went out for a quiet walk with Professor G, but there was no other noise than the sound of footsteps. The silence of Professor G and the girl proved that they were in love, had a love that was intimate and healthy. Only this condition could make a couple so silent.

The girl's outstanding feature was her eyes; they seemed to be constantly warning, constantly arousing. If you looked at her, they seemed to say, "You be careful. Don't look at me that way." If an acquaintance said something impertinent to her or behaved in a manner that would not bear scrutiny, those eyes had only to look at him in that way. They could inhibit excessive behavior yet at the same time encourage impudence. They could make the roguish too reserved and fearful to act recklessly, and they could give the staid illusions of making progress with her. They seemed always to possess a timid, sensitive light. If this light represented chastity, it was at the same time full of desire.

Because of curiosity, or something like curiosity, Mr. Dashi wanted an opportunity to learn a little more about the relationship between these two. From his observations, it couldn't be very ordinary. There was some question about it. There was a story. Moreover, the girl's silence attracted him and made him feel that he just had to know a little more about her. And her eyes seemed already to have aroused feelings in Mr. Dashi. "I know who you are, Mister, and you don't put me off. Come to me; get to know me; worship me. You aren't a simpleton; you know that this is fate and not anything that human power can resist." This was a challenge, a silent challenge. But Mr. Dashi cared nothing about it. He was just a little curious, that was all.

Just now magazines throughout the country were adding various colors to Mr. Dashi's love stories, arousing the interest of many people. This girl must know who Mr. Dashi was, whom he was going to marry, and many things that Mr. Dashi didn't know himself – that is, all those exciting rumors so remote from reality that were being spread around.

Mr. Dashi had told his fiancée all the things he had seen and heard since coming to Qingdao, except the things and feelings related above, which he kept in his diary.

Mr. Dashi sometimes went walking alone in the big meadow or up the hill along the road lined with ginkgoes to look at the sea, and three or four times he had run into the economist and the girl. You might say that these accidental meetings had been arranged. Although they only nodded casually to each other before going their separate ways, a good sort of impression imperceptibly accrued. Whenever

Mr. Dashi noticed a little something in the girl's eyes, he avoided those slightly dangerous orbs and walked on a little farther.

He thought, "This is funny. A year ago, this business would have made me fall very ill. But now it doesn't matter. My life has an immunity, so the sickness that makes one go hot and cold at the same time can't touch me." He felt that his avoidance was just a way of keeping another from suffering the same illness. The girl couldn't take such an illness, and if Professor G could avoid it, so much the better.

But all human events are as if arranged by an unseen hand. Everything happens by accident, everything changes under unexpected conditions. One day, when the lectures at the Qingdao University summer school were almost over, Mr. Dashi suddenly received an anonymous letter, a note only two lines long:

SCHOOL WILL SOON BE OVER. CAN YOU GIVE UP THE SEA?

(FROM SOMEONE)

What someone? It was really very amusing.

When this note reached Mr. Dashi's hand, he could tell from experience who had written it. It came from a trembling heart and a trembling hand, very timid yet very cleverly smiling. The author had posted it herself. Whoever it was, however simple the message, whatever its diction, Mr. Dashi clearly saw the meaning the letter expressed. As usual, Mr. Dashi silently put the letter into a big envelope. As usual, he felt neither fortunate nor proud. Perhaps he couldn't help feeling a little disappointed now and then. And because of his sangfroid, when he knew whose letter it was, ostensibly he paid no attention to it, as if he were more or less ungrateful for that young girl's passion and friendship. Still it couldn't sway him. If tranquillity was his customary manner, then he maintained that tranquillity throughout. The customs of mankind should bear some responsibility for Mr. Dashi's attitude. An influential word – one that restricts human behavior, prohibits its development toward superior purity, and keeps it from transcending the real world – should bear some responsibility. Mr. Dashi was engaged to be married. In the name of "virtue" he had locked the door to love, rejecting all friendship with other women.

Mr. Dashi stared at the note, thinking that it must have been written by an infatuated girl; holding it in his hand, he called to mind his six pitiable colleagues in the dormitory, and his heart involuntarily slipped into depression. "If you want it, it doesn't come; if you don't want it, it does come. Is this life?" He mumbled softly to himself, "If I don't go, what will happen? Can a true classicist really become sick? If I don't go, I still won't get sick!" Very definitely, even if he stayed because of business and still didn't go, he wouldn't go so far as to get sick. He had experience, confidence. He was a man who wasn't afraid of any demonic temptations. At another time he had stood on the brink of hell and hadn't been dazzled, hadn't gotten dizzy. The girl then had been one of those who makes men jump right down into the pit of hell itself. Sometimes he thought that this letter, which was almost a dare, was a young girl's game, the product of an audacious and reckless passion. He thought that ignoring it was the best way to discipline this reckless and audacious girl.

YUANYUAN:

TAKING LATE TRAIN BACK TO —— TODAY.

D.

After Mr. Dashi had taken this short telegram to the telegraph office, he noticed that it was only five o'clock. The departure time was already arranged, and this was the last day he would be in Qingdao. He remembered Professor B and the seashells on the beach. Mr. Dashi had told Yuanyuan that Professor B picked up a shell on the beach, and she had written in reply, "Don't forget to bring me back a few shells; I'd like some!"

So, when Mr. Dashi left the telegraph office, he went to the beach.

When he got to the bathing beach, the tide was just going out. Apart from several foreigners from the riding club galloping their black horses along the beach, there were only two beach attendants, who were taking in the boats and clearing up the sand. Mr. Dashi walked along the beach, his head bowed, searching the white sand for the pearly flash of a beautiful shell. He remembered the way Professor B had picked up the shell and thought it rather amusing. When he had almost walked to the eastern end, he suddenly discovered two rows of words written slantingly in the wet sand with a stick. He walked over to look at them and saw these words:

IN THIS WORLD SOME PEOPLE DO NOT UNDERSTAND THE SEA AND DO NOT KNOW HOW TO LOVE IT; OTHER PEOPLE UNDERSTAND THE SEA BUT DO NOT DARE TO LOVE IT.

Mr. Dashi thought about the idea and laughed. He was a handwriting expert. He recognized the characters, and he knew what they meant. He looked at the tideline and saw that the person playing this game had left not long before. This was a little strange, after all. Did this person know that Mr. Dashi would arrive at the beach this evening and there-fore come just before he did, leaving these two lines? Or did this person come to the beach and write these words every day, in the hope that one day Mr. Dashi would see them? No matter which, this evidently went beyond audacious reck-lessness; it was much more clever, more cunning. Mr. Dashi frowned at it for a minute, then left, his head still bowed. Almost defensively he thought, "Clever one, you're still going to lose. You're too young. You don't know that, once a man's suffered a certain illness, he can't get infected again! You're really quite clever. Someday this will help you accomplish something great, but this time you must admit that you've lost. It isn't your mistake; it's fate. You're one year too late – "

Yet he unconsciously faced the sea and heaved a soft sigh.

Don't understand the sea, don't love the sea, yes. Understand the sea, but don't dare love the sea, no. Could that be right?

As he walked he counted softly, "Yes – no? No – yes?"

Suddenly, something new on the sand made him stop dead. It was a pair of eyes, a pair of beautiful eyes drawn in the sand. Beside them was written,

LOOK AT ME, YOU KNOW ME!

Yes, Mr. Dashi knew very well who it was.

A beach worker came walking along the beach with a shovel. When he passed Mr. Dashi, Mr. Dashi hurried after him and said, "Slow up a little, will you? Let me ask you, do you know who drew this?" Then he pointed to the horseback riders.

The worker corrected his mistake, pointing to a pale yellow building by the hill. "Naw, a woman teacher drew it!"

"Did you see for yourself that it was a woman teacher who drew it?"

The worker looked at Mr. Dashi and said, a little offended, "How could I miss her?"

He finished speaking and walked off, his head in the air.

Mr. Dashi stood in front of the eyes in the sand for about a minute, still frowning slightly, then walked silently along the edge of the water. A light breeze wrinkled the surface of the sea into little waves. Mr. Dashi bent down, picked up a handful of sand, and threw it into the water. "Foxy thing, you're gone."

At twenty minutes past ten, Mr. Dashi went back to the dormitory.

Lao Wang, the porter, brought the train tickets from the school. He told Mr. Dashi that the train would leave at 11:25 p.m. and that half-past ten wasn't too early to board.

At eleven o'clock, the porter came to ask Mr. Dashi if he wanted him to take his luggage to the station. He returned *Divorce,* the novel he had borrowed, to Mr. Dashi. With an understanding smile, Mr. Dashi picked up the book and flipped through it, then gave the porter a telegram to take to the telegraph office.

It read:

YUANYUAN:

    AM SICK AND CANNOT RETURN TONIGHT. WILL STAY AT COAST THREE MORE DAYS TO GET BETTER.

DASHI

A true story. This doctor who called himself a healer of humankind's illnesses of the soul had definitely contracted a very extraordinary disease himself. It could not be cured if he left the sea. It had to be treated with the sea.

Later Elegies and Meditations on the Country Folk

Winter Scenes in Kunming

This section and the next sample works from Shen Congwen's later years as a writer, which for China were years of imperialist encroachment and outright warfare: war with Japan and civil war between Nationalists and Communists. The works in this section are less a continuation of Shen's urban concerns than of his inquiry into the condition of the country folk. The tone is meditative, and the terms of discourse are Chinese rather than avant-garde or Western. Shen Congwen was given to dark meditations on China's future. He wrote less and took to religious brooding about a pantheistic élan vital that he called simply "Life" (shengming). Love was his solution for China's problems. His religious concerns were not mystical, but clearly he was seeking another world beyond the corruption he saw occurring in this one.

To Shen Congwen and many other Chinese intellectuals of the day, the southwestern city of Kunming, in the province of Yunnan abutting Burma, represented the very best and worst of times. Professors and students from North China's top three universities took refuge from the Japanese together in Kunming at the Southwest Associated University. It was a time of the most abject poverty for them; wartime editions containing "Winter Scenes in Kunming" ("Kunming dongjing"; also titled "While in Kunming" {"Zai Kunming de shihou"}, with the postscript "6 February 1939") have covers evidently printed on the backs of scratch paper from the mathematics department. Yet, spiritually, Kunming was strangely exhilarating: a nearly self-sufficient and independent community of scholars and writers, free from political interference from either the Nationalists or the Communists, because the province was ruled by a warlord only nominally allied with the Nationalists. Everyone was equal, and everyone was free to ask ultimate questions. How different from the self-sufficient life in the countryside enforced on sent-down intellectuals by the Communist Party decades later. The appeal of this essay, as an evocation of the rare mood of the times, has risen accordingly, despite its topical subject: the decay of Chinese social and moral virtues, offset only by the resilience of the common people, who volunteer for war and haggle over provisions just like their ancestors.

If the subject is wartime corruption, the theme is much more abstract. Shen leads ever outward in contemplation and analysis, from the mundane world to the world of noumena, the cosmos, and Love. As in "Quiet," the animate props, some live, some not, provide reflections on freedom in the human condition. Shen Congwen's metaphors may indeed beckon one to look at the cosmos, not just in religious terms, but through the atomic particle theory of his scientific colleagues on the faculty. The idea that one could write about the war and simultaneously transcend it was unique in those stridently patriotic times. Only in Kunming could such ideas germinate. Yet Shen's apposition of ideas and images gives the piece a traditional flavor, too.

The new residence was on the high grounds, in a place called North Gate Slope. There from the little balcony you could see the name plaque "Tower for Gazing toward the Capital" on the northern gate turret of the city wall. To while away the idle hours, armed comrades in the tower were gazing down at the many people and horses passing below. A big open field lay in front of the house, with a grove of many different trees in one corner. The eucalyptuses were tall and lean, their catkins blue-green limned with silver, rippling in the gentle breeze. Each was like a silken flag, wound up into a bundle as if by an external force, wanting to open up, but bound by some invisible constraint and so unable to.

A clap of the hands would send round-headed squirrels with long tails leaping among the branches in startled confusion. These little creatures tossed themselves back and forth like balls, as if such caroming about could bring happiness, the joy of affirming the existence of Life through activity. From time to time they would stop and rest a while, looking all around them to see if they had succeeded in attracting the attention of some other creature. Perhaps they would discover that actually all creatures had their own private concerns. The man on the balcony who clapped his hands had already lifted his gaze from the eucalyptuses and fixed it on the great void above. That emptiness was an expanse of luminous blue, devoid of other existence. Here, too, was a kind of "man," one among all creatures, a man among the multitude of men: the meaning of Life. His imagination and feelings were at that very moment climbing up and leaping about branches of an invisible kind. He likewise was somewhat startled, somewhat perturbed, as he passed from one place to another through time, endlessly, without cease.

Though in the open field there were a great many women

Translated by Wong Kam-ming and Jeffrey Kinkley

and children, they all seemed to find this incident quite ordinary. No one looked up. In Kunming there were squirrels everywhere. Many people knew no more about these tiny creatures than that they could catch them and sell them to "the Shanghainese" for twenty cents to a dollar in "Central banknotes." The person on the balcony happened to be one of those the locals called a Shanghainese. He'd been spending Central banknotes to rent a house in Kunming where he passed his days. That he should have moved to this place was something of a coincidence, but on the other hand, because it was, it didn't arouse anyone's attention.

Most of the women were employees of a nearby stocking factory. They were in the field all day long, working spinning wheels to make cotton yarn. The children had very little to do, so they chased about and screamed at each other in the open field or picked up broken tiles and pebbles and threw them at dogs. Roads bounded the field on all sides. Stray dogs were constantly scavenging in the garbage pile in the wood, sniffing everywhere, their noses pressed to the ground. As soon as they saw the children crouch down, they knew the jig was up and fled nimbly toward a corner of the field. Sometimes they would only show their heads and look gently at the children, as if to say, "Suppose you play your games and let me play mine."

And sometimes it worked. That was when someone peddling beef or mutton arrived on the field shouldering a square wooden stand with a certified scale, a square cleaver, and a glistening, pointed "ox-ear" knife, then set them down to look for customers. Most of the women would put aside their work and come over to the meat stand to haggle over prices. As the children's interest shifted focus, several of the stray dogs would wander boldly into the field. At first they would sit in a corner convenient for a quick escape, looking on at the excitement from afar. Then, in a kind of probing movement, slowly, slowly, they would make their way through the crowd until, forgetting themselves, they would edge up to the meat stand. They would move off a little when the butcher caught sight of them and, brandishing his long-handled cleaver, shout, "You beasts, get away with you!" Then, standing outside the ring of humans, they would quite earnestly and passionately admire the fore- and hindquarters on the meat stand, the fleecy little sheep's tail, and the strips of suet hanging from the sides of the stand. By the look of it they seemed to feel that one part was just as good as another, that they were all beyond criticism. So the dogs kept silent. They kept waiting, hopelessly and helplessly waiting.

As a rule the women in the crowd would yell at the butcher, smiling all the while. On top of this would be oaths of all sorts to the effect, "As the gods on high are my witness, each will receive his due." The one testified that he was selling at a loss, the other that what was weighed out on somebody else's scale was hardly on the high side. But one way or another the transactions were completed. The meat was weighed and the money counted; the one getting the money went on his way, and the ones getting the meat would go home and hang it on hooks. Only after the children followed the women inside would the dogs take advantage of the situation and return. Pressing their noses to the spot where a while ago the butcher's stand had been, they would sniff here and there. If they chanced to come across a bit of bone or a scrap of meat, they would snatch it up with one bite and run away with it as fast as they could to a vacant spot in the field or under a eucalyptus. Just then a squirrel would be up in the tree, gnawing at a nut. The nut would fall to the ground. When the Shanghainese walked over and picked it up for a sniff, it would smell like mentholatum, slightly pungent and aromatic.

Six o'clock in the morning. The sun spread a silver-gray luster through the twigs and leaves in the tops of the eucalyptus; the air was cold and crisp. It was very quiet in the open field, with not a soul about, not even a dog. Several bamboo spinning wheels, gaunt as fine-boned skeletons, had been left sitting by a small clapboard shed. Standing on the balcony, looking down at these primitive, old-fashioned tools, one realized the multiplicity of the forms of "Life." Although the open field was completely empty, voices seemed to be issuing from it. They resounded in his ears.

"Too many bones. I don't want this big bone in the leg."

"My dear lady, without the bone, how could it have walked?"

"Do earthworms have bones?"

"Do you eat earthworms?"

"Good heavens, Buddha have mercy."

"Buddhas are made of wood and clay, not bones."

"Sounds like you're cursing Buddha. You'll go through every one of the thirty-three hells when you die and be ground up by millstones, burned by roaring fires, and bitten by hungry ghosts."

"All my life I've been a butcher, slaughtering sheep and pigs for religious believers like you and losing money in the bargain. When I die, I'll end up sitting on a lotus flower, flying up and up, straight to a pond in the Western Paradise. There I'll take a good, long bath and once and for all cleanse myself of a lifetime of sins and sheep stench!"

"You think the Western Paradise is a place for you butchers? Dream on!"

"All right, I'll stay here and let *you* go. But if none of us butchers go, you'll have no meat to eat when you get there! And when you all go on permanent vegetarian diets, you'll get tired of the Western Paradise one day and start worrying the Holy Buddha sick. He'll blame us butchers for having been such bad businessmen. All my life I've been doing business at a loss. In the end, if I don't get blamed by mortals, I'll be blamed by the Buddha. If you don't want that piece, I'll take it back."

"Go ahead! When that meat turns bad, I'd love to see you feed it to the dogs."

"If it goes bad, I *will* feed it to the dogs. If it isn't too bad, I'll share it with somebody. I'll invite him over when it's nicely stewed and throw in three bowls of wine. Don't be surprised if he feels like calling me Uncle or Daddy out of gratitude and promises to chant the *Lotus Sutra* for me a thousand times daily. Then, when I die, I'll mount to the Western Paradise on a lotus blossom the size of a card table!"

"You can go straight to hell! May you be reborn as a frog and croak your heart out, day and night."

"I won't go up to the Western Paradise or down to hell, either. The head of the Zhongxian district said to me, 'Zeng, you might as well quit selling your meat. You live in the eighth ward of Zhongxian district, and yesterday you were drafted in our conscription lottery. That's all there is to it; you're going to Hunan to fight. You're tall. When you put on your uniform and go marching off, right at the head of the column, you'll look terrific!' I said, 'Fine. I'll go whenever you want me to. I may be afraid of the Death Demon, but the Jap devils don't scare me. Since you've drafted me – want me, Zeng, to go – go I will.'"

. . . .

"I'll go off to war, to protect Wuhan. I can shoot, and my older brother commands a company of machine gunners. He's got three stars on his epaulets and three silver stripes! They'll make me squad leader the moment I get there and promote me to platoon leader as soon as I've won a battle. We'll fight our way to Peking. Then I'll drive a flock of sheep back to Yunnan and go into business. I'll really be doing business at a loss then!"

There followed another round of oaths, from both the butcher and the women. Everything was quiet and still in the open field. Faraway somewhere there were troops; the call of a trumpet summoning them to the drill ground reverberated in the damp air – motion in stillness. It occurred to him, "It's three months already since Wuhan fell."

A family out front had just whitewashed their walls. But the next day some gung-ho civil servant took notice and emblazoned a twelve-character slogan on them. The meaning came clear only after one mulled it over quite a lot. However, a phrase in the middle, "Nurture Up Hygiene," remained unclear. One of those words must be either superfluous or incorrect. This was a small matter. But if in small things they confused people so that the task at hand could not be carried out, just imagine what they did with serious business.

A lean horse with a copper bell around its neck passed by, carrying barrels of night soil.

A fellow with a gaunt, monkey-like face poked his head through the tiny, dark door of someone's house, calling out a child's name: "Wawa, Wawa."

What he saw had its effect on him; he mumbled to himself, "Where've you gone? Off eating shit again?" Wawa was already eight years old and had been to school, but his school had been moved out to the countryside in the evacuation. Now that he had no school to attend, he spent his days playing among the coal piles in the field. "Where does coal come from?" "It's dug up from underground." "What's it for?" "For burning." There was hardly any difference between what Wawa knew and what some experts knew. The Shanghainese thought to himself, "If you can go on to college, child, you might want to major in mining and metallurgy since you already know the origin and use of coal. Quite a few people are called experts on the basis of as much knowledge as that. They've gone on to important careers!"

Wawa's father, though, had been dreaming great dreams for his son's future all along. He thought that when his son grew up he ought to be chief of the Bureau of Planning and Management, a superintendent. Out here it was usual for anyone holding such an office to get rich. After you got rich, you bought somebody's house across the street. More Shanghainese had been coming, and they were willing to pay huge prices for houses. They paid high rent deposits, too. If you lent out money at 30 percent interest and let it compound, you could double your investment in three years. Hence the extraordinary fertility of this father's imagination.

Pity was, just now so many people had these naive, guileless dreams. And this is precisely the basis on which a place's stability and prosperity rest.

It's painful to admit this, isn't it? So let's drop the subject.

For if you've fallen in love with a patch of blue sky, a piece of the earth, and a group of honest, genuine people, you can hardly keep from shouting, "This won't do, this won't do! Heaven will not betray you. Don't give up on yourselves! Don't! Try hard to think of a way out! You should be getting a lot more out of life! You could be getting a lot more!"

Which would cause some people to ask, "Sir, what are you talking about? Whom are you criticizing? Whom are you lecturing? Whom are you trying to stir up? What is your motive in all this?"

When the questions were put to you that way, you wouldn't know what to make of them. Not only would you fail to understand them; you'd even get confused about what you'd originally had in mind yourself. Without dialogue, neither side can be right. You love *humankind;* they fear *change.* You are *devoted;* they are *suspicious.*

Beauty is an easy word to write, but it seems quite difficult to recognize. And although everyone knows the word *Love,* few really understand its meaning.

Amah Wang

"Amah Wang" ("Wang Sao"), written in 1940, *is a character sketch of an actual Shen family servant during the war years. It is also a paean to the strength of Shen Congwen's archetypal country folk, who were at the time of writing under the extraordinary duress of war. Hence, it is one of the few "patriotic" pieces in Shen's oeuvre. At the same time it shows unconditional, unpatronizing sympathy with a kind of lower-class consciousness and "worldview" that most Chinese intellectuals, Shen Congwen included, would have liked to reform if they could. Yet Amah Wang as a mother, like Mother Yang in "Qiaoxiu and Dongsheng," exemplifies nothing if not "Love." When at the end of the story Amah Wang burns incense, it could as well be for the daughter who was not spared as for the son who was. Thus, translator Peter Li feels, this piece is really about the mother-daughter relationship.*

Suddenly it was bustling in the kitchen. What could be the occasion? Just ask Amah Wang – her daughter was home for a visit! Only eighteen, with big, shiny eyes and her hair done up in a neat bun in back, she had a mouth as small as a cherry and a face that was round as could be. A gray-blue scarf covered her head; her apron was embroidered with a big red flower and decorated with red and green sequins. She was very shy. She blushed when she spoke, and in the company of strangers she just didn't know what to do.

Amah Wang, the housekeeper, explained that her daughter had been married only five months. Her husband farmed fifteen miles outside Kunming; she was wearing her new bridal clothes on this visit home. "Mrs. Wang – Wang *Sao*," said the mistress of the house to Amah Wang, "your daughter is our guest today. Why not fry up some eggs and ask her to stay for lunch?" Amah Wang turned to her daughter with a big smile and said, "The mistress says for you to stay. You don't have to leave right away." The daughter smiled back. Everyone in the family knew that Amah Wang had a good daughter, so they all came to have a look. They agreed that Amah Wang was indeed blessed with a nice girl. She was so lovely everyone liked her. Amah Wang beamed with happiness and did her chores with even greater enthusiasm.

Amah Wang had not only a good daughter but a fine son. Twelve years old, he had gone to work as a messenger boy at the tea bureau office in the western part of town, for fifteen dollars a month. The bureau was quite strict, so this son had to dress neatly and walk smartly in his gray uniform. All who saw him said from the look of his face that he was blessed with good fortune and would grow up to really be somebody. Only Amah Wang, fearing that he might go astray, frequently scolded the boy, pretending to be angry and telling him to get back to work quick. Although he was

Translated by Peter Li

her only son, he was unspoiled and well disciplined, and he spent his money prudently.

Amah Wang worked elsewhere for five months but came back when her other job apparently didn't work out. Her work for the household consisted of cooking and laundering and sometimes bickering over money with the people who came in from the country to sell eggs and clean the latrine — which she did for the sole purpose of protecting the honor of her employer. Because she was always honest and cheerful in disposition, so clean, and so careful and frugal about expenses, she was highly regarded and well liked by the whole family. The attention she received gave her a sense of pride, and she did her tasks with great eagerness.

One day another country woman came to town to see Amah Wang, bringing a bag of broad beans. The two women sat down and smoked as they talked. When the visitor had gone, it developed that Amah Wang's daughter, married just a year now, had died two months before. The visitor was her mother-in-law. The daughter had given birth, and there were no medical facilities there in the countryside. Two days later, when she began hemorrhaging, the rest of the family had all been at work in the fields. Thirsty and without any water, she ended up drinking sediment from the bottom of the water tank. She complained of a stomachache the next day and died shortly after. The baby had survived for two months and died, too. Despite this tragic news, Amah Wang went on with her life as usual. It was the ancient proverb, "Life and death are predestined; wealth and prosperity are decreed by heaven," that steadied her life and her emotions. She believed in those words.

Regarding her daughter's death, she said, "Her family were busy in the fields harvesting and loading barley onto the horse carts. My daughter wanted water, but there was none in the house. So she scooped up what was left at the bottom of the tank and drank it. Poor thing, she cried out that her stomach was in pain and then just up and died! Her husband cried and wouldn't let the coffin out of the house. After that, he decided to become a soldier. When his lot came up, he joined up at the Coiled-Dragon Temple. 'Life and death are predestined!' " Amah Wang never spoke very much, but when she did, her words were poignant.

At supper, Amah Wang added a dish of fresh beans — those brought by the mother-in-law earlier in the day. The two women had talked brokenheartedly about their daughter, their eyes wet with tears from invoking her name. But she was already moldering in the grave.

Amah Wang's daughter was dead, but her son was fine. Every month he would come to see her, bringing all his pay. She counted it out and gave him two dollars' spending money.

Like most other families, Amah Wang's employers raised chickens and had a dog and a cat. Each had its special place in the family, but it was Amah Wang who looked after them.

After serving lunch and washing the dishes, Amah Wang would sit on a stone stool in the inner courtyard and feed the chickens. When she saw the tyrannical big rooster picking on the young hens, she would kick it away and shout, "You lousy, no-good feather duster! How much can your little craw hold! I'll beat you to death!" But the rooster went about quite unperturbed, for this feather duster knew that Amah Wang was good at heart. The rooster belonged to a philosophy professor, Mr. Jin,[1] who lived upstairs in the Tang mansion across the way.

Every day early in the morning, the little black dog in the family was full of energy and looking for something to do. There was no one else to play with, so when he heard the rooster stretch out its neck to announce the day, he got his fun out of chasing it. This was a pretty fierce game, and the rooster couldn't take much of it. It had to give up its dig-

[1] Jin Yuelin.

nity and run around the house cackling by way of protest and in hopes that someone would rescue it. The noise of course drew everyone's attention, but they all knew it was just the little black dog up to his tricks, so they paid no attention. In the end it was Amah Wang who came to the rescue and no one else.

Sometimes she was already up and heating the water in the kitchen. She would pick up a pair of tongs from the fireplace and chase after the little dog. But sometimes she wasn't up yet, and the racket made her angry. Then she would pick up a long bamboo pole and beat the dog from the doorway. This pole, used for laundry in the daytime, was taken inside the house in the evening for this very purpose. The little dog was very smart, and he knew where his food came from – Amah Wang – so he treated her with due respect. He recognized the bamboo pole as the instrument of his daily punishment. But since he was terribly lonely in the morning, the little dog just had to chase that rooster. After Amah Wang had beat the dog a couple of times, he would slink to the wall like a naughty child, relieve himself against it, and willingly give up his little prank. No matter how much beating and scolding he received, the little dog knew very well that Amah Wang was the one who took care of him.

Amah Wang usually fed the dog first, then the chickens. Having eaten his fill, the dog would then sleep on the veranda. Amah Wang would clap her hands after feeding the chickens, as if to say that the feed was all gone. At this sign, the chickens would move to the other side of the courtyard to peck at the ground under the big eucalyptus tree. Now Amah Wang was ready to begin her own work. The afternoon was her time for washing the clothes. There were two large baskets of laundry to be washed, with the dirty clothes of all three generations in the family: the grandfather, the mistress and master of the house, the young ladies, the boys in school, the baby – and also those of her twelve-year-old son at the tea bureau. Amah Wang got it all done without getting ruffled. There was no end to her chores, but she just did them one at a time. As she rubbed and kneaded the laundry, she would sing a song from her native place. She had a pleasing soprano voice. Occasionally the mistress of the house would overhear this and ask her to sing out loud, but then she would blush to her ears and refuse to open her mouth again. Her singing was for herself only; it was to transport her into her own world of hopes and dreams.

Amah Wang earned twelve dollars a month, three less than her son. But they had no place to spend their money. They'd save it for a year, then send it back home to purchase a quarter-acre of farmland. As the war continued, the cost of food was rising. Even though their earnings were paltry, the interest slowly accumulated, and in five years' time it amounted to quite a bit. After eight years, the son would be grown, and the director of the bureau was going to recommend him for officers' training school. Then he would take a wife. Amah Wang would not ask for a big dowry, just an acre of land and a water buffalo. Her life was simple and practical, and it had made her healthy and happy. The world was always changing, and so were people's hearts — maybe the dogs and chickens were changing, too. Only the hopes and values of this country woman in the city remained the same, through it all.

After March, the weather improved. It was sunny all day long, but air-raid sirens began to wail in the city. When they did, the whole family, young and old, formed two groups. There were those who joined the evacuation and took shelter outside the city and those who stayed put inside the house. Amah Wang usually laughed at those who were evacuating. She would smile and tell them, "They're coming, they're coming, hurry, hurry!" She didn't say much, but her shout bore a lot of meaning. She was a bit sarcastic and proud of it. It showed that she was not afraid — not even when the airplanes flew overhead. And why? Because the ideas of Confucius were engraved on her simple heart: "Life and death are predestined; wealth and prosperity are decreed by heaven." She remembered a story about the Tang dynasty rebel Huang Chao, reputed to have killed people by the thousand. "Those destined to die couldn't get away if the escape route were right before their eyes. Those not destined to die couldn't pass by the judge of the underworld if they sat on his doorstep." This simple story and its moral calmed the woman's heart. All her life, she had worked to the best of her ability and been wholly reliable. In time of chaos, she was not afraid. The chances of a bomb falling on her head were not very great, and if one didn't fall on her head, what was the use of being afraid anyway?

After those who were evacuating were gone, the ones inside resumed their normal work and study. The courtyard was quiet, with Amah Wang left all to herself. She continued washing the clothes, and, as she scrubbed, she counted the airplanes flying overhead so that later she could report it to the master of the house or make small talk with any visitor who might come by.

Amah Wang also needed a kind word once in a while, either of praise or of respect. That was enough to elate her. Every afternoon at four o'clock, Professor Jin would come to look at his rooster. He would bring a big sesame cake and sit on the stone steps under the eaves, feeding the chickens as he chatted with Amah Wang. If the sirens were sounding, he would ask, "Amah Wang, are you afraid?" When he found that she wasn't, he would stick up his thumb and say, "Amah Wang, you're number one. You're the bravest one in the house!" Amah Wang was a bit embarrassed and said with a smile, "Yes, Mr. Jin, you're right. I'm not afraid. 'Life and death are predestined; wealth and prosperity are decreed by heaven.'" Knowing that she was talking with a professor of philosophy, she quoted the saying of the sages to regain her composure. The philosophy professor would repeat the words, adding, "Isn't that so, isn't that so. Straight from the mouths of the sages."

Amah Wang smiled and said, "And how could the sages be wrong!"

Amah Wang never left town to escape an air raid, and, as if "life" were in fact "decreed by heaven," not one bomb fell on her. Amah Wang only saw Chinese airplanes circling overhead, never any Japanese ones.

On May Ninth, the weather was especially clear. As usual the air-raid siren sounded, and thousands of people rushed out of the city. In Amah Wang's house there were, as always, those who rushed out and those who stayed in. But this time it was a little different. At about three o'clock, twenty-seven planes flew high over the city and dropped bombs on the airfield. The shape of the airplanes, the sound of their droning, the explosions, and the news of the bombing left a deep impression on Amah Wang. But afterward business went on as usual. At supper, Amah Wang brought on the soup and listened to the news. A guest said to her with a smile, "Amah Wang, did you see the Japanese airplanes?"

"Twenty-seven of them, very high. Then the antiaircraft guns started firing and the machine guns, too. Then, boom, boom, the airfield exploded. I didn't hide; I wasn't afraid."

"You're really not afraid? Those bombs are big as water tanks. This house wouldn't protect you."

"If they bomb, let them bomb. 'Life and death are decreed by heaven,'" Amah Wang said, and the matter was closed.

The next afternoon, the weather remained clear, but there was no air raid. Around two o'clock, Amah Wang was washing clothes, her eyes and ears on the lookout for Chinese airplanes. Suddenly the little dog started barking wildly. It was her son from the tea bureau.

The child's face was dirty, and his pants were ripped. He had come for his mother to mend them.

"Fushou,[2] where have you been?"

The child said, "I just came from the French Ganmei Hospital, near the Jinri Building district in the middle of town."

"Where were you during the air raid yesterday?"

"In the village of Hedianying."

Amah Wang was startled. "What were you doing at the airfield? Didn't the Japanese bomb that place to kingdom come? Lots of people got killed. You wanted to see the excitement? What's so great about that!"

"I was there on business. The planes came and dropped twelve bombs and three incendiaries. The building caught fire and collapsed. People's hands and feet were flying all around me, and three horses were blown to bits. Machine guns fired wildly all around without letup. I thought I was a goner, buried alive under the debris. Then someone found me, felt my heart beat, and saw that I was still breathing, so they put me on a truck and took me to Ganmei Hospital. This morning at nine o'clock I woke up. So you've come to, they said, and asked me my name. All right, Master Wang, they said to me, you get on home. At the office, they told me my mother was looking for me. My pants got ripped on the truck when they took me for a dead man. . . . They said I was very lucky. I'm not hurt at all. I was just a hair's breadth from death."

The boy told her what had happened clearly and in detail, without any sign of fear or boasting. He sat by his mother's laundry tub and felt the big rip in his pants. His skinny leg was wholly exposed. Amah Wang's voice was hoarse as she said, "Aiya! You're lucky you weren't killed! And you saw people die and the houses burn? And hands and feet flying up in the air? And then they took you to the hospital, and you only woke up at nine this morning? Was your boss angry with you when you got back? Come over here, let me see your pants!"

[2]"Good luck and long life."

The child went over to his mother. She pulled his pants down and smacked him on the rump three times. "You're not afraid to die, huh? I'll beat you to death first. That will save you the trouble of being blown to bits by bombs as big as water tanks!" Her son chuckled, but he could see that his mother's eyes were wet.

"I'm not afraid of the Japanese," he said. "I'm going to be a soldier when I grow up."

Amah Wang wiped her eyes with the corner of her apron and said to her son angrily, "All right then, you go ahead and be a soldier. You think the army will take a pint-sized soldier like you? The crows will think you're a mouse and snatch you away."

"I'm not a bit afraid of war. I'll take a prisoner and bring him back alive to show you. I'm going to tie him up with telephone wire – he's got to be alive so we can make him work on our farm!"

"The only prisoner you'll take will be a toy soldier made of straw!"

"But I'm growing up. I swear I'm going to fight in a big war."

Amah Wang decided not to argue with him anymore. She got out her needle and thread and sewed up his pants – meanwhile giving him a couple of endearing spanks. The son felt her love and asked, "Ma, are you afraid?"

"Me, afraid? What's there to be afraid of? The heavens are above us."

She looked up at the sky, all blue with a few puffy white clouds. Just then three crows flew up to the top of the eucalyptus tree and lit there. The child clapped his hands to scare the crows away. Amah Wang finished her sewing, bit off the excess thread with her teeth, and stuck the needle in her topknot. Amah Wang pulled her son over by his dirty ear and said, protectively, "If you become a soldier, the crows will snatch you up into the trees. Fushou, do you think you really can become a soldier?"

Fushou just smiled. He thought, "Why can't I become a soldier? When a man grows up, he can do anything."

When Amah Wang's son left, the whole household learned of his adventures that day. They all thought Amah Wang was such a good person with a kind heart and blessed with good fortune. Amah Wang didn't say anything but returned her mistress's smile. That night she sneaked out of the house to buy incense and paper money, which she took outside the northern city gate and burned. She thought about her daughter and how she had suffered. She certainly hadn't had a good life. Amah Wang felt bad; she hid in her room and cried all day, skipping supper. The family knew nothing of this because she thought people might laugh at her, or ask her questions, or offer consolation. She didn't need any of that.

Qiaoxiu and Dongsheng

"Qiaoxiu and Dongsheng" ("Qiaoxiu he Dongsheng"), written in July 1947, feels unresolved and uneven in tone; it was to be one chapter of a novel or story cycle. "Truth Is Stranger than Fiction," finished on the eve of the Revolution and available elsewhere in a translation by Gladys Yang, continues the tale, but still without achieving closure.

"Qiaoxiu and Dongsheng" begins with a Proustian attempt to recapture memory and lost youth. Fantastic images from nature and ghostly figures from Pu Songling's seventeenth-century masterpiece Strange Tales from a Chinese Studio *lend an air of eerie nostalgia. There are also dark hints, more or less red herrings, about the fate awaiting the heroine; she could end up a prostitute or drowned with a millstone around her neck for offending local mores, like her mother.*

Shen Congwen was dispirited when he wrote this story and its sequel because of the impending victory of communism and the decay of the old order that made it possible. He might have intended that to be the subject of his unfinished novel. "Qiaoxiu and Dongsheng" sets the stage, showing a deceptively peaceful countryside on the eve of upheaval; the locale is, as usual, West Hunan. The middle part of the story is close to sociology: an entire capsule history, pointedly non-Marxist, of the breakdown of the local social fabric. Shen tries to explain the origins of the rural bandit gangs and to show the highly dysfunctional reaction to them of the landed elite. Militia Captain Man, the local landlord and military head, personifies the latter, not unlike the unseen commander in "Sansan." Captain Man, the narrator's friend, is based on a real friend of Shen Congwen's, so his fallibility is particularly wrenching.

In the story below, there are merely hints that Captain Man makes illicit money from his office – unless one is shocked to see that the militia's business is escorting opium merchants. In "Truth Is Stranger than Fiction," Dongsheng and Qiaoxiu are held captive for ransom by a band of highwaymen, the Tians, who want money and also to tweak the nose of the powers that be. That of course is Captain Man, whose misjudgments set the stage for a blood feud sure to lead to the ruin of the whole countryside. In life, Shen's friend Man was hacked to death in bed by his blood enemies. In the 1940s there was a buzz phrase for people like Man and his enemies: tuhao *(local bullies). Shen Congwen retains his sympathetic eye, but clearly he sees his West Hunanese "paradise" slipping from imperfection into depravity.*

The postscript of "Truth Is Stranger than Fiction" was penned on the last day of 1948, just a month before the surrender of Peking to the Communists. "I believe that this story already has no hope of being completed," he wrote. And in fact he never wrote another work of fiction.

The snow was melting. Everywhere in the ditches between the fields, drops of melted snow water formed into rivulets, as if aching to join some distant ocean, as if uniting in a joyous dash to the sea. More, even than the flowers and grasses of the dry ground, wild bird calls from bamboo thickets by mountain streams still canopied by snow revealed a hint of spring, like an invitation just for me. Particularly the turtle-doves that lodged in the bamboo garden outside my window, wearing embroidered necklets over their bodies swathed in gray — their songs were becoming more and more complex — fantastic — like a dialogue in my ears, of my own voice in conversation with Qiaoxiu:

"Qiaoxiu, Qiaoxiu, do you really mean to go? You mustn't!"

"Oh, it's you, Elder Brother. Were you calling me? You never paid me any attention before. How can you blame me now?"

But I had heard this strange and impossible conversation only in the twilight between dreaming and waking. Full consciousness brought an acute sadness. Now I was completely lucid; what entered my ears had turned slightly derisive. I couldn't live on this estate any longer. So, with the excuse that I liked to be alone, I moved to a new place on the outskirts of the village, to a little upper-story lodging in a wing of the medicine god's temple. I could not have picked a better spot; the temple was wholly apart from the village, separated from it by a ridge of the kind that separates paddy fields. To have solitude was to have everything — everything, at least, that I, an eighteen-year-old, could want.

I had been to many strange places in my day, crossed many kinds of bridges, sailed in many sorts of boats, slept in many styles of beds. But never had I experienced a night so eerie as on that mammoth carved cedar bed in the Man

Translated by Jeffrey Kinkley

family mansion a fortnight before when the songs of mountain birds from far and near and the bubbling of water in the kettle at my bedside gave wing to the figments of my Life. Now that I lay on a mere hard plank up in these humble rooms, birdsong once again filled the vacuum in my heart – with feelings still more obscure and unfathomable.

Though the courtyard outside was sizable enough, it was half covered over by a canopy of delicate bamboo leaves. That left only a path of black flagstones on which to stroll and be by myself. Within that luxuriance I discovered bamboos of the arhat and palm varieties good for making walking sticks, purple and white bamboos suitable for flutes, even the snake-tail variety that makes a good fishing pole. Though these bamboos differed in their form, their gentle rustling in the breeze cascaded splinters of jade, evoking a cold that was different from the snow's. Even more secluded was the roof of my little building. The elevation of the site made it ideal for gazing into the distance; at almost any hour, unidentifiable birds warbled on top. Some, singing the joys of life, enjoyed their own music and at their own pace, in an unconscious *wuwei*[1] spirit. Others seemed to be anxiously seeking companionship, expressing an unrequited longing for life and love. The turtledove was a more familiar guest on my rooftop. Arrival here was like unto fleeing. But now here, I found myself closer to it than ever. Its continual whispering – deep, with a hint of desolation – kept reminding me of a matter that I ought to but never could put aside: Qiaoxiu's departure.

I had first come to this snow-capped village to partake of the wedding feast of my friend. Afterward, the mistress of the house lit a torch to escort me to my lodgings. Following the old lady, and bearing the silken bedding to my room, was the seventeen-year-old country girl Qiaoxiu. She spread out my quilt in silence, biting her lower lip. I was thinking

[1]"Nonaction," a Daoist principle.

of comparing her eyebrows with the bride's, to check out a story I'd heard.[2] Her braided hair and sturdy but shapely arms and legs had roused the wild fantasies common to most eighteen-year-olds.

Little did I expect to hear, at breakfast the next morning, that she had made up a little bundle of her things and stolen away, following a *suona* player from the countryside. It was as if, in her little bundle, she had borne off something of mine – a heart, or at least a dream.

It was already a fortnight since she'd run away, and still there was no news of her. My attempt to imagine the whereabouts of this country maiden with shiny black hair, bright eyes, and full bosom, how the two of them were getting by, and how it would all end, left me more lost and bewildered than ever. Not only was that which had by chance been carried away irretrievable; the girl herself – the warmth stored in her limpid, innocent eyes, the vitality in her quietness – all of it was far away now, corroded by a new life that kept on coming, forgotten in time, lost forever, gone.

At the West Gate in Changde, in You Family Alley in Chenzhou, on countless little boats moored at wharves all the way up and down the Yuan River valley, were thousands of young prostitutes who served the travelers and merchants. Girls with broad faces and fine, arching eyebrows, sitting in the bow or the stern by day to get some sun and singing the little ditty "How I Want My Man" till the sun went down, they stitched soles to cloth shoes or embroidered ornamental belt pouches, hoping to bind the hearts of passing boatmen to them with these little gifts. Though

[2]It was said that a Miao maiden kept her eyebrows thick, black, and luxuriant, plucking them into a thin, high arch only the day before her wedding. That was to enchant her husband, for she stayed in seclusion until wedded, and during the ceremony her eyebrows remained masked under a red turban. Only the next day could one see the "new" woman the bride had become.

their faces might be plain, an eternal glow shown through from the youth in their hearts.

But, however ardent, they were constrained by their lives and could not struggle free. This led to tragic outcomes. Because their loves were entwined with resentment and their ability to forgive was limited, one heard daily of those who hanged or drowned themselves. Most of these girls had come from backgrounds like Qiaoxiu's and started out not too differently. Wild infatuation had struck them as they neared womanhood; blind passion made them throw over the traces, break village tradition, and run off, heedless of the consequences. They say that a person can no more be stopped than the Yellow River can be kept from meeting the sea. But most of the waters from these mountain springs never even made it to Dongting Lake. They got dammed up at some little town or wharfside, there to spend the rest of their days. They could not move forward or retrace their steps, and that was that.

The temple of the medicine god where I lived was the highest meeting place of the village. It was headquarters for the village *baojia* head, the site of the school he had founded, and offices for the militia that kept order in these parts. It being the New Year vacation, the students and teachers had all gone home. Ordinarily there were only two kinds of meetings. The happy ones came in spring and autumn, to hire a troupe for putting on a puppet play requiting the gods, and to solicit donations from prominent villagers to that end. The unhappy ones occurred only when there was business handed down from the county government; the gentry and other villagers would assemble to decide what to do. Keeping the peace was not much of a problem locally, and the militia had few obligations, so apart from my friend Militia Captain Man, who doubled as head of the *baojia* police system, the only other regular officers were a bespectacled old secretary, who liked to read *The Recipes of Yuan Mei* and wrote his documents with a little green fountain pen, and a simpleminded office boy of fourteen. The local self-defense forces had thirty-odd rifles of assorted types, but most of them were kept at home by their owners, the wealthy families, just for emergencies; ordinarily there was no need for them. In other words, this district was normally very quiet. Since keeping order was no cause for concern, the primal peace of the village seemed, on the surface, to have been maintained quite well.

I hadn't been out much in my two weeks at the temple. I went to market with the militia captain, to buy tiger and leopard skins and scout out fighting cocks to bet on, and we got up a party of men and dogs to hunt rabbits in the hills. We went round and round under the cliffs and along the brooks, in ravines made slippery by the first melting of the spring snows, until we huddled together, all tired and sweaty. The rest of the time I simply watched the senior clerk play chess with the office boy. The one was forty-six or forty-seven, the other not yet fifteen. What they lacked in expertise they made up for in concentration. The militia bureau also had half the volumes of a lithograph copy of the *Strange Tales from a Chinese Studio.* The surroundings and the atmosphere made this just the place to read it.

But it was through a newer discovery, namely a brood of newly hatched chicks in a corner of the bureau's living quarters and bundles and bundles of herbal medicines I couldn't even name stacked at the head of his bed, that I bridged the generation gap with the secretary. And it was by other routes that I came to be a virtual confidant of the young boy. After a few days of reading the *Strange Tales,* I began to expect its characters Qingfeng and Huangying[3] to pay a visit, and I imagined their mincing footsteps as they ascended the stairs. I did hear the scampering of mice, but

---

[3]Young girls noted for their surpassing beauty and excellent conversation, the former a fox fairy, the latter a chrysanthemum spirit – both in human form.

the girls never appeared. These suspenseful fantasies, in which dread mixed with delight, were of course quite enjoyable to an eighteen-year-old. But, as I got to know the two militiamen, I felt good about casting aside those little old tattered books because, whenever I wanted to, I could browse through a much bigger book,[4] finding in it vitality and enchantment no matter what chapter I picked.

Qiaoxiu's mother had come from Xikou. She was widowed at twenty-three, with one-year-old Qiaoxiu and an acre of fields up in the hills to look after. Young and not content with her lot, she secretly began to see a tiger hunter from Huangluozhai. When her clansmen found out, they plotted to catch her in the act with her lover, the better to seize her paltry fields. In the end they succeeded. Swarming around the lovers like wasps, the clansmen herded them over to the ancestral temple for a public trial. They only meant to make a scene and throw a scare into the couple, giving them a good beating so that everybody could get some perverse satisfaction from the wrongdoers' misery. Then they could marry her off to someone far away, making a little money from the bride-price into the bargain, all in the name of saving face for the clan. They would spend a little of it on spirit money to be burnt for the dead, then split the rest, with the largest cut going to the busybodies who had taken the lead in the matter. This was the old custom of the place, and outsiders did not intervene when things were handled according to tradition.

But it so happened that the current clan head had borne Qiaoxiu's mother a grudge from before she was ever married. He had wanted her as a daughter-in-law, but she had refused to marry his son on account of his clubfoot. Full of smoldering resentment, the clan head subsequently kept finding excuses to take liberties with her. But the feisty young widow turned the tables, cursing him as a shameless

[4]That is, the book of Life.

old lecher. Hereafter, she would have something on him that could be exposed any time she wanted. Now that she was involved in the scandal, memories of the old grudge came back, and he resolved to get even, insisting that the dashing young tiger hunter from Huangluozhai suffer both his feet to be broken while the young widow looked on. The tiger hunter clenched his teeth and made not a sound while this irregular torture was being carried out. He just kept his eyes fixed on the widow. When the punishment was over, two elders prepared to bear him home on a stretcher the seven miles back to Huangluozhai. He had been caught red-handed, so his fellow villagers could hardly protest.

Yet the young widow went before her own clansmen and insisted on following her man, even though it meant abandoning her land and her daughter. The clan lost all semblance of face after that – particularly the clan head, who, bearing malice and mixed emotions in his heart, feared that this would not be the end of it. Better go all the way and extirpate the problem at its source. He proposed that the shameless hussy be drowned in a lake, according to tradition, rather than let her feed the gossip in Huangluozhai. He was a scholar with a petty official title and lots of quotations from Confucius to prove it, plus the powers of seniority and position, and a known disposition of stubbornness and imperiousness. For all these reasons, even the younger clansmen who did not agree with him were a little afraid of the man. He made his titillating proposal on the pretext of upholding the clan's good name, adding that the question of Qiaoxiu's adoption could be discussed afterward.

A crowd is easy to move; everyone of course raised their voices in accord, without much deliberation. No sooner was the whole clan in unison than ignorant young busybodies were already out scouting for ropes and a millstone, raring to go. In the confusion, the clan's moral values got mixed up with its latent sadism. The women and girls gathered at a distance, upset and afraid but quite helpless. "Heavens!"

they murmured, having no other way of protesting. Outside the ancestral temple, young men of the clan stripped the young widow completely naked, bound her hands behind her back, and weighed her down with a millstone, fastening it with vines drawn tightly around her neck. Then they all gathered around in a circle, wantonly taking in the attractions of her bare young flesh, even as they continued wildly reviling her for being so shameless.

The young widow took it all silently, her dewy eyes sweeping the crowd for signs of her tormentor, the clan head. But he, still mortally afraid of being exposed, had made a show of being enraged while looking her up and down as she was being stripped. "Disgusting, disgusting," he kept yelling. Then, pretending to be too busy and too proud to watch further, he made his getaway into the temple. There he and the other clan elders discussed how they would explain it in their report to the county government. They would all sign it, pushing the responsibility off onto the group in hopes of avoiding further trouble. At the same time, he kept reassuring the cautious old men who were of two minds about the matter, quoting them lines from the classics about their duty to root out evil, lest they get cold feet later on.

As noon approached, the clan head and his contingent of activists dragged the young widow to Xikou, put her on a boat, and silently rowed her upstream to the reservoir. The woman kept her head down and said nothing, staring at the briskly running waters and the reflections of clouds and starlight in them, fractured by ripples from the oars. Maybe she was thinking about how she would be reincarnated, or how she had spurned the advances of the clan head, or the many little scores not yet settled and favors not yet repaid between herself and other people. Maybe she was only worrying about the tiger hunter and how he would manage in the future. Her Qiaoxiu was only one year old. Would someone strangle her the moment her mother was gone? Just before they headed for the river, an old kinswoman had brought her the baby, so innocent of all that had happened. She wanted the young widow to suckle it one last time. At the sight of this, the old clan head kicked her away and cursed, "Damned she-devil, get the hell out of here!" Yet, strangely enough, the woman looked neither indignant nor perturbed. Nor did she seem particularly anxious, as if anything was out of the ordinary.

The clan head for his part was now seated in the stern. He seemed to be avoiding the young widow with his eyes. In reality his feelings were in turmoil. To cleanse his conscience, he kept muttering to himself that this was the right thing to do, that the reputation of the whole clan was at stake, that he couldn't have done otherwise. As head of the whole clan, a man educated in the classics, it was his responsibility to uphold morality. Needless to say, he felt no aversion to the woman's young, healthy flesh, now so bare; rather, he objected to the fact that someone else had enjoyed it. "Don't let good water run off into the fields of others," went the saying. Jealousy burned in his heart, strengthening his moral outrage and intensifying his obsessive vindictiveness. He pressed the rowers to set off. And the other clansmen, perhaps they were thinking only about who would get the widow's fields. They were ill at ease, for now that their fleeting lust had cooled down, they felt a little worsted by the young woman's quiet poise. As the little boat reached the deepest part of the pond, the rowers shipped the oars. The boat yawed, first to the left, now to the right. They all knew what came next. One of the older men exclaimed, "Qiaoxiu's ma, blame has to fall somewhere, just as debts fall to the debtor. You know that. You might as well accept it. Do you have any last wishes? Now's the time."

The young widow looked at this man who was trying to comfort her. After a pause she said, in a low voice, "Third Cousin, do a good deed; don't let them strangle my little Qiaoxiu. She's the sole continuation of our family line.

When she's grown up, don't hold all this against her. That's all I ask." Everyone fell silent.

In that beautiful twilight air, all was still. At first, no one was willing to make a move. So the old clan head put on a display of will, though inwardly he felt fearful and embarrassed. He went over to the girl and without warning threw her over into the water. After the shift in weight he scrambled to the other side, sending the little boat rocking from side to side. At first she put up an inevitable though feeble little struggle, but the weight of the millstone hanging from her neck sent her swirling downward. Bubbles rose to the surface, and then the water went quiet. The boat slowly left the scene, following the current, the young men on board still staring fixedly and silently at the surface. Because death had carried away with it all her personal shame and sense of wrong, it seemed to have left an invisible gift for each of the living. Though she had asked that her daughter be allowed to grow up without any encumbrances from the past, how could any of the participants forget their stupid action?

They turned the boat around, as if having completed a solemn and momentous duty. The deceased had died for her sins, but death became a part of the burden of each of the living. They must quickly get back to the ancestral temple and kowtow, set off firecrackers, and hang red silks to exorcise the evil vapors as well as show that their "brave," "decisive," and at the same time "truly stupid" act had already won back the tarnished "honor" of the clan. In reality, they were using all this to exorcise that bit of invisible self-reproach that might grow in the stillness and come to contaminate their consciences and their souls. It was because of such dread that, four years later, the clan head went mad and killed himself in the ancestral hall. But, because of the widow's last request, Qiaoxiu was sent away to live at the Man family estate at Gaojian, ten miles away.

As Qiaoxiu matured, an uncle who had witnessed her

mother's tragedy and brought the child up – the secretary at the militia bureau – got the idea of giving her to Militia Captain Man to be his concubine. That way she would have a home and a protector. Since the family matriarch was infertile and prone to illness, Qiaoxiu could hope to be promoted to a legitimate wife if she bore the captain children. Both he and his wife were agreeable to the idea. Only Dongsheng's mother, older and wiser and having bitter memories of her own, was in favor of taking the long view and not rushing things. Without any knowledge at all of her own family's past, Qiaoxiu was unwilling. But she was still young, so the matter was put off for the time being.

Coming often to the militia bureau to mend clothes for her uncle, Qiaoxiu got to be acquainted with Dongsheng. His mother, Mother Yang, was poor enough to be kind and virtuous. She was always praising Qiaoxiu in front of the secretary. Dongsheng would cut in to remind his mother, "Ma, I'm not even fourteen yet." "Fourteen this year, fifteen the next, you'll be a man in no time!" They would put on a little argument in front of the secretary, one that outsiders would be hard put to understand. But the secretary knew that both of them liked Qiaoxiu and were very concerned for her.

Like my arrival, Qiaoxiu's secret departure had little effect on the village. Everything that was fixed by history transpired as of old, and all the little things that were done out of habit continued without a hitch.

The whole village called Dongsheng's mother Mother Yang. When her husband died ten years before, he had left her only a tiny house and a plot of land no bigger than the palm of your hand. She lived in poverty, but her character was honest and good; not having taking ways about her, she typified a "woman of the old school." She trusted the gods, and she trusted people. She felt it was simpler and less trouble that many affairs of this world be given over to the gods. But there were some problems they couldn't handle, and those people had to do their best to solve. If people set their minds to it, there was no calamity they couldn't find their way out of; but, if they couldn't, best to leave it to the gods again. Like other village folk who worked close to the soil, she did her level best and left the rest up to the will of heaven. She seemed like a simpleton in every aspect of her life, and in everything she seemed to trust to fate or what educated people called the "Dao."[5]

With such a mother at his side, Dongsheng grew up tending water buffalo, cutting hay, gathering mushrooms, and doing the other things that fill the lives of rural young people. And he grew strong and healthy as well as quick and clever. After only a year of primary school he could write standard print-style characters in a small hand, and from the secretary in the militia bureau he learned a little about the prescribed forms of bureaucratic documents. An office boy didn't earn much, but room, board, and clothing came with the job. Besides that, he got a basket of sieved grain and a small stipend every month. The grain he brought home, and it made Mother Yang's life much easier. Moreover, the militiamen that the 250 households of this village supplied were volunteers, without any remuneration at all. The official salaried class here amounted to only four or five men; apart from the militia captain cum *baojia* head and his secretary, there were only the two schoolteachers. All of them were paid a mere pittance. So Dongsheng's position was enviable, one that the other village lads would be only too happy to fill. Besides the emoluments, the job carried more intangible rewards: draft exemption and relative immunity from the extraordinary levies always being exacted by the military and civilian officials in town. Anyone who had grown up in such a village knew how inexorable these impositions and decrees were – unbearable to all, but unavoidable by all, except for those on the public payroll.

Take the militia captain, the local "everybody all in one"

[5] The "Way."

who arranged village affairs. Whenever he sent a man with a gong to summon the village elders to the medicine god temple for a meeting, he would declare that public responsibilities would be borne publicly, with the rich families taking the lead. He, what with his flour mill and oil press, and others present, with their distilleries and general stores, would pay the lion's share, though he complained, with a worried frown, that the turnover was so slow he sometimes had to borrow money at interest. Still, the villagers couldn't fail to note that, every time the captain went to town, he brought back some uplifting new modern gadget or sported a new felt hat or a foreign fountain pen. When it came to signing official documents, most citizens drew a cross or left a fingerprint; a few had a chop they could use; but the captain reached into the front pocket of his Zhongshan tunic and drew out that smooth and gleaming little marvel. It was experience enough to see him write his name with it. But the price! More than a prime water buffalo! If that was poverty, who wouldn't volunteer?

Dongsheng got to follow behind the captain's white mule on trips to the county town five or six times a year, so he was more savvy than the average villager. His good character and his mother's had further won him special standing. The most open acknowledgment of this was that several small landed families with twelve- or thirteen-year-old daughters were eager to have him for a son-in-law, thinking that such a promising lad could help build up the family fortune.

The village was fifteen miles from the county seat and half a mile off the only highway. Not being in a strategic location, it had never quartered troops. Its two springs ran all year round, supplying the paddy fields with water through the winter. The terraces were surrounded by hills on all sides, and the slopes were thickly planted with tung trees, tea bushes, bamboo, and lacquer trees. A wise rule of the village forbade indiscriminate tree cutting and clearing of the hills as well as diversion of the streams and haggling over water rights. The many years of peace had given the place an atmosphere different from that of all the other villages, which had declined into poverty; everything was regulated. These time-honored traditions had allowed some families to get the upper hand economically, to gain control over the long haul, to run things. By the same token, others had been forced into tenancy generation after generation or to become seminomadic farm laborers, their lives dictated by circumstance. The contradiction between the two groups was manifest. Yet, though they lived different kinds of lives, the distance was not that great; both groups had their hands and feet in the earth, engaging in productive labor. No one was completely idle.

But, in accordance with broader social trends, the disparity in living standards still created some untamed spirits, who were known as rural revolutionaries. There seemed to be a pattern in the way they were formed: small beginnings led to larger consequences. In their youth they were just bad boys, out to break the rules whenever they could, cutting down other people's bamboo for fishing poles, picking the tangerines and grapefruit in their orchards, draining their paddy fields for the fish, and poaching the game caught in other people's snares. Having discovered as boys how easy it was to "reap without sowing," after growing up they of course never let a chance go by to cheat others. As their romantic spirits soared, they inevitably changed from peasants into people who "hung out." Since society was still stable, there was no outlet for their derring-do or way for them to get ahead, so they just opened a little storefront on the village street, where they could make fast money by running a gaming table and loansharking.

They had lots of connections and knew village business like their own ledger – they knew who held power and who was hard up – and how to extort money from wealthy widows without heirs. Usually they had no fixed employment, nor did they hire out in the fields. They followed the periodic markets, circulating from one village to the next, and gambling at each one. They had three or four cronies in every village for fifteen miles around with whom they could eat and drink and who could get them out of scrapes. They might butt in while livestock were being sold, so as to claim a small commission – drinking money – when the deal went down. When a village hosted an opera performance, they would have to get in on it. If they knew the troupe manager, they'd be invited to the big feasts at the beginning and end of the festival and be honored at the opening sponsors' ceremony by having their names called out, at which point they would have to make a contribution in a little red envelope with all the others. Aspiring opera stars – the young men playing female roles – had to socialize with these boys and get on their good side, or they might without warning find themselves assailed on stage one day with stones and catcalls.

If they got into trouble, offended a bigwig, or ran into some other difficulty and lost face, the rowdies would have to change their base of operations – gather up their things in a little bundle and take it on the lam. Even more of them became Xue Renguis[6] and enlisted. They of course were never heard from again. The majority became cannon fodder, later if not sooner.

But what about the women? Their case was a bit different. Developments and sudden changes in their lives were not so obtrusive while they were little; most occurred as they grew up and were related to their sexual maturation. If tradition ground them under and they could not struggle free, they ended up going mad or committing suicide. If they were to break through all the visible and invisible restrictions and make their own way, it usually meant eloping. But that, too, inevitably ended in tragedy.

Yet society had been changing for a long time – for the

[6]Tang dynasty general whose original enlistment is celebrated in a Peking opera, *Toujun bieyao* (Leaving the hearth to enlist).

last twenty years. These years of self-destructive and self-inflicted civil war, of division into separate military satrapies, had dissolved all there once was of rural society. It had of course left a marked influence even on this little place. As soon as the rural spirit of knight-errantry gained knowledge of certain social realities, this village of fewer than three hundred households found itself hosting several dozen extra firearms of assorted makes, a dozen or more retired officers who still liked to answer to the name of captain, lieutenant, or sergeant, and two or three men of still higher rank who were harder to figure out.

Most of them belonged virtually to a new class; they earned their living without laboring and were little different from parasites. Those with estates of their own could become local despots, and those without such standing could become hooligans and highwaymen. What both groups shared was an increasing detachment from the people, the soil, and productive labor. That was replaced by a new slickness and cruelty – particularly among those who had learned to use modern weaponry but lacked the ambition and the opportunity, as well as the money, to do something big. Naturally, when they came home, they were fit only to run a small business that didn't require much start-up money. And in this new kind of life they developed a utilitarian sort of philosophy. No one has ever described or analyzed it, but this outlook was in fact adopted by the vast majority of those who knew how to make the most out of the environment. "I was forced to" became their eternal refrain, so they found themselves forced to kidnap people for ransom and plant opium. The degeneracy born of all these things they were forced to do led to the continued spread of these ominous conditions.

However, villages that found themselves in such straits in those days responded instinctively with new forms of self-defense, that is, advanced techniques for rich families to protect their property. They sent their sons and nephews to military schools and put their money into firearms, supposedly for the defense of their families and the village, but in reality in defense of their own special prerogatives. Of course the two different groups came into conflict. Armed clashes might break out at any time and any place, leaving blood debts that lasted for generations, particularly in little villages, where there were basic conflicts of interest. During these twenty years when the villages were dissolving, their seemingly irreconcilable problems and contradictions, like those in the dissolution of society as a whole, could always find compromise solutions so that, under certain conditions, there were still hopes for a temporary equilibrium. One side held onto its land and its mansions, its oil presses and distilleries, while the other escaped the law up in the hills. Each considered the other "still one of us," lessening the antagonism and friction between the two groups and allowing each to go its own way and satisfy its own needs.

This state of affairs might look odd, yet it was very common, for it was characteristic of the development and continuance of the contradictions throughout society. Most of the plans for national reconstruction had neglected to trace and analyze these realities and therefore ended in a string of tragedies that encouraged warfare. This little village was in an isolated, inaccessible spot on the Guizhou-Hunan frontier, where "special goods"[7] were strictly prohibited, yet also taxed. Under such conditions, the opposition between the two privileged groups often disappeared, through "equal division of the profits." Being off the government highway, the place was good for smuggling; the illicit opium and salt traffic it attracted maintained the balance of power. That it was a balance between opponents was a fact of life, but each side seemed to have stashed its arms out of sight. At least those who went traveling on business found it safer to go unarmed than to carry a weapon. Passing a barrier or enter-

[7]That is, opium.

ing a mountain village, it was safer and more convenient to have on you a calling card with the right person's name than a rifle.

Dongsheng's duties at the militia bureau occasionally took him traveling, just to guide and protect some small traders with a pole load or two of opium or a little salt.[8] There was nothing to it, for he didn't have to cross into any other jurisdictions. At three in the afternoon it was time for him to be back, after escorting two opium merchants to the provincial border by the back roads. He talked to me about Qiaoxiu just before setting out. He wrapped his feet in coir cloth while I fixed the heels and laces of his straw sandals.

"Dongsheng, when Qiaoxiu ran away that morning, why didn't the captain send you after her to bring her back?" I teased.

"When people run, they aren't like a stream of water. A dam won't hold them back. She's a human being. I couldn't do much if I were her own maternal uncle. Chasing after her would be no use."

"Precisely because she is human, how can she forget all that the captain and the old lady have done for her the past ten years? And how could she let go of the secretary, the mill, and the fishermen's embankment upstream? They're like friends to her. As I see it, you can hardly let go of her!"

"The mill doesn't belong to her. You like it because you're a city boy, but that doesn't mean we do. Qiaoxiu knows the meaning of womanhood now, and she's gone off with someone. Good deeds and bad deeds get repaid in kind; so will this affair be, in time."

"Do you think she'll come back on her own?"

"Back here? No good horse grazes where it's been before, and the Yangtze River doesn't flow backward."

"I'll bet she's at some river port downstream right now.

[8]Salt, too, was subject to a special tax and therefore worth smuggling.

She can't have flown off to the ends of the earth. You can catch her if you try."

"She's a cracked pitcher,[9] so who wants her now?"

"You don't? If you don't, then I do! She looks like a girl of character to me, not some wild young thing."

My pitch was only half serious, but it stirred something in Dongsheng. So he said to me, again, almost as if he meant it, "If you love her, I'll be sure to tell her if I see her. She's a fine hand at needlework. She can make a nice embroidered waist pouch and fill it for you with pumpkin seeds of her own germination. Too bad you didn't speak sooner – the secretary could have fixed you up!"

"Speak sooner? I've only seen her once since I got here, my first night in the village. She'd eloped by daybreak the next morning! I couldn't have gone after her by lantern and torchlight."

"Then why don't *you* go after her now? You know the ports downstream. Go ahead and look for her, like Xiao He chasing after Han Xin."[10]

"I came here to hunt with your captain all right, but only deer, fox, and rabbit. I'd no idea the mountains were home to such a beautiful species as this!"

Naturally this was all said in jest. The secretary, who was closing in on fifty, must have got a lot more of my joke than fourteen-year-old Dongsheng. He'd been silent so far, but now he chimed in, "Understanding comes only with time. It takes a long while before you can recognize all the trees and plants up here, they're all so different in nature. Heart-

[9]No longer a virgin.

[10]The reference is to an ancient historical episode immortalized in Peking and perhaps local opera; strategist Han Xin left in anger when Han dynasty founder Liu Bang gave him a military command unworthy of his talents. Xiao He, who had recommended Han to Liu, pursued Han to beg him to come back. Liu Bang then made Han a grand marshal and was repaid by the many victories he won.

break grass is poisonous; the water buffalo know enough to avoid it. Fire nettles sting your hands. Be careful that they don't hurt you!"

About an hour after Dongsheng left, Mother Yang showed up at the bureau, her shoes covered with mud. The secretary and I were with the just-hatched chicks. We counted out twenty little black and white balls of animated fluff. A glance at her muddy feet and the goodies in her basket told us she had just come from market.

"Mother Yang, been doing your shopping for New Year's? Your Dongsheng is out on business. He'll be spending the night at Red Crag and be back tomorrow. Did you want him for something?"

"Nothing much," said Mother Yang, patting the cakes in her basket.

"Has that brown hen of yours hatched her eggs yet?"

"She's already gone to dinner in town." Mother Yang put the basket on her knees to count her purchases: a catty of "snowy date" rice candy, a catty of pork, a pair of black cloth shoe uppers, all the necessary incense, candles, and spirit money, and also a string of hundred-pop firecrackers. She showed them all off to the secretary.

Asking what it was all for, we learned that Dongsheng had turned fourteen this very day. Mother Yang had counted out the days on her fingers long in advance and determined that his birthday would fall on the day the market came to the village of Camp Yala. She'd been muttering to herself about it for some time before she got up the gumption to take the twenty-four large eggs her hen was to have hatched out of their crate, one by one, then carefully put them into her carrying basket, atop a layer of rice bran. Then she seized her mother hen, put on her straw sandals, and went off to market to deal with the city people. Although settled on this course of action, when she'd walked the mile and a half to market, she acted as if she were there just to see the commotion and join the fun — as if she had no other business there.

Among the villagers, a chicken is practically a member of the family. Lonely old women in particular love them whether they're naughty or nice and have simple and pathetic dreams about them that add a bit of variety to their lives. So when she got to market, where people and horses had splattered mud all around, and started milling around waiting for a customer, Mother Yang couldn't believe she was doing this for real. When someone asked the price of her hen, she deliberately named a figure double the market price and took an antagonistic attitude of "you may have money, but I've got the goods – I don't have to sell it to you," as if she didn't really want to let go of it.

Her price was so high that the poultry merchants from the city just stroked the hen's back and left without bargaining. That naturally made Mother Yang adopt a scornful, pearls-before-swine attitude. She pursed her lips and turned away so as not to pay them any more attention. Poultry merchants knew the psychology of country women, and they could tell this one by the clothes she was wearing. They knew it was early in the game, and they were in no hurry to buy. Since her asking price was so out of line, they decided to get her goat by offering a rock-bottom price in return. And they needled her, "What precious treasure is this that's worth so much!" In a huff, Mother Yang countered, very gruffly, "That price will get you some bean curd. Why don't you go buy some?" Most apologetically, as if the price offered had insulted not just her but the estimable fat mother hen by her side, she turned, stroking its feathers and patting its head, as if to reassure it, "We're in no hurry. A quarter of an hour more, and we'll go home. I only came here for amusement; I couldn't sell you!" As if fully aware of its own importance as well as Mother Yang's sentimentality, the hen shut its small red eyes and gave two little clucks, apparently fully in accord with the plan. Both of them seemed to be saying, "Never mind, we'll go home soon. I'll really be glad to get back. It'll be just like it was before."

When she was beginning to be offered prices within reason, a friend who wanted to help her make the sale put in a word from the side. "Go just a little higher, and she'll sell. This hen is nice and plump, raised on mung beans and corn!" Then, when the customer wasn't paying attention, she whispered to Mother Yang, "If you want to sell it, now's the time. The market is loaded with city merchants today, and they pay top dollar. You couldn't get this much for it if you went to the city in person." Because that well-meaning advice to "unload it quick, if you're really here to sell" didn't suit Mother Yang's mood, her retort was, "You might sell it, but I wouldn't. I don't really need the money."

Someone put in, "If not, what're you here for? Because you've got nothing better to do? Maybe you're here to officiate at a duck fight. Your shoulders seem to be free just now, so why don't you go tote a millstone?"

Mother Yang couldn't pick that wag out of the crowd. It wasn't the place to make a scene, so she just cursed under her breath, "No-good bastard, let's see your mother and your mother-in-law bring on the millstones! That'll be a pretty sight for everybody!"

It was fifteen or sixteen years since the incident with Qiaoxiu's mother, so the special use of millstones had passed into legend; even in the village, hardly anyone remembered the incident.

Who would have braved the cold winter winds to lug a chicken to market unless they needed the money? She was lucky that city folk needed lots of presents to give for New Year's. So, toward the end, Mother Yang scored a surprising victory – her hen brought more money than even she had dared to hope. After the exchange went down, Mother Yang visited all the little covered stalls. Amid all the chickens, ducks, sheep, rabbits, kittens, and puppies, and all the people wrangling, cursing, and holding out for a better price, she traded for the goods that filled her basket. Finally, as if to have a laugh at her own stubbornness, she even bought four pieces of bean curd. Then, feeling a strange mixture of loss, fatigue, pleasure, and vague anticipation, she made her way home to the village.

Along the way, she saw other villagers driving their piglets along the road with a leash of vines wrapped around their necks, while others carried theirs in a bamboo basket on their back. This reminded her of the problem of Dongsheng's marriage. When he turned twenty, he'd need four pigs for his wedding – that was just six years from now. Presently she would visit him at the militia bureau, give him a big "snowy date" candy to eat, and measure his feet to see if she'd bought enough material for his new shoes. Then she'd bring him home for his birthday supper, before which they'd light incense and candles and kowtow to his ancestors. Dongsheng's father had died exactly ten years before.

Mother Yang liked to tell everybody, "The heir of the Yang family is fourteen years old. Maybe you think hatching chicks is easy, but his father left us with only a sickle and a flail – you don't know how hard my life has been." By this time she'd be all sad and weepy. Someone would try to console her, "No matter, you're doing fine now, Mother Yang. You've had a lot of troubles, but you've overcome them all. Dongsheng is a young man of promise, and the captain has pledged to send him to school. When he comes back, he can be a captain, too. An only son gets double the inheritance and can marry himself two wives. The daughter of Constable Wang at Camp Yala has a dowry of eight sets of bedding. You'll have servants to fill your pipe and pour your tea. The best times are yet to come, so what is there to worry about?"

Mother Yang was peering over the secretary's coop at his chicks, and in fact she was smiling. Possibly she was still concerned over the fate of the hen and the twenty-four eggs she'd just sold and was covering up with this smile so the townsfolk wouldn't know. It was already growing late. The snow was melting. So many people had gone to market today that all the paths had turned to mud, almost impassible. The medicine god's temple was a few hundred feet from the village, across the fields. Two rolling brooks, fed by the melting snow, lay between them, each spanned by a one-plank bridge. Mother Yang thought to herself, "Dongsheng won't be able to get back to the bureau tonight, so he won't be coming home." She hesitated a bit over the thought of whether she ought to leave the big package of winter dates in her basket at the bureau for the secretary, but in the end she went ahead and picked up the basket to go home. We stood behind the stone balustrade at the front of the temple to watch the old lady, who was already slightly stooped, wend her way along the ridges between the wet fields. She took the trouble to remind me, "The roads are slippery. Be careful you don't fall into the water. The hired hand over there will bring you your meal!"

At about half past five, smoke from the kitchen stove began to rise from the chimneys of all the houses in the village. First came individual plumes that floated straight up without getting entangled. Then, fantastically, cold air from above collapsed them together sideways into layers of milky white mist. Soon after, the mist had enveloped the village, taken possession of it. It was not easy to imagine how Mother Yang was making supper that night. Her kitchen was a little colder and more desolate, for the hen was no longer there to hop up on the chopping block and peck at her spinach. At feeding time she scooped up a handful of seeds for the hen as usual before realizing that the bird was already sold. Still less could she ever have imagined that on that very day, at that very hour, five miles away in Red Crag village, Dongsheng and the two opium merchants had already been captured.

That evening the secretary and I sat around by the light of an oil lamp discussing Pu Songling's *Strange Tales*. He considered them all fantastic legends about ancient times that could not possibly come true in our world, so he never had any fears about corpses or ghosts. Having his tongue loosened by a cup of wine, and being aware of how I yearned to catch a glimpse of a young girl like Qingfeng or Huangying – not to mention someone else who had been in my thoughts – he told me the whole story of Qiaoxiu's mother. By the by, he advised me to give up my studies. He felt that riveting oneself to a chair in a tower, however lofty, was not half as good as sitting in a little "water skimmer" boat. Certainly the latter offered more opportunities for encountering the sort of miracles that could set a twenty-year-old lad's heart pounding and his spirit dashing. He simply meant that I should see the world rather than spend my life in one small place or within one tiny sphere of experience. If I could get around more, it would broaden my outlook. He didn't want me to keep thinking about that little boat that he once sat in, that boat that had now long ceased to exist.

I could almost see that little boat being rowed out to the middle of the reservoir, and I could almost feel myself sitting squarely in its prow. Someone seemed to have gone overboard, and the boat was already turning back. The sky and the waters were calm. The whole affair was over. Nothing is eternal. Only one thing could really last forever: the gentle stillness of that evening twilight and, in that instant of gloaming, the reflection of clouds and starlight in the water fractured by two oars – as seen by the bright, tender, all-forgiving eyes of a twenty-three-year-old widow who had been filled with love of life but whose love society had taken away. It was already a fortnight since Qiaoxiu had fled, already sixteen years since her mother had sunk into the reservoir with the millstone around her neck.

And yet nothing was resolved. It was only the beginning.

Modernist Works

The Housewife

The final three fictional works of this anthology show Shen Congwen the modernist, writing philosophically and contemplatively about problems of modern life, often using avant-garde technique, and certainly adopting a relativist, nontraditional moral viewpoint rather than the contemporary "patriotic" one.

Shen Congwen wrote "The Housewife" ("Zhufu") in Peking in 1936, just when the story takes place. The portraits of himself, his young wife, Zhang Zhaohe, and the details of their courtship are so exact that one must suspect that this piece was his way of working out problems that had already surfaced in their young marriage. Although intelligent and educated (after 1949 she became an editor for People's Literature), Zhang Zhaohe was raised to become a traditional housewife and must have been so treated by Shen Congwen. The difference in their ages, almost eight years, also began to tell. She was bored, while Shen was wrapped up not only in his writing but in antiquarianism, the hobby that became his profession after 1949.

Shen Congwen's "he says, she says" approach to narration, in which he enters the mind of his wife — partly to develop his own confession — is innovative and titillating. He dresses up the universal story of how the excitement, the infatuation ("surprise" or "wonder") of romance fades in marriage with his philosophical concepts about coincidence and "surprise" in human fate, the irresistible power of beauty to control human beings, and the meaning of dreams. The rare psychological analysis of this piece is further developed, and sometimes obscured, by the difficult and abstract prose of the original Chinese. Perhaps that is just as well if this piece is an apology to his wife. Beyond all the confession there is an attempt at self-justification for knowing no limits. At one point Shen Congwen may be trying — despite evident guilt feelings — to justify "transcending" the vow of marital fidelity.

Bibi was asleep on the fresh white sheets, a thin quilt covered in amber silk wrapped around her warm body. Her head with its long wavy hair lay buried in the big white pillow, but when she turned over, she revealed a petite face bearing red impressions from the pillow. She appeared to be sleeping peacefully. Her closed eyes formed a slightly curved line; her eyebrows were long and black, and little dimples at the corners of her mouth betrayed a smile.

Finished with sweeping the outside court, the maid tiptoed to the inner window and let down the curtain. Bibi was awakened by the sound. She opened her eyes and looked around; it was already light. The silk blankets lay piled on the bed like small mountains, and the bed's other inhabitant was nowhere to be seen. (She knew that he had risen and gone to wash his face at the well in the courtyard.) She stretched out her hand and picked up the square clock from the bedside table – exactly six o'clock. It was early, yet she had overslept by twenty minutes. They had talked a good deal the night before, and she had slept straight through, not waking even when he got up. The weather seemed rather nice. Closing her eyes, she could make out through the clear air the cooing of the pigeons drifting in and out.

She earnestly closed her eyes again, letting the sound be a cradle that gently rocked her senses.

A dazzling golden sunflower was swaying before her eyes, the stamens a glossy purple constantly in motion, impossible to pluck. She thought of her life. It too was like an illusion one could not grasp: it was always changing. She could not say herself what part of it was real, what was most credible. She was very happy. Remembering that today was a strange and wonderful day, she smiled.

Today was the fifth of the eighth month. Three years ago exactly, on just such a day as this, she had married a man

Translated by William MacDonald

whose life was completely different from her own and whose personality also seemed a little odd. To set up housekeeping they had hired a car and traipsed from East City to West City, from the Heavenly Bridge to the North Gate, selecting all manner of things for their new home. Laughing, arguing, compromising, grumbling, they went from bedding for the boudoir to pots for the kitchen and brought it all home. Bibi's elder sister from Shanghai, her mother's relatives who lived even farther south, two little sisters still in school, three or four friends – all were like invisible clock springs attached to her that spun around busily like wheels.

After all the gauze curtains, the red lamp shades, the red paper envelopes for gifts, the gold-flecked thank-you notes, after everything had been taken care of, the great day finally arrived. While she and her elder sister were cutting out little red characters to put on the cake, her outfit arrived from the dressmaker. "Whose is it?" "The young lady's." She ran with the gown into a little room at the back of her bridal suite to try it on in front of a mirror. While changing, she thought to herself, abstractedly, Everything happens by coincidence, and nothing remains constant. Go out and try to find your own mate, and it's not easy; find him and try to flee, and that's a waste of effort, too. A year ago I'd planned to don an all-gray student's uniform, to disguise myself as a man and go to Peking to study. What a romantic idea! Who could have known that today I'd be preparing to become a bride – giving myself over quite willingly to a man to become his wife?

The doorbell rang. Someone outside said, "The Chen Estate of the East City sends this present of four small plates." The groom quickly ran into the bridal suite with the present. "Come look, darling. What pretty little plates. Are you still changing? Hurry and look. Let's tip him a dollar. They're beautiful."

Someone else was talking in the courtyard. A guest had

arrived, a woman cousin, a second Shi Xiangyun.[1] From the courtyard she shouted, "Congratulations! Congratulations! Where is the bride hiding? What do you mean not letting anyone see the bridal chamber? What's this setup that you don't want anyone to see?"

"Cousin, please have a seat in the parlor. Elder Sister is cutting out flowers and waiting for your help."

"When bride and groom go off to bed, the go-between knows it's time she fled; and I'm not even the go-between, so I can't be of any help. Since I've still got things to do, I can only stay a minute. I'll wait till the ceremony to congratulate her. Then I can watch Mother Wang flee!"

The florist came too. Then someone came with a gift from the Wangs, and someone from the Zhous; one sent a porcelain vase, the other a ceramic figurine. The groom hurriedly took these things into the apartment. "A beautiful vase, a beautiful figurine. Bibi, come look! What? Haven't you changed into your gown yet? Doesn't it fit? Can't I come in and look?"

"No, no! Please don't come in, don't come in!"

Clothes had arrived from another tailor. "More bridal clothing is here. Let me come in and have a look."

At that the two met in the little room, laughing and grumbling at each other as she tried on the bridal clothes. Although the groom appeared to be enthusiastic, still he felt that the affair about to take place wasn't real. And because of this he had to verify it somehow, concretely: he wanted to embrace her, to kiss her.

"Don't!"

"Darling, you're really quite beautiful today."

"My goodness! Don't touch me, sir. Don't wrinkle my dress! I want it to look nice. Get out! You can't stay here and fool around!"

"You're not as forward as you were in school."

[1] As in the *Dream of the Red Chamber.*

"Okay! Enough! Hurry up and leave; someone's looking for you! Enough, enough!"

The noise outside, of course, meant that someone else had arrived. The groom took her hands and kissed them, then ran out, smiling.

When she had put on her pale red silk gown, she quietly opened the double doors and went out. The groom was just then arranging a vase in front of the window. He turned his head and saw her. Looking her up and down, he smiled.

"What a beautiful treasure. Simply – "

"Oh! Don't touch me. Your hands are filthy. Who sent that vase?"

"Third Elder Brother Zhou."

"What's going on here? You really like to play with fragile things. The ones you buy for yourself don't seem to be enough; you want your friends to buy even more of them for you as gifts. You're really odd."

"Not at all. This is my hobby. Don't you like this vase?"

"Oh! Don't do that! Wash your hands first. If you're going to keep on playing with your hobby, then let me go look in on the parlor. Cousin's calling again."

The commotion passed; it was evening. Some had gone home, and the guests that had come up from —— dispersed one by one. Elder Sister had performed an act from a Kun opera, then coaxed the younger sisters to go off to sleep in a side room off the parlor. The couple had been busy all day. Both appeared to be dead tired and in need of rest. She straightened her clothing and silently watched her "friend." The friend was just then moving a white jade box from the top of the dresser and replacing it with a green flowered dish.

As if admiring the dish, and her, he said, "My treasure, you are wonderful! Are you tired? You must be dead tired."

She laughed and thought, "You must be more tired than I because I've seen you move that dish five or six times."

"Darling, we're married now."

Her smile seemed to say, "I think you married some old piece of porcelain today. One minute you call me your darling, your treasure, and the next you say the same thing about a tray or a vase."

"A man must have a hobby. And when he has a hobby, he develops an addiction to it. I can't afford to collect bronzes and jades, and I don't have an eye for collecting painting and calligraphy, just these little things. They don't cost much, yet they're not trifles. What others don't want, I do – "

Still smiling, she said, "What did you say? What others don't want, you do – "

He stopped a minute and realized he'd said something wrong. He hastened to clarify, "Fooling around with plates and vases, that's what other people don't want and I do. As for people, what people want and can't get is exactly what I want and finally got. Darling, you can't imagine what a wreck you've turned me into these past few years."

She still smiled, as if to say, "I still think that what you really love, what can really bring you happiness, are those things that are easily broken."

He said nothing; he just smiled happily. Perhaps she was right. She didn't know that his hobby actually had a deeper significance. He seemed to be searching for something forgotten in the back of his mind; after a while he mumbled to himself, "Bibi, this year you're twenty-three, and you've become a bride! When you were twenty, did you think this day would come? Such sweet eyes, such a sweet face, to let a totally unimaginable man come to spend his days with you. He simply flew into your life. A very strange and wonderful thing! Do you think this is personal choice, or is it a coincidence of fate? If you say it's fated, then suppose I hadn't gone to the south last year; would today have been possible? If you say it's due to human will, could it really be that we arranged this all by ourselves?"

She sighed. Nothing should be gone into too deeply, or

there would be no end to it. Yesterday, tomorrow, today —
there was no way of connecting them in her mind. If nothing was fated, at least it did not seem to be due to human
will. There would still be many unexpected things in the
future. She saw that he was going to continue discussing
this question that couldn't be answered, so she said, "I'm
tired. It's late."

The days passed.

The things that continued coming into the lives of the
couple, of course, were the usual happinesses and irritations,
the winds and rains, the minor colds, the brief separations,
the household accounts, the household moves, the hiring of
new cooks, the entertaining and going out, the weddings
and funerals. As for her, she became pregnant and gave
birth. Because of the child she had gone to the hospital
again and again, then down to the south, and from there
back up north again. An accumulation of days, an accumulation of human affairs suddenly came and anxiously went.

Three years had passed. The little child who had been sent
to live with Bibi's grandmother had imperceptibly grown to
be two years old. This young shoot that had come from her
own body could already shout and laugh and also sit on a
small bench and pretend to drive a bus, making the toot-
toot noise of the horn. He had two fat little wobbly legs, a
pair of high, arched eyebrows, and an outgoing and agreeable nature. Everything about her was a witness to unceas-
ing change, particularly this small child, a maturing solitary
life hinting that each new day had special significance. Was
she or was she not also following this unending stream of
days and ending up as another person? When she thought of
this, it was like standing on the edge of a vast boundless sea;
she seemed to lose herself a little. She quickly bowed her
head and washed her hands in the lake. She loved her child,
and she was spellbound by his tears and laughter. Because of
the child she forgot about yesterday, and didn't much worry

about tomorrow. The broadening of her maternal feelings made her a little more practical.

When she had graduated from middle school and was a freshman in a private college, all classmates who were close to her had called her *beautiful.* She was a little surprised and didn't quite believe it. She thought, What is beauty? Things that are seldom seen are often considered wonderful. Purposeful flattery she didn't often permit, for she did not need it. So she was cautious and carefully avoided becoming close with those men who flattered her.

Later she came to know *him.* He found her warm and sweet, intelligent and uncomplicated. And when he was permitted to speak with her, he told her that he thought he loved her. It was almost the same thing she had heard from the others, just spoken a little differently. At first she thought it was nothing more than the "usual" thing. And of course she ignored it, as usual. The obstacles to human affairs made her feel she should be especially distant toward him, show no warmth or sweetness, ignore him. She spent two years playing this diffident and standoffish role. During this period many of her fellow students naturally tried to embellish her student life with improper attentions. She secretly enjoyed these improper attentions and at the same time gradually became used to, even came to expect, receiving letters from that stranger. They were full of self-deprecatory adoration, mixed with a hopeless, helpless melancholy. She read every letter from beginning to end, then softly sighed, marked the letter, and put it away in a small box.

Undoubtedly those extralong letters gave her a secret happiness and helped promote certain illusions. Sometimes she even thought of replying, but she didn't know how to choose the words. Their lives were too far apart, and their personalities were too hard to understand. To tell the truth, her impression of him was of a diminutive and cowardly man, hardly remarkable. There seemed to be a sort of barrier between them; perhaps time could remove it, but who could say. However, she had already slowly become accustomed to seeing the many self-deprecatory and bold words in his long letters. She was no longer afraid of him. A little love was growing, in secret. As before, she paid no attention to him; outside her deep silence, she had never done anything to encourage him, and she very carefully maintained a distance. She did this, she told herself, not so much for his benefit as for the benefit of some others wholly unrelated. She was afraid people would find out, that they would ridicule her; she didn't breathe a word even to her own sister. But was that possible?

Naturally it was impossible. After graduation she lived at home. He knew. He supposed that her attitude toward him would be a little different, so he impetuously took the train from the north coast to see her. It was a strained meeting full of bashful and nervous affection, a kind of meeting at which he didn't know where to start talking. As the time for departure neared, he asked her about her future plans. She told him that she was going to Peking to study for a few years and see the big city. When she had been there half a year, again he came from the coast to see her. And, as before, it was a meeting full of bashful smiles and silences in place of words. When he was about to leave, he told her again that her life could take more than one form. Each had its good points, its correct points; was that not worth considering? It was up to her. Thus a new question came into her head: Ought she to enter a school or a home? She was undecided. Finally, she thought, Everything was opportunity, and if good things came in pairs, as they said, then what happened yesterday might happen again today. He had endured this for three years; one more year wouldn't make him take flight, wouldn't make him run away; better to put it on hold. And she really did put it on hold, for half a year. And now a new opportunity made them colleagues at the same school.

When they were together, he said to her, very obliquely, that he'd about written all the letters he could, and that was why heaven had allowed them to work together. If she didn't find him too terrible, she ought to think of how to keep that foolish adoration of his and let it become an ornament of her life. When a woman was young, she needed such an ornament.

For the sake of prudence, she said with a laugh that she really didn't understand this question, for it was too complex. If he had really written all he could, then there was no need for any more; wouldn't it save him trouble? She perceived a trace of unhappiness in his expression. She then asked him why he didn't bother all the other attractive girls, but only kept pestering her. She, after all, wasn't so attractive. Actually she was very ordinary. She was honest but not very clever. He should speak frankly, without flattery – simply speak his mind.

His answer was very interesting. Beauty is an unfixed and illimitable term. Whatever can arouse affection, induce wonder, surprise, and cause comfort in someone is beauty. Because she was clever and cautious, she seemed affectionate and pure; this easily drew people's attention and admiration. He felt that her warm glances could subdue his wild ambitions and purify his disordered thoughts. He knew many girls, but only she had the kind of fascination and power to overcome him, to control him. She thought the explanation interesting. Not completely honest, but beautiful. It was close to flattery, but at least it was different from the usual flattery. She still didn't quite understand what it meant for one person to be passionate toward another, yet she delighted in his trust and his acknowledgment of her power. Although she had planned that the two of them might get to know each other a bit more, become a little closer, and see if that attraction, that "surprise," didn't disappear, still she became engaged to him. And they married.

When they were married, she remembered everything he

had said to her and very happily passed her days in the new life. Their habits were entirely different, so she tried hard to adjust. She wanted to become a model wife at home as well as a model wife in society. She was loving and responsible, modest and disciplined. And her efforts were not wasted. From her friends and relatives she won universal praise and sympathy, while at home nothing was out of place. But she discovered, as if it were inevitable, that, because of their excessive closeness, the "surprise" of the one at her side seemed to erode away with daily life and wane day by day. Furthermore, the willfulness and heedlessness to which his past had accustomed him became daily more apparent. She now understood what passion was, and she knew that he retained that nearly childlike passion for her, but this had no meaning in daily life, nor had she any great need for it. On the other hand, this passion, overused and abused, added all the more to her dread. She wanted to subdue him and control him, as he had said before, but she could not, so sometimes she could not help feeling a little disillusioned and tired of her household duties. And, like most women, she considered her marriage a mistake, a mistake for which she herself was partly responsible. She loved him, yet she also hated him a little. Perceiving a change between them, he became a little cooler.

This change was of course unavoidable. She needed more understanding of this, a deeper knowledge: an understanding that the ebbing of "surprise" was very natural and that its re-creation was never impossible, if only she was good at adjustment and control. But limitations owing to her age and disposition made her unable to do that. Since she was ignorant of natural changes that take place in the feelings between the sexes, a few tears naturally fell into her happy life. So the short-lived monthly depression, boredom, and mild bouts of anger that had come to her in a cycle became nearly fixed. She was only twenty-six, not quite old enough yet for cool self-analysis. Because she loved him, she retreated and sought compromise in forbearance. She did not try to understand his actions, only to tolerate them. This tolerance was just one aspect of her generous, accommodating character. However, it had its limitations. She often worried that there would be a time when his actions would exceed the limits of her tolerance.

For his part, he was a man with too much iron in his blood, too many illusions in his head, and too many headstrong habits in his life. He used society as his school, as his home. He was quick witted, and he was naive. He was passionate but not warm, and he loved visible success but lacked patience. Although good at observing human relations, he was awkward at adjusting to them. He loved her, but he was poor at pleasing her. He was sincere in his feelings but neglected responsibility. What hurt her most easily was that disposition of his, always passionate about life and rich in imagination, but neglectful of reality. Such a disposition might have been an asset in his work, but it was an incurable weakness at home. He had long recognized this fault and realized that in preparing for marriage he would have to reform, to adjust to the feelings of another person. The most material method of reforming himself was to put aside his main work, change his hobbies, and curb the development of his personal fancies. He understood that giving in to his hobby wasted his ambition, yet he wanted to collect a few small art objects to increase the felicity of his home just a little.

After marriage he got to know her a little better and understand that her hope was "to help him keep his good points and get rid of the bad." She was not yet old enough to understand that "what may be a personality's strength in one context may be a fault in others." He hoped that she would understand him better, for he needed that understanding more than the benefit of her tolerance. In the end he realized that this was impossible. He thought, In life, gaining one thing often means losing another. If something is to be accomplished, then something must be destroyed. Accepting fate does not necessarily lead to happiness, or to unhappiness, either. Now, since I cannot transcend the ordinary and become a saint – cannot merge with the infinite and be untroubled by the outside world – then I had best discipline myself and respect a certain fact. I have no intention of flying high, so I must clip my wings. In the past three years, his spirit had appeared to become somewhat lazy, somewhat given to self-abandonment, a little decadent, even vulgar, yet, because of this, his domestic life seemed to be a bit happier.

When she noticed this and heard his explanations of it, she naturally experienced a dilemma: a conflict between pure logic and her desire to monopolize him. She believed part of his explanation. When she thought deeply on this question, she felt love and resentment intertwined, suffering and happiness in equal measure. She was quite terrified, did not know where to turn. She therefore clearly saw the complexity of life, but she tried to put the whole thing together, in quest of simplicity. She tried to forget, and let bygones be bygones, and worked hard to fulfill her obligations in her daily affairs. She gave up her personal ideals or converted them into concern for the child. In other words, she did all she could and let fate command. When these two were proclaimed "a perfect couple" in front of their friends, they would smile, as if to say, "But also antagonists"; yet when their friends made as if they were "antagonists," that subtle smile came again, to say, "But we're really a perfect couple." In the eyes of most people, she seemed very happy, and she had discovered no melancholy in herself. She acknowledged reality, and when reality did not excessively wrong her, she was as happy and lively as ever, passing her days full of the spirit of life.

Three years had passed. He dreamed that he broke a vase. When he awoke, he counted the little dishes and bowls he had collected, and there were almost three hundred. They were sandbags weighing down his spirit, scissors clipping his imagination. Remembering now what day it was, he turned toward her, she who was still deep in sleep, and reviewed the many things the two of them had been through in the past three years. He thought of their efforts to adjust to one another because of the differences in their personalities and of the change that had taken place in their lives due to their inadequate strength as well as some unforeseen contingencies. And he examined himself, in all his relationships with others: how in certain aspects he had planted the seeds of happiness and in others reaped bitter fruit. He analyzed himself still more mercilessly, dissected himself: how clumsy he could be while in the throes of love and hate, yet at other times how clever. Finally he mused about how he had clipped his wings with his material hobbies; he rehearsed the lives of some people who had been free these last three years, and as the ancients said, "The cripple does not neglect his shoes"; the one with the fault is the one most conscious of it.

In the struggle within his emotions between the ordinary and the extraordinary, his brain had gradually become confused. He felt he ought to leave this room and go walking in the courtyard, where there was wind and sunlight. So he dressed and quietly left the bedroom. When she awoke, he had been standing out there by the well for an hour.

While at the well he quietly and unconsciously peered at the ginkgo tree, finding the direction of the wind from the way the leaves blew and anticipating how they would move in the next breeze, as if that could reveal the secret of life. He thought, When the breeze in one's heart blows on the life of another, is this by coincidence or of necessity? Which is more reasonable: the person who is so often controlled by the climate, her age, and the environment; or the one who seems forever untrammeled, illimitable, unrestrainable? Is the ideal of life to restrain the emotions to just the right degree, or is it to let them run free, without limits, without restrictions? Is it best to live for the past, the present, or the future?

As he fixed his eyes on the azure sky, his emotions swam boundlessly, as though there was nowhere that he could not freely go: the past, the future, the great void. He was an abstraction. Only when he came to and felt a little giddy did he realize that he was still standing beside the well in the vineyard. He plucked a leaf and thought of the woman with whom he was attached. Like the grapes, tightly rooted in the earth, so was life attached to reality. For some reason he could not fathom, he felt a little sorry for himself, a bit of love mixed with pity. "The light and heat of the sun give all things the enjoyment and happiness of life. I can do this, too, and I must. Living things cannot dwell in the sky, so I must stick close to the earth."

For the woman who lay in bed it was different.

She first reflected on the changes in their material environment the past three years and the slight disappointment and slight wonder that they had brought. Then she saw something in the changing material environment that didn't seem to have changed at all. She thought this rare (it *seemed* rare). Actually, in the course of the changing seasons everything mutates, but she was still about the same as years before when she was a college student. This could be proved by the words and glances of strangers and acquaintances as well as by a glance in the mirror.

She remembered something a friend had said about her, adopting an amused expression of wonder: "You all say that Bibi is older than her sister-in-law; she's already twenty-six and has a child. Twenty-six, who would believe it? Her countenance and appearance aren't at all like an adult's. The child is already two years old, and she herself is still like a child!"

The jesting of an old paternal aunt was even more interesting: "Bibi, when I saw you year before last, you seemed a little younger than your oldest younger brother – now that I see you this year, you look younger than your youngest little brother, number five. You were prettier than your older sister when you married, and now that you've had a child you look prettier than your younger sister, too. You're twenty-six this year, but to me you look only twenty-two."

When she thought about it, this seemed funny. She was already twenty-six, four years away from thirty, the peak of a woman's youth, after which it was all downhill. From woman, to housewife, to middle-aged wife – getting plumper and more affable daily – before long, she'd be an old grandmother, with grandchildren around her knees. It was a predestined change that no one could avoid. To some it seemed to occur rapidly and to others slowly, yet it came about eventually. But to look at her now *she* still had ten years before coming to the turning point of thirty. Many people, seeing her eyes and sweet face, guessed her to be between twenty-two and twenty-four. They all thought she was still in college. No one believed she had been a housewife for three years and even had a two-year-old child. Come to think of it, what a funny mistake it was! It seemed to have really reduced her age. The jesting of her old paternal grandmother and the passion of the man near her proved that it was a very natural mistake, one that was going to continue.

While it seemed that in all human existence time was creating and destroying endlessly, that the new was always replacing the old in human affairs, still there was an occasional exception, like the permanent beauty of one's youth. This beauty was of little significance in itself, especially today, when artificial adornment was also called beauty. Its advantage lay in the past. If it had ever stirred certain people, got entangled in their feelings, then it would be preserved in the present with no diminution. All those boys, strangers and friends, come from near and far – the silly infatuation and rash actions brought on by her youth, the despondency and depression that arose from the slightest hint of her friendship, the newborn love that came from a smile or a glance from her – all these were preserved without the slightest diminution. She felt happy. She was very satisfied with her own clean and delicate light-brown hands. She believed that God had known what he was about when he created her eyebrows, her eyes, her ears, her nose. She sensed instinctively that she could excite especially intimate good feelings in friends of a certain temperament and that, if she desired, she still could give those strangers a little vexation or happiness (her sensitivity toward the many virtues of a woman and her practice of them were enough to gain the praise of those around her and to increase their admiration). She felt that the beauty of youth could subdue others and that virtue could assist. She did it not for pride, or for vanity, but only for happiness; her beautiful appearance and beautiful virtue gave her equal pleasure.

Just then she remembered the words of a poet: "Time, like ever-flowing waters, carries away everything on earth, but never the figments of love, the dreams of youth, or the laugh and frown of a loved one." She was a little embarrassed, as though ashamed of the ridiculousness of her own imagination. He returned to the room.

She thought he seemed a little downcast and asked, "What's wrong? Don't you remember what day it is? Why would anyone get up so early and sneak away?"

He said, "Because I love you, I've been remembering all the experiences we've shared."

"I've thought about them, too. Kiss me. Look how pretty and happy I am! Today I'm full of joy because today is our most memorable day."

He forced himself to smile. "Darling, you're a good wife. You really are. Many others think you are, too."

"Many others? What others? Everyone thinks that I'm all right, but you don't care about me, don't even pay attention to me. You don't love me! At least you don't belong completely to me." Although what she said was quite true, she wasn't the slightest bit angry. She intentionally put on an unhappy expression and covered her face with the blanket, laughing quietly.

In a moment she suddenly threw back the silk blanket and stretched out her gentle arms. She wrapped them around his neck and said, happily, "Darling, you don't know how much I love you!"

A thread of newborn sorrow invaded his feelings. He didn't know what to do to make her happier and more satisfied, make her understand him better and know herself more clearly. He thought her too young, her spirit rather more youthful than her age. Because she didn't understand him very well now, she wouldn't be able to understand him much better in the future. But she loved him, loved him intensely. And he? He wanted to "belong completely to her" as she wished, but he didn't know how to go about it.

Suicide

"Suicide" ("Zisha") is another presentation of the dilemmas of modern life in a bourgeois setting of the sort Shen Congwen knew intimately during his own midlife. Written 7 August 1935, about a year before "The Housewife," this piece presents its modern "problem" by means of a more exterior and clearly plotted narrative, reinforced with deft symbolism and foreshadowing through double entendres in the characters' words. It is to be sure a comedy of manners, with ironic overtones even in the characters' names; Professor Zhao Gongyu's given name, for instance, is an inversion of yugong, *"foolish old man." And the name of the main protagonist, Xishun, seems rather stodgy. Literally it means "Taking after the ancient sage-king Shun." It is, however, the psychological analysis and occasional stream-of-consciousness technique (loosely defined), along with the dark subject, that give this story a modernist feel.*

"Suicide" is not experimental autobiography in the sense that the last piece was, but it may still have reflected Shen Congwen's condition. He actually attempted suicide in 1949, and in 1985 Liang Shiqiu claimed that students at the Wusong China Institute, where Shen taught in 1929, spread the rumor that he contemplated suicide because his courtship of Zhang Zhaohe was unsuccessful.

Professor Liu Xishun was considered fortunate by his colleagues. At about three o'clock in the afternoon, following his lecture "Love and a Sense of Surprise" for a psychology class at the university, he remembered a date he had made with his wife some time before and got into his personal automobile to be driven home. He arrived just as his wife was getting everything ready in the small parlor, including blue flowers she had put into a white porcelain vase. When the professor arrived, she hurried past the window and out of the parlor to greet him.

"Come, come, look at my flowers!"

The professor entered the parlor to watch his wife arrange them. "Very beautiful!" he said, in praise of both the flowers and the one who had arranged them. The wife wore a pale yellow gown. It matched the ripples of lustrous black hair that fell across her shoulders, the pure white of her perfectly oval face, and the delicate white hands among the blue flowers. The flowers were peculiarly blue, like a rare flame, just as bright and just as quiet. This scene – these flowers, this woman – was too lovely to behold. Remembering the foolish words with which a northern friend had once complimented his wife, the professor couldn't help smiling. He felt very fortunate – blessed in a way that really did merit the envy of others.

Wanting to open a conversation, he asked, "Aren't these forget-me-nots?" His wife seemed not to have heard, for she took no notice.

While balancing the arrangement, the wife glanced at the professor and asked, cheerfully, "How much do you think these flowers cost? Guess!"

"A dollar – "

"A dollar? One dollar, two dollars, that's all you know to say. Sixteen cents I tell you, and not a penny more. See how beautiful they are in that vase."

Translated by Jeffrey Kinkley

"Really, very beautiful."

After the flowers were arranged to suit her, the wife took the vase in both hands and set it down on a long table of red sandalwood in a southern corner of the room. They didn't look quite right to her, so she moved them to the window sill. Then she lay back on the little black couch to appreciate the blue blooms before the rice-colored background of the gauze window screens. She smiled at the way they looked.

The professor took the lovely hand of his beautiful wife and kissed it. "Darling, you really know how to make things nice. A little blue is just what this parlor needed." His wife seemed enlivened by the compliment. She smiled, but said nothing.

"They don't look like forget-me-nots," said the professor.

"Who said they were?" chuckled the wife. "You can't even tell the difference. I'd originally meant to buy a little pot of forget-me-nots, but they aren't in season yet, so they weren't on the market. We needed a little color in that corner. Red wouldn't have done; it needed blue. They should be spread out in a row, not all bunched up. Only if they're spread out will they fit the window and balance the vase. Don't you think?"

"That would be perfect. It just seems to me that the vase is a bit too tall."

"Uh huh, naturally it would be better if it were wider at the mouth and narrower at the bottom."

The housekeeper entered the room to pour tea and clean up the broken twigs and flowers on the table.

"Have the guests arrived, Amah Wang?"

Amah Wang cleaned up the table and said, "Mr. Zhou from the agricultural college called to say that old Mr. Zhao has arrived from Nanjing and, if the master wants to visit him, he can see him at Mr. Zhou's house."

"Is that Zhao Gongyu?" asked the wife.

"Who else?" answered the professor. "He's going north in

the spring to inspect three provincial administrations, and he says while he's at it he'll get a divorce from Mrs. Zhao in Tianjin. The world is really changing when even fifty-year-old men are eager to get a divorce. What do you know but his wife wouldn't grant one. So old Mr. Zhao told his daughter, 'If Mama doesn't grant me a divorce, I'll kill myself!' The daughter was furious. 'All right, Papa,' she told him, 'if you're going to commit suicide, then go back to Nanjing and do it. We can't interfere with such things. You may not want your wife, but I want my mother. After I graduate from Peking University next year, I'll support her.' After that, old Mr. Zhao spoke no more of committing suicide."

"That's what I call a Daoist's revolution."

"It's an epidemic," he said, reviewing some interesting cases. "Mr. Zhao isn't as old at heart as he is in body. Putting in his time there in the new bureaucracy at Nanjing, naturally he'll be making some waves. Then there's Mr. Yu. They say there was nothing wrong with his wife except that she didn't acknowledge his talent, didn't look up to him, so he felt he had to divorce her. And he really did. Someone asked him if that was really why he divorced her, and he denied it. 'If that really were the reason,' the person said, 'it would be quite unfair to your wife.' Then Mr. Yu pretended to be very serious and said, 'Society misunderstands me. It's so unforgiving. I want to commit suicide!' It got that acquaintance worried about him. He was afraid the conversation would push him over the edge and cause him to take his life. He finally relaxed when he saw that Yu was still writing his seven-syllable romantic poetry for his old friend, with the rhymes and allusions all in the right places, so it looked like he wouldn't be killing himself for the time being! Previously, this contagious disease was quite virulent among the young. Now that they've developed an immunity and it doesn't threaten them anymore, it has spread to the middle-aged. When they've caught it, they get chills and fevers and rant and rave. There doesn't seem to be any cure for this strange illness yet."

"How could there not be," his wife said, grinning.

Noticing the professor's big briefcase, Amah Wang remembered that he'd got an express letter that day. She said to the professor, "Four regular letters and one express are on your desk in the northern study; do you want me to bring them?" Off she went to get them.

Resuming the previous conversation, the wife said, "I think that illness you spoke of is easily cured. Ask yourself, did you ever get sick, or were you always well? Maybe when little Yuanyuan grows up to be eighteen, she'll ask you, 'Papa, would you like to commit suicide? Here, I have a gun.'"

A little defensively, the professor explained, "Those who have had the sickness before have an immunity to it. If I do get it again, eighteen years from now, our little Yuanyuan is bound to really give me a gun. But with a daughter like her, it would be hard to carry out!"

When Amah Wang brought in the letters, she carried little Yuanyuan into the parlor. Yuanyuan was the couple's only daughter, the family treasure, one year old. As she had learned to do, Yuanyuan grabbed the letter away from Amah Wang and gave it to her father with her own little hands.

He took it, patting Yuanyuan's tiny hand and teasing her, "Yuanyuan, did you see the big white crane in the park today? It flies on the water! Flies!"

Little Yuanyuan imitated her father: "Flies, flies, Papa flies!"

The professor kept up a patter with his baby daughter as he read the letter. "Papa flies to the park, he flies up in the sky." He couldn't suppress a smile. He quickly handed the letter to his wife. She saw at once that it was from Mr. Shi, editor of the *Eastern Miscellany* in Shanghai, asking him to write an article. The topic was just what the two of them had been talking about: "Why People Commit Suicide." "It's a pity I can't write fiction," the professor said, "or I could make a very interesting piece out of the stories of Mr. Zhao and Mr. Yu."

The professor's wife handed him back the letter and cradled Yuanyuan in her arms, warmly kissing the palms of her little hands. Pointing to the blue flowers in the vase, she said, "Look, Precious, pretty flowers!"

Yuanyuan softly called out, from her mother's embrace, "Flowers, flowers, Mama flowers! Flies, flies, Papa flies!"

"Mama flowers, and Papa flies. And what about little Yuanyuan?"

As if pondering the meaning of her father's words, Yuanyuan aimed her big, beautiful eyes at her father and said, "Papa, Papa, fly!"

The telephone rang in the hallway. Amah Wang picked up the receiver and learned that Mr. Wang of Popo Lane wanted to talk with the professor. After taking the call, the professor returned to the parlor looking somewhat put out. His wife guessed what it was. "You have to go to a meeting in the park again, don't you?"

"That's it. Yuanyuan, in a little while Papa really will have to fly over to the park."

Looking at the blue flowers, his wife said, softly, "Must you fly?"

"I don't want to. But how can I leave the school to its own devices? I'll go with you to the east side of the city tomorrow when you go to buy material for dressmaking, all right? Darling, your eyebrows are beautiful – " The professor looked at his wife as he spoke and heaved a soft sigh. He really was fortunate. Her long eyebrows reminded him of a line of poetry: "So worried that her long eyebrows were knitted all the way to the temples." But what was there to worry about? He couldn't quite remember.

Seeing that the professor was in a mood to flatter her, and knowing why, the wife said, "You have business, so go do it."

"I hate to leave you."

"How can that be?"

"I'll go with you. Amah Wang – " he said, intending to telephone.

"Stop it."

"Flies, flies," said little Yuanyuan.

The professor took out his gold pocket watch. It was almost four o'clock. The meeting was scheduled for four-thirty, so time was running short. He stood up to go to the lavatory in the western wing.

"Papa, flies, flies," little Yuanyuan said.

"Yes, little Yuanyuan," he said joking, "Papa really will fly." And he spread his arms out like wings to tease her.

Without a word the wife left the parlor with the professor, cradling Yuanyuan in her arms. They went into the yard to view the sunflowers. "The sunflower has a mind to face the sun always, whereas willow catkins can but twist in the breeze." She counted them: eight, nine, thirteen. An unlucky number. So she brought in a little bud from the side, to make fourteen.

The park was especially crowded when the sky cleared after the rain. It was as if the trees were fresh from a bath, bright and pleasing to the eye. The professor found his colleague Mr. Wang in a secluded spot at a table for tea. Mr. Dai the Beard, Mr. Zuo, and tall Mr. Song arrived forthwith. Just as the men had seated themselves and were discussing various personnel changes in their department for the second half of the year, a little girl suddenly came up and shouted, "Uncle Wang, Uncle Wang." She was about eleven or twelve, with fine long eyebrows, lovely eyes, and a particularly beautiful nose. As she approached Mr. Wang, she said, "Uncle Wang, why aren't you at Auntie's house so we can play? Are you angry at someone? . . . Who is this?" she said, looking at the man with the full beard. "It's Uncle Dai," Mr. Wang said. "Uncle Dai," she addressed him. Then she turned to look at the tall one. "Who is this?" she asked.

"This is Uncle Song," said Mr. Wang. And so the girl greeted him as "Uncle Song." Then, after asking who the other bearded man was and being told it was "Uncle Zuo," she greeted him by that title, too.

Finally the little girl caught sight of the professor. She stared at him. "Who is this, Uncle Wang?"

"Uncle Liu," said Mr. Wang.

"Uncle Liu?" The little girl sized up the professor for a moment and then softly hailed him as "Uncle Liu," but this time used the term for "uncle" reserved for younger men. That brought a laugh from all present.

"Say, Dalian," Mr. Wang said, "why do you call Mr. Liu a younger uncle? Do you remember that picture of a beautiful woman you saw in the *Northern Pictorial Magazine,* the one you thought looked like Mama? You said you liked her so much, and then you cut her out and stuck her picture on your mirror. She's the mother of the family; she's Auntie Liu!"

The girl tilted her head to give the professor a good look. "Really, Uncle Wang?"

"Would I fool you?" said Mr. Wang. "Someday, when we go to Uncle Liu's house, we can visit Aunt Liu."

"Really?"

"You'll see when you get there."

"Does Aunt Liu have a little baby?"

"Yes she does, and you can see the little baby, and play with it!"

"All right, one of these days I'll go. Is it really true, Uncle Wang?"

"Why don't you ask Uncle Liu?"

The little girl bashfully bit her lip, exposing a row of fine white teeth. She stared at the professor for several moments and then, as if she had found a secret in the way he looked, suddenly mumbled to herself, "It's true. It really is."

"You and Uncle Wang come to my house to play!"

"All right." Nodding her head, she flew away, like a little swallow.

As she left, Mr. Wang followed her with his eyes and heaved a long sigh. "Whose child is that?" Professor Zuo asked him.

There was a long pause from Mr. Wang.

They were all bewitched by the girl. They talked about the extraordinary beauty of her eyes and how different she was from ordinary little girls. They learned from Mr. Wang that she was an orphan, retribution for the sins of the famous Yao-Li suicide case that took place six years before in Shanghai. Her mother had been a famous beauty. The daughter of a dentist, she had married a Mr. Li, the son of a rich family. They had got along admirably after the marriage, without any grudges or bad feelings at all. Then, seven years after the marriage, for no apparent reason, the woman had killed herself. The reason for her suicide being so unclear, all society thought that the man must have been in love with another woman, but there was no evidence for this conjecture. His subsequent behavior also proved beyond reproach. After that there was another theory, that the woman had fallen in love with a very ordinary man — some said it was a high school student who was related to her; others said a painter. Hemmed in on all sides, the woman had no choice but to commit suicide. Three years later, the man ran off to Mount Huang in a fit of depression, and he committed suicide, too. His suicide note proved that the secret of the woman's suicide was something altogether unpredicted. As to what it was, the note said that the girl could find out from a document when she was twenty years old and engaged to be married. An aunt had taken in the orphan they left behind, to live with her in Peking. Her uncle was the biologist Professor Yang.

Back home, when Professor Liu had finished supper with his wife, he got to talking about that little girl he'd met in the park and the story of her mother's suicide, which he found so inexplicable. "There are a lot of things in human behavior that one can never figure out," his wife said, "but a suicide of this kind isn't very unusual." The professor couldn't figure out how that could be. He asked his wife what she meant by "not unusual." She just smiled and said nothing.

That evening, the husband was in his little study, writing the article "Why People Commit Suicide." He looked through lots of reference books. All their theories and case studies were well thought out, but when he contrasted them with the cases he had heard about that day, he wasn't sure which to believe.

Yes of course, the professor thought, some suicides cannot be classified. They fall outside of economic hardship, failure in love, or any other category. One *might* kill oneself from a misconception, an illusion – from a fast-striking physical and psychological infection (a sentence, or an idea, from a book). One might also commit suicide as a luxury (if one reasons that squandering life itself is the supreme luxury). But if one kills oneself because of the difficulties of surviving or losses in business or in love, society will consider one to be avoiding pain and responsibility, too cowardly to get through the difficulties of existence, and will take the act to be a sin. For one's suicide to be praiseworthy, one must be lucid at the time, unaffected by any abnormality. One must understand life as being one's own and understand and cherish it – must die to attain a lofty ideal or complete a beautiful plan or to give one's life a beautiful form, as if death were a necessary subplot in a great drama or narrative that one must carry out calmly and according to plan.

Some such suicides are on behalf of human freedom, cultural progress, historical change, and others are for oneself – to bring one's life to a climax. Society considers all these deaths difficult and commendable. But what is the real difference between the child bride who secretly takes an overdose of opium in her rustic kitchen and Socrates, who took his cup of hemlock in prison? Many people die to leave behind a deep or beautiful memory for the living, yet we consider all sorts of behavior that are a good deal stupider than this to be deeper. Many people fear to go on living, and that is akin to cowardice. Many others die just to impress the memories of others, and that is akin to being greedy. "To be greedy for life out of fear of dying," to save one's skin at all costs, is a phrase of reproach, but there are also people who are greedy for life regardless of death. Is their behavior moral? . . . And perhaps there are others who take their own life without giving it much thought either way. . . . He pondered the matter, but it remained quite inconclusive.

The professor felt a little upset, a bit unsettled. He looked at the clock. It was already five past twelve. A stack of books and papers lay in front of him. Lamplight gently caressed the rosewood desktop. Tiny insects were on the window, trying to climb up, or softly throwing themselves against it. All was quiet. The whole household was asleep – the cook, the housekeeper, little Yuanyuan – they were all quietly dreaming in their own beds. The professor pointed the tip of his writing brush at his heart. He could almost hear the gunshot: "bang," and he was gone. Everything was all over. He slumped back in his chair and dropped his brush. His heart told him, in a prosecutorial tone of voice, "I am not one to choose suicide by an act of will; I am a cowardly person escaping my responsibilities. Yet now I am finished. My good fortune has left me. . . . And what is it to be fortunate? Everyone says I have a good wife – even the little girl from the Li family tragedy has cut her picture out of a magazine and gets absorbed staring at it from time to time. A college student once committed suicide because he couldn't have her. Some can feel themselves blessed because of her beauty, others unlucky. I am the one closely tied to her. Why is it I who find her just ordinary? Why does she never fill me with a sense of surprise, of wonder?

A small black door in the professor's study-bedroom connected with his wife's bedroom. At this time it was gently pushed open. She had seen the light still on in the study and realized that the professor hadn't gone to bed.

Reaching in and waving her white hand, she said, gently and affectionately, "Why aren't you asleep? Still at work? The clock has struck midnight. You ought to rest. Listen, that's thunder! It'll be raining before daybreak. Would you like a cup of tea? What are you writing? May I come take a look?"

The professor said nothing. Still standing by the door, the wife said again, "Why are you at your desk all the time? *Must* you write that article? Would you like a – "

"I don't want anything, darling. Go to sleep; I still have work to do."

"You don't want anything. Not even me?"

"Darling, I'm working!"

Like a little child, the wife stood at the door for a while and then, without asking the professor's permission as she usually did, went up to his desk on her own accord. "I'm here whether you want me or not. As soon as you get to working and studying, you find me repulsive. I come to see you, and you say I'm bothering you. This is unfair!"

The professor's wife had changed into a thin, white, velvety nightgown. She had taken down her hair and tied it into two braids. The skin of her face and arms was smoothly white, as clear as if carved from jade. Her long eyebrows and lovely eyes, the slightly flirtatious blush of her cheeks, made her even more dazzlingly beautiful. The professor had to smile. She knew that her husband was thinking through a problem. She forgave her husband's neglect of her. She patted the professor on the shoulder and leaned toward his chair. After getting her husband's kiss, she returned to her own bedroom in high spirits. The professor sighed as he looked at that little door and mumbled to himself, "People!"

The professor grabbed a novel off the little bookshelf at his side. It was written by a Russian. He turned to the part describing a man while he imagined the country girl he loved: wrapping her hair up in a head cloth, taking off her clothes, and getting ready for bed. And how, lying in that sweet-smelling hay under a new quilt, he tossed and turned all the night long. The author's skilled pen brought the reader directly into the world of which he wrote, as if only the circumstances he had created amounted to love.

Rain began to fall, and the thunder grew louder, too. The light went on in the baby's room. The professor knew that his wife had gone into Yuanyuan's room to check the windows and see that she was covered up. Ordinarily they would have done it together, but this time he did not get up. He remained there at his desk, motionless, still thinking of the girl Dalian he had met during the day. There was a clap of thunder, and the rain came down hard, making a racket on the mat shed in the courtyard. The little door to the wife's bedroom gently opened again.

"Darling, why aren't you asleep yet?" said the professor.

"There's thunder, and I was a little scared. I couldn't get to sleep."

"You're no child — still afraid of thunder?"

"It's raining hard. Why haven't you come to bed yet? So you're not afraid of the sound of thunder. What about storms?"

"I'm not afraid of them!"

"Really? If you don't pay more attention to me, I'll rain on you, too!" She slammed the little door.

A line of poetry: "Tears like spring rains, never clearing up." The two of them had come across this poem the other day while reading together from a collection by a modern poet. The professor suddenly awoke to something. Hurriedly he rose and entered his wife's room. She had draped herself over the bed, and her eyes were already bright with tears. As the professor tried every way he knew to bolster his wife's spirits, he noticed the extraordinary beauty of her face. "Darling," he smiled and said, "You are so beautiful."

"What were you thinking about just now," she said, "that kept you tied all the time to your desk?"

"I was thinking about the problem of suicide," he said in the voice he typically used for joking. "And you?"

"Me? The same as you."

"I don't believe that. Not the same as I."

"I don't think you love me anymore!"

"That proves we weren't thinking the same thing! I've never doubted that you love me."

"You don't doubt it because I do love you!"

The professor felt uncomfortable continuing in this vein, so he changed the subject. "Darling, it just now occurred to me, ten years from now, when that little girl I met in the park gets to be twenty, she'll find out her mother's secret, all by herself. It's hard to imagine what that will be like."

"You don't love me any more," the wife repeated intently.

And she thought, When the girl is twenty, you'll be forty.

A thunderclap startled little Yuanyuan awake, and she began to cry. The wife hurriedly rose and went to her room by another door.

The professor lay inert on the bed. He pushed the middle finger of his left hand up against his chest, pointing at his heart, and imagined that he heard another "bang." He slumped, prostrate, and kissed his beautiful wife's white pillow – and kissed, and kissed. It was as if to answer his wife with an "I love you." He recalled the descriptive passage he had just read in the novel. A note of sorrow seemed to keep flowing into his life, from where he wasn't sure. He wanted to be rid of it, but he could not.

Gazing at Rainbows
(The Shape of One Person's Life in a
Twenty-four Hour Period)

"Gazing at Rainbows" ("Kan hong lu"), written in July 1941 and revised in March 1943, represents the peak of Shen Congwen's avant-garde technique and also of his eroticism (although the figure of the rainbow itself actually represents a beautiful and evanescent ideal – or woman – rather than carnal pleasure, according to the author). The lovers in the story communicate with each other both vocally and subconsciously, giving conflicting answers to each other's respective conscious and unconscious lines of thought. Strange resonances and contradictions exist between a character's own open and hidden thoughts, too, and the less regulated speech of the private self delivers, among other things, satiric jabs at the false, patriotic wartime discourse of the times.

In its day, "Gazing at Rainbows" was condemned as salacious and perversely out of step with the wartime spirit of "resistance to Japanese aggression." It also raised a scandal because the woman depicted resembled Shen's own extramarital girlfriend at Kunming's Southwest Associated University, an old flame from his Qingdao days in the early 1930s named Gao Qingzi. The room described below appears to be from Shen Congwen's actual Kunming residence, Shen's friends attest, although in the story it comes to the protagonist in a flashback, possibly from memories years earlier. In any case, it seems much more likely that Shen imagined the object of his adoration in his Kunming home without ever having actually invited her in. Indeed, the story reads like an exercise in sublimation, and by most accounts his affair with Gao Qingzi was "passionate" but platonic. The love, like the story, may have existed largely in Shen Congwen's mind. Still, he refused to show this story to his wife!

This retranslation of the piece, made from a newly recovered Chinese text, restores passages deleted in a previous English version. Typically the parts deleted were about God and Life, which to the pantheist Shen Congwen were the same thing.

I

Eleven at night.

One half hour ago I returned here from another place. I reached an old-fashioned memorial archway not far from home and paused an instant under it, stirred by the clear, glimmering moonlight. This place was a raucous farmers' market during the day, but in the night it felt opened up and silently deserted. The vast empty space seemed to be broadening out my feelings, though the silence was changing those "feelings" – formless, shapeless, and compressed into a block of time – into something of substance. Suddenly there came a distinct fragrance of plum blossoms, and I felt my eyes fixed on the "emptiness." Slowly I stepped toward this "emptiness"; I found myself entering a little courtyard, and then a plain and simple little room, with a stove. The perfume of plum blossoms filled that tiny little room. It seemed to be New Year's eve, for the sound of exploding firecrackers reverberated from all directions in the crisp night air. In this absolute isolation, I began to read a strange book. Cautiously I opened it to the first page. It bore an inscription that was completely intelligible:

"God dwells within our Life."

2

The fire in the stove begins to blaze, making the room warm as the spring, making one want to take off one's heavy clothes and exchange them for something lighter. Lamplight coming through an orange lamp shade tinges the walls, the carpet, and everything else that meets the eye in an otherworldly color, steeps them in an otherworldly atmosphere.

Translated by Jeffrey Kinkley

A tiny yellow lemon is placed on the vermillion lacquered desk by the window, in a porcelain dish shaped like an autumn leaf; the pungency of lemon is in the air as well.

The curtains have been drawn over the windows, tan curtains with brightly drawn pastel horses that look as if they are bounding into the room. By the time the visitor reaches this point, he is wholly lost in a fantastically solitary state. But just for a moment, for then it falls away from him. The master of the room – that is, the mistress – has quietly stolen in, unawares; her image appears in the great mirror opposite the stove. Her face is white; her eyebrows are long; there is the warm breath of spring in her smile. Her hair fluffs out at the temples, in a style that clusters tiny blue flowers behind her pale ears. They appear to be hailing the beholder: "See how wonderfully placed we are, how lovely."

Her fingers are soft and slender. As they ruffle her hair, the smiling face tilts to the side, breaking the silence in her guest's mind.

"I am so sorry, putting you through this wait; it must have been oppressive."

"No. Not in the least. A room so warm, so quiet, is pure enjoyment."

The smiling face disappears. The chair by the stove slightly shifts, and the black kitten with the white nose and paws sleeping atop the rose-colored satin cushion jumps to the floor. Now that it can no longer enjoy the warmth of the stove, it arches its back, expressing disapproval at this unreasonable banishment, and slowly ambles away.

The small clock on the table ticks away, the little hand over the eight. Eight o'clock in the evening.

The guest's eyes continue to roam, intently taking in the surroundings. Again he sees the herd of little colored horses decorating the curtains, caught in the midst of every sort of gait.

"How warm this room is. It's almost like a little green-house."

"Are you hot? You must be wearing too many clothes. I'll open the window for a moment."

The guest had only wanted to compliment her on the warm and comfortable room; he hadn't found it too hot at all. But, seeing the windows being opened, he can't very well object now.

Light snow is drifting down outside the window. From the open window chilly air penetrates with a rasping sound. The window closes again.

"I am beginning to feel hot, too. I'll go change."

She leaves the room for a time.

He sees the horses on the curtains again. The tiny things seem to be galloping and jumping, for he is solitary again. The plum blossoms smell wonderful.

Returning in a gown of green silk gauze, she looks slimmer now.

"That gown is too light – won't you be too cold? Catching cold is no fun. The medicine for it is bitter, and sugar may make it sweet, but not tasty."

"I'm not cold! This dress is thick enough. It was made seven years ago. When I found it, rummaging through a trunk in the fall, I feared it wouldn't fit me and thought I might give it away. But then, to whom, I wondered. I tried it on, just to see. And in the end I was the recipient." She leans toward the stove and holds out her dainty hands toward the fire in a way that is exquisite. Before he can compliment them, the hands are withdrawn and turning up the hem of her gown. "I made this gown myself. I love the soft weave of its silk gauze, so heavy. It gives it substance."

"Yes, it suits you wonderfully. The heavy substance of the material sets off the vivacity and slender gracefulness of your figure perfectly." What he wants to say completely dissolves into a smile. The mistress of the room understands. She responds only with a smile of her own.

The turned-up hem reveals delicate legs enclosed in mouse-gray gossamer silk stockings, looking like a pair of stunning white poplars, like a pair of polished stakes – no, simply a pair of perfect legs. This is a road, a road that leads one's imagination into heaven. The scenery in heaven is unadorned and yet marvelous, an expanse of bluegrass – lush, running riot, still, silent.

Without a word his eyes caress her softly protruding anklebones, the shins modestly pulled back, her rounded knees – they are all perfectly made. Beholding them makes one feel very much at ease, yet also slightly jittery.

As if feeling the slight blasphemy in this gaze and its journey made in reverie, she pulls down her hem again, tightly wrapping it around her knees, and gently sighs. "How do you like my stockings? The color isn't very good, but the material is." As her slender white hands stroke those stockings under her gown, she seems also to be saying, "The material is good – it makes my feet look much prettier, don't you think?"

"When the weather's hot, it's much less bother, isn't it?" But what he really means is, "When it's hot and you can go without stockings, your feet are prettier still."

Her hem blows up again. "Yes, it's much less bother when it's hot." She really means to answer, "They all say my feet are attractive, but how can that be?"

"When it's warm, young ladies can wear lighter shoes, too." (Your heels and toes are just as pretty.)

"Fashions change every year. It's expensive." (Do you like them?)

"Think of all the millions that countries across the world spend every year on all sorts of outrageous and ridiculous things. What does it matter if a young lady changes her shoe style once a year?" (What does the expense matter if they're pretty? The technician in a shoe factory contributes no less to human welfare than the technician in an arms factory!)[1]

"That question is too deep for me to comment on. I'm more like an untamed child. When I get to the seashore, all I want to do is kick up the sand with my bare feet." (I'm not afraid to be stared at, or kissed – but not everywhere.)

"There must be new fashions in bathing suits this year, too." (You're a lot prettier naked than other women.)

The unvoiced words seem to have been understood by both parties from the ones they have spoken. There is no mistake in their intent. At this point the mistress of the room smiles and falls silent. As a rule an intelligent woman's shyness is a mixture of her commitment to chastity and her passionate desire. Within the smile and the silence are both elements: beckoning and avoidance.

The mistress of the room quietly lifts her feet. (*I* know all your foolish notions! But they're not so foolish that I find them offensive.)

Then she draws her feet back a little, as if they are fleeing after having been kissed by him. (Enough. Why must you always be so foolish?)

"You cannot imagine how beautiful you are when you walk. Everywhere you radiate joy and good health." But what the visitor really says is, "Do you prefer hiking in the hills or strolling on the beach?"

"I prefer the sea of course. It can liberate me, and it can satisfy you." But she only says, "The seaside is much more fun. The outgoing tide leaves the sand wet and cold; it's such a thrill to walk on it barefoot, unfettered, unreserved."

"I like to go looking for those lovely little shells in the sand. Beauty is such a strange thing." (A thing of beauty is

[1] "Arms factory" is the translator's conjecture for the phrase " —— —— factory," which appears in the original. Such deletions generally were made by wartime censors.

an object of worship. To encounter it is to bow one's head. To discover beauty, to draw near to it, gives one a feeling not just of happiness but of solemnity, for it is like being face to face with God.)

"You find so many strange things in this world." (Surely you jest. You only *think* that you are adoring, that you bow your head in humility. You wouldn't ever really bow your head to me. You're a strange one, thinking up so many frivolous things, without ever having done anything naughty yourself. You really know how to protect yourself.)

"Yes, I see what the others overlook, and my knowledge never seems to be 'true,' but something different from other people's. Perhaps that's a 'tragedy.'" (For instance, do you really want me to treat you so courteously? It seems to me that you are beckoning me to act a little differently.)

"Have you been writing much poetry lately?" (There is a hint of sarcasm in her voice, as if to say, When you write all day, your passion is dissipated in your composition, so you spend your days quite as properly as a respectable gentleman.)

"I've been writing a story. The thoughts and sentiments behind it are fantastic and baroque, while the writing is dazzling without being serious. It's a story that is absurd yet romantic, about hunting deer alone in a snowstorm. As if by a miracle, the hunter captures one. It's like a children's story, for only little children could believe in the reality of it, and only they could appreciate all the things it speaks of, in a spirit that goes beyond words like *reality* and *fiction* and partakes of the tragic feelings of the characters." (You will understand if you read it. Your Life, too, yearns for the fantasy and beauty of fairy tales and is prepared to accept the unpredictability of living. You might want to read it, but be careful!)

The mistress of the room seems to understand him perfectly, for she smiles and says, "You've finished your story, haven't you? You must let me read it. Let me test my childlike innocence with your story. I myself am not so sure I have it anymore!"

The visitor speaks. "Indeed, I for my part would like to use your thoughts and feelings about this work to test my understanding of human nature. Often I doubt my grasp of it. Many have complimented me on this aspect, but I still feel unsure of myself."

This makes her bow her head (the drooping of a lily) to read the fanciful story. Before beginning to read, as if worried about her forsaken visitor, she raises her head and looks at him. There are spring breezes and summer clouds in those eyes; they are both comforting and attractive. Whereupon the visitor says, "Don't look at me; read the story. And you mustn't be unnecessarily offended by anything in it."

"It is your story, so I must read it slowly."

"Yes, this is fiction. It can be understood only if read slowly."

"You mean because it's too deep or because I'm too stupid?"

"Neither. I mean that the language is too obscure – not in accord with ordinary usage. Surely you're aware that all thought and behavior not in accord with custom run the risk of being seen as very dangerous, as leading to anarchy!"

"Fine. Let me see if I can discover something in this work."

At this the mistress of the room quietly goes on with her reading. And the visitor quietly goes on with his scanning – of the horses on her curtains. The horses seem to be galloping into a boundlessly vast and empty expanse of lush vegetation, where they disappear.

The visitor feels a need for more such conversation, to fill up the emptiness of the time.

– Simply too beautiful. A beautiful woman, as a rule, cannot imagine how much disappointment her beauty brings to others, or how much happiness.

— Really? You must be joking. Why do you stare at my feet so constantly? You look honorable on the outside, but you are wanton at heart. I know that once upon a time you kissed my whole body with your eyes. But what you said was, "The horses are well drawn. They look to be running off in all directions." What was running away was your heart! And right now you are practicing that very kind of journey again. When you speak of these things I become a little ashamed for you, but I am not afraid. I have known all along that you are incapable of any behavior that is truly frightening. You are capable of these pleasure trips, like a traveler aimlessly strolling through the temple of another people's religion. And from this I know that you bear the sincerity that comes of terror and dread, for a sense of sin weighs heavily on your mind.

— Yes, your guess is perfectly correct. I want to kiss your toes, the soles of your feet, your knees and legs, and those places too embarrassing to speak of. I want to linger here and there on your body. You must know how honest are my desires, how unselfish.

— I understand everything, except why you do not act as you fantasize.

There are just the two of them inside, and outside it is quiet, with only the sound of snowflakes floating down on the windowpane. Occasionally accumulated snow falls to earth from a pine tree, but that sound is very soft, too. The visitor thinks he can almost hear this conversation between them, but what he really hears is only his own heartbeat.

The fire in the stove is now blazing.

The mistress touches the tips of her toes to the floor as she reads, as if to instruct the visitor, "Please start here. I do not fear you, however much you may act up. I know what you are up to, how many silly things you have in mind, how flustered you are."

Her hair is soft and dark, her neck as white as carved jade, her eyes bewitching and inviting. Her cheeks are dimpled, her breasts protruding; perhaps her gown is a little too thick.

His eyes kiss her hair, hair glossy as lacquer and soft as silk; they kiss her white forehead, her elegant eyes, slightly narrowed. And then, as they kiss her cheeks, there comes an intoxicating fragrance. As they reach her neck, they seem to suck out a little red seal. When they come to her breasts, the left, and then the right, her gown is decidedly a little too thick. So he asks her: "—— ——, aren't you too warm, so close to the stove?"

"I'm not afraid of heat, I'm afraid of cold," she murmurs, chuckling without lifting her head. "I'm a cat, a pretty Siamese cat that doesn't like to move, particularly when I'm by the stove. Ordinarily I sit here all day long without having to do or think a thing." She giggles again as she speaks.

"How far have you got in the piece?"

"To the part where the deer stands on the lonely crag where the storm cannot reach. She turns her liquid eyes away, thinking herself quite safe, unaware that the hunter is already stalking her. The hunter is confident he can capture her by her slender hind leg. He closes one eye, the better to appreciate the down on the deer's foot. He seems to be taking his time. Your description is funny, for your imagining of the events is unreal. Beautiful, but not authentic."

"Please read on. Criticize it when you've finished."

Her smile gradually fades as she reads. He knows that she has reached a chapter describing another part of the doe's body and how human that soft and gentle creature is. The tenderness flowing from her gaze because of her new love is depicted even more touchingly and likened to human feeling.

She places the book on her knees, open to those pages, and heaves a gentle sigh. The visitor seems to have used writing to strip her legs of their stockings, leaving her feet white as the frost. She thinks she hears the visitor whisper, "Do not think it blasphemous; I like to look at them. Do not be angry, for I shall kiss them with my lips. I want to travel up that road of white poplars, until I reach my intended resting place. I want to reach that place hidden in the shade, taking the twists and turns, to the little well-spring, and the lush pasture, where the white kid may be let out to graze. In short, I want to pass through all that the hunter has. It may be slightly foolish, slightly idiotic, but still I want to do it."

Feeling that her position is not quite proper, she hastens to draw her feet back together and to pull down her hem. No longer daring to read the story, she reaches out to warm her hands by the fire, pretending to be cold. Yet unconsciously she opens the stove door, throws in three lumps of coal, and stirs the blazing fire with a bronze poker. "The fire ought to burn full blast. I so like the heat."

"Have you finished reading the story?"

She shakes her head. Although she lowers her head immediately, both of them feel between them a new and unfamiliar emotion beginning to mingle in their Lives, bringing with it a hint of terror.

The second time she shakes her head, her meaning is entirely different from the first – no longer a mixture of denial and acknowledgment, but an expression of fear that there might be someone outside the window. In fact there is nothing there, only the light snow coming down.

The visitor goes to the window, pulls up a corner of the curtain, wipes the condensation off the window, and looks out. But all he sees is an expanse of white, simple and pure. As the curtain falls: "Whiteness, covering and concealing everything, making it disappear. Symbolizing – God!"

Meanwhile there is, by the stove, another whiteness, simple and pure, symbolizing the very pinnacle of morality.

"All right, tell your story. And tell me about how you really captured that doe."

"Fine. Let us warm ourselves by the fire, and I'll tell you. . . . Heaven knows what I was feeling as I stalked her. As my fingers stroked the smooth down on her feet, I wondered, Had I taken a pulsing, living doe in my hand, or captured an image of beauty, using the most delicate mental tendrils of my Life? I wanted so much to know, but I was not allowed to. I thought of how the ancients once described the beauty of a woman's fingers. Like catkins, spring shallots, or jade-green bamboo – spartan or luxuriant, such descriptions are ridiculous. One who has never seen the maternal tenderness in the clear, liquid eyes of a doe will puzzle over why my lips lingered so long a time upon her eyes. Still more absurd, of course, is that my lips lightly bussed each of the creature's four legs, then planted kisses all the length of her spine and down her slender yet rounded tail. There I discovered a delicate whirlpool, like a nest of hidden kisses of which the poets speak. The finest down covered her face. Her waist was slimmer, her neck more perfect, than I had ever before imagined in a dream. More unimaginable still were the two breasts with which she nursed her fawn, so soft, so lovely. Yet she seemed to have no thought of fleeing from my side; she betrayed no fright, no dread. Without my having to utter a single word, she seemed fully aware of my benevolent intentions. It was I who felt a little panicked, who knew not what to do. I looked into her eyes: What shall we do? I wanted to take my answer from her tender gaze. I thought I heard her say, 'I am in your power.' "

"No, never, not a chance. She must have wanted to escape – far, far away, for the sake of freedom, that measure of freedom that she deserves."

"Yes, she wanted to escape, yet she chose not to. For, once outside the cave, there was only snow. It was quite cold. And – the instinct to flee is related to that of danger, and what real danger did she face? – "

"How do you know she didn't care to escape? If she was intelligent, surely she would have wanted to go."

"Yes, she went through that stage. She wanted to precisely because she thought it was intelligent – the conclusion an intelligent deer ought to come to. But if I had allowed her, I would have been a fool indeed. It seemed to me she wasn't understanding me very well, so instead of using words I explained with my fingers and my lips, caressing her, calming her. I did all that I knew. In the end, as I stroked her heart, I saw that we were already familiar with each other. It was of course a miracle, for I began to hear her softly sighing – a deer's sigh for ideal love. You're skeptical?"

"Wholly impossible!"

"Perhaps, if you put it that way; it could never happen. For she was but a deer! But as for people – for instance – oh, God, let us not go on. I have already said too much."

They fall silent for a moment.

"Aren't you too warm? You are still wearing too many clothes." And as the visitor speaks, he does something with her. And he recalls something, something very abstract.

A poet said it, if not a madman: "Poetry sets Life ablaze, as does fire. As it burns through, it leaves but a figment of blue flame and a pile of ashes."

Twenty minutes later the visitor softly asks her, "Aren't you cold? Haven't you something to throw across your shoulders?" while pulling a delicate mouse-gray shawl from a pile of silk clothing. He puts it over her. "That pattern on the window curtains is peculiar. It always seems to me to be in motion." In fact, the colored horses on the curtains already seem to him completely still.

Stirring the stove fire, the mistress of the room gently tells him, "I am still thinking of that doe. Why didn't she flee a while back, when she had the chance? It must have been fate." She seems almost to be excusing or consoling herself, for the event now belongs to the past.

Silence continues to envelop this room with its orange lamplight and raging fire.

The next day, the mistress sits alone beside the stove and reads a letter:

—— ——: I still feel as if I am dreaming, my heart and body floating in air. It is as if I were still kissing your eyes and your heart. In this dream you are everything, and you are mine. Revealed before me is not simply an immaculate body, but a radiance, a bouquet of flowers, a wondrous cloud. All words lose their power here, for poetry is but an inferior decoration for the springtime of Life. Whiteness is the highest virtue incarnate, but you have already surpassed the meaning of the word.

In the Song of Solomon it is written, "Thy navel is like a round goblet, which wanteth not liquor." I touched it for the first time, fearing not that I might become drunk.

When the fruit of the vineyard ripens, becomes plump and sturdy, this is a symbol that Life is ready to render up, to expand. If it is not picked, it will slowly wither.

I am fond of fine porcelain, pure and lustrous. What I saw yesterday far surpassed any piece I have ever beheld these twenty years.

I like to look at that Yuan dynasty landscape painting: a lush, thick mat of fine down between the hillocks and the depressions, triangular in shape, neat and fine, curly and soft, twisting and tangling, like clouds and silk. The most wondrous concealed scenery I had ever seen in my life. I would happily stay there a lifetime, secluded among its delights.

It was as if I had seen a sculpture, not of bronze or jade, yet precious and resplendent – infinitely rare. Legs long and slender, the abdomen rounding out and suddenly drawing in, a quite perfect line unfolding from between the cheeks down to the ankles. The form is ideal, like a replica of elegant sculpture from ancient Greece. Works of art bear the sculptor's Life and precious feelings, but in the replica before me I faced God's will and the solemnity of his feelings.

The marvels of its shape are beyond belief. In one place there is a bulbous bluish sheen, in another a pair of small, dark areolas, and in still another marvelous swirling curves. From these places one can see the wonders of God's handiwork. These vortexes of curves lie hidden in the joints of her hands and feet, between her cheeks and her neckline, below her waist – as the poet said, "in the goblets where warm kisses are kept." These places not only make one want to lightly touch one's lips to them; they engender a fantasy of implanting one's whole Life among them.

Lily stalks are thin and delicate; your neck and shoulders are quite like them. When your beautiful head was tilted back from your long neck and the lamplight shone down on your alabaster forehead, it was like a white lily on the cusp of blossoming. My fingers trembled – I dared not pluck you – for in this flower I had seen God. And when you smiled, you were a white lily in full flower, coursing with Life. You were silent, and in that silence nobler still. You knit your long brows involuntarily, your tiny frown but heightening your captivating beauty; and this, too, was like unto a pale green lily, which on opening reveals its own tiny yellow pistil, amid black mottling. . . . But all this is only abstraction.

3

After reading this account, my eyes were dazzled, confused. This book became a blue flame, disappearing into emptiness. I stood once again beneath that old-fashioned arch; at some time, I know not when, I had left that "room." Only that blue flame was preserved within my Life. Preserved elsewhere must be a small heap of ashes. During the time of my imaginings, the withered plum blossom had lost the remnant color and fragrance of its Life. I remembered only the opening words of the book: God dwells within our Life.

I had reached home.

Eleven thirty. Yellow light from a rapeseed oil lamp covers my black table and spreads through my tiny room. Wherever my eye roams, I see books: some written two thousand years ago, others written thousands of miles away; some by myself, some by strangers of my own time. A gray mouse scurries to and fro in the recesses of the book piles where the lamplight does not penetrate. Its calmness attests that it, too, is a living creature, but wholly unconnected to these piles of Lives. I am reminded of the many scholars who have come to this study in the last ten or twenty years or sat studying or lecturing in a classroom. I cannot help saying, under my breath, "God, how many more books will I read in this life? And how many will I write?"

I must have rest for a while, yet I do not know where to find it.

I feel very tired, yet still I live in a fantastic realm that will go on and on.

The end of the lamp wick has effloresced; a little blossom has opened up within the flame. It occurs to me, "The flower will wilt and drop only when the fire is extinguished. Truly it is a symbol of Life." My heart also seems to burn and rage. I know not why.

Although the fragrance of the plum blossom is gone, I want to search through the world that it has conjured up. I wish to discover something there, as if the existence of it all justified my own existence. Within a figment of "the past," I found a patch of yellow and something withered and burned black, representing the form of "Life" of someone else, or perhaps only the form of another "dream" of mine – which, it matters not. From these withered and blackened vestiges, quietly I peer deeply into emptiness, and see all kinds of doings by someone of another time, in happiness and in madness. And I vaguely see my own image in the happiness and madness of others, and in the hesitation, the vacillation, between love and hate and give and take.

Like a ray of sunlight imprinted on the wall. Like a young heart beating. As though everything had regained its significance and its meaning.

I surmise that there must be another book, recording the dazzled amazement a woman feels in the weak sun on a cool autumn day – from her own beautiful and delicate flesh, her silky black hair, the lipstick on her thin lips, the perfume between her full white cheeks, matching the purity, the smoothness of her limbs and neck, the gentle songs streaming from her eyes, transparent as tears, and the unavoidable conflict of love and hate when her body melts. Oh, how beautiful are these Lives, which all are lost in the sunlight and forgotten in time! All disappear, all are lost, and when you search for them, all that is left is just as withered and charred. Is it a flower of hair plucked from my own temple or a scrap of paper picked up from the roadside? I cannot tell.

When I search for the meaning of "Life," I simply reencounter a list of names: passion and love, resentment and hatred, giving and taking, God and the devil, human being and human being, meeting by chance and ships passing in the night. After half an hour, all these words lose their significance and their meaning again.

It is about five minutes before daybreak; I have dispelled all my "past" and "present" experiences and abstractions, giving up the power to analyze the meaning of their existence. I have never fashioned the patterns I understand of Life into language and forms that create a new model for

Life and the soul. My head is spinning; I have been driven to the brink of madness again by my quest to preserve these images in my memory, forms that are materially and spiritually perfect. Ultimately, the "I" dissolves into the "story." I have already written five thousand words in the composition book that lies on my table. I know there is a place I can mail this little composition where others will consider it "fiction" and try to ferret out the factual and the fictitious in it. But to me – just a vestige of Life, the remnants of a dream.

This account lies before me. I love the "Abstract" with a passion; staring into emptiness, I dissipate the time. Stubbornness in the face of absolute perplexity, and the persistence of this stubbornness, is my only way of coming to terms with "existence." All other "knowledge" and "facts" are of no use in the present, for I live wholly in my thoughts, not in the real world. It is as if I use the Abstract to torment my own soul and flesh. It is painful, yet at the same time enjoyable. Time flows through my Life, going on without leaving anything behind.

I gently open the door and see that the day has already begun. Early morning sunlight, so familiar from before, rushes into my room, shooting obliquely onto the white wall. The golden lacquered Burmese boxes before my bookcase reflect a magical dazzle in the faint sunshine. All seems new. But, recalling that "there is no new thing under the sun," I am both saddened and heartened. I await all that comes with the "night": the odor of plum blossoms and the fantastic lessons that this faint fragrance has imparted.

To my surprise it is ten at night again. The moonlight is bright and clear as it floods the veranda. So I open the door, to let the moonlight in.

It is as if someone has quietly followed the moonlight into my room and, standing behind me, asked, "Why do you torment yourself so? What is it for?"

My eyes moisten as I force a smile, but I do not turn around: "I am writing about Qingfeng, the character in *Strange Tales from a Chinese Studio*. I want to bring her back with my pen."[2]

The sound of a gentle sigh brings me to. Twenty-four hours have passed, and I have not so much as drunk a cup of water.

[2]Qingfeng was an unattainable young woman who filled the dreams of a young bohemian scholar, a girl of surpassing beauty and intelligence when he met her at the age of fifteen. She became a source of visual inspiration and good conversation ever after, when by a happy stroke of fate the scholar reencountered her, reincarnated as a fox spirit, and was able to take her into his family.

Appendix
Nonfiction Works

Songs of the Zhen'gan Folk

The Miao and other nonliterate minority nationalities of Southwest China are known not only for their memorized myths and legends but also for their extemporized songs. Still today they have intervillage singing contests. And young people with good voices still find good mates. Some types of songs are sung in unison at times of greeting, parting, festival, and rites of passage. More notorious are the songs in which stanzas or lines are sung in alternation by members of the opposite sex. According to the practice of some groups, girls and boys line up on facing mountainsides to sing in unison and then pair off to make love under the sky, after gauging the partner's wit through the inventiveness of the lyrics he or she has put to the standard melodies. Examples of how a singing sparring partner may be outwitted, insulted, or otherwise outdone appear in "Meijin, Baozi, and the White Kid," translated above, and in "Long Zhu," but few Miao consider Chinese translations of such songs adequate. The originals use multilayered symbolism and double entendre, with botanical tropes being graphic stand-ins for human sexual organs.

Another custom comes at festival time, among these mountain villagers who may otherwise be hard pressed to gather in one place. And, as Marcel Granet fancifully imagined was true in all of ancient China (he was inspired by the botanical tropes in the Book of Odes*), festivals can become marriage fairs. One practice is that facing files of girls and boys toss embroidered balls back and forth. It is up to the young person to decide whether to catch the ball, thereby initiating friendship (song 8 below refers to an "iron embroidered ball," meaning something that would really be too fine for a blacksmith to make). A young man (or a young woman) may on the other hand initiate amorous contact with a stranger out on the road simply by singing an appropriately saucy song that piques the other's interest, or at least demands a riposte.*

The verses below are authentic folk songs from Shen Congwen's home town of Fenghuang, known during his childhood as Zhen'gan. Although in Chinese, not Miao, they were sung by the mixed Sino-Tujia-Miao country folk of the old Zhen'gan military colony. Surely they are much influenced by the humor and mores of the aborigines. They may in fact be pale imitations of Miao songs, but, because they are in Chinese, few of their "merits" were lost on young Shen Congwen. He often inserted these songs and others into his later fiction.

"Songs of the Zhen'gan Folk" ("Ganren yaoqu") is, however, an early piece by Shen Congwen, written in November 1926. (Songs 43–49 were inserted in sequence by the translator, from a sequel that Shen published in August 1927 under the name of his cousin Yin Yuangui.) Shen Congwen was homesick and not afraid to confess to weakness and melancholy. The sardonic foreword to the songs thus represents a whole genre of Shen Congwen's earliest writing, in the May Fourth autobiographical belles-lettres tradition previously plowed by Yu Dafu and Zhou Zuoren. Unlike them, Shen was a struggling literary wannabe with no outside income, which may explain his peevishness and belligerent attempt to define himself as a poor fellow from the countryside, thereby drawing a line against the Peking monied classes and their pastimes: romantic poetry with lots of exclamation points (that of Guo Moruo), dating and kissing, and amateur Peking opera. Like Lu Xun, Shen disdained the shrillness of northern opera, although he liked the more melodious dramas of his own region. It was in his "Cramped and Moldy Studio," as he called his student lodgings near Peking University, that he finished this piece, while listening to his noisy neighbor; other portions of the foreword were written in his spartan room in a temple gatehouse on Xiangshan, in the Western Hills. Today the gatehouse overlooks an I. M. Pei hotel. A monk must have lived there before, hence the reference at the beginning.

These are not songs for polite society, which is partly why Shen Congwen wrote them up and "seriously" annotated them in a literary supplement – to shock the bourgeoisie. References to sparrows (song 7) and long things like yams and tall trees (song 10), and perhaps "inflating" turnips (songs 27, 33), are really to the penis. The figure of a "flower garden" in song 42 is not so common, but surely it refers to the female. To call someone your brother-in-law is to imply that you're illicitly getting it on with his sister – that she's a whore. References to "elder sister" and *"younger sister" really mean "you" when sung by the boy or "I" when sung by the girl. Third-person references to males, such as "her darling," "elder brother," etc., mean "you" when sung by the girl, "I" when sung by the boy. Most of the songs have lines of uniform five- or seven-syllable length in the original Chinese, with an AABA rhyme.*

Foreword

I've been up in the hills a long while and with too much time on my hands, like a novice monk. Unaccustomed to his new life, the monk dreams day and night of returning to the laity. But that is not allowed. I need something to do to get me through the days; they are so very long. If I really were a monk, I'd be crawling out of bed each morning before dawn and toting a big wooden clapper pole to a giant iron monastery bell, letting it ring out for Buddha to my heart's content. That life might have some fun in it. But there are no bells or drums to pound on here or any other kind of amusement. I'm embarrassingly idle, like seven years ago, at Huaihua town. There, my army buddies and I would tote our swords and rifles deep into the bandit country and pass the time watching beheadings and such. And not just us impulsive child-soldiers. The judge advocate or the staff counselor would read out the guilty party's crime in a monotone, the way we used to memorize texts at school, and then rush down the path, hookah in hand, to the bridge so that he could take in that solemn and moving spectacle of a criminal on the path to extinction. It happened all the time. Right now I can't even participate in such refined ceremonies as that. I really am lonely, aren't I?

When I go down the hill to the stone road they call a national highway, sometimes I see an automobile go by. I look through the windows at the passengers inside, all fat as pigs, and they're as bored as I am.

There are of course more sophisticated things to do, like follow Old Man Zhou into the thicket to hear the crickets chirp and then compose an ancient-style five-syllable regulated verse about it with a title like "Sentiments on Attending the Chirping of Orthoptera in the Glade." But that isn't for everyone. Good poetry comes only from one who is truly inspired. I find I can't

Translated by Jeffrey Kinkley

make a poet of myself just out of love of exclamation points, so I'm alienated from the genre.

Unable to make anything interesting out of the meaningless din of crickets, I just shut the door and sit myself down to read the classics and histories. Whereupon the gentleman in the next room is kind enough to share the screeching of his *huqin* fiddle with me. He plays the same thing day in and day out, never asking me if my taste is as refined as his. Having to listen to his second-rate fiddling all day long keeps me angry quite a lot of the time. Yet the sound does remind me of opera performances.

The red painted faces charge onstage as the black painted faces charge offstage; men stripped to the waist enter one after another, turning somersaults; others come on in gaudy clothes and painted faces, strutting about like prostitutes and singing falsetto like women, to old-fashioned rhythms; according to a lot of people who still wear pigtails (in spirit!), this is the sole art of China. And people who so believe are therefore artists. Professors today are in that category. Ah – such a lofty entertainment, why don't I rush to learn it? If it's because I'm too ugly for the male and female spectators to get their respective jollies from watching me sing, why not sing the role of a bearded man? If I could go into falsetto like that opium junkie Tan, I'd not only be rich but able to seduce the professors and their wives – to invite a professor to be my secretary or a Ph.D. to write an article about me, to hype me in the newspapers abroad. That would be an interesting and profitable enterprise. And yet –

And yet this is just a dream, however wonderful. Suppose I went about studying it with all my heart, until my vocal chords were in their prime, as they say. Let one or two of those famous professors and old fogies with their unhealthy lusts, those still strong enough after giving their daily lectures on Shakespeare and Ibsen to stand by the mirror and fix their bow ties just right, bring their wife or lover to a theater to appreciate me. Or let those young fogies that our national universities have newly reared to appreciate these spectacles come and cheer for me, so I won't feel lonely and ignored while I'm studying. But I can't hear anyone clapping to urge me on just now, although I hold in my anger and perform like a nonspeaking extra, running on and off stage on cue. So I think I'll decline to take it up.

The aggravation of the sound of fiddling from next door has dashed my desire of learning to sing opera — or so it seems. I wouldn't know whether he's taken up the instrument to pursue some greater purpose.

Now that fall is here, I'm more bored than ever. The crickets seem to have chirped themselves to exhaustion; their tone is gradually changing from singing to sighing. The fresh air of autumn in the hills makes it just right for a stroll. I could go to Bada to see the steles with poems at the temple, but there's no one to share the mule ride with me. I've no choice but to race through the hills all day by myself, climbing up and down the untrodden paths, seeing how far my legs will take me. There are others who scramble among the hills as hard as I, but for another purpose: the young girls from poor families who come up to gather firewood and brush. They're as sturdy of body as wild boars — beauties, all — with good complexions, smooth and pink, that remind one of newly ripened wild peaches in mountain forests. Their bodies are just the right place for any youth to make sensual love, if only both partners are willing. I feel myself at a loss for words to praise the virtues of such girls, so I won't try; it would be overreaching. I'm not one to act on those wild impulses myself, but whenever I see them, or faintly hear their voices in the distance, I can't help but spin out my own fantasies of laying them down for that healthy amusement.

I recall how it was in the countryside back home. In such weather, weather just right for digging potatoes and harvesting corn, the rest breaks would provide the young girls and boys with unimaginable pleasures! Strange, however, that, in these parts, one doesn't even hear the mountain songs that can express the desires of the two parties. Could it be that folks here have no such needs? I hardly think so. From what I've seen with my own eyes of the young people at rest down by Senyuhu, there's hardly a one that's not just made for taking into a mountain hollow, laying down under the sun on a bed of leaves, and taking up into that healthy amusement. Perhaps the people who live too close to the city have learned that you're supposed to keep deathly silence during a "hot kiss." But I wouldn't know about that.

I just said that I'm not one to act on those wild impulses myself. Still, when the weather's just right, neither too hot nor too chilly, and partners are all around you, everywhere you look, even I can't be completely unmoved. I feel compelled to go out onto the slopes, day after day, to softly croon the few mountain songs I know. To praise natural things like nakedness, plain folk songs are more appropriate than poetry of the more refined sort – no need for me to explain that. I sing these songs so softly that probably only I can hear them, partly because I don't have a good voice, partly out of fear. (I fear what might happen if my songs brought a sympathetic response from the girl!) Some hear me sing as I pass by, only to lower their heads and go on their way giggling. At that point I'd like to say, "Young woman! Let me sit down with you, to get to know your silly smile and tell you the songs a young singer ought to know – and then we can do as they beckon." But of course instead I become speechless, while the "big sister" from the countryside flying so fast down the hillside continues on her way.

I lived this way for two weeks, with no one having the faintest idea what I was doing up in the hills all by myself. But I've slowly come to feel that I know too few songs. I can imagine so very, very many things that go on between boys and girls without being able to find the right song for them. That gave me the idea of writing a letter back home to West Hunan to get some more.

So many petty illnesses came over me in succession after I moved to the city, tethering my heart to a futile kind of work, that I completely forgot the girls who gather firewood out on the hillsides and that I had asked my younger cousin to collect folk songs from home. A group of more than four hundred was compiled. My thanks go out to my cousin and his fellow soldiers for their diligence, for it is by their hands – and what awkward hands they write in! – that these songs are before me now. Nearly every song is enough to move mankind, and nearly every one is able to touch a young country boy or girl's heart. But, having so many love tonics before my eyes, and not being able to sing them to people on the plain or willing to copy them out for my eyes only, I find that they've only increased my vexation. And the letter from my young cousin says this is just a small portion of them – there are more than two thousand more, and that's from Zhen'gan alone. He says he and his army buddies will copy them all out for me soon. But, to tell the truth, I've been wondering for some time what to do with just the few I have here.

My cousin is in the service in Hunan, just recently promoted to sergeant. When I was a sergeant first class in the pacification headquarters of the Thirteenth District, he was only a bodyguard at the judge advocate's office. It was as a guard that his romantic fortunes soared, allowing him to learn untold numbers of mountain songs. But the songs below were compiled with the help of other soldiers in his squad, for the handwriting and layout differ from page to page. Some songs are carefully written out on copy paper, one character per box, while others are messy. Though I'm quite familiar with the vulgar expressions from those parts myself, I wouldn't be able to read them but for the help of my cousin. I believe that many of these soldiers must have been my own fellow classmates when I was little. They all graduated from primary school, then left home to join the army, as is the custom in my home town. Young reserve soldiers don't have many duties, don't even have to drill, so they go outside the camp, three or four at a time, and raise hell. It's great for going up into the hills and singing to entice the girls. The songs below are undoubtedly the ones that this lovable little band of scalawags used for their fooling around two or three years ago. Some of the songs are handed down and known to everybody, and others were made up by these monkeys themselves. I wouldn't doubt it for a moment.

My cousin writes that he'll mail me the others soon. I only hope he hurries. If he can mail them this year and I'm still in the mood, I'll select half of them, add my own appreciations, opinions, and West Hunanese background to the poems, and make a neat little book of them – if the manuscript is long enough and the printer isn't afraid of losing money. Maybe this harmless little trifle will at least gain praise from the minority who are interested in such things.

Lately my life has gotten to the point where I simply must write again. Poetry is easy, but I feel extremely embarrassed to use such words as *nightingale* and *rose.* This is a "tragedy," though one without a "swans-down" lining; I can't say if my heart has "splintered into pieces," nor have I broken any "heartstrings." Perhaps I'm not fated to write poetry. After poetry there's fiction, but that's no good, either. Perhaps it's because I hear another voice, shouting out opposition to the old literature and old knowledge – asking for the creation of something new – and I want to see what others have created. So I feel dejected.

I must thank my cousin and the other soldiers for mailing in these songs. They have given me some interesting work to do. There aren't a lot here, but among these cheap local products – these turnips and stalks of celery – I've found some fatter, more substantial sweet potatoes. Until I can put together that book, I've culled out the ones here and added some explications. I present them now for everybody to taste. If the editors can exercise a little indulgence and the readership is short on members of the Board of Rites, then I ought to be able to print a few hundred of them in literary journals. That would make me very happy indeed.

Let me say once more that these mountain songs were collected by a group of soldiers just barely in their twenties. Soldiers, in other places, like Peking – although they do evoke admiration for their *bravery* and *capability* – well, ours back home are simply very lovable. They are as naive as children and filled with artistic sensibility – not all of them, but most. They may not look very strictly disciplined, but everyone does his duty and is content about it. It's not at all unusual to see a regimental commander squat down on the ground with the troops and drink with them. And when the troops form into ranks and march off, you never hear about anyone taking French leave. For all the top commanders are fellow townsmen, and everybody is addressed as "uncle" in front of his rank, from the little bodyguards on up to the battalion commander. It's funny, but nobody laughs. During the two and a half years that my little brother and I were reserves (in name), we did nothing at all but learn to fish, swim, and set a dog onto hunting wild boars. And I learned to write my characters square and proper, so people could read them, not in primary school, but during the six months of 1918 I spent in Yushuwan as a reserve. My ability now to write what I want to say, so that it comes out smoothly when you read it, can be attributed to the year or so that I lived as a sergeant.

It's been more than two years now since I've left that wild and undisciplined life, but what changes have there been in my circumstances? That's something to think about. I'm still hoping to earn enough money in the next year or two to go back and have a look, so I can introduce to the outside world the comic skits for requiting the gods that we perform in our region in the tenth lunar month. That's when pledges are redeemed to the Nuo gods, and those plays are even more interesting than our folk songs. And there are the Miao people's fascinating customs and their valuable legends. I really ought to master the Miao language so as to introduce Miao songs to the world through both transcription and translation. But in my present circumstances, with a cold, and a nosebleed, I haven't even the twenty cents necessary to register at the hospital. The severe winter weather is coming, and I don't know when I'll be able to replace my thin little blue gown. So returning home must remain a golden dream, far in the distance and ultimately unrealizable.

I

Big sister's comin', smi-smiling,
Her pair of boobs 'a stretch-stretching,
How I'd love to have a feel,
Oh my heart is leap-leaping.

From what I know, "big sister" *(da jie)* ought to be written
"sister" *(jiejie)* and pronounced *"jiazai"*; that's more in accord
with the dialect of Zhen'gan's southern townships. In the village
of Brigade Commander's Battalion, near the Miao country, and in
Xikou and the other districts east of Zhen'gan city, they find the
pronunciation *"jiazai"* much more natural. Here's the meaning of
the song: it expresses the exquisite feeling you have when you're
out on the road and you see this country woman with a bosom
that sends your head reeling. You want to "appreciate" it, but you
know you don't dare. The song lets us imagine how alluring a
"big sister" can be, bearing a heavy basket on her back brimming
over with vegetables, wearing a blue woolen outfit and new straw
sandals, her pigtails done up in circles round her head, her cheeks
all rosy, and her hefty thighs bouncing, racing down the road like
the wind! The repeated syllables make the song even more moving. It's the best one of all. Another is:

2

Clouds rise up in the sky – cloud on top of cloud,
Under the earth are buried graves – grave on top of grave,
Dainty younger sister [i.e., you] washes bowls – bowl on top of
   bowl,
Dainty younger sister is on the bed – lover on top of lover.

That song is for a different occasion, but it, too, uses repeated
syllables to enhance the effect.
A slightly humorous one is the following:

3

Dainty younger sister has grown whiter than white,
Her darling has [i.e., I have] grown blacker than black,
When black ink is written on white paper,
Just look, don't they go together well?

The boy uses this to tease the girl when she thinks he's too dark for her. Now, song 4 is used to defend yourself when she thinks you're too young.

4

Younger sister is eighteen, her darling seventeen,
Yap, yap, she scolds him for not being old enough!
Tree leaves in the mountains are not all the same size,
And who ever heard of all ten fingers being the same
    length?

This song is also popular in Yuanzhou and Huangzhou. The sound of the lines, particularly the second one, leads me to suspect that this song was transmitted to West Hunan from Guizhou. If my guess is correct, the fifth song did not originate among the Zhen'ganese, who are plain and simple and not very literate.

5

Younger sister is being beaten, and her darling knows why,
Whack, whack sounds the beating, on sister's body,
A fire burns in the blue mountains, but I dare not go to the
    rescue,
The foot steps on a turtle, but the hurt is in my heart!

In Zhen'gan we use a different word, "treads," for the word "steps" in the fourth line, but in this line "treads" would be a tongue twister.

A purely Zhen'ganese song that wouldn't make sense in any other dialect is song 6.

6

Here's a song for you, here's a song for you,
Your old man got himself a Miao wife,
And she raised him some Miao brats,
So go ahead – you and all your Miao forebears and descendants
    sing us some Miao songs!

Children cutting firewood up in the mountains sing such songs back and forth in alternation, to curse each other. Very few places outside Zhen'gan call their father their "old man" *(laozi)*. You score big when you can call a person a Miao brat, and it's only the Zhen'ganese who are always using the term. There are an awful lot of interesting songs you can use to curse people, but the ones that make the best use of lots of dirty words, like this one, aren't suitable for publication where a young lady might see them, so here I picked just a few such songs.

7

I had an early breakfast but it wasn't any good,
Went outside and ran into someone who was singing,
Sing me some of your best songs,
"The male sparrow enjoys renown however far he travels."

Song 7 is the opening shot in a little monkey's fusillade when he wants to lure someone else into a war of songs. Judging by its sound, the song must come from the Guizhou-Hunan border, for the words and lines are rather mild and gentle. You'd never hear a song like that in the pure Zhen'gan territory, like the country districts of Xikou or Liao Family Bridge.

Whether it's a girl and boy singing to each other or two boys competing, custom says that, whenever one responds to the song of another, the verses can go on and on. But let me assure you, the result of any singing between a boy and a girl is usually that each one is moved and goes up to meet the other; they end up in that healthy amusement on a mattress of leaves. When two males sing, apart from wrapping it up in mutual curses, they have a hard time coming to such a peaceful solution.

When you're willing to be addressed by another person in song, you sing this one:

8

Mountain songs are easy to sing but hard to start,
Hard as a carpenter starting up a house on stilts,
A stone mason sculpting a stone lion,
Or a blacksmith forging an iron embroidered ball.

One way of cursing a person is to address him as if you were the husband of his elder sister, as in song 9:

9

A fan is yellow on both sides,
You be the brother-in-law, I'll be the lover,
As brother-in-law, you can have some wine at my wedding,
But as the groom, I'll take [your sister to] wife!

Or you can get your jollies by having your opponent eat your "sparrow," as in song 10:

10

A five-foot tung tree, tall and thick,
I eat bean curd, the yam's your lick,
I get my bean curd from your sister,
Out of yams? Then eat my prick!

Then the other person returns the honor with, "Your prick isn't as big as mine. . . . "

To praise your own abilities after conquering another in song, you sing:

11

You don't know as many songs as I do,
I know as many as there are hairs on three oxen!
If I sang for three years and six months,
I'd just make it through one ear's worth!

They wrap it up by yelling and cursing at each other, and each then goes on his way to cut firewood, whack, whack, whack. Bystanders can derive much fun from these bloodless conflicts.

In songs 12 and 13, two lovers lightly tease each other while out picking hot peppers:

12

The peppers are green in the field apart,
Hot peppers, peppery stomach, peppery heart!
You've a wife in your bed, but your mind's elsewhere,
On your dewdrop [illicit] lover [me], that little tart!

13

The peppers are yellow in the field 'cross the rut,
Hot peppers, peppery stomach, peppery gut!
You've a husband in your bed, but your mind's elsewhere,
On your dewdrop lover, that awful lout!

You could also explain these as the woman poking fun at herself in the former song and the man at himself in the latter.

14

The sun sets on the slope, the mountains turn to gold,
Come a pair of wildfowl – hens, I needn't be told,
The only ones about, they're on the prowl for a beau,
Sister won't you come and try to keep me in the fold?

That's the best of the four songs that you can sing at dusk while waiting for your girl to come meet you.

There's another you can sing when you suspect your lover's gone elsewhere for her pleasures:

15

I've sat all day long by the road for my lass,
I've sopped up the dew and then worn out the grass,
My sandals are off so please read me my fortune,
What man do you think has stolen my lass?

To change song 15 into a song for the woman to sing, you just have to change a few words; the straw sandals, for instance, become embroidered slippers. These aren't alternating songs as such, but in practice they're sung as if they were. The parties sing to tell each other how anxious and upset they are waiting for one another; after waiting so long that the dew has dried out and the grass has turned yellow, it's time for some divination with trigrams to help decide what to do next!

I've sat all day long by the road for my fellow,
I've sopped up the dew and then turned the grass yellow,
My slippers are off, so please read me my fortune,
What woman do you think has stolen my fellow?

"Worn out" means "wilted" only in Zhen'ganese dialect; from that one word, you can tell that, even if the song was not made up by the Zhen'ganese, it was reshaped by them.

There's also one for when you can't make up your mind. Some of the well buckets go up while others come down, with no trend in sight, and you can't bear the shilly-shallying any longer, so there's song 16:

16

Raft waft grass – grass waft raft,
Ten in water, and ten float aft,
If you're gonna take the plunge, then now's the time,
Neither floating nor sinking you're bound to go daft!

Only in the border counties of West Hunan can they get those words to rhyme, so this, too, must be a Zhen'ganese song.

17

The maiden's front door is far up the hill,
Few ever go there, but I'll visit still,
Even iron-soled shoes can't take it too long,
It's for thee that I do it, not just for the thrill.

Song 17 is used to display one's loyalty to one's girl. To express one's happiness on seeing the face of one's lover, there's:

18

How happy this lad, to approach his dainty maiden,
Closer and closer, I have almost reached her,
Happy as the dragon king getting his precious pearl,
Happy as an exam taker getting his official post.

We can't very well picture the ecstasy of the dragon king when he gets his precious pearl, but we can fully imagine the elation a civil service examinee feels when he finally gets a post.

There are songs making fun of a boy who sees a girl and wants to approach her but is too scared to go up and give chase, like me, in what I referred to as my suppression of my own desires. But, of the songs that attribute it to a deficit of lustiness, song 19 is the wittiest.

19

Little bitty sparrow just left the nest,
Winging to a field, he alit for a rest,
Sparrow's so 'fraidy, he looks quite distressed,
The grain is ripe, but sparrow won't test.

With a few alterations of the pronunciations, it's a perfect old Zhen'gan song.

The woman may think her family too rich for the man's and refuse him with these words:

20

For hill thrushes, the hills are where you look,
And only a fish will get caught on a hook,
Lover boy, please don't get carried away,
If this match is not fated, I just won't get took!

For warm words to each other at the time of parting, there are:

21

Clouds rise in the sky, clustering blue,
Be patient, younger sister, when you go home,
Don't let your husband beat you and scold you,
And don't worry about your little darling!

22

My words are already out, my heart is busted open,
I beg you pity me, pretty maiden, for I'm like
Linseeds in August, all busted open;
Steeds running atop a city wall can't easily turn around!

In song 21, we can see the moving admonitions of a young
man who is strong but very gentle at heart as he accompanies his
lover back home. Song 22 is sung by another kind of person. It is
his pathetic pleading before a girlfriend who's not paying him
any attention. The [Chinese] word *can* in the first line, meaning
"out" or "open," is used in our country districts to mean "the rice
has already been cooked," "spilt water can't be put back inside
the jar," or "since my words are already out, please take pity on
me!" In the countryside, the only kind of metaphors they can
think of for "busting out" or "busting open" are ones like lin-

seeds busting out in August. To the old gentry or the new-love romantics, this is not elegant enough, but from this very lack of elegance we can see the sincerity with which country folk plead for affection and how true is their dejection when their hopes are aflame.

Song 23 shows a life-or-death obstinacy in the quest for a lover:

23

I fear not to climb a tree, however tall,
I fear not to love you, maiden, though my head should fall.
How could I fear to lose my head by the sword?
I'd still have a soul for you, 'twould come to call!

Another version changes the last line to "The yang soul will have his yin soul to ball!" That intensifies the meaning a bit, though at the expense of crudity.

If a *daipa*[1] is bent over, head down, at a stream to wash clothes or vegetables and we want to twit her, then we sing:

24

I'm singing a mountain song to get a rise out of the maiden,
To see if I can get her to raise her head,
When a horse doesn't raise his head, it means he's eating
    tender hay,
When a girl doesn't raise her head, it means she's not amorous!

If she doesn't pay any attention, it's not really that she's not "amorous"; it's just that you've got no hope with her and you'd better proceed to another.

[1]Sino-Miao word meaning an unmarried Miao girl.

If you want to get her to smile, then you sing another verse.

If you observe that she can be dallied with, then you sing song 25 to get the flirtation off to a quick start and move the maiden during her moment of indecision:

25

Elder sister! Seventeen or eighteen, this is just the time,
But you haven't loved me yet, so tell me when, what time?
The king of hell takes people, regardless of their age,
I fear you'll repent too late, when you're covered with lime!

You can make the following word substitutions, just as in the *Book of Odes,* where you have the same verse over again, with one or two words different:

Elder sister! Seventeen or eighteen, this is just the year,
But you haven't loved me yet, so tell me when, what year?
The king of hell takes people, regardless of their age,
I fear you'll repent too late, when you're on your bier!

If you're afraid the girl will refuse you because you see yourself as too lowly, or because your clothes are too dirty or something like that, and you want to give her an explanation, song 26 is one that will do:

26

If you want to make love, then make love,
Mustn't be like a little cowherd boy, looking on at the meadow
    from so far away,
The high slopes and level ground are one as grassy as the
    other,
People are alike, whether rich or poor!

There's another, similar verse that adds the words "your darling" at the end of the rhyming sentences.

If such an explanation were used in other boy-girl relationships, such as modern urban romances, it would of course simply seem stupid. But it has its effect on the heart of an honest and straightforward *daipa*. There's no doubt at all that such a defense can make her attitude go resolutely down the path you want it to.

To prove that it isn't just love at first sight, that your love has been burning in your heart for a long time, there's the following song:

27

The other vegetables have died since the turnip sucked away
    their nourishment,
Only because Elder Sister is so fine did I come to love her,
I did not fall in love just today,
The turnip has got so big since being planted!

There is the following, which you sing when you can't bear to let your girl depart:

28

Don't get in a flurry, don't be in a hurry,
A day has so many hours, nearly an etern'ty,
Won't you come on over, come take a rest,
I'll cut your fodder, no need to worry.

This song is said to be for a boy who sees a girl gathering grass for the pigs. He wants to rendezvous with her and thus teases her with these words to arouse her interest. The next one is quite urgent in its plea that she stay:

29

Don't be flustered, don't be in a hurry,
When the sun has set, the moon comes out,
When the moon goes down, there are the stars,
And after the stars, there is daybreak again!

A song for the woman who really wants to resist is:

30

You're no child, elder brother, don't you know better,
The sun is already setting on the slope,
This maiden wants to go home and cook dinner!
My husband may be away, but not my in-laws!

Another song like song 20, in which the woman refuses the man trying to seduce her, but expressing Zhen'gan local color, is:

31

You're no child, elder brother, so don't be rude,
No match in this quarter, if I'm not in the mood,
Each *baba*[2] on the fire is promised to someone,
So don't let your fancy take a turn toward the lewd!

32

You're no child, elder sister, I *want* to be rude,
My fated match is right here in the neighborhood,

[2]Rough cornmeal biscuits, a staple of the Miao and other West Hunanese.

Which *baba* on the fire already have their masters?
All it takes to land a mate is aptitude!

In song 32, the boy simply adapts the wording of the prior song to respond that the *baba* biscuits baking over the fire have no claimants yet so he can eat any one he wants to reach out and take; to woo a woman, all you need is the knack. My young friend Yepin is proof positive of the truth of this one.[3] You win final victory because you have the knack — that's a phrase that works everywhere. But, up in the mountains, one with the knack just sings a couple more songs to the girl, and the heart of the girl who initially refused him ultimately turns around — nothing to it. Try that in the city; it's not so simple. In the countryside, love-making doesn't require any other technique than singing. It's not like courting a modern woman of the city. Singing won't work. Something a little more elegant, like poetry, won't either. Better to get with it quick and put up your money, right? Perhaps you can still get a girl to fall in love with you through the techniques country folk are good at, but that would be the exception. The boy below is slow to get the picture.

Let's look at song 33:

33

Planting turnips in the big fields and on the broad slopes,
The turnip has grown myriad yards tall.
If only you are willing, Elder Brother, darling,
How can you fear journeying ten days for a meeting!

Here the girl is pleading with the boy, saying that no geographic separation is too far if he's in love. Even a tryst once

[3] When Hu Yepin successfully wooed Ding Ling at about this time, Shen Congwen was the loser, or so speculate the historians.

every ten days would be worth it. I've got more than a dozen such songs for the women, so tactful and sincere. I considered this one a worthy representative. But I don't think it's of local origin; judging by the rhyme and meter, it's from the Guizhou borderlands. Folk from the border counties of Sichuan and Guizhou, like Sinan, Songtao, Tongren, Youyang, and Longtan, and Hunan's Huang county, which borders Guizhou, have less of the Miao character, so their songs are much gentler and more tactful than those of the Zhen'gan people. Their songs are filled with the same burning passion, but a little more dreamlike mistiness and autumnal melancholy, while lacking some of the unrestrained willfulness and crudity. Readers from other areas may find this willfulness and crudity objectionable, but the people from my region, who appreciate the audacity and frankness, think of these qualities as assets, indeed, necessities. The difference is very clear in song 34, which we can use for comparison:

34

'Neath ramrod maples, from which sap disperses,
Make love to the maidens, till they beg for mercies,
Having made it with oh so many virgins,
I've worn through scads of velvety pursies!

That one obviously came from a woodcutter. It's more flavorful than those stale ancient literary phrases about a man and woman fondling each other and undoing their clothes. Moreover, to have been friends with so many virgins and earned the privilege of wearing their embroidered purses on your belt is something that young woodcutters might justly be proud of among other fellows. But when we read it, we can see the humorous side, too.

35

There's a well by the wayside that has very cool water,
Folks stop to drink from it, but none comes to keep it in
   repair,
Your little darling is of a mind to come fix it up,
He's afraid the well water won't keep on flowing!

The flirtatious song above uses a well as a metaphor for the woman and expresses the fear that this love won't last. I can vouch for the fact that others besides the Zhen'ganese sing this one. You use it to provoke a girl into singing back to you.

Verses like song 25 must be answered with a song by the woman. Of course there are different kinds of responses. She can reject the man with, say, song 31, but how should she answer him if she's willing? I haven't a clue.

If the man thinks one woman isn't enough and that it only gets interesting when he has two or more, he sings song 36:

36

In gathering kindling, you must gather bamboo,
When the bamboo has been taken, shoots come to replace it;
In making love, you must do it with two lasses,
When big sister has been taken, little sister comes to replace
   her.

The woman uses a song like the following to correct the man's error:

37

Leaves of the maple tree are three cornered,
Darling, when you pick flowers, don't pick too many!

If you make love to two sisters,
They'll quarrel you to death!

Another, which advocates universal love, goes like this:

38

When picking flowers, pick enough to adore,
When lighting a pipe, you smoke three or four;
Three or four girls, too, when making love,
If this'un's too weak, maybe that'un has more.

The woman has song 39 as a response:

39

A new-made pick-hoe has two points,
Darling, don't you make love with too many women,
No matter how many stars may fill the night sky,
They're not as bright as half a moon!

In another version, it's not a half moon but a full moon. The full moon makes more sense, but it's easier to say "half a moon." Songs 36–39 seem to be from Zhen'gan; whether they exist elsewhere, with a few words changed, I can't say. If they *are* popular in other parts, then at the very least that "quarrel you to death" at the end of song 37 would have to be changed, and so would portions of song 38. Yet the artistic achievements of these four verses lead one to doubt that they were entirely composed by people from Zhen'gan. To be frank, the long suit of the Zhen'ganese is abuse, not subtlety. Hence, song 39 is really quite an achievement for them! What a pity that Tang the Beard, who was so good at mountain songs, is no longer here, or we'd ask him about dialect variations from Huang county and Guizhou.

Setting aside the private lovemaking of girls and boys altogether, let's look at a song that is purely for singing to oneself:

40

It's a long distance, going up the slope in the morning,
Halfway up, there's a Tudi[4] temple,
Granddaddy Tudi asks me for a donation of spirit money,
And I ask Granddaddy Tudi for a wife.

Here, a little monkey who carries his load up the mountain every day at the crack of dawn suddenly breaks into song as he passes by the Tudi temple. The purpose of his song is to amuse anyone within earshot – hence the wisecrack in the last two lines. But even when you sing for your own benefit, you can't help being overheard by a young woman on the mountain facing, so the real point is that "wife."

Now here is a longer one:

41

So long without a meeting, don't be offended, Elder Sister!
So long without a meeting, don't lose your ardor, Elder Sister!
Don't give your flower garden to anyone else,
Don't get red eyes [be envious], like sorghum!

Don't get red eyes, like sorghum,
Don't let your heart grow black, like the wild pepper!
Don't show a thousand eyes [casting light in all directions]
    like the lantern,
We are a single heart, like a burning candle!

[4]Tutelary deity.

You must grow straight up, like a bamboo,
Don't fray into a thousand ends, like a horse whip!
You must return to your nest, like a pigeon,
Don't sing [everywhere] half the spring, like a sparrow!

There's another verse for the woman to sing to the man, with the change of a few words.

I'm aware of half a dozen songs of the type that follows:

42

The bitter bamboo's sprouting, black umbrellas are all
    around,
The ground is all white with tung tree blossoms;
My darling, my honey,
When will you get home from your mother's?
Tell me the truth, and
I'll go to meet you, rain or shine!

The bitter bamboo's sprouting, black umbrellas are all
    around,
The ground is all white with tung tree blossoms;
My darling, my honey,
Come on the fifteenth, not the first of the month!
If it's clear, I fear my brother may send me off, and
If it rains, I fear my husband may come to meet me!

The bitter bamboo sprouts and the other two images at the start of the song are indications that the season is early summer. This is a plain and simple love song for when you're escorting your sweetheart to her mother's house and you stop along the road where the tung trees are just blossoming and shedding their petals. Being married, the woman is afraid that her lover will get into trouble, so in her response she tells him not to come get her on her way back.

That song must be the creation of the districts out west of Zhen'gan, for only in their dialect does that repeated "my darling, my honey" sound so forceful.

43

When it comes to vegetables, stay away from *bak choi*,
When it comes to lovers, best shun the soldier boy,
He'll leave you stranded, a million miles away,
When three months later, comes his time to deploy.

Response

The pomegranate's red as soon as you pare it,
When it comes to lovers, a soldier has merit,
Just wait three months, and he'll get his pay,
Stay around long enough, and you too can share it!

The words are pronounced a little differently in the Zhen'gan dialect. This song is for the woman, and the man matches it. The woman fears being stranded – cast aside – so the man proposes a little "communism" to persuade her.

Now that's a song about the perils of loving a soldier. But there are others about the pain of parting with a soldier one loves:

44

We're furling the red flag, pulling up stakes,
Good-bye at the crossroads, for that's just the breaks,
Maple seeds flutter where'er the wind takes them,
Go AWOL to see you? That's about what it takes!

Response

They're furling the red flag, loading up the camp mare,
This kind of good-bye leaves your lass in despair,
When you're settled again, you'll know just how to get me,
I'll wait for the call of your palanquin chair!

This is a song for when the soldier has to leave. The woman
can only try to persuade him to send for her.

45

You're furling the red flag, going off to the front,
Lover, when the big war starts, don't you bear the brunt!
No need for promotion to sergeant or captain,
Let peace reign forever, you just be a grunt.

Response

We're furling the red flag, we're going off to fight,
Little Sister, don't let the thought give you a fright!
Firing once, firing twice, oh we'll surge through the lines,
You're a wife-mother-grandma in whatever light!

We laugh to read song 45 the first time, but on the second
reading we're moved by the sincere sentiments it expresses. Who
can deny that a soldier will brave artillery fire and risk his life just
for the sake of a lover?

I've always suspected that this song didn't come from the
Zhen'ganese. Even if it did, it must be the product of the border
region, for, although Zhen'gan recruits a lot of soldiers from its
own men, this song clearly comes from a temporary encampment.
Zhen'gan has never known occupation by troops from other prov-
inces or counties, apart from the new troops that come down

yearly to each county for garrisoning. Maybe it was composed jointly by a woman from Yuanzhou and a soldier from Zhen'gan. My educated guess is that everybody learned to sing it after Zhen'gan soldiers brought it home with them. The last sentence, with the "wife-mother-grandma," offers proof of my conjecture. In the West Hunan border area, only in Yuanzhou do they string those three words together like that.

46

I'm going, I'm going, Sister, don't think I'm teasin',
Must leave a road to go down, and that is my reason,
For flowers leave roots that go down in the ground,
And that is the way they survive every season.

Response

You're going, you're going, but come back Big Brother,
For I just can't bear it and won't take another,
Brother, you be the moon, and let me be the ground,
Let your light flood my heart, and gladly I'll smother.

The word for "road," or "escape route" *(lu)* is pronounced *"liu,"* like the word for "leave." These lyrics are relatively refined. They were composed by the people from around the village of Victorious Battalion (Deshengying), near the county border with Qiancheng.

47

Fir trees are crooked, their ashes are fine,
Find me a mate, Sister, please make her mine,
I'll give you a nice gift on my wedding day:
A big box of *baba* and a large jug of wine.

Response

The fir trees are straight and their ashes are gray,
I won't be your matchmaker no matter the day!
By the time of your wedding you'll 've long cast aside
Your poor little matchmaker, far, far away.

This is a song for engaging a matchmaker. It's the custom to reward her with a box of *baba* and a jug of wine, but it's also clear that the male intends to induce her to help him by using a little bribery. The woman refuses him on the grounds that, "once you've got a wife in your bed, you'll kick your [loving] matchmaker out of the house."

48

The golden vine will wrap 'round the fir,
Hear her bawl him out, that awful cur!
Comparisons for you, my Younger Brother:
You're a dirty sow that's stunk up the place,
And so many times,
That's what I call base!
You're a trash collector, you'll take anything,
Even if it's damaged, you're sure to give chase!
Smithy, your furnace needs so very little fuel,
You've already a blaze in each fireplace!
Like drawing chi-chi sticks at the city god's temple,
First come, first draw, them's the words you embrace!
Any wonder at all that I won't go with you?
If anyone saw me, I'd die of disgrace!
You've heard all my nos, and you've heard all my neighs,
The girls suited to you are your old easy lays.

I was never in love, but you went all the way,
And now I'm not fresh, so you say with dismay,

You can drink bloody wine in the city god's temple,
But the offering is still on the threshold today!
You can't get off by saying it's all just too naughty,
The ears of the heavens are not far away!
I'll tell the whole world of my lover's dishonor,
Too much to live down, though you try as you may!
If you're going to take off, then you go right ahead,
To the latrine, hungry dog, get your food for the day!

I suspect that this one was taken out of a songbook. Yet everybody in the countryside outside Zhen'gan can sing it. I find that very peculiar. If they had the chance to select, they ought to have selected something better. But the evidence to the contrary is convincing. If it was composed locally, why are songs of this length so rare in those parts?

In fact, the language of every line is suggestive of local sayings and adages. And when we read the last stanza, the living image of a country woman jumps out at us, of a woman cursing back at her man even as her eyes stream with tears. So I thought I'd record it, even if it isn't a local composition.

49

I moon all day long as I think about you,
I sit on the ground and never come to,
You must've put a spell in the hat on my head,
You must've put a potion right down in my shoe.

Response

I'm dazed by my man, and I'm the only one,
I forget to stir the soup till it's already done.
I lay out the straw in the sties for the pigs,
And pig fodder out where the buffalo run.

This is only one of about a dozen songs telling of daydreaming about one's lover. The couple tell each other how much they suffer when they're apart. Suffering and happiness are the same among all people in love. There are no distinctions between classes and different races or ethnic groups. The only thing that differs is how they express what they feel.

Coda

The songs you know can't be as many as mine,
I've one for each hair on the hides of three kine,
In three years of singing and six months beyond,
I'll be through just one ear, and you'll have to resign!

The Celestial God

"The Celestial God" ("Xiaoshen"), composed about 1925 or 1926, when Shen Congwen had been writing for only a year or two, may be the most unusual piece in this anthology. It is not modern literature at all but a rewriting of folklore materials, perhaps even a close approximation of a folk play that Shen Congwen remembered from childhood. Besides offering a window on the folk mind and insights into Shen Congwen's later sense of humor, works such as these showcase, in rawer form, local expressions that Shen used in his mature fiction (e.g., the phrase about luck being unstoppable by a door plank, which is voiced by Uncle Duck Feathers in "Guisheng").

China's modern folklore movement coincided with the new culture movement out of which Chinese modern fiction was born. Among the folklorists, Zhou Zuoren was known for his work on Greek mimes and Japanese kyōgen; taking Zhou's translations as models, young Shen Congwen wrote his own kyōgen-style plays in Chinese, adapting anecdotes from West Hunanese folklore for his plots (examples are his one-act plays "Duck" and "New Year's"). He also wrote a mime, based on a Buddhist tale.

"The Celestial God" is not, however, classed by the author as kyōgen or any other genre; it is intriguing to imagine that this little farce recreates a hometown folk play. That would be a masked Nuo drama performed near the end of the year. Shen as a child witnessed torch-lit three-day-and-night Nuo exorcisms, which took their name from a two-millennia-old Chinese rite but locally were directed by Miao shamans. Friends and relatives sang in unison and then donned masks to play stock characters, or perhaps themselves, to act out their own problems or satirize local customs. The relationship between a man and his mother's brother, featured below, is particularly close in Miao society and communities that have intermarried with the Miao.

At some Nuo ceremonies performed by Han people (as in Mayang), the major gods of the sacrifice were not the Miao people's, "Lord and Lady

Nuo," but the Xiaoshen ("Celestial Gods," or according to another tradition, which used a different Chinese character to write xiao, the "Little Gods"). They were small, colorfully dressed, and loved music and mischief making. When displeased, they stole or ruined household objects until propitiated. Like West Hunanese magicians, they could also make objects disappear into thin air and turn up someplace else. That particular power of the Celestial God motivates the farce below. From his being addressed as "Commander," we also see that this West Hunanese god may have taken on a bit of the martial bearing of his worldly counterparts. (The nephew, clearly, is a Zhen'gan soldier.)

Were this a real Nuo play, it would be performed at night, before the spirit tablet of the Celestial God, inside the house or courtyard of a well-to-do supplicant who has laid out sacrifices to the god. The setting would be both real and symbolic – in this world (the yang world) and the other world (the yin world), with the Celestial God in the audience, enjoying the spectacle performed for his amusement. Real sacrificial animals laid out to the god would double as props in the play. A local boy and his maternal uncle, known for getting in each other's hair, would play the leading roles, and Village Head Liang would be in the audience, too, enjoying jokes made at his expense. Such a play would not be disrespectful, for these gods have a sense of humor.

NEPHEW: Ya, ya, ya, "the time's not right, and the luck's not right, the wife loves her outside man at night – " I, Pimply Zhu the Second, have no wife, though, so let it be. Gooloo gooloo *(rumbling)*, my stomach has begun to speak; it must be hungry. Stomach, oh stomach, about my soldier's rations of two taels silver, six cash, and three bits – in a single breath, like "a fast horse under the whip," I got up into the "sedan chair" and was "taken for a ride" by the three sharpies at my table.[1] Three hands of Casting Tens and one of Matching the Six Old Gents just wiped me out clean, and I have no hope of winning back my losses. Stomach, I may have wronged you, but you'll have to put up with it for the time being. That damned son-of-a-bitch Fifth Yang just isn't fit for human company. He lets other people play on credit in a big way; it's only me, Zhu the Second, he looks down on. The day will come when luck strikes, "you can use a door plank to stop it, but even that won't do the trick." When that kind of luck comes, you dog-fucked Fifth Yang, just you wait and see! But with the kind of luck I've got now, "how frustrating it is, the great hero, the great sport, is bound from head to foot." Gooloo gooloo, my stomach is calling out again. Let me think of a good plan. *(Lowers the head.)* Hm, hm, I've got it, I've got it. I'll go to the house of my maternal uncle and play like I've turned over a new leaf, asking Uncle to forgive me. When I've finished the meal he lays out for me, I'll wait for the right opportunity to slip away, then off to the gaming tables again! Yes, perfect! It's not too late, so why don't I beat a path to my uncle's right now.

UNCLE: *(Kneeling before the image of the god.)* Divine One, oh Divine One, thy humble servant addresses thee: looking up in awe, he entreats that thou deign to listen. I have received thy blessings, Great God, Great Commander, thou who hast given

---

[1] A common form of sedan chair in West Hunan had three bearers; reference is therefore to three men ganging up to cheat one.

Translated by Jeffrey Kinkley

health to my family, young and old, and made my livestock prosper. Thy humble servant has today set out offerings of incense and candles, and meat from the three sacrificial beasts, respectfully to repay thy divine favor! I shall obey thee in all things hereafter, relying only on thee, Great God, Great Commander!

NEPHEW: Having taken flight, as if mounting the clouds and riding the mists, I've arrived at the entrance of Wang Family Lane. A gold character for *happiness* is pasted on the front gate. Isn't this none other than Maternal Uncle's house? Let me go up and take a peek. Hah, the gate is closed. Let me take a look through the crack in the door. Hah, he's kneeling. Let me listen to what he's saying. He's going ohmm, ohmm, intoning prayers to the Celestial God! If the Celestial God may be so entreated, wait till tomorrow, and I, too, shall buy three cash worth of incense, and two of spirit money, and go to do a kowtow. Gooloo, gooloo, my stomach is rumbling again. Don't those fowls and the suckling pig laid out in the middle of the hall make awfully good-smelling sacrificial beasts? "There was a beautiful woman, her face like the hibiscus";[2] you can look but you can't touch; isn't this frustrating? Let me think *(dramatic action of bowing the head),* first this, then that . . . , and then this . . . , and then that . . . , I've got a plan. Why don't I take this opportunity to sneak into the house, climb the stairs, and take the place of the Celestial God for a while? I'll manifest a bit of his August Power to trick Uncle out of a little wine and food. If discovered, I'll say I was in a trance, not in control of my faculties, and was forced to go upstairs in Uncle's house under the influence of the god. Uh oh, uh oh, don't turn around, don't turn around! Made it inside the door. He didn't turn his head, so he doesn't know I'm here. Let me go upstairs. Now I'm up there. Let's listen.

[2]A phrase from the *Book of Odes* that, like the other phrases in quotation marks, probably is known to the character from its quotation in a local opera.

UNCLE: I have a special request, Great God, Great Commander –

NEPHEW: He's praying, isn't he. How irritating! He's speaking so softly that even I, his nephew, can't make it out. Surely the Celestial God doesn't have keener ears than this little nephew of his! Let's find something to throw down at him and see how he reacts. Ping! That fragment from a broken bowl that I threw landed right on the wine pot – boy, the wine inside smells good!

UNCLE: Eerie indeed! There is no breeze – how did this get here? Oh, Great God, Great Commander, thine August Power is everywhere. Thou art on high, looking down into thy subject's heart, and hast given me this sign! Takest thou note of this, Great God, Great Commander: Your humble subject, Zhou Who Must Get Rich, so honest in his dealings with other men, and who has never given offense to any of thy creatures, has taken this occasion –

NEPHEW: He thinks it's real, doesn't he! Watch me throw down a little something else. Thump! That brick landed on one of the three sacrificial beasts – on a rooster, with a lone feather still sticking straight up from his tail. Boy, does that chicken smell good!

UNCLE: Great God, Great Commander, thy disciple kowtows before thee! *(Aside.)* Is this god deaf? Can't he hear how I'm bribing him? Let me raise my voice. *(Action of modulating the voice.)* Great God, Great Commander, let me tell thee: Thy humble subject Zhou Who Must Get Rich, so honest in his dealings with others, and who has never given offense to any of thy creatures, has on this occasion carefully prepared candles and incense, the three sacrificial beasts, fine liquors, and spirit money, in hopes of receiving more favor from thee, Great God, Great Commander –

NEPHEW: Gooloo, gooloo, my stomach is rumbling again. I'll try throwing down something a little bigger this time, to scare him into fainting. Then I can come down and pluck the sideboard with the three sacrificial meats at my leisure. Won't it be grand when I'm back home with all this food, washing it down with wine as a midnight snack?

UNCLE: *(Aside.)* How eerie, how out of this world! How can the god be in such a foul mood? Surely it can't be that the wine I laid out was too strong, causing him to get roaring drunk? Or that –

NEPHEW: What a pain, he still hasn't fainted! Get a load of this object from heaven, then! Sploosh, splash! Hurrah, hurrah, this time I've knocked the wine pot over onto the floor!

UNCLE: *(Aside.)* Is the Great God angry? Is he saying that I am insincere? Or is it really that he's already plastered, drunk out of his mind? If he's crazed with wine, I'd better sober him up with a batch of kudzu root soup. *(Modulates the voice.)* Great God, Great Commander on high! Thy humble servant kowtows to thee! If the Great God is angered by his humble servant's insincerity, wait until I have atoned by slaughtering another pig, or a lamb, to wish the Great God a long life. The Heavenly Majesty being so near to me, not a cubit away, though I know not where, I entreat the Great God to givest me another sign, that I might –

NEPHEW: More sacrifices, huh? Then let's treat him to another brickbat. Better be careful this time not to hit the three sacrificial beasts, though. Oh no, oh no, the brickbats are all gone. What else might there be? Oh no, oh no, there's nothing left to throw! Let me throw my felt hat down there. Hah, your heavenly harbinger is among you!

UNCLE: Ooh! What could this be? It has descended from above – don't tell me that it's – hmm, let's have a look at it. Ah, a hat, and still warm. The Great God must have snatched it off somebody's head and brought it here, to give me a sign. Let's try for another. *(Modulating the voice.)* Great God, Great Commander, hear my humble petition! Thy sign to me has been received. Mayest thou not send down another article of clothing, that thy humble servant might take the one to a temple and keep the other in his humble house, where he might keep it supplied with fresh flowers at all times!

NEPHEW: What shall I do now? That still wasn't enough. Don't tell me I have to hurl myself down on him. All right, all right,

I'll throw down this worn-out old shoe I'm wearing. Hah, take a gander at this sign from above.

UNCLE: *(Aside.)* Another spooky object! This isn't just some thing he grabbed off the street; this is the fulfillment of my request. It's obvious that today the Great God has come down among us! Let's see what it is. Oh my goodness, it's an old shoe! Still warm are its insides, like unto a fine fragrance – might it not be from the Great God's own foot?! It is said that he who puts on the Great God's shoes and hat can make himself invisible. Why not ask for the mate to this shoe? *(Raising his voice.)* Great God, Great Commander on high, thy August Power is bright and glorious, though it fills one with terror. Great God, please bestow on me the mate to this holy object.

NEPHEW: If he thinks these holy shoes are useful to him, I'll have to send him down the other one. Let me take it off. Aha! There's your holy gift.

UNCLE: *(Aside.)* That's really it; the Great God is favoring me. I must express my thanks! *(Dramatic action of kowtowing.)*

NEPHEW: There he goes kowtowing again. Let's listen to what he's saying.

UNCLE: Having received these gifts bestowed on me by the Great God, I am duty bound to put them to good use. *(Aside.)* Let me take off my own hat and shoes and put on these holy objects so I can go out and test them. I recall that Village Head Liang has just smoked several hams and hung them up in his house at the head of the lane. How nice it would be if I could steal one or two of them. If it works, good-bye troubles, I'm set for life!

NEPHEW: He's changed into my clothes. Gooloo, gooloo, my stomach is rumbling again. You'll just have to put up with it a while.

UNCLE: Great God, Great Commander, may I humbly explain! Having received the gift of thy crown and thy slippers, I know thee to be of inexhaustible resources; allow thy humble servant to presume to wear them outside. If I may become invisible like the gods, I shall surely lay out a thanksgiving feast with sacrifices for three days. Never would I renege on such a pledge!

(Exit the UNCLE.*)*

NEPHEW: He's gone out. Let me quickly go down and get myself dressed again in Uncle's own hat and shoes, and then I can pick up his tray with the food and be on my way. One, two, three, four, five, six, I'm down on the ground; there're only seven steps. *(Eats.)* Gooloo gooloo, my stomach can't stand it, I've treated it so unjustly, let me cut off a pig's ear first of all, to settle it down. Gulp, gulp, num, num, how delicious! Let me try that other ear. Gulp, gulp, really good! Ha, how stupid of me. What's that chicken head any good for; I can't stand you looking at me so arrogantly even when you're dead. I'd better eat you up, hadn't I? Gulp, gulp, ah, delicious. And wouldn't it be prejudicial of me to eat the head but not the legs? Better polish them off, too. Gulp, gulp, very tasty. I must be crazy! What kind of boiled chicken can lose its head and legs and still keep its wings? Better eat 'em up! Gulp, gulp, quite a treat!

(Enter the UNCLE.*)*

UNCLE: Some devil from I don't know where really put one over on me! No sooner was I out the door than Old Tian, the water seller, made fun of me. He said I'd rented this cap from the city god temple to rid myself of some evil spirits. Isn't that awful? Then I ran into that young buck from the Zhao household. He laughed and yelled as if I were mad. "Everybody look at the crazy man!" he said. Now that's aggravation for you. I'd better give up the idea right now of running over to Village Head Liang's to steal those hams. I'd better hurry back to have a look at those three sacrificial meats. If I'm gone too long, the cats will get them. Back I go. Before I know it, the front door is in sight. That was a quick trip! Hmm, there seems to be someone inside. Let me take a closer look. *(Gesture of rubbing the eyes.)* Could it be the Celestial God? Perhaps when the Great God saw that I meant to use his holy objects to commit theft, to steal somebody else's hams, he made these magic gifts lose their power? But they say that the Great God is only a foot tall. He wears a red cap and an embroidered gown and has handsome good looks. This god is much too tall! It's so hard to see in the dark, I can't make him out through all the clothes and flowers. Let's wait until he turns around, to see what his face looks like.

NEPHEW: Ha ha, how come I hear no more gooloo gooloo? *(Gesture of patting the belly.)* A small injustice to you, handsomely requited, so stop your groaning. What a pity that I knocked over the wine pot with a brick. Not a drop left. If I could have drunk it dry, wouldn't that have been even more fun? Hey, now that my stomach's completely stuffed, let's gather up this leftover chicken and fish to take home! Good, good, I've got it all gathered up. Now let me get out of here before Uncle returns home. *(Sings.)* First this way, then that way; out the door I jog, and run into a dog.

(The NEPHEW *is grabbed by the* UNCLE *as he goes out the door.)*

NEPHEW: Oh! Don't hurt me, dear old Uncle! The Celestial God grabbed your nephew's shoes and hat right off him. I ran here barefoot, and here you are dear old fellow, going all over creation with your nephew's clothes on!

UNCLE: You little devil, why I'll – you made a fool out of me! I'm going to give you a good beating.

(Casting aside the tray with the meats, the NEPHEW *breaks free and runs for dear life.)*

Bibliography

Select Writings about Shen Congwen and His Milieu

Chow Tse-tsung. *The May Fourth Movement: Intellectual Revolution in Modern China.* Stanford, Calif.: Stanford University Press, 1960. (On Shen Congwen's intellectual milieu.)

Dong Yi. "Shitan Shen Congwen bufen xiaoshuo sixiang qingxiang de fuzaxing" (Tentative thoughts on the ideological complexity of some of Shen Congwen's fiction). *Wenxue pinglun,* no. 6 (November 1983): 48–61. (Contains interesting tidbits about Shen's fiction.)

Gunn, Edward. *Rewriting Chinese: Style and Innovation in Twentieth-Century Chinese Prose.* Stanford, Calif.: Stanford University Press, 1991. (Comments on Shen's style.)

Hsia, C. T. *A History of Modern Chinese Fiction.* Rev. ed. New Haven, Conn.: Yale University Press, 1971. (Still the best critical introduction to Shen Congwen's works; see esp. pp. 189–211, 359–366.)

Jishou Daxue xuebao (shehui kexue) (Journal of Jishou University [social science edition]). Jishou, Hunan. (This quarterly publication provides a steady source of new views and tidbits about Shen Congwen; it is published at a university that organizes research and conferences about him.)

Kinkley, Jeffrey C. *The Odyssey of Shen Congwen.* Stanford, Calif.: Stanford University Press, 1987. (History, criticism, bibliographies, and contextual information about Shen, his homeland, and his works, with materials from 1980s interviews.)

———. "Shen Congwen and the Romance of Chu Culture: Their Legacy in Chinese Literature of the 1980s." In *From May Fourth to June Fourth: Fiction and Film in Twentieth-Century China,* ed. Ellen Widmer and David Der-wei Wang. Cambridge, Mass.: Harvard University Press, 1993.

(How Shen Congwen influenced China's new literature of the 1980s.)

Larson, Wendy. *Literary Authority and the Modern Chinese Writer: Ambivalence and Autobiography.* Durham, N.C.: Duke University Press, 1991. (Discusses Shen's autobiography.)

Lee, Leo Ou-fan. *Voices from the Iron House: A Study of Lu Xun.* Bloomington: Indiana University Press, 1987. (On Shen Congwen's greatest contemporary competitor for literary fame.)

MacDonald, William Lewis. "Characters and Themes in Shen Ts'ung-wen's Fiction." Ph.D. diss., University of Washington, 1970. (Literary criticism and thematic analysis.)

Nieh, Hua-ling. *Shen Ts'ung-wen.* New York: Twayne, 1972. (Biography and criticism.)

Prince, Anthony John. "The Life and Works of Shen Ts'ung-wen." Ph.D. diss., University of Sydney, 1968. (Literary history and criticism.)

Rabut, Isabelle. "La création littéraire chez Shen Congwen, du procès de l'histoire à l'apologie de la fiction." Ph.D. diss., Institut National des Langues et Civilisations Orientales, Paris, 1992. (Literary history and criticism.)

Schwarcz, Vera. *The Chinese Enlightenment: Intellectuals and the Legacy of the May Fourth Movement of 1919.* Berkeley and Los Angeles: University of California Press, 1986. (On Shen Congwen's intellectual milieu.)

Shao Huaqiang, ed. *Shen Congwen yanjiu ziliao* (Research materials on Shen Congwen). 2 vols. Guangzhou and Hong Kong: Huacheng & Sanlian, 1991. (Recent scholars' writings on Shen as well as historical documents and commentary about him.)

Shen Congwen. *Shen Congwen wen ji* (The works of Shen Congwen). Edited by Shao Huaqiang and Ling Yu. 12 vols. Guangzhou and Hong Kong: Huacheng & Sanlian, 1982–1985. ("Authoritative" for the time being and yet not wholly reliable, owing to state politics and authorial/familial scruples about reprinting erotic works.)

———. *Shen Congwen bie ji* (Other works by Shen Congwen).

Edited by Liu Yiyou, Xiang Chengguo, Shen Huchu. 20 vols.
Changsha: Yuelu shushe, 1992. (Unpublished letters mixed
with other works, some already in print; not a rectification of
the blind spots in the *Shen Congwen wen ji*.)

———. *Shen Congwen quan ji* (The complete works of Shen
Congwen). Forthcoming in China. (Bids fair to be the largest
collection of Shen's works yet, but for political reasons it
cannot be "complete," even apart from nonextant works and
privately held letters and scrolls. Shen's essays will surely be
abridged as in the *Shen Congwen wen ji;* pre-1949 editions are
likely to remain authoritative on Shen's social thought.)

Wang, David Der-wei. *Fictional Realism in Twentieth-Century
China: Mao Dun, Lao She, Shen Congwen.* New York: Columbia
University Press, 1992. (Literary criticism.)

Sources for More Translations of Shen Congwen's Works

Acton, Harold, and Ch'en Shih-hsiang, trans. *Modern Chinese
Poetry.* London: Duckworth, 1936. ("Ode.")

Birch, Cyril, ed. *Anthology of Chinese Literature.* Vol. 2, *From the
Fourteenth Century to the Present Day.* New York: Grove Press,
1972. (A chapter of *Congwen's Autobiography,* trans. William L.
MacDonald.)

Chai, Ch'u, and Winberg Chai, eds. and trans. *A Treasury of
Chinese Literature: A New Prose Anthology Including Fiction and
Drama.* New York: Appleton-Century, 1965. ("Long Zhu.")

Hsia, C. T., ed., with the assistance of Joseph S. M. Lau. *Twentieth-
Century Chinese Stories.* New York: Columbia University Press,
1971. ("Quiet" and "Daytime," trans. Wai-lim Yip and
C. T. Hsia.)

Klöpsch, Volker, and Roderich Ptak, eds. *Hoffnung auf Frühling:
Moderne chinesische Erzählungen: Erster Band: 1919 bis 1949.*
Frankfurt am Main: Suhrkamp, 1980. ("My Education," trans.
Helmut Martin and Volker Klöpsch.)

Lau, Joseph S. M., C. T. Hsia, and Leo Ou-fan Lee, eds. *Modern
Chinese Stories and Novellas, 1919–1949.* New York: Columbia

University Press, 1981. ("Baizi," "Xiaoxiao," "The Lamp," "Quiet," and "Three Men and One Woman.")

Munro, Stanley R., ed. and trans. *Genesis of a Revolution: An Anthology of Modern Chinese Short Stories.* Singapore: Heinemann Educational Books (Asia), 1979. ("Seven Barbarians and the Last Spring Festival.")

Richter, Ursula, trans. *Shen Congwen Erzählungen aus China.* Frankfurt am Main: Insel, 1985. (Nine short stories.)

Shen Congwen [article says Shen Ts'ung-wen]. *Green Jade and Green Jade.* Translated by Emily Hahn and Shing Mo-lei. *T'ien Hsia Monthly* 2, nos. 1–4 (January–April 1936). *(The Frontier City.)*

———— [article says Shen Ts'ung-wen]. "Hsiao-hsiao." Translated by Lee Yi-hsieh. *Tien Hsia Monthly* 7, no. 3 (October 1938): 295–309. ("Xiaoxiao.")

———— [article says Shen Ts'ung-wen]. "Old Mrs. Wang's Chickens." Translated by Shih Ming. *T'ien Hsia Monthly* 11, no. 3 (December–January 1940–1941): 274–280. ("A Country Town.")

———— [book says Shen Tseng-wen, or Shen Tsung-wen in the reprint ed.]. *The Chinese Earth.* Translated by Ching Ti [Di Jin] and Robert Payne. London: George Allen & Unwin, 1947; reprint, New York: Columbia University Press, 1982. *(The Frontier City,* a chapter from *Congwen's Autobiography,* and twelve short stories; with new author's preface in the reprint ed.)

———— [article says Shen Ts'ung-wen]. "Little Flute." Translated by Li Ru-mien. *Life and Letters* 60, no. 137 (January 1949): 20–29. ("Xiaoxiao.")

———— [article says Shen Ts'ung-wen]. "After Rain." Translated by David Kidd. *East-West Review* 3, no. 2 (Summer 1967): 182–189.

————. *The Border Town and Other Stories.* Translated by Gladys Yang. Beijing: Panda Books, 1981. *(The Frontier City,* "Xiaoxiao," "The Husband," and "Guisheng.")

————. *Recollections of West Hunan.* Translated by Gladys Yang. Beijing: Panda Books, 1982. ("After Snow," "Qiaoxiu and Dongsheng," "Truth Is Stranger than Fiction," and chapters from *Congwen's Autobiography, Discursive Notes on a Trip Through Hunan,* and *West Hunan.*)

————. *Le petit soldat du Hunan.* Translated by Isabelle Rabut. Paris: Albin Michel, 1992. (*Congwen's Autobiography,* complete.)

Snow, Edgar, ed. *Living China.* London: George G. Harrap, 1936. ("Baizi.")

Wang, Chi-chen, trans. *Contemporary Chinese Stories.* New York: Columbia University Press, 1944. ("Night" [1], also known as "Night March.")

Yüan Chia-hua and Robert Payne, eds. and trans. *Contemporary Chinese Short Stories.* London: Noel Carrington, 1946. ("Black Night" and "The Lamp.")

Contributors

Jeffrey Kinkley is a professor of history at St. John's University, New York. He is a translator of modern Chinese fiction and has written a book about Shen Congwen's life and works.

Peter Li is an associate professor of Chinese at Rutgers. He has published books on Chinese literature and most recently edited a book on the Tiananmen crisis.

William MacDonald is an associate professor of Chinese literature at the University of Illinois, Urbana-Champaign. He has published translations of Chinese literature and written a doctoral dissertation on Shen Congwen.

Caroline Mason is a lecturer on Chinese at the University of Durham, England, and a published translator of modern Chinese fiction.

David Pollard is a professor of translation at the Chinese University of Hong Kong and coeditor of *Renditions.* A noted translator from the Chinese, he has published books on modern Chinese literature and literary criticism.

The following stories in this collection were originally published in Chinese in the periodicals indicated. "The New and the Old" ("Xin he jiu," 1935): *Duli pinglun.* "The Vegetable Garden" ("Caiyuan," 1929); "The Lovers" ("Fufu," 1929); and "The Husband" ("Zhangfu," 1930): *Xiaoshuo yuebao.* "Quiet" ("Jing," 1932): *Chuanghua.* "Meijin, Baozi, and the White Kid" ("Meijin, Baozi, yu na yang," 1929): *Renjian yuekan.* "Ah Jin" ("Ah Jin," 1929); "The Inn" ("Ludian," 1929); "My Education" ("Wo de jiaoyu," 1929); and "Ox" ("Niu," 1929): *Xinyue.* "The Company Commander" ("Lianzhang," 1927); and "Songs of the Zhen'gan Folk" ("Ganren yaoqu," 1926–1927): *Chenbao fukan.* "Staff Adviser" ("Guwenguan," 1935); and "Eight Steeds" ("Ba jun tu," 1935): *Wenxue.* "Black Night" ("Hei ye," 1932): *Shenbao yuekan.* "Sansan" ("Sansan," 1931): *Wenyi yuekan.* "Life" ("Sheng," 1933): *Renmin pinglun.* "Guisheng" ("Guisheng," 1937); "Big Ruan and Little Ruan" ("Da xiao Ruan," 1937); and "Qiaoxiu and Dongsheng" ("Qiaoxiu he Dongsheng," 1947): *Wenxue zazhi.* "Winter Scene in Kunming" ("Kunming dongjing," 1939); and "Amah Wang" ("Wang Sao," 1940): Hong Kong *Dagongbao.* "Suicide" ("Zisha," 1935): Tianjin *Dagongbao.* "Gazing at Rainbows" ("Kan hong lu," 1943): *Xin wenxue.*

"The Housewife" ("Zhufu") was published in Shen Congwen's *Zhufu ji* (1939) by Shangwu yinshuguan, Shanghai. "The Celestial God" ("Xiaoshen") was published in Shen Congwen's *Yazi* (1926) by Beixin shuju, Beijing.